THE FAERIE KNIGHT

A Gothic Romance

DAVID NIEMITZ

This book is a work of fiction. Names, characters, businesses, organizations, places, events and incidents either are the product of the author's imagination or are used fictitiously. Any resemblance to actual persons living or dead, events, or locales is entirely coincidental.

ISBN: 979-8-8842563-0-9 (Paperback)

ISBN: 979-8-8842573-4-4 (Hardcover)

Cover design and map by Sarah Murphy

https://www.instagram.com/artbysarahmurphy?igsh=MTVpaDJ0eWFvcTFjbQ%3D%3D&utm_source=qr

Formatting by Ben Schenkman

CONTENTS

DEDICATIONS

To my wife, Sarah Murphy, not only for her beautiful art, and her insightful suggestions as my first reader, but for her support and enthusiasm for this project over the past year;

To my sister, Alyson, who spent successive Thursday evenings over the course of an extended stay in Connecticut convincing me that I needed to learn how to market my work - enjoy LA!

To Ash and Ben, who not only put up with my daily tracking of word counts, but clapped every step of the way, and who shared ideas on topics as varied as marketing, audio recording, and everything in between;

And to my friend, Sarah Gabbey, who passed too soon. Pieces of you live in this book, and you will be remembered.

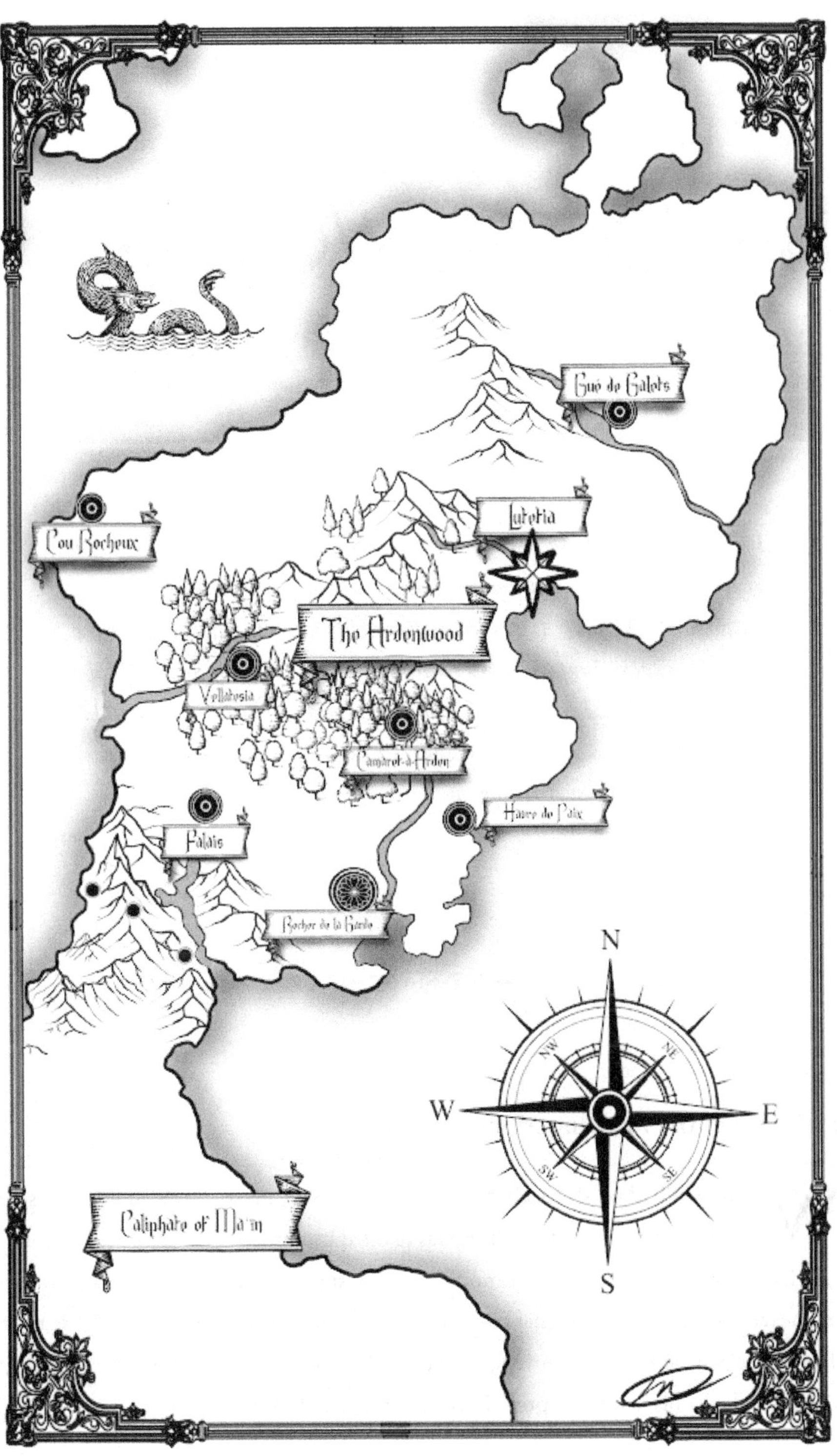
Gué de Galets
Cou Rocheux
Lutetia
The Ardenwood
Camaret-à-Arden
Havre de Paix
Falais
Rocher de la Garde
Caliphate of Ma'in
N
NW
NE
W
E
SW
SE
S

Chapter One

Into the Woods

It is tempting to think that, with the benefit of hindsight, we can point at clear signs of the coming Cataclysm. The truth, however, is that by all accounts Decimus Avitus led a thoroughly unremarkable life for the son of an Etalan Emperor, and that prior to the arrival of Sammā'ēl the Sun-Eater there was no reason to think he would ever rise higher than his post as a provincial governor, or indeed do much of historical note at all.
-François du Lutetia, A History of Narvonne

19th Day of the Planting Moon, 297 AC

When Trist had nearly reached the end of the woodcutter's paths, not far outside of where the edge of the village was marked by a stockade of dark Iebara wood, he reined Cazador to a halt and dismounted. The steel rings of his chain mail rustled, and he readjusted his broad leather sword belt to settle it on his hips comfortably. Rather than tie the gray destrier to a convenient branch, Trist pulled a carrot from his saddlebag. Caz snuffed over his hand, accepted the offered treat, and happily munched away.

Trist took a few more things out: two unlit torches, which he thrust through his belt; a wineskin; and a sack with a slice of cold roast boar, a wedge of cheese, and a loaf of last evening's bread from the kitchens of Foyer Chaleureux. He checked the newly forged dagger in his boot, to be certain it was still there, and then turned back to the destrier.

"Good boy," Trist murmured, cupping the horse's head with his left hand and leaning his own forehead down against the white blaze that stood out from Cazador's otherwise gray coat. "Don't wait for me," he said, after a moment, then stepped away and raised his voice. "Go home, Caz." He turned into the forest, ignoring the whinny from behind him, and set off through the Ardenwood for the Chapel of Saint Camiel. He knew the way: he had walked it since childhood.

7th Day of the Flower Moon, 285 AC

Trist du Camaret-à-Arden didn't have a destination in mind when he fled the manor: he only wanted to get away from his tutor, Brother Alberic, before the old monk could switch his knuckles raw again. Mother would never have let the old man hurt him, if she was still alive.

"It isn't fair," Trist grumbled to himself, sprinting down the beaten dirt track to the forest, away from the center of the village, the river, or the fields to the south. Even Percy had yelled at him, finally, in frustration, when Trist had knocked over a pot of ink with his elbow. Trist's half brother - elder by just over two years, and their father's heir - was usually his protector, the one who stepped in when Trist was in trouble. But this time the ink had spilled on Percy's parchment of Old Etalan translations, and even he'd had enough.

Trist ducked off the path when he heard the woodcutters singing their tree songs up ahead in the distance, the thunk of their blessed axes, and their occasional shouts to each other in the cool morning. To the west, a carefully tended Iebara grove provided the village's most prized crop: a fine, black wood nearly as strong as steel, used to create longbows of incredible power, stringed instruments that sounded more truly than any other wood, and a dozen more goods besides. He jumped a fallen tree as he moved away from the woodsmen and the grove, cut around a patch of blooming sweetbriers, and followed the gentle sound of flowing water until he came out of the undergrowth to a broad, shallow stream, rippling over pebbles and around rocks. "It must flow into the Rea," Trist decided, talking out loud to himself. Another habit that Brother Albernic and his parents deplored. He sat down on the mossy bank, removed his boots, then his wool socks, and dipped a foot into the water, finding it cold.

He was just selecting a good rock for skipping when the wind carried the sound of someone humming to him. "Hello?" Trist called, and, forgetting his boots on the bank, picked his way upstream. He climbed a small series of cascades among the wet rocks until he came to a golden pool, sandy beneath the water, where a break in the green canopy overhead let fall a shaft of sunlight. A slim girl, perhaps ten years or so of age, like him, was standing in the pool in a white linen shift, singing softly to herself.

"Oh, do not tell the Priest our plight,
For he would call it a sin;
I've been with my love in the woods all night,
Conjuring Summer in!
Now is the Sun come up from the South,
With Oak, and Ash, and Thorn!
Sing Oak, and Ash, and Thorn, my love,
All of a Midsummer morn!
Surely we sing no little thing,
In Oak, and Ash, and Thorn!"

The falling sun lit up her pale hair like fine strands of fire, her shadow danced on the rippling water, and Trist stumbled, his foot coming down heavily, with a loud splash, as he caught his balance.

The girl gave a cry of fright, eyes wide as she saw him, frozen in the moment like a deer startled by the hunters. Trist knew that she would run.

"Wait!" he called, holding up his hands. "I won't hurt you. I just heard you singing, and wanted to see who it was. I haven't seen you in the village before."

She trembled, there, hesitant. "I'm not from the village," she said softly.

"My name is Trist," he introduced himself, but didn't dare bow. He felt, somehow, that he had trapped her eyes with his, and the moment he broke the connection, there would be nothing holding the girl here. "Trist du Camaret-à-Arden." He swallowed. "You don't need to be afraid. This is my father's land. I won't let anyone harm you."

Something flickered through her eyes at his name, too fast for him to judge what it meant. "Call me Linette," she said.

"What were you singing?" Trist relaxed a bit; she seemed to be calming.

"An old song," Linette said, after a moment. "A tree song."

"It was pretty," he said. "Teach it to me?"

Linette nodded, and they sat on the bank, bare feet in the brook, until he'd learned the words and the tune, while she wove roses from the sweetbriers into his nut-brown hair.

19th Day of the Planting Moon, 297 AC

Trist had expected that something would bar his way, but that it was a knight all armored in thorns was a surprise.

"Let me pass," he said grimly, but the wood-helmed knight gave no response, and Trist could not see his face. His armor was all of a pale green, almost faded to gray, in large, thick plates of bark. Sharp thorns extended from his pauldrons an inch or more, from his cuirass and greaves and everywhere that Trist could see. His shield was blazoned with the pink rose of the sweetbrier, and his sword was serrated beginning a hand's span below the tip. If drawn across his bare flesh, Trist expected it to leave horrific wounds: he was thankful he wore a shirt of good mail over his padded gambeson, with steel pauldrons and vambraces over that. Trist stepped left, and the Knight of Thorns mirrored him; two steps to the right, and the knight moved again. He pulled the unlit torches from his belt and dropped them, and then the sack of food. He had no shield to match, but his blade had the better reach.

"I have business with Linette du Chapelle de Camiel," Trist said formally.

The Knight of Thorns raised his shield and set the tip of his blade in line with Trist's chest. Trist's longsword slid free of its leather sheath with a sigh, thirty-six inches of well-kept steel. He raised it to his right ear, both hands on the hilt, blade parallel with the ground, tip aimed at the chest of the Thorn Knight. *Ox.* John Granger, his Master at

Arms, had always said that Trist favored the guard too much, but for all that, Percy could only rarely break it. For a moment, all the sounds in the forest died away, save for the soft babble of water over stone, somewhere just past the knight, from the brook that ran into the Rea. The twin shadows cast by the two knights leaned toward each other, barely restrained.

Trist pushed off with his back foot, more clumsily than in the practice yard, his blade coming around in a diagonal cut, down and from right to left. The Knight of Thorns raised his shield to take it, and stabbed with his shorter arming sword.

Trist smiled. His enemy had taken the feint; he hadn't been certain it would work.

Instead of remaining committed to the cut, which would never have pierced plate in any event, Tristan kept moving forward, spun tight counter-clockwise around the shield, keeping it between him and the arming sword, planted his right foot inside the knight's left, and shoved him hard from behind. The Knight of Thorns stumbled, falling forward, and Trist quickly switched grips, holding his sword by the lower blade, and swung the cross-guard above the hilt into the thorn knight's helm like a warhammer. The metal crossguard punched through the helm like an axe through rotten wood. Trist wrenched it out, then swung a second time, then a third. By that point, the knight had stopped moving.

The Thorn Knight's armor began to fall apart, twisted vines unraveling like threads. No longer tightly pressed together into plate, they curled up, stretching for sunlight, and green leaves sprouted all along their length. It was as if Trist watched winter pass through spring and into summer in the space of a moment. Where a knight had sprawled on the ground, defeated, a patch of sweet-briers now blossomed, the roses delicate and pink.

Blood rushing in his ears, Trist looked at them once, then sheathed his sword and sat down to catch his breath. It was the first time he had ever been in a real fight, with live steel. Once his heart slowed, he picked up the things he'd set aside, and made his way through the wood to the brook where he'd met Linette du chapelle de Camiel, twelve years ago.

18th Day of the Harvest Moon, 287 AC

"You really live here?"

They were thirteen, now, and after a day of dancing and cider at the harvest festival, Linette had finally agreed to take him to where she lived with her mother. Trist had a sack full of turnips, bread, a wheel of cheese, and salted dried meat, all slung over his shoulder. He'd made a habit of bringing Linette and her mother food for years now, from the manor's kitchens. He also carried a knife in a sheath on his belt, though he would have wished for a sword, instead. Not that there was any danger so close to the village, not like in the depths of the haunted Ardenwood. Still, he liked the feel of a sword at his hip: it seemed to be the one thing he was good at, or at least the one thing he could do better than Percy.

"I do." Linette nodded, reaching out her pale hand, and Trist took it. The briar-roses were still in her hair, from when she'd met him at the edge of town in the morning, just as the monastery bells were ringing terce. She tugged him along up the worn stone steps, beneath a canopy of oak and ash boughs, and his boots rustled through the dry autumn leaves as he followed her up the path. There was a stone arch, and the foundations of crumbling walls running away from it to either side, covered in moss. Beneath the green he could make out faded carvings of the Angelus Saint Camiel, sacrificing himself against the Sun Eater. Past the arch, Linette led him to a small chapel on top of the hill, rectangular in shape, built of regular stone blocks. They were mossy, too, and discolored by long exposure to the elements. The door had long since rotted away, and the roof, as well, and a great oak tree had grown up from the floor, spreading its branches over the structure. The oak retained most of its leaves, with the effect that the chapel was roofed in bright autumn scarlet.

"But there's no actual roof," Trist protested, their voices echoing around the inside of the chapel. "How do you keep warm in the winter?"

"The cellar," Linette said, motioning to a stair in the corner that descended down into the earth beneath the chapel. "You can leave the food at the top of the stairs," she suggested, and Trist set the burlap sack down.

"I wish you would come live in the village," he said again. "My father would take your mother on as a servant, if I asked."

Linette shook her head, as she always did when he said this. "We like the forest. There's too many people and too much fuss in town. We're quite happy here. Though I did like the dancing!"

"I worry about you," he admitted. "Especially in the winter."

"Oh Trist," Linette said fondly. "You don't need to worry about me." Suddenly, she leaned into him, flighty as a bird, and brushed her lips against his cheek. "I've shown you where I live. Now go, before my mother gets back."

He did as she asked, as if asleep, and hardly knew where she was until he'd crossed the brook again and was nearly back to the village, only pausing once when he heard an old woman's sharp voice from the ruined chapel. "Where've you been, girl?" her mother said. The thought of fleeing Linette's mother displeased Trist, but he knew she was old enough to be betrothed now, if not married quite yet, and he didn't want to ruin her reputation.

Trist grinned as he stepped back onto the beaten earth of the woodcutter's road. He was thinking of Linette as if she were a lady, the daughter of a knight or a baron, when she was a peasant girl with no father, living in the woods. He doubted anyone else in the village would say she had much of a reputation to ruin, in the first place. But he still wanted to protect her. His birthday was High Summer Day, in less than a year. After that, he would be fourteen years old, and that would be old enough. He was the second son, and would never inherit land, no matter what. He could support Percy just as well with a peasant girl for a wife, as with some western knight's third daughter. When he was fourteen, Trist decided, he would ask his father's permission to marry Linette.

His fingers rose to touch his cheek, where she'd pressed a fleeting kiss, and Trist hurried home.

Chapter Two

The Labyrinth

The Angelus, our prayers implore,
Heralds of glory evermore,
Angelus of all grace and might,
To banish sin from our delight:
Our mind be in their keeping placed,
Our body true to them and chaste,
Where only Faith her fire shall feed
To burn the weeds of daemon seed.
-Narvonnian Hymn, early 2nd century AC

19th Day of the Planting Moon, 297 AC

As a child, Trist had hopped from stone to stone when crossing the brook where he'd first met Linette. Now, armored in chain, longsword sheathed once again, he tromped through, careful of his footing, relying on the oiled leather of his riding boots to keep out the water. Once he'd reached the far bank, he set off up the familiar game path that led to the hill upon which the ruins of the Chapelle de Camiel rested.

When he came upon the worn stair, however, and the mossy stone arch above it, Trist did not see crumbling stones tumbled off to either side. Instead, the walls looked as if they had been built yesterday, the granite smooth and well fitted, stretching out to surround the chapel in both directions. Placing his left hand on the pommel of his sword, Trist strode up the steps and passed beneath the arch.

Before him stretched another stone wall, parallel to the walls leading out from the arch itself, creating a sort of outdoor hallway or corridor, open to the blue sky above, but paved with broad, flat stones beneath Trist's boots. He looked up, measuring the walls, and guessed them to be at least ten feet in height, and too smooth to climb easily, especially armored.

To the left, then, as one direction seemed as good as another. The walls curved, and he tried to imagine how, from above, they would form a circular fortification around the chapel. His father would have loved stone walls like this. The curve had taken him out of sight of the arch when Trist came to the first branching: the wall opened to his right, leading into another curving corridor. Or, he could continue on the outside ring.

"It is a labyrinth," Trist realized, with a sigh.

13th Day of the New Summer's Moon, 288 AC

The great hall of Sir Rience du Camaret-à-Arden's manor, Foyer Chaleureux, was filled to the brim with relations and guests. His old friend and battle companion, Tor De Lancey, a gregarious man with a red face and a great belly that Trist guessed must have grown since the stories of their youth as squires, had brought his wife, Jeanette, and their daughter. Three great banners hung this evening: one with the black Iebara tree, sprinkled with white flowers, on a field of green, the heraldry of Trist's own family; and another, a red warhammer on white, shaped just like the weapon hanging at Sir Tor's belt when he'd rode into the courtyard. The last was the white sea shell on blue of their mutual liege, Baron Urien.

Percy and Trist's older cousin, Sir Lucan, had come, newly knighted and soon to be wed, escorting the young Lady Clarisant, who was to be Percy's wife, all the way from Rocher de la Garde, on the sea, where Trist dimly recalled spending a single, golden summer. The family's Master of Arms, John Granger, sat near the foot of the table, his hard eyes scanning the room as fiercely as he watched Trist and Percy in the practice yard. Brother Alberic sat next to Brother Hugh, the Abbot, deeply involved in a discussion of theology. Trist had caught just enough out of the corner of one ear to come to his own conclusions about how interesting the subject matter was, and the answer was 'not at all.'

And while they were commoners, not nobles, Sir Rience had invited many of the more important people in the village, as well: James Miller, whose father and grandfather before him had run the lumber mill fed by the woodsman, for instance. His family had mastered the songs for the working of the Iebara wood cut from the grove. William Chapman and his wife, Anne, were the most prosperous merchants in town, enough so that they'd rebuilt their shop in the market just two winters past, to be two stories tall. The only person missing was his mother, but Trist put that thought aside firmly.

Trist took a long drink of watered wine; building the bone-fires with the other young men had been long work, even with - especially with - the help of the younger boys of the village, who were more interested in playing with the fires and running around, shrieking, with smoking brands. He didn't know whether the bone-fires actually kept dragons, witches and faeries away, but it was a Midsummer's Eve tradition, and he couldn't remember a year where he hadn't been running around on the errand the night before his birthday. He was fourteen tomorrow, on the Feast Day of Saint Madiel, and he now wore an arming sword on his hip, though he would have preferred something longer. Trist had come more and more to prefer a blade he could wield with both hands, though Percy told him he was a fool to give up a shield. Of course, Percy could hardly beat him one time in three, now.

"And Angelica root - wild celery? - that's good for aches and pains when you get older," Enid De Lancey went on, seated to his right. She was younger than him, though Trist forgot by how many years, a wisp of a girl with brown hair and a quiet voice he had to strain to hear over the sounds of the feast. The current course was Tartes de Chare, a pork pie containing currants, dates, raisins, and pine nuts, spiced with pepper and ginger, and all mixed with honey. It was one of Trist's favorites, though Enid didn't seem to be eating much of it. In fact, while she'd moved her fork around a bit, he wasn't sure she'd actually swallowed any.

"I wonder if Brother Hugh is aware," Trist said courteously. "It might be good to grow a crop in the Abbey herb garden, for the older Brothers. How do you like the pork pie, Lady Enid? It's one of my favorites."

Enid looked down at her plate. "I don't usually eat meat," she admitted, in a voice that was barely audible. Trist opened his mouth to ask whyever not, but thought better of it. A knight was courteous.

"Well," he said, after scraping his mind for a moment, "You might prefer the mushroom and cheese pie, in that case. I'm not certain what course it will be, but I helped gather the mushrooms yesterday. They grow on the oaks around here, and they taste a bit like lemon-chicken."

The younger girl brightened, giving up on moving pieces of pork around, now that she'd been honest with him. "Yes, that sounds wonderful! That sounds like Chicken of the Woods? There are a few that look much like it, but are poisonous..."

"Don't worry, I had expert help," Trist assured her. Linette had helped him, and she knew every berry, nut or mushroom that could be eaten in the Ardenwood. She had to, or she and her mother would have starved long ago. Trist's eyes flicked to his father, Sir Rience, at the head of the table, dignified in his white beard. Perhaps between the courses, Trist could find an excuse to sneak over and speak to him. He'd practiced the words in his mind - and even out loud, in the privacy of the Ardenwood - a thousand times over. How he'd admit Linette was not of noble birth, but describe her beauty, her intelligence, her loyalty.

"-Glad you're so kind," Enid said, and Trist realized he had no idea what had come before. "Father said you would be, but you never know until you actually meet someone. But now I see I had nothing to be frightened of."

Trist smiled politely; the footmen were coming in to clear the course. "Of course. You are absolutely safe here. Would you excuse me, for just a moment? I need to speak to my father about something." He rose even before the girl had responded, and threaded a path carefully up to the head of the table, where he greeted his father.

"Ah, Trist!" His father reached out an arm and wrapped it around Trist's shoulders, pulling him down and in for a loose, one armed embrace. Down the sides of the table, to the left and the right, Sir Tor and his wife, Percy and Lady Clarisant and everyone else who'd been seated near the head of the feast-table, greeted him with smiles and raised glasses. "Fourteen years old tomorrow. I remember when you were small enough I could hold you in the crook of one arm!"

Trist blushed. "You've told me, father," he said, and waited till nearly everyone had turned back to their conversations before lowering his voice. "I had hoped to speak to you, actually. Now that I'm old enough to be betrothed-"

Sir Rience leaned in and lowered his voice. "Sharp boy. Figured it out, eh? What do you think of her?"

Trist's mind caught like a wagon wheel in the mud. "Think of her?"

"Little Enid De Lancey. She'll make a good wife for you; best to give it a few years, let you both grow up, like we're doing with your brother," the older man motioned with his goblet to where Percy and Clarisant were sitting side by side, speaking with their heads close together. Percy was sixteen, but his betrothed a year younger. "But she's kind, and that's a good thing in a mother. Tor says she's crazy about plants, which is a bit odd, I'll grant you, but harmless."

"I wasn't going to ask you about Enid De Lancey," Trist finally blurted out. His father frowned, but he went on anyway. "There's a girl who lives just outside the village - her name is Linette."

"Who's her father?" Rience du Camaret-à-Arden asked gruffly, narrowing his eyes.

"Her father's long dead," Trist said, "and she cares for her mother. Which shows her loyalty, father. They aren't wealthy, I know, but I am only the second son. Percy's your heir. I care for her, father, and I want to ask your permission-"

"Angelus above, tell me you haven't already put a baby in her belly?" Trist just about choked. He'd never had more than a dance and a kiss on the cheek from Linette - not that he hadn't thought about more. He shook his head, and his father let out a sigh of relief, leaning back in his chair. "Good. You're not to see her again," Sir Rience ordered, with a decisive chop of his hand. "A dalliance with a peasant girl can be overlooked, so long as nothing comes of it, but your future wife won't like it if she finds out, so best to end it now."

"I don't want to wed Enid De Lancey," Trist protested. "She seems nice enough, but I don't love her. I barely know her."

His father grabbed him by his linen shirt and pulled him in close. "You will not refuse the daughter of a knight, of one of my oldest friends, a young woman of good breeding and quality, for some ragged peasant girl living in the woods. Now that's the end of it. The betrothal will be announced tomorrow, so go get to know the girl, and be kind to her. I should have put a stop to you sneaking off into the Ardenwood years ago - it's dangerous. We lose woodcutters every few years, and the merchant wagons have it even worse. By all that's Holy, boy, the Bissets lost a child there just this past winter. You're to stay out of it from now on. Focus on your training with John."

Trist opened his mouth to protest again, but Sir Rience clenched his fist, balling up the linen fabric and pulling Trist's shirt tight. Trist's eyes flicked down the table to Sir Tor, sitting just two spaces down on the left, with only his own wife between him and Trist's father. *A knight is courteous*, he reminded himself. "I'd like to speak more of this tomorrow morning," he told his father.

"We can speak," the older man said. "It will not change anything, but we can speak. Now go and see to the comfort of your guest." Sir Rience released his grasp, and Trist stood straight, then set off to find his way back down the feasting table to his empty seat. Enid De Lancey, it seemed, had been craning her neck to watch him, and now that he was returning, she offered a tentative, hopeful smile.

At that moment, Trist realized the feasting hall was the absolute last place he wanted to be. Turning away from the girl his father had decided he would wed, he strode out of the hall and into the warm summer evening, quickly, before his father could stop him.

Chapter Three

The Shadow Knight

Young knight, learn to love the Angelus and honor women,
so grows your honor; practice knighthood and learn
The art which dignifies you, and will glorify you in battle.
Wrestle well and wield lance, spear, sword, and dagger manfully,
whose use in others' hands is wasted. Strike bravely and hard!
-Johannes of Skandia, from his introduction to Sur les Combats

13th Day of the New Summer's Moon, 288 AC

Foyer Chaleureux stood upon a low hill, little more than a gentle swelling of the cleared land at the edge of the Ardenwood, but it overlooked the River Rea, and had enough of a view of the fields to be the most defensible part of the town of Camaret-à-Arden. Two of his father's men-at-arms guarded the door, but they didn't stop Trist from hurrying out and down the cobbled road that led to the stone gatehouse. Iebara wood was near enough as strong as stone, but limestone didn't burn, after all. His father had wanted to complete the work of turning the wood palisade atop the earthen ramparts into stone for years now, but had only ever been able to afford importing enough limestone from the quarries near Rocher de la Garde for the gatehouse. To either side, Trist passed the barracks and the stables, and then the guards at the gate, and then he was headed down into town.

Despite his father's command, he turned onto the beaten road of bare earth that the woodcutters took into the Ardenwood early each morning, and down which fresh lumber was hauled to the lumber mill on the River Rea. Past the sweetbriers, as the sun sank low on the horizon, then with a light step over the rocks and the brook, painted gold and fire where the sun shone through the forest leaves. Trist found Linette just inside the ruined chapel, where a cookfire of banked embers smoked. She stirred a clay cookpot with a wooden spoon, her left hand absently tucking the fall of her hair back over her delicate ear.

"Trist?" When she saw him, Linette leaned the handle of the spoon on the rim of the clay pot, stood up, and walked to meet him. She was barefoot in the summer heat, her hair unbound, the light from the fire glowing through the white linen of her dress to make it nearly transparent. When they met, halfway between the fire-pit and the rotten out doorway, she reached up to cup his face in her hands. "Are you well?"

Trist swallowed. "My father wants me to wed his friend's daughter," he said, the words tumbling out faster and faster. "His old friend, Tor de Lancey - he even brought the girl along and sat her next to me. They planned it, and he didn't tell me. Nothing, until I caught him to ask about you..."

Linette closed her eyes. "Is she kind, at least?"

"She seems to be," Trist admitted with a sigh. "She knows quite a bit about herbs and roots... you might even like her."

"I don't think I like her if she's going to wed you," Linette said, turning her face away from him. "Is she pretty?"

"Not like you," he murmured, reaching out awkwardly to catch her about the waist. He'd never done that before. Trist could feel how warm her skin was, beneath the thin linen dress.

"You should go," Linette said, her voice breaking. "I'm sorry, I never should have believed this could actually happen. I'm just a bastard girl living in the woods, I don't even have a roof..."

"I don't care where you live," Trist said. "I'll speak to my father again in the morning," he decided. "I'll tell him that I won't wed her, that if he tries to force me, I'll leave. I promise you, Linette, my heart belongs to you." The world rippled at the words, and he could feel them echo in his bones.

She sighed, but seemed to relax. "You should leave now. The stew's almost done, which means I need to feed my mother."

"I could help," he offered. "I'd like to meet her."

"You will," Linette promised. "One day. But she isn't well, and... I don't want to upset her. When you've convinced your father, when it's all done, I think she'd take everything better."

Trist nodded. "Alright. I understand." Releasing her was more difficult than getting back on his feet after an hour of being knocked down by John Granger, but he did it, and headed back through the twilight and the summer fireflies.

The next morning, when the bells rang with the dawn, Sir Tor De Lancey was missing.

19th Day of the Planting Moon, 297 AC

By the time Trist had reached the fourth ring of the labyrinth, he guessed that it must be at least nones, but strain as he might he could not hear the monastery bells through the forest. There'd been half a dozen dead ends along the way, forcing him to backtrack, and while he could now see the arching branches and leaves of the old oak that grew out of the ruins, well overhead, he found it difficult to judge exactly how close to the chapel doorway he might be. If the seemingly endless corridors even led there.

"Linette!" he called, not for the first time, craning his head up to try to shout over the walls, but heard no response. Nothing more than the wind rustling the oak-leaves. Trist kept on, heading to what he thought was the right. The hallway ended and turned a corner, leading him into the fifth ring, and Trist was just thinking that he must be making progress when something caught his attention at the corner of his eye. With a scrape, his blade left the sheath on his left hip. Trist brought it up in a smooth motion, spinning to set aside a black sword that would have sheared his head in half. That could have killed me, he realized in terror.

For a moment, as his eyes roamed over the stone wall, Trist thought there was nothing there. But his blade had impacted something. The beams of light coming down through the foliage of the old oak, and over the walls of the labyrinth, picked out his shadow against the stone of the wall. His shadow was using a different guard than he was. Trist had settled into the Plow Guard, with his sword gripped in hand near the level of his hips, while the shadow was in High, dark sword pointed to the sky above its head. Why wasn't it in the same stance as he was?

The realization came just soon enough for him to parry the Shadow's downward cut. With dawning horror, Trist realized the Shadow fought like he fought. It parried his riposte and shifted into Ox, moving just a hair's breadth ahead of him at every turn until they met in a bind, blades crossed at an angle before each other's chests. The face of the shadow was blank, featureless, only a silhouette with edges of shadowed hair waving in the breeze. There were no eyes to read, and it wasn't sucking breath from exertion. Did a shadow tire? Could you move faster than your own shadow? Instead of winding, Trist pressed hard in the bind, trying to force the Shadow off balance, but it moved with him, gave way before him. They both backed off a step, and the Shadow fell back into High guard as Trist desperately tried to think of what he could do. Nothing the Master of Arms had taught him had prepared him for an enemy like this.

He was breathing hard, feeling the weight of the armor he was wearing. He'd already tramped through a stream, and then the Ardenwood, fought a Thorn Knight, and then had to walk back and forth for an hour through this maze of corridors. Trist had a grim certainty that he would tire before the Shadow did, and if that happened, he was done. He needed to end this quickly. The Shadow was solid enough to fight him, to parry his blade and struggle in the bind. He didn't know for certain that he could hurt it, but he would act as if he could, and pray it worked.

Trist lowered his sword into the Fool's Guard, inviting an attack. The tip of his sword was pointed at the ground, extended out before him, and the Shadow came, cutting down diagonally across his chest.

Trist let the swing come.

He didn't even try to parry it: instead, he moved forward, swinging his long sword up in a rising cut and trusting his chain mail to save his life. Trist was wearing armor; the Shadow was of the same consistency everywhere, a simple silhouette with no further definition. A burning line of pain moved across his chest, and half a heartbeat later, Trist's sword sliced the Shadow in half. It fell in two pieces down to the ground, where it coalesced back into simply his own shadow, moving with him naturally, and nothing more.

Trist staggered and hit the ground, dropping his sword to clutch his chest. Metal rings had been broken and torn apart, his thick gambeson sliced open, and blood was leaking out. It hurt a lot more than the bruises he'd gotten from the practice swords, and he felt faint.

14th Day of the New Summer's Moon, 288 AC

The morning after the bone-fires and the welcome feast, Trist was up with the first light of dawn, cutting the clock in the courtyard with Percy and the Master of Arms, hoping that cousin Lucan would join them, as he'd promised he would. Percy was sixteen, already, and the two years between them now made quite a difference in size. Trist's older brother was now two hands taller than him, and outweighed him by a good two stone, if not more, all of which meant that Percy lately preferred wrestling to swordplay, so that he had the advantage.

They began in high guard, cutting straight down, then diagonal, followed by horizontal cuts and then rising diagonals, all from right to left. Then, they changed feet and cut the entire sequence from the other side, making each cut ten times. That made eighty cuts from High Guard, forty on each side. They worked their way through Ox, Plow, and the Fool's Guard. Trist knew that Percy would have stopped there, but Trist moved into the secondary guards, as well, beginning with Key. By the time they were done, all three of them had each made six hundred and forty cuts, and they were bare-chested, dripping with sweat. Granger gave them both a moment to take a drink of watered ale - the servants always made sure there were mugs waiting for them in the yard.

Trist heard a muffled giggle, and looked up to find both Enid De Lancey and Lady Clarisant watching their practice from one of the windows on the second floor of the hall. Percy must have noticed them, as well, for he turned and gave a wave. Clarisant waved back, but Enid turned away from the window. Even from down in the yard, Trist thought he could see her blushing.

"Wave to the girl, Trist," Percy said just loud enough for him to make out. His older brother had come up on his right, and put a hand on his shoulder. "You're going to wed her one day, after all. Best to get on her good side right off."

Trist couldn't help but frown. "We should get back to it. The morning is wasting." He turned to look for the Master of Arms, but found that John Granger now had his head together with their father, and two of the household guards loitered nearby. The older men's eyes fixed on the two brothers, and then Granger nodded sharply.

"Practice is over for the morning, m'lords," the Master at Arms said gruffly, turning away from their father and striding in their direction. "Get dressed and meet us at the Gate House. Wear your swords."

"What's wrong?" Percy asked. Trist probably would have got a cuff on his ear for questioning Granger, but then again, Trist wasn't going to inherit the hall and the village after their father's death.

"Sir Tor isn't in the manor," Granger answered, lowering his voice after a quick glance at the upstairs window where the two young women stood. "Apparently he was up drinking quite late last evening, and seen wandering the grounds with a bottle of wine after nearly everyone else was abed. Your father's assembling a search party to find him."

Trist sighed. His father in law to be was a drunken sot. "They will probably find him passed out beneath the mill," he grumbled, irked at missing the morning's swordplay. It was about the only thing he could do right, the only time of the day when he felt like he was better than Percy at something, at least.

"Let's hope you're right, Trist," the Master at Arms said grimly. "And that he wasn't fool enough to wander off into the Ardenwood."

Chapter Four

THE SEARCH PARTY

The ghost stories of the Ardenwood date back to even before the Etalans conquered Narvonne and made it a province of their empire, and many of the names of monsters and faeries in those stories are in old Narvonnian: Volonté des Feux Follets, the dancing lights in the fog that lead a traveler off their path and to their doom in some swamp or rocky gorge; or Hellequin, the Huntsman, who rides at night in the pursuit of anyone fool enough to offend the faerie king...
-François du Lutetia, A History of Narvonne

14th Day of the New Summer's Moon, 288 AC

Sir Rience du Camaret-à-Arden kept twenty armed men as guards for his hall, men whose training and equipment he paid for out of the taxes due to him from the village industries. Adding to that Rience himself, his two sons, the Master at Arms, and finally Trist's cousin Sir Lucan, who had escorted Lady Clarisant from Rocher de la Garde, that made twenty five armed men gathered in the yard not half a bell later. The servants had not found Sir Tor, nor had anyone in the village. Trist had observed Lady

Clarisant ushering a panicked Enid De Lancey back into the manor, and did not envy her in the slightest.

"Each of us will take four men," Sir Rience said. "Trist, you stay here in case he returns, or, Angelus forbid, something else happens. I'll go north, Percy east. Check all along the river, mind, both banks and the ford, all of it. Round up some men and take poles to dredge the shallows. Lucan, go south, you've been on the road to Rocher de la Garde not two days past, you'll best notice anything different. John, take the Woodcutter's path west."

"Father," Trist spoke up, and every eye turned to him. "I know the forest better than anyone else here."

Rience scowled, but to Trist's surprise, John Granger spoke first. "The boy's right, m'lord. He's been gallivanting around the woods since he was waist high. If anyone should go west, it's him. I can hold things here well enough."

"Fine." His father's scowl did not leave his face, but the matter was decided, and Trist took four men onto the woodcutter's road heading west into the Ardenwood. He wore too large a shirt of rings, an arming sword at his hip, and rode Cazador, the five year old destrier his father had purchased for him the summer before.

"Here, m'lord," one of the younger men at arms called to him, crouching down to examine the beaten dirt path. Trist saw that he had smallpox scars on his cheeks, and remembered that his name was Henry. While it annoyed him a bit that he missed the tracks, it didn't surprise him; Trist had never been great at hunting. He'd never been great at anything, but swordplay.

"What have you found, Henry?" Trist asked, urging Cazador a few steps closer. His father had always taught both he and Percy that a lord should know the names of the people who served them, and use those names. It showed people that you knew who they were, that you took your obligations as a lord seriously, that you cared what happened to them.

"Two sets of footprints," Henry said, after a moment. "The boot prints are deeper, the man who made them was heavy. And then here?" He reached across the dirt, pointing at scuff marks that Trist could barely make out. "Bare feet. Whoever made these was much lighter."

Trist sighed. Wonderful. The man who was supposed to be his father in law had gotten drunk and wandered off into the Ardenwood with a woman. Not his wife, of course.

Trist wondered if they'd find Sir Tor with a serving girl, or with someone from the village. "Can you follow the tracks?" Henry nodded, and they were off.

It was slow going; Henry paused regularly, to examine the ground, to point out a broken branch, grass that had been crushed underfoot when trod upon, moss that had been scuffed off of a stone. Trist knew the forest well enough to keep a mental map of where they were, and what direction the tracks were leading them in. They weren't headed for the ruined chapel where Linette and her mother lived, he realized quickly, and that was a relief. He didn't want a drunken knight anywhere near them.

No, they were heading roughly southwest, which brought its own problems, because that meant they were coming up on the falls. The brook which spilled into the River Rea wasn't large enough to have a name, but it did have one feature that every parent in the village cared enough about to warn their children away from: a series of small cataracts, where the brook tumbled down a rocky twenty foot fall before continuing on its path to the Rea. Trist and Linette had picked their way among the rocks many times, wading in the pool at the bottom; she'd even slipped on the wet rocks once, a heart-seizing moment that he would never forget, her arms pinwheeling before he'd grabbed her by her dress, and pulled her tight against his body.

That a drunken Sir Tor and some random woman had made their way to the falls late last night did not fill Trist with hope. "Damn it all," he growled, the moment he understood where the trail was heading. "One of you stay with Henry and keep on the trail in case it turns aside. The other two, follow me as fast as you can."

Trist kicked Cazador into a canter and leaned forward, rising up in the stirrups, letting his legs hold him and flex with the destrier's gait as hundreds of hours in the saddle had made second nature. Caz leapt fallen logs and veered around oak and ash trees as they made their way to the falls, leaving the two men at arms following them some way back.

"Sir Tor!" Trist called out, as he reined Caz in at the bank. He slid out of the saddle, looped the reins around a convenient branch, and began to clamber out onto the rocks, left hand on the hilt of his sword. At first, he saw nothing, but when his eyes scanned across the bottom of the falls, a dark shape caught his eye.

Trist ended up having to wade into the brook. The pool was hip deep at the bottom of the crashing water, and cold as winter. Tor De Lancey was not alone at the bottom of the falls: one of James the Miller's daughters was there as well, broken on the rocks, the both of them, half-dressed in sodden clothes, flesh pale and bloodless. Their heads were cracked on the wet stones like rotten gourds. He recognized her by her black hair:

Percy had commented once, before he was betrothed, that he thought her pretty. Anne, maybe? Tor's breeches were lost somewhere, who knew how far downstream. Neither of them was breathing, and there were dark stains everywhere the splashing water did not reach.

When his two men got within shouting distance, Trist sent one back to fetch everyone else and to carry word to his father; the larger of the two, a man named Luc, he urged into the water to help him pull the bodies out. It was the first time that Trist had ever touched a dead human being, and after they had gotten the girl onto the grass, and Trist had put a saddle blanket over her for modesty, he had to take a moment to be sick into the water. After he'd heaved up his breakfast and washed his mouth out, they tried to get Sir Tor out, but he was so heavy and waterlogged they couldn't pull him up onto the bank until help had arrived.

It was Sir Rience who broke the news to his old friend's wife and daughter, and Trist was glad he didn't have to do it. Enid De Lancey collapsed in great, heaving sobs at the news her father was dead, her face red and blotchy. Trist was uncharitable enough to wonder if Linette would still be pretty when she cried. The celebrations of Saint Madiel's Feast Day, and of Trist's fourteenth birthday, were muted and awkward.

Lady Jeanette, he noticed upon observation, was somewhat less distraught. Trist caught her grumbling something about a 'besotted fool' at breakfast one morning, but the new widow was agreeable enough to Brother Hugh laying Sir Tor to rest in the burial ground behind the Monastery of Saint Kadosh. Trist didn't blame her; he wouldn't have wanted to cart the corpse all the way back to their lands on the coast - all of which now fell under the widow Jeanette's control, by Narvonnian law.

Brother Hugh gave the service, and Trist would have avoided it if his father would have let him. After it was done, and he'd left flowers for both Tor De Lancey and Anne Miller, he stayed behind to put a wreath of briar roses, which Linette had helped him weave, outside his family's crypt,where his mother was buried. Linette's mother wouldn't have let her come to the funeral, she'd said, but she wouldn't send him empty-handed. Inside the granite crypt, Cecilia du Camaret-à-Arden rested, along with Percy's mother, who had died birthing him, and all of their ancestors.

The two women departed Foyer Chaleureux, along with their guards, the morning after the funeral, escorted by Lady Clarisant and Cousin Lucan. Trist watched their carriage leave from his window, and after that there was no more talk of wedding him to Enid de Lancey.

19th Day of the Planting Moon, 297 AC

When he didn't bleed to death on the bare stones of the labyrinth, Trist eventually got up the strength to do something about his wound. Pulling the shirt of mail off hurt enough to make him gasp and swear: half-broken rings had been pushed into the wound, and tearing them out again made the bleeding worse. The thick gambeson came next, and then he tore his linen shirt into strips, which he soaked with a splash from his wineskin, then tied as tightly across his chest as he could. The gambeson went back on, and then the chain shirt, turned around so that the gash of broken rings was over his back, instead of his front. Trist didn't plan to be running away from anything. The steel pauldrons he ended up not being able to strap back on over his shoulders: it simply hurt too much, so he left them lying there on the stones.

He staggered a bit against the walls, at first, but kept drinking watered-wine as he went to dull the pain, and eventually Trist was able to move almost as well as before the fight with his own shadow. His thoughts skittered like a waterbug, and it occurred to him that if he had married Enid de Lancey, she would have packed his wound with some sort of poultice to help him heal. He hadn't been fair to her. If he was still alive in a few days, he would see what he could do to rectify that. Not a quarter hour after setting out again, he followed a final turning and emerged from the labyrinth at the entrance to the Chapelle de Camiel.

Bracing himself, Trist closed up the waterskin tight, let it hang at his waist, and drew his longsword. "Linette!" he called ahead, and staggered heavily into the ruined chapel. There was no one waiting for him under the shade of the oak leaves, and the fire-pit was cold. He shivered; the entire chapel was cold, for that matter, as if the sun did not warm it. Trist's eyes fell on the stairs leading down to the cellar. Linette never had let him down there, but the time for seeking her permission was past.

Sword in hand, Trist descended the stairs into the cool dark beneath the hill on which the ruins of the Chapelle de Camiel stood.

Chapter Five

The Wedding

If you say that you can't, then I shall reply
There's never a rose grows fairer with time
Oh, Let me know that at least you will try
Or you'll never be a true love of mine
Love imposes impossible tasks
There's never a rose grows fairer with time
But none more than any heart would ask
I must know you're a true love of mine
-Traditional Narvonnian Ballad, Author Unknown

18th Day of the Planting Moon, 297 AC

Colored light fell from panes of stained glass overhead. Trist was now twenty-two, since last Midsummer's Day, and Percy twenty-five. Standing at his older brother's side, he dragged his eyes down from bright depictions of Angelus, and scanned the small crowd again. He didn't think there was actually any threat to Percy's life in the chapel at the Monastery of Saint Kadosh, but in accordance with tradition, Percy was not wearing a sword, and that meant that his safety was in Trist's hands. He almost wished someone would be fool enough to try something, just so that his years of training would finally be worth something.

Brother Hugh stood in front of the small altar; he had just finished fasting Percy's right hand in Clarisant's left, wrapping cloth gently around their fingers three times. There had been words, prayers to the Saints Theliel and Lailahel, but Trist had let them pass him like water over rock. His new sister-in-law's maid stood by her side, and in the pews, Baron Urien's retainer, Sir Cador, looked on impassively as witness; Trist's father, Sir Rience, had a smile on his face. There hadn't been many smiles from the aging knight since his old friend's body was dragged out of the brook, but apparently watching his eldest and favorite son wed was enough to break through the gloom. No doubt their father was already looking forward to grandchildren, and the security of another generation of their lineage. Trist wondered how Clarisant felt about that: her most important duty wasn't something you could train to be good at, like jousting or fencing. Her most important duty was to give her husband a son, and whether that happened or not was in the hands of the Angelus.

There had been no further attempts to betroth Trist; his father stirred less and less from his solar as the years passed, as if something in him had died that morning by the falls. He was like an old tree, half rotted but still standing, only a few leaves to speak of. Everyone knew it was coming down sooner or later, but somehow it hadn't happened yet. Which left the actual business of running things to Percy, and plenty of opportunity for Trist to find his freedom in the Ardenwood, with Linette.

Cheers rang out from the pews; the ceremony must be concluded. Trist felt slightly guilty for not having paid more attention, but he was only here for Percy. Perhaps the whole thing would have been more interesting if it was his hand being wrapped in cloth, but he'd never had much tolerance for listening to Brother Hugh drone on. The only thing that made him slightly curious was that Lady Clarisant's parents hadn't arrived with her five days ago, on the eve of the Feast of Saint Lailahel. Percy had confided to him that there were rumors of war with the Caliphate, south of the Hauteurs Massif.

For a moment, he wondered what Linette would look like under the stained glass, painted in colored light, hand in his. Would they all cheer just as loudly? Trist pushed the thought aside; he would see her tonight, after the feast.

The remains of roast boar had been cleared away, the bowls of venison stew and eel from the river, and Trist ducked back into the great hall to pop one last raspberry tart into his mouth.

"Sir Cador just came down and bid me farewell; he's riding south tonight. You've seen them up to their rooms?" his father checked gruffly. Nearly everyone had already departed, but Sir Rience was still drinking his wine. They'd put a new bottle in front of him on the table, Trist noticed.

"Yes," Trist said, after washing the tart down with a sip of ale. "Saw them upstairs and into your old rooms. The door is closed, there is a guard outside, and I have no desire to listen from out in the hall. Kind of you to offer them the suite."

Rience shrugged. "I haven't needed the space since your mother passed," he admitted, words fumbling and slow from drinking. "Too many memories. I'm already happier on the north side."

"Well," Trist said, pocketing a few treats to take with him, for Linette. She enjoyed sweet pastries with the innocent glee of a child, and she never got any unless he brought them. "I could do with a bit of fresh air. I will see you in the morning, Father."

"You're going out to the forest again, aren't you," his father called after him, voice echoing through the hall, just before Trist passed through the doorway. He paused, and looked back.

"I am," he said, "And I am sick of pretending otherwise."

Sir Rience sat in the gloom of the hall, the torches burned low and guttering. Trist couldn't quite make out his father's expression. "I should have put a stop to that when you were a boy," he muttered. "After the first time."

"The Ardenwood is not nearly so dangerous as you think, father," Trist sighed.

"More dangerous than you know!" Rience du Camaret-à-Arden lurched to his seat, spilling his goblet. Wine ran off the table onto the floor. "Have you ever counted how many lives that forest has claimed? I have! Hardly a winter goes by when some traveler isn't dragged off and eaten by wolves. Four children since your brother was born. Four! As if I could forget that number - every one of them, I thought, 'that could have been one of my boys.' Tor," he coughed over the name of his old friend, "And the Miller's daughter. And then there's the ones who just go missing. Over two score claimed by that damned forest in the past twenty years, Trist! Do you really think that is normal?"

Trist frowned. "I do not understand what you are saying, Father," he admitted, at last. "It is a deep forest. We know there are wolves and bears, and sometimes people who go in get lost. But every forest is like that."

"No!" Rience strode across the hall toward him. "No other wood is like this one. None that I've ever been to. And I've let it be for too long. I should have gone in years ago, when you were still young, with iron and fire and priests, and hunted down whatever evil is nesting there."

"There is nothing in the Ardenwood but animals and ruins," Trist said sadly. His father used to be such a confident, strong man. It was hard to see him broken, like this, and harder to admit it. "Animals, a few old stones, and a couple of people living out their lives on what they can gather. There is no great evil there."

"Why do you think they consecrated that hill, boy? It-" Rience broke off as a woman's scream echoed through the building, from somewhere on the second floor.

"Clarisant," Trist realized, in an instant.

"Go!" Rience shouted. "Protect your brother!"

Trist turned and raced out of the room, then up the curving stairwell, left hand on the pommel of his blade. Sir Rience tried to keep up with his youngest son, but the drum of his steps faded behind Trist by the time he'd scrambled out onto the second floor landing. Age and food and drink had ended the days when his father could outrun him. Down the hall to the door of the master suite, where Trist drew his longsword and then kicked the door with one boot. It flew inward, and he froze.

His new sister-in-law, Clarisant, wore nothing but a thin shift; her eyes were wide. She was backed into the pillows like an animal cornered up against a wall, and she clutched his brother, Percy, to her chest as if she would protect him. Percy's skin was pale, bloodless, and his eyes closed, his head lolled to one side. Between the newlyweds and the doorway was a woman in a white dress, blonde hair tumbling down her back, and she spun to face Trist when the door gave way with a bang.

"Linette?"

Trist's sword dipped toward the floor, and his gaze caught on her ears. They framed her face differently, threw his familiar image of her off so that everything felt fundamentally wrong. Instead of being rounded on top, they rose upward in a gentle arc, elongated to a delicate point at least an inch higher than the top of an ear should go. Linette's hair stirred as if caught by a playful breeze, but he felt no wind in the room. So, too, all the colors of her were somehow more intense: her hair as bright as the full moon, her eyes the blue of a cloudless summer sky, her lips as red as if they were stained with raspberry juice.

"Trist, my love," she said, "Look at me. I came to protect you. To protect us."

"She's a monster!" Clarisant wailed. "Percy," she moaned, burying her face in his older brother's hair. "My sweet Percy..."

"They were going to send you away," Linette spat, as Trist's eyes swung back and forth between his brother and the girl he loved. "It was all a plan with your father, to get you away from me."

Clarisant, in the meantime, shook Percy, trying to wake him, and then tapped his cheek with her hand. "He's not breathing, Trist," she sobbed. "He's not breathing, help!" Tears streaked her cheeks.

"What did you do?" He asked Linette, mouth dry, tongue thick.

"The only thing I could do," she said, eyes shining. "One for each, a Tithe to the King of Shadows, and a Tithe to me. Let me finish. Turn and walk out of the room, my love. She won't feel any pain, and then it will just be you and I, and we can be married, and live here together. I'll even give you a son, my love, I promise. We'll be so happy together, I know we will."

"Percy!" Sir Rience du Camaret-à-Arden, gasping for breath, barreled through the doorway, dagger in hand, pushed past Trist, and swung at Linette. She hissed and spring backward to the window, arching like a cat, and Trist would not have been surprised to see a tail flick behind her from the way she moved, nothing like a human being.

"Daemon," Rience growled, while Clarisant sobbed Percy's name over and over. "What have you done to my son?"

Linette's eyes narrowed. "You should have let me have him years ago, old man," she hissed. "For fear of losing one son, you've lost the other." Her gaze flicked back to Trist, but none of it seemed real. "Come to me under the hill, my love," she said. "Two oaths you've given me: you swore to protect me from harm, and you swore that your heart is mine. Now I give you one in return: I will love you until the end of the world, undying, as only one of the Fae can. Come to me."

The faerie woman threw herself backward, and glass shattered, but there was no blood. For a long moment, there was near silence, broken only by the sobbing of a young widow. "My boy," Sir Rience said, the words ripped from his heart, and stumbled forward to the bed to wrap his arms around the corpse of Trist's brother.

Feeling nothing, Trist walked to the window and looked down. For the space of a single heartbeat, Linette's wind-tossed hair shone in the moonlight, and then she was gone, but he knew where he would find her.

Chapter Six

Acrasia

The station of Knight was an invention of General Aurelius, the first King of Narvonne, during the dark years following the Cataclysm. After the fall of the Empire, the support structure of the Etalan Legions was gone, and Aurelius needed to reorganize his army. From that need, we have the Knights and Barons of today, all holding land from our Crown, in return for their fealty and service.
-François du Lutetia, A History of Narvonne

19th Day of the Planting Moon, 297 AC

Dust billowed into the air, boiling in the shaft of sunlight that speared through the windows of the scriptorium. Brother Alberic coughed as he flipped carefully through the pages of the third manuscript they'd pulled out of the monastery's archives; Trist had waited through the monks' prayers at prime, then immediately pulled his tutor aside. Two well-scraped bowls of stew sat on the table, thrust to one side, and Trist ran an oiled cloth once more along the blade of his longsword while his former tutor read.

"Here we are," Alberic croaked finally. "The account of Brother Accolon, the first Abbot of the Monastery of Saint Kadosh, nearly three hundred years ago, after the fall of the old Etalan Empire. General Aurelius had sent people to settle here and to harvest the grove of Iebera trees, you'll recall from your histories, and the monastery was built to shepherd their souls. But woodcutters kept disappearing into the woods, and so a knight was sent for from Lutetia, a certain Sir Baylin, an Exarch who fought with a sword in each hand." Trist rolled his eyes; he regarded people who used two swords as more concerned with flashy appearances than skill at arms.

'And he went into the Ardenwood," Alberic read out loud, "And to a certain hill, whereupon he found a maiden surpassing fair, who called herself Acrasia, and the entire hill was her bower, of Oak, Ash, and Thorn, where she wove flowers into her hair and sang. Sir Baylin was passing courteous to her, and asked her whether she might know of any monster in the wood that might have taken so many wood-cutters, whereupon she spake that the trees of the wood were in her charge and in her care, and to fell them a grievous harm. Sir Baylin apologized and made as if to leave, but hid himself in a patch of sweet-briar, and saw where the Lady Acrasia descended into a cave under the hill. He followed, and under the hill there he found all of the lost woodsmen. Pale they were, and laid upon stone biers in row after row, their lips starved in the gloam. And then he knew what the Lady Acrasia was, truly: the Faerie lover who enslaves men with her love, and then lives upon their lives, as they waste away, ever her slaves."

"Acrasia," Trist said, the words from the manuscript pounding in his heart. "But there's no roof - How do you keep warm in the winter," he'd asked her, years ago. He heard Linette's voice again, clear as bells: "The cellar." And she'd pointed to a stair that descended down into the earth beneath the ruined chapel.

"Is that her mother, then?" He wondered, frowning, but with a feeling of relief. If Linette's mother had forced her to do this, Percy's death was not truly her fault. "Did she keep me away from her mother because she knew what might happen? Because she wanted to keep me safe from Acrasia?" Trist sighed. "And how did the chapel come to be there?"

Brother Alberic flipped ahead, scanning the pages. "Accolon writes that Sir Baylin returned with a group of monks and woodcutters, and with iron and flame drove the faerie into the ground, where they sealed her up with great stones, and then built a chapel. They consecrated it holy ground, so that as long as the chapel stood, Acrasia would be sealed beneath, unable to leave."

"But the chapel has fallen into ruin," Trist said, understanding. "And so now she is free. Has been for a while - that is why my father has records of all the people missing or dead. This monster has been stealing the life from innocent people for years." And holding her daughter captive.

"The Chapelle de Camiel has been a ruin for as long as I can remember," Alberic admitted. "People forget, Trist," he said, sadly. "Even when we write things down... people forget. After three hundred years, we forget quite a lot."

"And now my brother is dead." Trist rose. "But I know what I need to do. Thank you." He sheathed his longsword at his hip.

"My dear boy," Alberic said, and his voice may have been the kindest that Trist could ever recall from his former tutor. "You are all we have left. Whatever you do, you must be certain you come back to us."

On his way from the monastery back to his father's manor, Trist stopped to visit Hywel, the village blacksmith, who had begun his morning work making horseshoes.

"That is an odd thing to ask for," Hywel said, his mustaches drooping over a puzzled frown as Trist placed four silver coins before him. "Steel would do you better, m'lord. There's a reason no one makes weapons like that any longer. Steel is stronger, and won't rust as easily."

"Can you make it?" Trist asked again, and Hywel nodded. "And is that enough? To get it done right away."

"It is," Hywel admitted. By the time Trist turned his steps uphill to the Foyer Chaleureux, the apprentice was pumping the bellows so that the blacksmith could begin. Trist thought that the guards at the gatehouse saluted him more crisply than usual, and his mouth twisted at it. Percy was supposed to inherit their father's lands, not him. None of this was right.

He went to the kitchens, where he took a wedge of cheese, a half loaf of slightly stale bread from the wedding feast the night before, and a slice of cold boar. Two torches, unlit, but with wrapped heads soaked in oil and then dried. He filled his wineskin with watered wine, and then made his way up to his rooms, where he began to pull his armor off the stand.

Trist's father hadn't wanted to have a full set of plate commissioned for him until Sir Rience was certain that his youngest son was done growing. Trist had a padded gambeson, however, which he put on first over his linen shirt, and then over it he wiggled into a shirt of rings, which Hywel had made him three or four winters past. It had hung down almost to his knees, at first, but now it fit him. He wrapped his sturdy leather belt around the mail twice, and hung his longsword back on his hip before going to Percy's rooms.

Clarisant wasn't there; she was preparing the corpse, he knew, for the funeral. As Percy's widow, it was her task to wash his body and shroud it, before it was taken to the monastery. With certain strides he walked over to Percy's armor stand, and began sorting through pieces to try what would fit him and what wouldn't. It was a beautiful set, each piece etched with the family heraldry, the flowering Iebara trees carefully detailed. The vambraces were fine, good steel that he buckled over the sleeves of the gambeson, and they protected his lower arms well. His elbows were left vulnerable, but there wasn't much to do about that.

The pauldrons he was able to make fit well enough, strapping them across his chest over the mail, and a trial at moving his arms convinced Trist that he wouldn't be slowed too much with his blade. He wanted to get the greaves on, but the straps just weren't long enough. He'd always had thicker calves than Percy - 'they're like tree trunks!' his older brother had complained when the Master at Arms had them wrestling. It would have to do. Trist tromped down the stairs, one hand on the pommel of his sword, and out to the stables, where he loaded Cazador's saddlebags with the food he'd taken and set about getting the destrier ready to ride.

His father found him in the stable.

Sir Rience du Camaret-à-Arden seemed withered, curled in on himself like an autumn leaf. Gone was the confident stride of the knight in his prime that Trist remembered from his childhood. "You're going, then?" His father asked, voice quiet with sheer exhaustion.

"I have to," Trist said, pulling the girth strap tight and elbowing Cazador in the belly to make the destrier exhale with a huff. The big baby liked to hold his breath and cause trouble when he was being saddled. "You were right, father," he said, though it pained him to admit it. "The Ardenwood is dangerous. I have been with Brother Alberic, reading over the records from the first Abbot. The Chapelle de Camiel - it was not built for people to worship at. It was built to seal that hillside, to trap whatever evil lives underneath there, to keep it from killing any more people."

"Sweet Angelus," Rience exhaled. "I should have dealt with this years ago, when you were children. Now I'm too old and too broken. I'll only get in your way, if I come with you, my boy." He coughed. "Get on your knees."

"Father?" Trist frowned.

"I said get down on your knees, son," Rience insisted, "And hand me your blade."

Trist pulled his longsword from where it hung at his hip in a leather scabbard, and offered it to his father, hilt first. Then, awkward in the mail and pieces of plate he'd scavenged from Percy's chambers, he got down on the ground, on one knee. Sir Rience put the sword between them, tip down on the packed earth of the stable.

"Hands on the hilt, with mine," his father instructed, and Trist swallowed. His mouth was suddenly dry. "Trist du Camaret-à-Arden, I charge you to never commit outrage or murder, always to stand against treason, and to give mercy to those who ask for mercy, upon your honor and the honor of your family, forever more. I charge you always to help ladies, and never to commit rape, upon pain of death. Finally, I charge you to never take up a battle in a wrongful quarrel—not for love, nor for any worldly goods. Do you so swear, by your hope of salvation under Heaven?"

"I so swear," Trist murmured.

"Remove your hands." His father lifted the sword, leveled it with the ground over Trist's left shoulder, which he tapped with the flat of the blade. Then, he raised it, passed it over Trist's head, and tapped his right shoulder. "Rise, Sir Trist du Camaret-à-Arden, Knight of the Kingdom of Narvonne."

Trist hesitated. "Father, I..."

"Get up and take your sword back," Rience said gruffly. "It's too big for me now, anyway," he grumbled.

Standing, Trist accepted the longsword and sheathed it. "I thought I needed to stand vigil, first," he said, after a moment.

"Hardly ever time for that, on a battlefield," Sir Rience explained. "Wasn't when Tor and I were knighted, after the massacre at the Hauteurs Massif. No, the oath's the important thing, and that it be another knight to give it to you. You renew that vow every year, you hear me?" Trist nodded. "Good," his father said. "Now go avenge your brother, and then come back to us."

"I will, Father," he promised, and then put one boot into the stirrup, before swinging up into the saddle. "I know we have often argued, but... I loved my brother. And I love you, Father." Trist steered Cazador out of the stable and into the yard, and turned his head toward the road that led down into town, and further on to the path the woodsmen took into the Ardenwood.

Chapter Seven

Under the Hill

Ides of September, 979th Year of the Empire
Another skirmish with the forest-men, today. They are practically the slaves of the things in the trees. This forest is like no Etalan wood, filled with all manner of fell beasts and temptations. The Narvonnians call them faeries, but they are monsters all by any name. When we find one, we stake it to the ground with iron spikes and then set it aflame, and that seems to do for them well enough.
-The Campaign Journals of General Aurelius, volume II

19th Day of the Planting Moon, 297 AC

"I barely had enough time to grind an edge onto it," Hywel, the blacksmith, admitted, showing Trist the dagger. "Full tang, because I knew I wouldn't be able to get a wooden handle onto it for when you got back. I wrapped the tang in leather cord, but it won't be comfortable, m'lord. In truth, I have far better already made. You can take any of those you like; this thing is so brittle it's liable to snap when you most need it."

Trist examined the dagger. The blade was a dark gray, darker than steel, almost black. Hywel was right, he found, when he gripped the leather-wrapped tang in his hand: it wasn't comfortable. "It will do. Thank you," he told the older man, and bent down to put the iron dagger in his boot.

Hywel followed him back out of the forge, and watched as Trist swung up onto Cazador's back. "Good luck, m'lord," he said. Trist waved once, and then he and Caz were off. "Iron," he could hear Hywel still complaining behind him. "Why does the boy want iron, of all things?"

The temperature had dropped noticeably by the time Trist reached the bottom of the stone stairs that led under the hill, beneath the ruins of the Chapelle de Camiel, and the cold made his fresh wounds ache. He had to stop halfway down the stairs, when the curve of the stone stairwell had begun to cut off too much of the light from above, to pull one of the two torches from where it had been thrust through his belt. Three strikes of flint and steel later, he got a spark, and the light from the first torch was enough for him to see by the rest of the way down. When he finally stepped off the last stone step, and the torch cast a circle of flickering light into the gloom, he saw that he was not in a cellar.

The floor was packed earth, but that was true of plenty of cellars. The gray sedge growing nearly knee high to either side of him, forming a bare path from the base of the stairs, stretched out to the edge of the light on every side, blades waving gently, though Trist felt no breeze. Frost coated the sedge, though it was summer.

Trist held the torch high, swinging it around to get a better look, and his eye was drawn to his own shadow. He frowned. His shadow's left hand rested on the pommel of his sword. Trist looked down at his own left hand, loose at his side. Back to the shadow, gripping the sword pommel. Despite himself, he shivered. He had no desire to repeat that duel.

"Linette!" Trist called, and his voice echoed in the darkness. Seeing nothing else to do, he set off down the path of packed earth that wound between the banks of sedge on either side. The circle of flickering torchlight moved with him, and the stone stairs were out of sight by the time he came upon the first pair of biers.

Unlike the wooden bier his brother's corpse had been placed on, these were of stone, and had no wheels. Trist knew what they were all the same, for upon both sides of the path, a corpse lay on each bier, draped in a gauzy shroud. Trist swallowed, and examined them. To his left, a knight, still in ancient armor, clutching a sword to his chest, all the metal long rusted. And on his right, a lady, her dress moth-eaten and sere. He did not recognize either of them.

Nor did Trist recognize any of the first half dozen corpses, for he passed more stone biers, each with their own shrouded remains, to right and left as he continued down the path. The seventh and the eighth corpses, however, he knew: a kind woodsman he recalled from his childhood, and opposite him, a young boy. Trist looked down at the child's face, and tried to remember his name.

Bill, he decided, after a long moment. He'd been part of the gang that was always fishing down by the bridge over the Rea, when Trist had tried his hand at it, once. It had been awkward, all the other boys calling him 'm'lord' when he only wanted to play. Bill had gone missing in the Ardenwood, and everyone had gone searching. The boy's father had fallen into a ravine that night, stumbling about by torchlight, and broken his neck.

Trist moved on to the next pair of corpses; he didn't recognize them, but they had the look of the kind of mercenaries who were hired to guard the wagons full of trade goods that passed through the Ardenwood between Camaret-à-Arden and Rocher de la Garde on the sea.

The eleventh and twelfth corpses, he knew immediately. On the right was Anne Miller, the drowned, black-haired girl he'd pulled from the brook beneath the falls himself, and on the left was Sir Tor De Lancey, armed and armored as he had been in life, when he'd come riding up to the gatehouse with his wife and his young daughter Enid and their men-at-arms. "But we buried you," Trist murmured, shaking his head. He stepped closer to Tor, leaned over the corpse and its thin shroud. "Five years in the ground," he spoke out loud, if only to break the silence. Shouldn't the old knight be rotten?

Tor's eyes opened, and Trist bit back a shriek. Now his left hand really did drop to grip the pommel at his belt, and his heart was so loud in his chest it nearly drowned out the croaking gasp from the dead knight's lips.

"Flee!" Tor de Lancey gasped, flesh pale, lips cracked. "Before it is too late!" With a sigh, his eyes fluttered closed again, and Trist retreated from the corpse. He swallowed a gulp of watered wine from the skin he carried, to give himself strength, and continued up the path. There was the sound of water, now, moving over rock, and wildflowers began to grow among the sedge. His eyes skittered over the next two biers with their shrouded corpses, but the fifteenth bier held armor he recognized, while the sixteenth was empty. They stood in front of a deep, dark pool, and an empty throne of black, knotted Iebara roots, rising from the ground.

Trist wanted to turn aside; wanted anything but to look upon the corpse that was on the fifteenth stone bier, but he was drawn forward as if in thrall to some dark fascination, and he could not look away.

"Percy," he moaned, choking back tears. His brother lay on the bier, pale under his shroud, wearing his full armor - even the pieces that Trist had appropriated before coming.

"His wife should be on the other side," Linette's voice came out of the gloom, and she stepped gracefully into the flickering torchlight, barefoot, her hair tossed by no breeze Trist could feel. The frosted wildflowers and sedge brushed her white dress, and she wore sweet-brier roses in her hair, just like she had on the day they had first met, as children. "Only half the Tithe is paid."

"How can he be here?" Trist demanded. "He was being washed for burial when I left."

Linette stepped to him, her shadow dancing and twirling about her, and he was damned for when she wrapped her pale arms around his neck he did not stop her. "Is a man's body all that there is of him?" she asked softly, bending her neck to one side, and as her hair shifted and fell away he saw the pointed, delicate tip of an ear peeking through the strands. He looked at her pale, soft neck and tried not to think of pressing his lips to her skin.

"No," Trist said, after a moment. "There is a soul."

"Call it what you like," Linette said, resting her forehead against the mail over his chest. "A stunted and deformed thing, like a stillborn child. Nonetheless, it exists. Unseen, like the stem of a lilly beneath the pad, under the water. There," she nodded to Percy's shroud and bier, "Is the lilly-stem of your brother. His soul, if that is how you name it."

Trist closed his eyes for a moment, then opened them with new resolve. "Listen," he begged. "I know you, Linette. You are kind, and I love you. I know your mother made you do this." She pulled back from his chest to look up at him with those blue eyes, but now he realized they were winter eyes, blue over a still land blanketed in snow. Trist wrapped his hands around her small waist, and she leaned her weight back into them, as if they were about to begin a dance.

"Yes, your mother," he continued, to get it all out before anything could stop him. "Acrasia. We found the name in the oldest records of the monastery, how Sir Baylin sealed her away, and they built the chapel here to make her a prisoner. She made you do this, did she not? But I am ready for her, Linette. I have brought iron and fire. Help me defeat her, help me put a stop to all this killing, and we can leave together."

"My mother?" Linette shook her head. "You mean this mother?"

In his arms, she changed: her skin wrinkled and spotted with age, her hair streaked with gray. "Where've you been, girl?" she said, in the same voice he remembered hearing from the ruins so many years ago. In a blink, Linette's mother was gone, and she was young again.

"What-" Trist shook his head, unable to make his mind work.

"Do you understand yet, my love?" Linette asked, and then she was as he'd first seen her, a girl of not more than nine winters. "It's all me. It's always been me. Your Linette," she purred, once again beautiful and a woman grown. "Your Acrasia."

Trist shoved her away, violently, and drew his sword, throwing the torch onto the packed earth of the path so that he could take the hilt in both hands. With a jolt, he realized he was in Fool's Guard, the tip pointed down at the ground instead of at her. How appropriate.

Linette - Acrasia, he corrected himself - looked at the torch, then at his sword. "Fire to drive away shadows, and iron to strike. But steel doesn't work as well, and you're missing a piece, my love," she chided him. "And you're mine by oath, twice over."

"You murdered my brother," he gasped, anguished, saying it out loud for the first time. Her mother hadn't made her do it. She had no mother. It had been her, and her alone. Now it was real.

"They were going to take you away from me," she said softly, as if soothing a wild animal or a wailing child. "I couldn't let that happen. And now everything can be perfect, my heart. Look. Wed me, take me as your lady, and I'll even give you a child." Acrasia waved her hand, and suddenly, a young boy was standing in the sedge. He had Linette's moon-pale hair, but cropped short and wild, and Trist saw his brother and his father and himself in the boy's face.

"I can give you everything you want," Acrasia urged, stepping around him, closer and closer, like a wolf circling its prey. "We'll rule these lands together after your father passes, and then our children in years to come. The Tithe is only a little thing... you can choose! Criminals, if you like. It can be a punishment for the wicked, just give them to me. They're all only shadows anyway, only half real, they don't matter."

"And me?" Trist asked, his sword wavering. "Do I matter? Am I only half real?"

"They're not like you, my love. You can be more, with my help... Only love me," she pleaded, coming around from behind him, and dropping her dress to pool at her feet. Naked, she slipped into his arms, soft and smooth; she pressed against his chest, and tilted her face to kiss him.

Chapter Eight

The Sixteenth Bier

The first seven Exarchs were raised from General Aurelius' most virtuous knights, in response to the new King's pleas to the Angelus to intercede against the daemonic forces of the Cataclysm. Not for himself or his own personal power did the first King of Narvonne beseech them, but for the protection of the innocent people of the land. Moved by Aurelius' humble sincerity, the Angelus created the Accords, and moreover recognized his claim to the throne of Narvonne by their divinity.
-François du Lutetia

19th Day of the Planting Moon, 297 AC

Afterward, they lay on a bed of moss beside the dark pool. The torch had gone out and somehow, impossibly, there were stars above them.

"...a Tithe to Auberon, the King of Shadows," Acrasia murmured, sleepily, from where she nestled against him. Her hand traced soft fingers along his chest, where she'd kissed him in the height of passion not an hour past. Her cool thigh was flung across his legs, still, from when she'd dismounted him. "Half the souls to him, and half to sustain me."

"Which was Percy?" Trist asked, the words sticking in his throat. Bile rose at her touch.

"I was going to keep him as mine," his first lover admitted. "I thought you might appreciate that. So that we could call upon him to defend us, in time of need. Your brother's sword, back from the dead..."

"So you still owe one to the Faerie King?" Trist asked, stretching beneath her, rolling his shoulders and reaching his arms up over his head. Once his back had popped, he let his right arm come back down so that he could rest his hand along her bare flank. She was so perfect in his arms. A perfect monster.

"I do," Acrasia admitted. "But it need not be that girl he was to marry if you don't want it to be. There's always rough men in the woods. Bandits, criminals fleeing the headman. I can take one of them."

"We can think about that tomorrow," Trist said, after a moment. "Now I just want to hold you."

"My perfect knight," Acrasia sighed, closing her eyes. "I'm so glad you've forgiven me. Like pulling a splinter," she yawned. "Just a little pain, and then it's all better. So long as you and I are together, no one can stand in our way," she said, voice smaller and smaller, and then she said nothing at all.

Trist held the faerie-woman against him, marveling at the fact that she breathed, like him. So this was what it was like. Would Enid de Lancey have felt as good? Acrasia's skin was cool, but she was hot inside, and the memory of it made him want to wake her and take her again.

Instead, he slowly, carefully moved his left arm down from where he had reached when he stretched his arms along the moss behind his head, and brought with it the rough iron dagger made for him earlier that day by Hywel, the blacksmith.

Trist hesitated then, for how long he could not say.

He imagined Acrasia beside him, Lady Acrasia du Camaret-à-Arden in truth, seated beside him in the great hall at the wedding feast. She was right: his father was old and broken by tragedy, and not long for this world. His mother was gone years past, and soon it would be just the two of them. Trist imagined children to come: the vision of a blonde boy she'd shown him earlier, and in his mind's eye he saw girls, too, pale-haired and playing down by the brook, weaving flowers in their hair as their mother had taught them.

And what would the people of the village think of their new lord and his faerie-wife? The faerie-wife who, it was said, fed on the souls of the wicked. Anyone who stole, or murdered, would be taken before her, so that she could pay the Tithe to Auberon, Faerie King of Shadows, and with each death she grew stronger and more terrible. And would her children be like her? Would they need to take a Tithe of souls, as well? Would rumors fly to the court of King Lothair, at Cheverny, and would he send one of his Exarchs?

Trist thought of his brother Percy, dead, clutched in the arms of the Lady Clarisant, half wrapped in the blankets of their marriage bed. The same bed that would now belong to Trist and his wife. The Faerie-wife who had murdered his brother.

Before he could think anymore, Trist stabbed the iron knife into Acrasia's chest. His hand gripped the angular, rough tang so tightly that it hurt his fingers.

She woke screaming, sucking in a great breath only to wail in pain again, and Trist scrambled back away from her, toward where his clothing lay scattered in a pile. Acrasia's fingers clutched the leather-wrapped tang of the dagger and jerked it out, throwing it aside, but where the iron had touched her, Trist could see the pale skin of her bosom blackening, as if she were a leaf held over a fire. He had the vague sense that she extended beyond what he could see, a luminous, incomprehensible thing out into the darkness. His eyes had adjusted to the starlight, and he picked his longsword up from the ground, drew it from its leather sheath, raised it to his ear, and pointed the tip at her center of mass.

"Oath breaker! Betrayer!" Acrasia howled, hunched over herself, half screaming and half sobbing. There was blood everywhere.

"Angelus help me, I still love you," Trist said, blinking away tears. "But you killed my brother."

He swung the sword.

Trist laid her body out upon the sixteenth bier, after he had dressed. "For Auberon," he said, and laid her dress over her so that she wouldn't be cold. By the side of a deep, dark pool he dressed, under the impossible stars and before the throne of black roots, but he couldn't cover what he'd done. What would Percy have thought of him, now? What would his father say? He guessed the throne was beneath the grove of Iebera trees where the woodsmen worked each day, oblivious to the evil waiting beneath their feet.

The iron dagger had burnt away to embers and ash, as if it had been a branch thrown into a fire. Trist sheathed his sword, buckled it round his waist, and set off back down the path through the sighing sedge. To either side, the spirits of those who had been Tithed stood next to their biers: Percy, Sir Tor, the woodsman and his son, and then all the others. Trist had no need of his second torch beneath the cold starlight under the hill.

When he broke into the ruddy light of the setting sun, at the top of the stairs, Trist looked around for shadow-monsters or knights of rose and thorn or mazes. There was nothing, now, but tumbled stone walls and then the Ardenwood, and a set of gleaming pauldrons lying in the leaves. He picked them up. With a rumble, the stairs leading beneath the hill collapsed behind him, swallowing up the world beneath. After he had crossed the brook and returned to the woodcutter's road, Trist found that Cazador had waited for him, so he swung back up onto the destrier's back and headed for town, where the bells rang for vespers.

When he turned onto the road that ran through the center of Camaret-à-Arden, past the blacksmith's shop, Hywel ducked out to hail him; the older man must have been keeping watch. "Is it done, my Lord?" he shouted from beneath his bristly mustache.

Trist did not rein in Caz, but let him keep walking. He was tired, his chest wound ached, and all he wanted was to lock himself in his room in the dark and try to remember what Acrasia's lips had tasted like when she'd kissed him. "It is done," he called back to Hywel.

"Hurrah!" The smith punched his arm into the air with a grin that looked to split his face. "The young Lord! Sir Trist!"

The cry drew others, and the village tumbled out of their cottages, from where the evening supper must have been served already. Every cheer bent Trist's back a bit more, and he could not raise his eyes from the road in front of Cazador.

"The forest is safe!"

"All hail Sir Trist!"

"Trist the Monster Slayer!"

"The young lord is avenged!"

Trist the Oathbreaker, he should have been called. Trist the Blind, whose brother had to die before his eyes were opened. Trist the Lecher, who lay with the murderess who slew his own brother. Finally, he passed beneath the gatehouse, where the men-at-arms looked at him with wide eyes. Sir Rience, Lady Clarisant, and Brother Alberic waited for him in the yard.

"You came back," his father said, trembling.

"It is done," Trist said dully. "Fire to drive away shadows, and iron to strike," he repeated her words. When he tried to dismount, he almost tumbled out of the saddle, and his father and the monk caught him. The cut he'd suffered fighting his own shadow must have opened, for he felt faint.

"Bring him in where I can wash his wounds," Clarisant said, and they did. It took all three of them to undress him, and by that time he felt feverish. They laid him on his bed, and the Lady Clarisant carefully pried the blood-crusted, torn strips of linen from his chest. Her fingers were delicate, but they weren't Acrasia's. He screamed when the needle went into his flesh, but he didn't know for whom.

"Whose name is he saying?" Clarisant asked, and Brother Alberic said something. Trist's eyes opened again when she began to clean the wound with hot water and wine from the kitchens, and he screamed then, but once she'd wrapped him in bandages he fell back into the darkness. The last thing he heard was his father asking, "Will he live?"

"Wake up, my love," Acrasia purred in his ear, wrapping her body around his.

"You're dead," Trist said, in the darkness of his room, in the agony of his dream.

"A part of me," she agreed. "Now we are even: a shell for a shell. Take up your sword, my lovely knight."

He pushed her off and stumbled out of his bed, to where his sheath hung, next to the stand for his armor. Someone must have taken his mail to be fixed and Percy's pauldrons and vambraces to be scoured clean, for he didn't see them. But his sword, when he drew it, had been oiled. His father. An old knight still knew how to care for a blade. The length of metal shone in the moonlight that fell through his window, pale as her hair.

"The Tithe must be paid," Acrasia's voice thrummed from the sword. He could smell her, feel her in the room with him. "The King of Shadows demands it. As you have taken one of his hand-maidens, it is now your Tithe to pay. No longer in two parts, but in three. One for Auberon, King of Shadows. The second part to the sword, which is me: Acrasia, the Faerie Blade, to sustain me. And the third part, to you, our Faerie Knight. Who to Tithe is your choice, but that Tithe must be paid."

"I'm dreaming," Trist gasped, cradling the sword.

"In return for your Tithe," Acrasia continued, and he could feel her lips along his neck, and he shivered, retching. "We give you power beyond that of mortals. First, the blade itself. Look, my love, with my eyes."

Cool hands passed over Trist's eyes, closing the lids, and when he opened them again, the room was spun with starlight. His sword burned dull red, one piece of something much larger, behind it, stretching back into the night: something luminous and incomprehensible.

"That is you, is it not?"

"Now you see me," Acrasia-in-the-sword said. "Now you see all of me, for true, my sweet, foolish mortal." Whirls of fire etched themselves into the night of his room, and Trist could not look away.

There were two threads of burning red, intertwined beneath the metal surface of the sword, and the sight reminded Trist of the way that a rope was made up of smaller fibers, wound together for strength. A cord stretched from the sword to Acrasia, behind him.

"What am I seeing?" Trist asked.

"Two Boons," Acrasia explained. "Earned beneath the hill, by your deeds, as all Boons must be. I could never give it to you, without you earning it. The first is my kiss, the Kiss of the Lhiannan Sidhe, inherited now by your sword. The soul of any mortal killed by your weapon will be Tithed. Every first soul to Auberon; every second to me; and every third, to empower you as my Exarch."

"Exarch," Trist groaned. "But the Angelus make the Exarchs."

"By the Accords," Acrasia explained, "Angelus, Faerie, or Daemon alike. Rarely do my people do this, my love, so rarely that you are only the second. But you are my Exarch now, for good or for ill, and we are bound together. The second thread, look at it."

"I do not want it. I refuse." But she did not go away, and finally Trist focused on the burning red line, and shivered. For a moment, he thought he heard voices.

"Once each day, the second Boon will allow you to summon our restless knights," the faerie explained to him. "Only one, at first, and only for as long as you can carry the weight of it - perhaps a moment or two, perhaps less. The knights I have slain are bound to serve me still, even in their death, and now you can call upon them as well." It was all meaningless; his brother was her slave still.

"Percy," Trist whispered, and fell to his knees, sobbing. Acrasia wrapped her dead arms around him and to his shame he let her hold him there, on the cold stones of his floor, under the moonlight.

Chapter Nine

A Cup of Qahwa

François du Lutetia is not worth the price of a camel's spit. No, truly, I say this not to be cruel or to insult the man. I have read his 'history,' and it is nothing of the sort. I would call him self-aggrandizing, but for the fact that his entire work is in the service not of himself, but the ghosts of his dead kings. Name it not a history, but a pile of dung buzzing with flies, and you would be more accurate. As if Narvonne were the only land to be protected by Exarchs. If you wish to truly see the blessings of the Angelus, look to the Caliphate of Maʿīn, the most perfect and holy land, guided directly by the chosen of the Angelus themselves.
-The Commentaries of Aram ibn Bashear

20th Day of the Planting Moon, 297 AC

Ismet ibnah Salah, Exarch of Epinoia, caught the delightful scent of freshly brewed qahwa as she approached the Garden of Paradise, in the palace of the Caliph of Maʿīn. If someone had pressed her to find words to describe that smell, she would have struggled;

she was no poet. Nutty? Sweet? Bold? Regardless of the words, the bouquet made her mouth water.

Six paved paths led to the fountain at the center of the garden, lined by small, cleanly trimmed green hedges. Beyond the hedges, fruit trees grew: lemons and oranges, pomegranate shrubs and apricots, and her favorite: figs, like her grandfather had given her as a treat when she was a small child.

Shadi ibn Yusuf, Exarch of Jibrīl, poured her a cup of steaming qahwa when he saw her emerge from the lanes of fruit trees. "Good morning, Exarch," he greeted her with a voice that effortlessly filled the garden. It was, Ismet concluded, a voice trained to be heard across the din of battle.

"General Shadi ibn Yusuf," Ismet returned the greeting, lowering her eyes. She was grateful for the niqāb, the long black veil which revealed nothing but her eyes. The feeling of a man's gaze upon her was uncomfortable, for a good many reasons, and so while it was not required, Ismet preferred to wear the veil whenever possible. If others took it as a sign of her devotion to the Angelus, all the better. At the wave of the general's hand, she took her seat on the cushions that surrounded the low table, using her hands to arrange the fine black fabric around her carefully.

"You have become known for your modesty this past year," Shadi remarked, watching her settle as he sipped his own cup of dark qahwa. "I cannot help but wonder whether this is related to the unwanted attention of one Nasir al-Rashid."

Ismet lifted her cup, inhaled the rich scent of the dark liquid, and then used her left hand to lift one side of the veil, revealing as little of her face as possible, so that she could take a sip. She could not help a small sigh at the taste of the well-roasted qahwa. "The eldest son of the Caliph is of course a great man, and it is an honor whenever one finds oneself in his company," the young woman replied, choosing her words carefully.

"An honor, indeed." Shadi's eyes seemed to bore into her own. "It is said you have refused his offer of marriage twice."

"I cannot help what is said or not said," Ismet stated simply, taking another drink. "For my part, I am interested only in my duty as Exarch. I have no intention of being wed to any man so long as that duty remains."

"It is a worthy duty, and one earned by only a few," Shadi said, putting aside his cup and lifting a piece of paper. "I have here the assessment of the University scholars. High marks in grammar, arithmetic, and geometry. Top marks in theology, law, logic, medicine, and astronomy. Your combat instructors praise your skill on horseback, and with the saif. You prefer the curved variety of sword, I understand?" She nodded. "Yes, they are better for use while mounted," Shadi concluded, putting aside the paper. "And your accomplishments were sufficient to earn the notice of the Angelus Epinoia, with whom you have made an Accord."

"I am humbled by the scholars' judgment of my abilities," Ismet said. "I worked very hard to be judged worthy, and the day of my Accord was the greatest day of my life." Next to her, a presence settled, and the cool, delicate hand of the Angelus moved onto her own left hand, where it now lay in her lap.

"Let me be open and honest with you, young Ismet," Shadi said, with a troubled look on his face that made her heart beat faster. He could not see her terror. The niqāb made certain of that. "Nasir al-Rashid is likely to be our next Caliph. Someone truly exceptional would need to emerge in order for Isrāfīl to make a different choice. Thus, he cannot accept being refused by you. It makes him look impotent. It is good for the ears of a general to hear many whispers, and my ears hear that you will be collected by the Caliph's guards, to be taken to quite luxurious apartments where you will remain a guest until such time as you agree to wed the Caliph's son. At which point, it will be necessary, of course, for the Angelus to release you from your Accord so that you may devote yourself to the duties of marriage, and provide Nasir with sons to continue the dynasty in their own time."

"No!" Ismet cried, then winced at her own voice and continued at a lower volume. "Please, General. I do not want him, and he does not truly want me." Shadi arched his eyebrows, signaling her to continue. "I am a... a sort of prize," she explained, grappling for words. "He says he loves me for my beauty, but I know I am too strong to be womanly. I have... wide shoulders, and arms, that are muscled like a man's. I worked for those, to use with my sword. But he says my face enchants him, so I wear the veil. That does not stop him, either. What he truly wants," she said with a swallow, finally able to put words into a fear that had been troubling her for so long, "Is to conquer a woman no one else can conquer. To prove himself on me. To take a woman chosen by the Angelus for her faith, and her learning, and her skill, and to reduce her to nothing but a brood mare to carry his children. Because if he can do that, he is better than me. He is better than all of them. And I tell you truly, General, that I will die before I let that happen. I wish I had been born so ugly that he would turn away from me with disgust, but I was cursed with my mother's face. It is my greatest grief."

General Shadi reached down to the table, lifted his cup of qahwa, and finished it. Then, he set the cup back on the table, lifted the pot, and poured for himself again. "Twenty-five years ago," he said, changing the subject in a sudden manner that left her head spinning, "I rode north into the mountains with the army of the Caliph. Do you know why?"

"The battle in the Hauteurs Massif?" The foreign words slid off her tongue easily: they had taught her Narvonnian at the University, too. "Forgive me, General. I did not realize you had fought there. I am told it was... hard fighting."

"It was as though Jahannam had come to our world," Shadi said, and she noticed his hand tremble for a moment before he lifted his cup. "My teacher died that day, slain by knights of Narvonne. They butchered him like he was nothing but meat." A sip of qahwa helped the older man to settle himself. "Afterward, while I cradled his corpse, Jibrīl offered me the chance to take up his Accord. How could I do anything but accept? Together, we rallied what we could of our men, and retreated. The Caliph said that if we had not, the day would have been a complete massacre. For twenty-five years," he continued, "I have worked to prepare our army for another march on those mountains. Not for vengeance," he assured her. "Do you know why we must bring the light of the Angelus to Narvonne?"

Ismet considered, remembering her history. "I know that kingdom was where the daemons came," she said slowly. "Where the first Accords with the daemonic were struck, and the old Etalan Empire began to crumble."

"It is so." Shadi nodded. "A night that lasted for weeks, while the crops died, and daemons slaughtered their way out from the provincial capital into the forest and the fields and the mountains. It was not until the Angelus came to lend their light to our cause that the daemons were pushed back, and bound. Ask your Angelus, young one, why we must cross the mountains and go to Narvonne."

"Epinoia?" Ismet turned her head to the side, where the Angelus appeared to her eyes. Epinoia's hair was dark as the spaces between the stars, her skin pale as marble, her eyes deep as the sea.

"What was bound three hundred years ago is stirring," the Angelus explained. "Old chains loosen and fade. The monsters of the past, the daemons that ruined an empire, wake again. They are starved now, but they will feed. They will make new Accords with wicked men. The daemon-haunted city will birth new horrors, drawing the worst of humanity to it."

"We have to warn them," Ismet said, turning to meet Shadi's gaze.

"The Caliph tried to warn the Kingdom of Narvonne thirty years ago," the general said sadly. "We tried everything we could before we marched into the mountains. But the Narvonnians have never submitted themselves to the Angelus, like we have. Their Exarchs make Accords, but they are ruled by kings who prize their own power above the will of the Angelus. Do you see now, Ismet ibnah Salah, why we must ride to war? Time grows short, and on our cause hangs the balance of the entire world."

"We." The one word stood out to her as if written in fire.

"Yes, we." Shadi nodded. "I cannot win this war alone, child. The Caliph will keep most of our Exarchs here, with him, to protect the capital and his family. I have been granted permission to bring only a single Exarch, of my choice, when I march tomorrow morning. Will you come with me?"

"Nasir al-Rashid would never allow me to go," she said, but hope sprung in her stomach like a sickness, so sudden and unexpected that she felt both faint, and at the same time as if her morning meal would come up violently.

The general shrugged. "I was granted permission to bring a single Exarch of my choice. I have it in writing. I suppose the Caliph and his son expected me to choose someone older, and thus made an oversight, but the choice remains mine to make."

"Tomorrow?"

"We ride with the dawn. I am told that Nasir al-Rashid often returns to his chambers after Fajr, and does not rise until quite late in the morning," Shadi remarked, casually. "By that time, we will be many miles north."

"I am untested," Ismet protested, though her heart cried out to go with the army. "Surely there must be better choices. Exarchs who are veterans of many battles."

"I was untested twenty-five years ago," Shadi said. "I believe there is a certain value in bringing someone with the eyes and mind of youth. Too often, as we age, we become set in our ways." All of a sudden, the general stood, and offered Ismet his hand, in defiance of all customary behavior between a man and a woman. "I have no child, Ismet. In this, will you become as a daughter to me, and allow me to teach you?"

"Choose, Ismet ibnah Salah, Exarch of Epinoia," he continued from above her, in a voice like the tolling of a bell. "Remain here, and wed that pig of a man, or come with me. Come with me, and ride to battle with the wings of the Angelus to shelter you, for the fate of this world and all of the people in it."

It was not, Ismet realized, much of a choice at all.

"As your daughter." She reached up and slipped her hand into that of General Shadi's, and he drew her to his feet as if she were nothing more than a child.

"Good. Let us see to your armor." Together, they left the Garden of Paradise.

Chapter Ten

The Widow

Vellatesia was already burning by the time we got there. General Aurelius had taken the 9th north to deal with an uprising on the border with Provincia Skandia, and we'd just sorted the savages out when word came. No one had any idea what was happening at the time; we just knew the sun didn't rise for a week straight, and we had to march in the dark. If we hadn't spent all those years building the roads, we might never have made it back through the damned forest. But anyway, we could see the capital burning three hours out, because there weren't any other lights. And it was only once we breached the walls that we found out what Governor Avitus had done.
-The Life and Times of Legionary Titus Nasica

20th Day of the Planting Moon, 297 AC

Trist woke up on the floor of his bedchamber, dawn light glaring in his eyes, naked but for the linen bandages wrapped around his torso. His sword, blade bare as he was, lay on the floor next to him, and he shivered. He'd slept through the bells that should have woken him.

"My Lord?" Brother Alberic's voice called from the hall, muffled by the door. "May I come in to inspect your wound?"

"One moment!" Trist croaked, and lurched to his feet. Fever dreams; he must have been tormented by fever dreams from the wound. Acrasia was dead, and his sword was just a sword. Nevertheless, he reached down for the hilt, to sheathe the blade before returning to his bed. The moment Trist's fingers touched the leather-wrapped hilt, a woman's arms wrapped around him from behind.

"Good morning, my love," Acrasia whispered in his ear. Trist dropped the sword back onto the floor with a clunk, and she was gone.

"I am coming in, my Lord," Brother Alberic called, and at the sound of the door swinging open in his sitting room, Trist left the sword on the floor and threw himself into the bed. The monk entered and paused, eyes flicking to the sword lying on the ground. Trist didn't see or feel Acrasia anywhere, but he thought he heard her giggle in his ear. "You shouldn't be out of bed yet, my dear boy," the monk said kindly. "I can get that for you."

"Leave it!" Trist nearly shouted. He didn't know what would happen if someone else touched the sword. Would the faerie be able to appear to Alberic, too?

Brother Alberic hesitated, and then simply said, "As you wish. Let's have a look at that wound."

Trist flinched as the linen bandages were peeled off again, but the old monk seemed satisfied. "Lady Clarisant has a deft hand, it seems," he admitted. "The stitches are small and neat. Better than I could do, in my old age. There were signs of infection last night, but it seems to have subsided. Good. I'll bandage you with fresh linens, then."

Trist gritted his teeth and suffered through the process silently.

"You should stay in bed for at least three days," Brother Alberic decided.

"Why the honey?" Trist asked, as it was slathered on the wound.

"Helps to prevent infection," Alberic explained absently. "Be thankful I don't need to use the maggots."

Trist shuddered.

"The humours in your body will be imbalanced from blood loss," Brother Alberic continued, finishing up with the bandages. "You need to eat a special diet to recover. I will speak with the kitchens. Lots of meat, especially beef and liver. Oranges and lemons, from Rocher de la Garde. Kale and spinach."

Though he had a few choice thoughts about liver and kale, Trist remembered his courtesies. "Thank you, Brother Alberic," he said, instead. "And thank you for your help in the scriptorium. If you had not not found that text..." he struggled over how to finish the sentence: then I wouldn't have been able to kill the girl I've loved since I was a child? Was Acrasia even dead? Linette was, that was for certain: he would never be able to look back on those memories without knowing them for a lie. Linette was a mask; Acrasia had been the truth. But could he even call what had happened a victory?

"My dear boy," Alberic said kindly. It was strange to see the fond smile on the face of a monk he'd considered his harshest taskmaster. "You were not the easiest student, I think we can both admit. I was hard on you because I felt I had to be. But I have always looked upon you with affection, even if I did not show it. I - all of us - are proud of you. Camaret-à-Arden will be in good hands when your father leaves us behind. Out of this tragedy, at least some good has come."

Shame roiled at the pit of his stomach until Trist thought he would be sick. "My brother is dead," he said finally, unable to meet Alberic's eyes. "I cannot see what good has come of that."

The monk gently laid a hand on his shoulder, then stood and headed for the door. "Your father wishes to speak with you, now that you are awake. I'll fetch him."

The door closed, and Trist's eyes shot to the sword lying on the floor of his bedchamber. "Nothing but fever dreams," he told himself, out loud. He swallowed, swung his legs around, and girded himself to cross the room and lift the sword.

"Let me get that for you." With a swish of skirts, Lady Clarisant crossed from his doorway and, before Trist could do anything about it, lifted the longsword. "It's ice cold," she said, with a frown, but slid it into the sheath, then hung it on the wall before turning to him in a business-like manner. "I didn't get my hands bloody stitching you up to have you ruin my work the next morning," she chided him, shooing Trist back into bed with her hands and tucking the linen sheets in around him.

Trist winced as he settled back onto a pile of feather pillows. "If you had warned me, my lady, I would have put a shirt on."

"Oh, I saw everything last night," Clarisant shot back, with a harumph. "I daresay there isn't a whole lot more need for modesty between us."

"As you say." Trist was pretty sure he was blushing, anyway. "Thank you, Lady Clarisant, for tending to my wounds," he said, his training as a gentleman providing a shield of courtesy to steer the conversation back to more comfortable territory.

"Nonsense. You saved my life." Clarisant looked to the door, and then back to Trist. He noticed that her eyes were red from crying. "Your Lord Father will be here shortly, and I expect Sir Rience will have things to speak to you about. One of them will be this: wed me, Sir Trist."

Trist blinked, and managed to close his mouth without saying anything idiotic.

"Allow me to explain." The Lady Clarisant took a breath, and then launched into it, pacing back and forth next to his bed, not so much as looking at Trist as she spoke. "Your brother's death places me in awkward circumstances. Obviously. As his widow, I should inherit his lands and properties; indeed, were he to have died years from now, even as a young man, and been survived by a wife and children, there would be little issue. But as only your father's heir - not holding these properties in his own right - and without any children, or even a pregnancy, Percy can be set aside. Your father will name you his heir, as the younger, but surviving, son. My family will want my dowry back, which I know for a fact your father has already begun investing. If he can't get it, my father will insist on my rights as a widow. Regardless, I have little to go home to: I am the fourth born child of a Baron, and a daughter besides; I inherit nothing of my own except my dowry, which as I have said is already paid to your family, and there will be some amount of doubt now as to whether I am even a widow, or if the marriage might not have been legitimate, due to lack of consummation. Which is only on my word, one way or the other."

Finally, she stopped to take a breath, and turned to Trist, the tumble of words having at last dried up, like the cascade in the Ardenwood after a hot summer. "Do you see?"

"I never had a mind for legal contracts or money," Trist admitted. "Percy was always the one who was good at those things. You are saying that if I wed you, in my brother's place, all of that mess is avoided."

"Precisely." Clarisant knelt down next to the bed. He'd never looked at her as a woman, before, but now he was forced to: instead of his someday sister, his brother's betrothed, Trist allowed his gaze to take in Lady Clarisant du Rocher de la Garde. It shouldn't affect his decision, he knew. If his brother had died in battle, before the wedding? There would have been no question of him taking up Percy's obligation and fulfilling the arranged marriage contract.

And Clarisant was pretty, of that there was no doubt in his mind. The purple of her dress brought out something in her dark hair, a cool shade that almost seemed to reflect the vibrancy of the dress. Her hazel eyes looked at him honestly. She'd prepared for this meeting, obviously, to present herself to her best advantage: her eyes outlined in kohl, her cheeks flushed, her lips red. The bodice Clarisant wore seemed to draw her waist in, and her skirts spread out, making the whole quite shapely. He's seen her in nothing but a linen chemise, and the memory of her pale skin came to mind now.

It wasn't her fault that Acrasia had been more beautiful than any mortal woman should be. Clarisant was a good woman; she deserved his honesty, if nothing else.

"You would do better without me," Trist said, closing his eyes to avoid the shame of hers. "I am not pure, Lady Clarisant; I am not chaste. What I have done is unforgivable."

"If you are thinking of the wedding night," Clarisant said desperately, "I swear upon my honor and my family name and my faith in the Angelus, that things had not... progressed so far."

"It is not you-" Trist began, but then the door banged against the wall as his father entered. He winced from the sound, and when he'd opened his eyes, he saw that Lady Clarisant had now risen, and stood a modest distance from the bed.

"Brother Alberic said you were awake," Sir Rience said, by way of greeting, then paused as he noticed his sometime daughter in law. "Ah, Lady Clarisant. It is good that you are here." The old knight strode over to Trist's bedside. "You are feeling better, now the fever has broken?"

"I am, Father," Trist said, "Though I am tired." His attempt to beg off from further conversation did not succeed.

"We will not be long. Indeed, I think it is best for all of us if this goes quickly," Rience said, with a sigh. "We will bury your brother today. Alberic has told me you can leave your bed in three days' time. Brother Hugh can perform the ceremony then. We won't throw another great feast," he continued. "I think that would be in poor taste. But it's important to set everything to rights, and then go on from there as best we can."

Trist did not have to look at Clarisant to understand what ceremony his father was referring to. "I would like to see my brother put to rest," he said thickly. The memory of Percy, pale and armored, standing beside the fifteenth bier, came to his mind. If, indeed, Percy's soul was capable of resting.

"We can have a few men carry you in a litter," his father allowed.

Trist shook his head. "I cannot marry you," he said, turning to Clarisant. "You do not understand what I have done."

"Lady Clarisant," Sir Rience said, after a long silence. "Would you let my son and I speak alone?"

"Of course." Clarisant offered them both a curtsy, and then withdrew from the bedchamber, leaving Trist with his father.

Chapter Eleven

A Broken Oath

The romantics would have you believe that Aurelius wed Elantia of the Narvonni because she was the most beautiful woman he had ever seen, but anyone who reads his war journals can tell you the truth: Elantia was the daughter of a Narvonni chief, and she brought with her the support of an entire tribe, including their fortified town at Lutetia. Vellastesia was a daemon-haunted, smoking ruin, and he needed not only a place to camp the remnants of the 9th Legion, but more urgently, supplies to feed his men.
-François du Lutetia, A History of Narvonne

20th Day of the Planting Moon, 297 AC

The door closed, and Sir Rience du Camaret-à-Arden dragged the single chair in the room over to the side of his son's bed. There he sat, with a sigh as he settled in. "Don't get old, boy," he told his son. "Everything hurts. The wound I got hauling Tor out of the muck at the Hauteurs Massif. Hurts every time it rains, too." The older man paused for a moment. "There's your first. Mark my words."

Trist looked down at his new bandages; it was better than looking at his father. "I cannot. She does not understand; she thinks it's about her, but it is not."

"Then tell me, son," Rience said. "Help me to understand."

Trist talked for the next hour, at least. He told his father, for the first time, how he'd met Linette as a child, when she was singing in the brook, with flowers in her hair. Instead of haranguing his son, for once, Rience listened. He didn't say anything when Trist described finding her on Percy's wedding night, until he relayed her words to him.

"She said you were going to send me away," Trist said.

"Yes," Rience said, with a sigh. "Yes. The Crown Prince has mustered a host to march into the mountains again - that's why Baron Urien couldn't come to his daughter's wedding. Prince Lionel intends to break the Caliphate for good, this time, though we've heard those words before. Your brother and I had thought to knight you, and send you with a few men to join the muster. My fighting days are past, and Percy would have been newlywed. We could have given his excuses, delayed at least until Clarisant was carrying a child."

"When was I to know?"

"After the wedding," his father said. "I had the thought that... if you took your girl - Linette - with you, as a camp follower... well, I didn't know what she was, at the time."

"Neither did I. You had never even met her, father," Tristan said. "But I should have known."

"The masks of faeries are things of legend," Sir Rience tried to comfort him. "You are not by any means the first to be taken in by their glamours."

"If I'd realized sooner, Percy might still be alive." Trist's voice broke on the admission.

"We both have enough 'ifs' to haunt us for the rest of our lives," Rience grumbled. "What happened when you went after her?"

Trist told his father of the Knight of Thorns, the labyrinth, and the shadow, and then of what lay under the hill. When he came to the stone biers, and the corpses on them, his father asked a few sharp questions, nodding at Trist's recollections, able to put names to some of the dead that the young knight had not recognized. Through Trist's description of his time with Acrasia, and how he had stabbed her in her sleep, then struck her down, the older knight was silent to the end.

"I believe," Rience said slowly, "I understand now why you feel you cannot wed Clarisant. Battle isn't like the stories they tell," he continued. "It's mud and piss and the smell of a man's guts falling out of his belly onto the ground. It's the scream of horses dying, and rolling around in the shit until you can jam a dagger into some poor boy's neck, because if you don't, he'll do it to you. Listen to me."

He reached out, and settled his hands on Trist's shoulders. "You never say these things to Clarisant. You go to Brother Hugh, or brother Alberic, and you make your confession. None of the other monks, mind: those two I trust. And whatever they tell you to do, you do. What happens at war, we do not bring that home to our families. We protect them from it. The same as what happened under that hill. As far as that young woman is concerned, you saved her life on her wedding night, then hunted down the monster that killed her betrothed and destroyed it, and when you came back she showed you how much that meant by stitching your wound with her own two hands. You're a knight who avenged his brother, who did what he had to do for the honor of his family. Don't ever let her believe otherwise. You hear me? It won't do her any good."

Trist nodded.

"Now," his father said. "Let me have the rest. Everything."

"The sword." Trist couldn't look at it. "When I touch the sword, I hear her voice."

"Linette? Or Acrasia, rather?"

Trist nodded. His father stood, walked over to where the sword hung, and picked it up by the leather sheath, careful not to touch the weapon itself. He sat back down, and set the sword on the bed next to Trist. They shared a glance, and then Sir Rience deliberately put his hand on the pommel.

"Cold as the river in winter," Rience observed, frowning. "I don't see or hear anything. Put your hand on it, son."

With about as much hesitation as he would have reaching into the fire to pull out an ember, Trist placed his hand on the hilt of the sword.

"I'd rather your father were gone before you talked to me, my love," Acrasia's voice purred in his ear. "We have much to speak of, yet. Oaths broken, oaths still kept. The Boons of the King of Shadows. And I want that girl gone. You're mine, not hers."

With a jolt, he pulled his hand back.

"She spoke to you, then?" his father asked, and Trist swallowed once before responding.

"She did. She wants to speak of Oaths, and... other things," Trist explained. "She does not care for Lady Clarisant."

"A cursed sword." Rience shook his head. "No good will come of that. What else has it told you?"

"Something about Tithes," Trist said. "I thought it was a fever-dream, last night, but now that I have heard her again - I remember. Souls, to be tithed to the Faerie King. That is why she killed, she told me. One of every three souls taken by the blade to Auberon, one to Acrasia - or the sword - and the third portion to me."

"Don't name the King of Shadows aloud," Rience warned him. "You might draw his attention, and that's the last thing we need. So you need to kill. To feed the sword, to feed the Faerie King. It isn't the worst thing in the world."

"Father - I refuse to be a murderer," Trist said. "I would rather drive this blade through my heart right now and be done with it."

"Who said anything about murder?" Sir Rience asked with a grin. "You're a knight, boy, and your Crown Prince goes to war. You'll have plenty of chances to feed your blade on the battlefield. But before you go, you need to do your duty to your family. You're my only heir, now, Trist. Swallow whatever misgivings you have, and do what needs to be done. We bury your brother today; in three days, you wed Clarisant. You put an heir in her belly, and then leave her with me. We'll be certain the village is still here by the time you come back."

Trist let himself fall back into the pillows, and close his eyes. "If I do not?"

"Then your family dies, son," his father said plainly. "One of us has to go to war, and if it's me, I won't come back. Either way, if you don't marry Clarisant, it has to be someone else, and as soon as possible. There's a price to setting her aside; and it would ruin us. This is what it is to be a man grown, and not a child. See what needs to be done, with clear eyes, and then do it. Because no one else will."

It felt like surrender, but Trist couldn't see any other way. "As you say then, Father." He didn't open his eyes. "I think I need to sleep."

The legs of the chair scraped on the floor as his father stood. "I can hang the sword for you."

"Better no one touches it but me," Trist said. "And I have things to say to Acrasia du Chapelle de Camiel."

Without another word, his father left the room and closed the door behind him.

Trist opened his hand, felt for the hilt of the sword, and closed his fingers around it.

"Let me kiss you to sleep, my heart," the faerie whispered in his ear. He could smell sweet-brier roses in her hair, and her lips were soft on his face.

"Not yet," Trist whispered. He didn't open his eyes; he wasn't certain he would be able to see her if he did, but seeing her would make this so much worse. "If I go to war, will men killed in battle be accepted as my Tithe?"

"Auberon doesn't care how you do it," Acrasia murmured, nestling her head down under his chin. Trist marveled at how he could feel her, just as if he had never laid her body to rest under the hill. Did the sheets move as she slid into bed next to him? "He only cares that you kill. It was two each year, for me. Three, now, for you, though he won't turn down more. It might win you his favor, in all honesty."

"I do not want his favor," Trist said. "Is there any way to undo what you have done to me? For me to be free of you?"

"Only when you die," Acrasia said. How could he even know whether she was lying?

"What is all this about Oaths and Boons, then," he asked, trying not to relax into her. A week ago, this had been all he'd ever dreamed of: alone in his bedchamber with the woman he loved in his arms. Now it felt like he was embracing a serpent - a serpent who'd taken his brother from him.

"Oaths are important to my people," she explained. "Any Oath or promise spoken in our presence, we can bind a mortal to; and any Oaths we take, are binding upon us. The very binding changes us - alters what you call a soul. The more that an Oath restricts someone, the more commensurate power it grants."

Trist frowned. "Why?" He didn't want to hear any of this; he wanted her gone.

"Put that aside for now," Acrasia said. "You've never been the scholarly sort, my love. You kept two Oaths true, when you left me under the hill, and broke a third. Threes are a sacred number, by the way. I approve."

"I promised to protect you," Trist said, thinking it through. Such an examination was not natural to him, but he could do it when forced by need. "And I broke that promise when I stabbed you."

"Stabbed me with an iron dagger, yes," Acrasia chided him. "That was horribly painful, you know."

"It does not seem to have worked," he shot back.

"You didn't kill me, but that is not the same," she explained. "That Oath is broken, until you redeem yourself. No power there - not that you can use, at any rate. Your father spoke of a cursed sword, but that broken Oath is the real curse hanging around your neck. Would you like to see it?"

"You can show it to me?" Trist asked, and she nodded against his chest. "Like you did the sword, last night? Make it easy to understand?"

"Yes. You could handle that? I worried simply enchanting your sight to see as I do might overwhelm you," Acrasia admitted. "And I would hate to watch your eyes burn out of their sockets."

"Let us keep my eyes, thank you," Trist agreed. "Show me the curse, then. Like you did with the sword." Once again, loops and twists of fire unspooled against the dark of his closed eyelids. One of them was obviously broken, the two ends ragged, though still it burned with power in that deep shade of red.

"That is the Curse," Acrasia told him. "Focus on it, my love. Let it burn into your mind."

The broken thread flared, and Trist saw himself armored, in battle. He cut a man down, but then fell to a knife, thrust into his back from behind. Another place, another field: his enemies were different, but what happened was the same: an arrow lodged in his back. Over and over again, he watched himself die, and every single time it was to an attack from behind, or an ambush, or some other sort of dishonorable trick.

And every time, when he died, the burning, ripped thread of the Oath finally fell away.

Chapter Twelve

BETROTHAL

Yes, I saw it. I was at the battle of Vellatesia, how could I not see the damned thing? There were plenty of daemons to fight, though we hardly knew what they were at the time. The names came later, you know. Legionaries were dropping left and right from fever, spitting up blood. When they fell, those damned birds either landed on them, or if we fought those off, the corpses sat right up in a couple of moments anyway. That wasn't even the worst of it; over everything, it was circling - the Cataclysm itself. Whenever it came down, men died. It gobbled up horses, dropped men's bodies from the sky to break on the stones. A swipe of its tail knocked an entire building down, right on top of my cousin Felix. We never did find his body.
-The Life and Times of Legionary Titus Nasica

20th Day of the Planting Moon, 297 AC

"What?" Trist exclaimed, opening his eyes. "Are you trying to get me killed? Someone stabs me from behind, or shoots me with an arrow, and I die? That is the only way the curse ends?"

"Seems entirely fair to me," Acrasia mumbled into his chest. "You did try to kill me in my sleep, after all."

"But is there not any other way that I can get rid of it?" He demanded.

"By protecting me, the way you were supposed to do in the first place, at great cost to yourself," the faerie explained. Why would he want to protect her, after what she had done?

"You are a sword."

"A piece of me is a sword," she corrected him. "The piece you mortals are most capable of interacting with, true. But not all of me. Not even most of me."

Trist felt a vein throbbing in his head, and decided to put this aside for the moment. "Fine. If a broken Oath is bad, then Oaths that I have kept are good?"

"They channel the restrictions on your soul to strengthen you, yes," Acrasia confirmed.

"Show me the other two Oaths, then," Trist demanded. Nothing happened.

"Ask me nicely."

"Acrasia," he said, more gently, "Could you please show me the other two Oaths?"

"Of course!"

Lines of red fire traced out to his right and left, and Trist observed again that it didn't actually seem to matter that his eyes were closed. In fact, it made things easier to see.

Trist focused on the line to his left, and, like the night before, visions flickered before him in the darkness, as slippery as fish in the River Rea, passing from his mind quick as dreams on waking.

He saw a daemon in the shape of a woman, ragged winged and horrible, forehead crowned with horns. She whispered in his ear, but he remained unmoved. A faerie lord, tall and pale, commanded him to kneel, yet he remained upright.

"Your Oath of Knighthood," Acrasia explained. "It strengthens your resolve against all manner of compulsion that would turn you aside from your duty."

Trist looked right, upon the burning thread that unspooled there, and saw visions of Acrasia. A monstrous shape, darkly massive, threatened her, and he lifted his sword in her defense. A man insulted her, and he fought in her name.

"Your Oath of Love," she continued. "So long as you are loyal to me above all other women, you are able to call upon the power of this Oath in my defense, when fighting in my name, or even when you are trying to reach me - such as if I was being held captive. The Oath will grant you increased physical strength, pushing your body beyond mortal limits."

Tristan winced. "That second Oath is going to be a problem," he muttered, and then yelped as Acrasia took his head between her hands. Out of reflex, he opened his eyes, and saw her face in front of his, nose to nose, gaze locked on his own eyes.

"What do you mean by that?" She asked, with a growl in her voice. "You're not thinking of abandoning me, merely because I no longer have a body?"

"Acrasia," Trist began, with an edge to his voice. Only a lifetime of training to treat others with courtesy, as a knight should, helped him to restrain his tongue. "You killed my brother. The Angelus teach us that forgiveness is divine, but I do not know that I will ever be able to forgive you for that. Even if you were not a sword, I would not marry you. You ruined what was between us, two nights ago."

"That's ridiculous," Acrasia said, sitting back to regard him evenly. "He was just a mortal. He would have died in a few years anyway. When your horse breaks a leg, you don't cry over putting him down. And you don't expect the dead horse's brother to be angry with you."

"My brother is not a horse!" Tristan nearly shouted, and despite himself, found his eyes wet.

"There's hardly much of a difference," Acrasia mumbled, with a roll of her eyes.

"I am going to wed the Lady Clarisant," Tristan growled, pushing a finger right up to her face. "Because it is my duty to my family. And if you want to blame anyone for that, blame yourself."

"But you don't love her!" Acrasia folded her arms over her chest and pouted. "You love me. I should have gotten around to killing her quicker."

"There are other reasons for marriage than love," Tristan spat. "Now. You are going in the sheath. I have to bury my brother today, and I cannot stand to look at you." He thrust himself out of bed, wobbled on unsteady legs, and, ignoring her protests, hung the sheathed sword from its hook on his wall, next to the armor stand. The moment his fingers broke contact with the sword, Acrasia disappeared, in the middle of her sentence.

Trist sucked in a breath, and put a hand on the wall to steady himself. He needed to dress for his brother's funeral service.

Trist had deluded himself into thinking that after he got dressed, he might go down to the great hall for breakfast, or even walk to the burial ground behind the monastery himself. Or ride. But by the time he'd pulled on a clean linen shirt and breeches, he couldn't do more than collapse on the bed, wincing at the pain from his wound.

He was only half aware of the door to the room opening, but Clarisant's voice brought him back to full consciousness.

"Leave it on the table by the bed," she directed two servants - one carrying plates of food, the other a small wooden table. They set up the table and the plates next to him quickly and efficiently, laid out fork and knife, then a bottle of wine and two goblets. One of them even dragged around the chair his father had used, and put it next to the table for Clarisant. Trist saw that she had gotten a black veil from somewhere, and put it on.

"Brother Alberic chose your food," she noted, and Trist scowled.

"He told me. A special diet to balance the humors. Too little blood," Trist recalled, looking over what was there with a grimace. "I have no intention of eating the liver." There was a steak with a couple of eggs next to it, however, and he found himself suddenly aware of a gnawing, sharp hunger, so he dug in.

Lady Clarisant poured two goblets of wine, lifted one, raised her veil, and took a sip. There was a stretch of awkward silence; though she'd made three or four visits to Camaret-à-Arden prior to the wedding, she'd always spent more time with Percy than with him. Which made perfect sense, Trist knew, only it also made things a bit off now, because they hardly knew each other better than strangers.

Once he'd gone from ravenous to merely hungry, Trist slowed down and took a sip of wine to wet his throat. "I beg your forgiveness, my lady," he said, pausing his meal.

Clarisant waved him off with her left hand. "You need to eat to regain your strength. I'm pleased you have an appetite, if anything."

Trist shook his head. "I beg your forgiveness," he started again, "For not stopping what happened on your wedding night. My brother's safety - and your safety - were in my charge, and I failed you both."

He might not have caught her hand shaking if it had not made ripples in her wine. "You could hardly have done more without being in our bedchamber with us," Clarisant said, after a moment. "And while that may be done for the wedding of a king and queen, it is not the custom for country knights."

Trist looked down at his half-scoured plate. "I knew her for years," he said, voice rough. "And I never suspected. Forgive me for my blindness, for being a fool."

Clarisant sighed. "Your brother was a good man, wasn't he?"

"He was," Trist said. "He was better than me at almost everything, you know," he admitted. "But I did not resent him for it. Well, not usually. It was hard not to be a little jealous when Brother Alberic had nothing but praise for him, and harsh words for me.

But it was right that he had a keener wit, a sharper mind. He was going to inherit. I just needed to be a sword at his side. And I could not even do that."

"Did you ever suspect her?" Clarisant took another sip of her wine.

Trist shook his head. "Never. I was so blind. You must think me such a fool."

"We all thought you foolish," she said slowly. "But a harmless sort of foolish. It makes a good song, for a knight to fall in love with a beautiful peasant girl. Less entertaining in real life. If anything, I suppose I was a bit jealous."

Trist looked up. "Jealous?" Why would anyone ever be jealous of him?

"Of course! When I was a little girl, I dreamed of marrying for love," Clarisant explained, with a sad smile that he could just make out beneath the veil. "Too many ballads sung at feasts, perhaps. But of course I dreamed of a gallant knight who would defy everything to have me. So romantic." She shook her head, and beneath the veil he could see her lip turn down.

"But when you get older, you realize that's only for songs. You hope your father finds you a good marriage, to a man who isn't ancient, drunk, or cruel. Percy was a good marriage, but we were never in love. And there you were, ready to defy your father for a pretty peasant girl, just like one of those songs. How could I not be a little jealous?"

"I never thought of it like that," Trist realized. He took a sip of wine. "Are you certain you want to do this? I cannot say that I love you, my lady," he admitted plainly. "But I do feel I owe you my protection, and whatever I can do toward your happiness. There is a debt I do not believe that I can ever pay."

"Of course you don't love me," Clarisant said. "I do not love you. We hardly even know each other, and today we need to bury Percy. You aren't ancient, Sir Trist. Are you a drunk?"

"No." Trist shook his head. "No, I always wanted to keep my head clear. If the only thing I am good for is my sword, then it would be a failure to be too in my cups to put it to use. And it makes men fat, makes you sleep late and miss your morning practice. Not a good habit to get into."

"Alright, then." Clarisant set her empty goblet down. "Are you cruel? Will you beat me, or our children? Cast me aside for a younger woman when my skin is wrinkled and my hair gray? Force yourself on me in the night?"

"I will not do any of those things," Trist promised her. "Though I may be cruel. I killed a woman who loved me. I do not know how I could do that if I was not at least a little bit cruel."

"Can you promise to turn whatever cruelty you have outward, then?" Clarisant asked. "To use it to protect your family - our family?"

"I can do that," he said quickly enough.

"Then I can be your wife." Clarisant stood. "It isn't love. But I'm also not going to betray you and try to murder you on our wedding night. Perhaps it will be enough."

Chapter Thirteen

THE FUNERAL

Angelus, who tellest the number of the stars, and callest them all by their names: heal, we beseech Thee, the grief in our heart, and gather together our tears, and comfort us with the fulness of Thy wisdom.
-Narvonnian Funeral Prayer

20th Day of the Planting Moon, 297 AC

Trist did not wear his sword to the funeral service.

Even if he could have endured Acrasia's presence while burying the brother she'd murdered, he was not in any fit condition to carry a weapon, or to wear armor, until he'd had a few more days to heal.

The burial ground behind the monastery took all of the village's dead, and Percy was laid to rest in the same granite crypt as his mother, and as Trist's mother Cecilia, and the unborn sister with whom she'd died during the plague. Trist's grandparents were there, as well, all of the family marked with the same coat of arms displayed in the hall: a great black Iebara tree, branches spread, with white flowers, roots exposed, for the Ardenwood.

It was engraved on the crypt door, and then again inside, where the stone walls kept the air cool.

It must have been the entire village crowded around the crypt, to bid their perfect young lord farewell. Trist was placed with his father and Clarisant, at the front. Brother Hugh spoke of the Great Cataclysm that destroyed the old Etalan Empire, when the Daemon Lords walked the world and the Wild Hunt rode in the suffocating darkness when the sun did not rise for days. He spoke of the coming of the Angelus, and how the town's patron, Saint Kadosh, was one of those who lent his strength and blessing to help humanity survive, rebuild, and eventually prosper. Finally, he commended Percival's immortal soul to Saint Abatur, the Angelus who weighed the souls of the dead on his scales.

Trist stewed in his litter. The stories of the Wild Hunt weren't quite as bad as the horrors committed by daemons during the Cataclysm: the fae hadn't ever skinned an entire city's population alive, for one thing, like the daemons had at Rumen. On the other hand, they hadn't actually helped humanity, either. In the end, the Angelus had forced the fae to abide by the Accords - mostly - but no one in their right mind voluntarily had anything to do with faeries.

And now he was going to carry around his dead fairie love in the form of a sword, and go off to war with the Crown Prince's army so he could Tithe to the faerie king by feeding the blade the souls of the men he killed. He could hardly keep his food down at the thought of it.

It sounded ridiculous. It certainly wasn't the sort of thing he imagined the Angelus would approve of, and while his understanding of the Accords was hazy, he suspected this went right up to the line of what was allowed. Which meant that if the truth about Acrasia got out, Trist might end up with both Angelus and daemons angry with him.

He watched as his brother's body was carried into the crypt, while he was too weak to assist. Trist felt as if he should be swearing vengeance, but who would he take revenge on? Acrasia? He'd already killed her once, and look how far that had gotten him. For a moment, he closed his eyes, and tried to recall his glimpse of her true self, extending out from her body. How was any mortal man supposed to kill something like that?

After a long moment of thinking, Trist made a different promise, silently, hoping that with the sword hanging all the way back in his chambers Acrasia wouldn't be able to hear it and twist it. I failed to protect you, Percy, he thought to himself. So I will do everything I can for the people most important to you. Our father, Clarisant. This town. If that means a wedding, I'll do that. If that means going to war against the Caliphate in the Hauteurs Massif, so that no one we love is Tithed to this damned sword, I'll do that too. I will try to make you proud, brother, even if you never forgive me.

Only after the last of the crowd had finally dispersed, and the crypt door had been closed again, did Trist permit the men-at-arms to carry his litter back to the manor.

Back in his bed-chamber, Trist grumbled but accepted help getting onto his mattress. "Bring me my sword," he asked the last man-at-arms to leave the room, a big man named Luc. Then, once the door was closed, he settled into the pillows, closed his eyes, and wrapped his fingers around the hilt. He had things to speak to Acrasia about.

How was it that he could feel the bed shift, as if she was a living woman and not some kind of ghost, crawling onto the mattress next to him? How was it that he could feel her hair tickling his chin as she tucked her head in, could inhale the scent of her? He hated how she made him feel, now.

"Are you using faerie magic to make a body?" Trist asked softly, unable to resist his curiosity, though this wasn't what he had intended to say.

"I'm only tricking your senses," Acrasia murmured into his chest. "Much easier."

"...are you telling me that you could make me, for instance, not see the edge of a cliff, and walk off it?"

The faerie giggled. "Your resistance to things like that - illusion, emotional manipulation, memory alteration - is even lower than most mortals. But don't feel bad, Trist. You have your strong points."

Trist resisted the urge to grumble. "You said something about Boons, earlier? Those are separate from Oaths?"

"That's right," Acrasia confirmed. "As long as your service continues to please the King of Shadows, he may offer you Boons to choose from. Each one costs a certain amount of souls, Tithed to him, from your portion."

Trist thought that through. "So one soul of every three I kill with the sword goes to him already. One goes to you, and one goes to me. But then I can trade mine for Boons."

"Correct."

"That sounds like an over complicated way of him getting my portion." Exactly like the sort of lopsided bargain faeries were infamous for.

"Blame the Angelus that negotiated the Accords," Acrasia grumbled. "They insisted that mortals get something for what they gave. Angelus, by the way, are absolutely no fun."

"How do I know what Boons I can Tithe for," Trist asked, ignoring that borderline heretical statement on her part.

"You ask me, silly. That's my job, now. You've earned the right to one by your deeds, and one other is offered to all Knights of Auberon, like my brother. Here, I'll show you. Same way as before?" Trist nodded, and coils of fire splayed across his vision.

"Fae Touched," Acrasia said. A line of fire extended from her and dipped into his chest, burning out to his toes and the tips of his fingers so that his entire body stiffened and his back arched. When Trist's muscles relaxed, all of the fatigue and pain had been wiped away, and he felt stronger than he ever had been before.

"When you are granted this Boon for true, your body will have taken the first step to moving beyond the capabilities of mortal flesh, and it will only grow stronger and faster as you Tithe more souls to the King of Shadows. The touch of un-alloyed iron, however, will become something you cannot bear without discomfort," Acrasia warned him. "Now, look at the second."

The other thread was an even darker shade of red than the first, and pierced Trist's eyes. He reached out, as if to grasp it, and when his hand touched the twining loop of fire, the shadows in his bedchamber seemed to draw in and thicken, hanging about them like a curtain of darkest night.

"You are a knight in service to Auberon, the Faerie King of Shadows," Acrasia purred in his ear. "And when you accept his Boon, as his Knight of Shadows, you will be able to see in darkness like a cat. The darkness will greet you as a friend, moving to conceal your passage, and it will enhance your ability to pass without being noticed, so long as you have shadows to move in."

"Stronger and faster." Trist's eyes went back to the burning thread of the first Boon, Fae Touched, and he considered, recalling the way that Acrasia had moved, cat-like, graceful and swift. "You were a lot faster than me, were you not? Is that what 'beyond the capabilities of mortal flesh' means?"

"Mmm-hmm." Acrasia rolled out from nestling into his side, to on top of him, where she straddled his hips. "Oh, yes. You could move like that, one day, if you Tithe enough to the King of Shadows."

"It is vague, though," Trist complained. "Hard to know exactly what you are getting. How much stronger or faster? I hand over a soul, take that Boon, and what, I can lift a horse?"

Acrasia arched her back, stretching her hands above her head, and squinted down at him. "I've shown you the way I see the world," she said. "If only in glimpses. Have you ever looked into a fire, my love? Looked at the different colors of the flames?"

"Yes," Trist confirmed, trying to ignore her thighs parted around his body.

"And the fire of a smith's forge is a different color than a cook fire, yes?" she prodded him on.

"Brighter," Trist confirmed. "Not just yellow, but almost white, after they have been working the bellows."

"And sometimes, even shades of blue," Acrasia agreed. "Learn to pick out the shade of the flames, Trist, when you glimpse them. That is how to see as I do. Red is the least powerful. Then orange, yellow..."

"So one Tithe gets me a red... thread?" Trist scowled.

"Yes. That's a good way to think of them. Like threads running through your body, each tied to me and to the sword, and to the Faerie King. Each doing something different, strengthening you in a different way."

Trist took a moment to try to absorb it. Having Acrasia's lithe body on top of him didn't help him concentrate: even if she'd admitted that her physical form wasn't really there, it certainly felt like it was, and brought back rather distracting thoughts of their time together under the hill.

"Enough for now," Trist said, and released the hilt of the sword before Acrasia could do more than frown. Immediately, her body was gone: he lay on the bed alone, and it was a relief to be free of her. No lines of fire splayed across his vision, though the knowledge they'd presented was now jumbled in his head.

He wasn't going to worry about either of the Boons right now, Trist decided. Until he'd killed at least three men in combat, he could safely put choosing between them aside. His instinct was that he would probably end up choosing Fae Touched, but until he had mustered with the Crown Prince's forces at... his father hadn't actually mentioned where the muster was happening. He would have to find out, and plan his route. But in any event, until he was actually at war, he didn't need to think about Boons.

That left the Oaths and the sword itself to consider. The Oath of Knighthood actually didn't worry Trist at all: he saw no downside, as he'd never intended to break his vows anyway, and it was only a benefit. It was something that he didn't expect to come up very often, but who knew whether the Caliphate would be sending Exarchs to war.

Perhaps the Angelus lending them strength would try to use some sort of divine magic to manipulate him; if it happened, he'd be glad to have the Oath helping him.

The Oath of Love he expected to break in three days time. That it hadn't already shattered surprised him: Trist didn't think he should be feeling any love at all for a woman who had lied to him about her nature for his entire life, and then betrayed him and killed his brother. The fact that he'd lain with her, and that he hadn't thrown the sword she was hiding herself away in down the deepest well in the village, didn't mean that he still cared for her in the slightest. Regardless, that Oath would no doubt turn into a stone weighing him down the moment he wed Clarisant, so he wasn't going to count on it ever helping him.

All of this meant, Trist concluded, that the only real advantage he'd gained from this whole ordeal was the sword itself. If the sword truly was sharper and stronger than any made by a mortal forge, that was amazing. The description Acrasia had given him also said that it could cut things that a normal sword could not. That, he would test in the practice yard as soon as Brother Alberic told him it was safe to do so.

The first of the sword's named magical abilities wasn't really for him: it was for the Faerie King, and for Acrasia, and simply allowed him to collect Tithes. Again, he could put it aside from his thinking. Summoning a ghostly knight to aid him in battle was, however, promising.

Trist considered. He wasn't likely to be fighting for his life for the rest of the day, he decided, after a moment. And he didn't want to trust in something he had never done before, when he needed an edge in the heat of battle. Before he could talk himself out of the experiment, he reached for the hilt.

"Summon Restless Knights," Trist intoned, firmly, and the temperature in the room dropped. Frost crackled across the small glass panes of the windows, and Sir Tor De Lancey appeared at the foot of the bed.

Chapter Fourteen

The Restless Knight

The Narvonnians speak of honor when it suits them, but when it does not, they are quick to resort to barbarity; the Massacre at the Hauteurs Massif is all the proof that anyone needs. What, however, can one expect of a people who refuse the rightful authority of the Angelus, and place their faith in all too fallible mortal kings? To be mortal is to sin and to err, and the Narvonnians do their share of both.

-The Commentaries of Aram ibn Bashear

20th Day of the Planting Moon, 297 AC

The restless spirit of Tor De Lancey was fully armed and armored, wearing plate that had clearly been forged after the older knight had begun to gain weight. He carried a kite shield on his left arm, and a warhammer hung at his waist. If Trist squinted, he could make out the doorway through Tor's ghostly form, as if he wasn't entirely solid.

"You called, boy?"

"I am a bit surprised that you can speak," Trist admitted. "I apologize for calling you without a battle for you to fight. I wanted to be certain I knew how this would work, before I relied on it." He could already feel, as Acrasia had put it, the weight of this: holding De Lancey by a red thread was like trying to keep hold of a strong fish on a line.

Sir Tor scowled. "If you would apologize, set me free of the faerie witch who enslaved me."

"I do not know how to do that," Trist confessed. "Or even whether it is possible. But I will try to find out. Until I do, are you willing to fight beside me when I have need of you?"

Tor De Lancey huffed in dissatisfaction. "I will fight for you if you do two things," he said finally. "First, call me to no battle that is not worthy of my vow as a knight."

"Agreed," Trist said easily. Motes of light began to unravel from De Lancey's ghostly form, as if the wraith was a piece of fabric, fraying at the edges, or sand blown by the wind. He was losing the thread. "And second?"

"See that my daughter is safe..." The voice cut off as Tor's form dissolved, leaving behind no sign he had ever been present.

"Once a day," Trist reminded himself, "And not for long, at all." Calling on Tor's aid would need to be saved for a moment of true need, when he was unable to win through a battle on his own. If he tried to call upon the restless shade of the former knight before a fight began, Sir Tor was liable to fade mid-hammer stroke. Still, it was comforting to always have the option of aid from a hardened veteran like Tor De Lancey. The man had let himself go in his later years, but from everything Trist's father had ever told him, you could ask for no truer friend to watch your back in the thick of battle.

"It is only a red thread," Acrasia explained, perching on the corner of the bed, turned away from him. She must have been angry he cut her off earlier. "When you Tithe a soul to me, I can make the magic more powerful. He will remain for longer. Give me enough power, and you will be able to call more than one shade at a time."

"You want me to spend souls like coin," Trist said, settling back into the pillows. "I do not like it. And I have the feeling that there will always be more power to be had, for the price of more souls."

"Of course!" Acrasia giggled. "That's how the Accords work, after all."

The Crown Prince's army, it turned out, would be mustering at Falais, a castle town that commanded one end of the Passe de Mûre, the primary route through the Hauteurs

Massif south to the territory of the Caliphate of Ma'īn. Trist's father had been there before.

"The castle is relatively new," Sir Rience explained, stabbing his finger at the map he'd brought to Trist's bed-chamber, from where he sat on the left side of the bed. On the other side, Clarisant had peeled off Trist's bandages and was examining the wound. She had brought fresh linen wraps, herbal poultices, and boiled water to clean him with.

"The whole village practically hangs from the side of a cliff," Rience du Camaret-à-Arden commented. "The most damned thing."

Lady Clarisant turned to fix him with a stare and an arched brow.

"My apologies, Lady Clarisant," Trist's father said. "I forget myself."

"I've sent word by pigeon to my father," Clarisant spoke up, not deigning to acknowledge the apology. "He knows you will be meeting him there."

Trist looked at the map, and frowned. "There looks to be a good road south of the Ardenwood from Rocher de la Garde," he pointed out. "Would it not make more sense for me to take the road south to your father's castle, and then travel west with him?"

"That was our original plan," his father admitted. "But with everything that has happened since the wedding, and the time you need to recover, the Baron will be on his way before you can get to him. You'll need to cut through the forest, southwest." Rience traced a finger from where Camaret-à-Arden was located, upriver and inland from where Rocher de la Garde was marked on the coast, through the Ardenwood to where the western road met the mountains, and Falais was marked on the border with the Caliphate.

"Are you not always saying the forest is dangerous, Father?" Trist asked, with no little degree of amusement.

"And so it is," Rience agreed. "But there is an old Etalan road that you can pick up here," he explained, tracing his finger west of the village. "Used to lead north from the mountains to the old capital, Vellatesia, before the Great Cataclysm."

Trist shivered. "Any road that leads to that daemon-cursed place is not one I want to step foot on," he muttered, then flinched as Lady Clarisant pressed a new poultice to his wound.

"The Old Empire built roads to last," his father argued. "Good stone from the mountains. Even a thousand years later, those roads are strong. You ride west, you'll hit the road. Then you turn south, and follow it. Do those two things, and you can't get yourself lost. It will be tough going through the Arden until you find the road, but once you're on it, you can push hard."

"You are confident it is still there? Not split by ravines or overgrown?" Trist frowned.

"It was still there twenty-four years ago," Rience said, "When Tor and I rode it during the last war with the Caliphate. It's lasted a thousand years; twenty more won't have broken it."

"Fine," Trist said. He could almost hear Acrasia laughing at the prospect of him going back into the woods.

By the time Hywel had finished measuring him, Trist was glad enough to sit back down on the edge of his bed. "So?" he asked the blacksmith. "What can you do?"

"There isn't enough time to forge any new pieces, if that's what you're asking," the older man grumbled from beneath his bushy mustache. Percy's armor rack had been dragged in by the servants, and now it stood to the right of Trist's. "I can adjust the leather straps on the greaves and the cuirass. Let them out enough for you to wear them. But there's no way I can make the fingers of the gauntlets fit you in so little time."

Trist nodded. "Just do the best you can. Even if you can only get one more piece fit for me to wear, that is better protection than I would have otherwise."

"There will be smiths with the Crown Prince's army," Hywel pointed out.

Trist sighed. "Yes, there will. But there will be so many knights competing for their services, if my father is right, that the prices will be exorbitant. He has been to war and I have not, so I am inclined to believe what he says."

"Capture one of those Caliphate knights and ransom him," Hywel suggested, with a grin. He looped the leather straps of the greaves around one of the straps on the cuirass, so that he could carry out all of the pieces he intended to work on.

Trist did his best to return the grin. "I will see what I can do," he said, but he wondered whether he would be able to capture anyone when he needed to be Tithing souls to the faerie king, and even to his own sword.

23rd Day of the Planting Moon, 297 AC

On the morning of the third day, Trist took his sword down to the yard at prime, as had been his habit before suffering a wound. He was stiff, it hurt when he pulled at his stitches, and having not made the cuts since returning from the chapel meant that he was winded and covered in sweat far sooner than he should have been. He had to stop twice as often to drink watered wine, but finally, he finished.

The entire time, Acrasia watched him, sitting to one side, and offering commentary. Everything from cheering when he first took his shirt off, to suggesting she knew far more pleasant ways for him to get sweaty. He did his best to ignore her. Once or twice, his eyes flicked up to the window where Clarisant and Enid De Lancey had watched he and Percy from the second floor of the manor, but this morning there was no one there.

"You won't be seeing her until the ceremony is over," John Granger told him. "Tradition, and all that." The Master at Arms looked him over critically. "You're not yet back to fighting strength, m'lord," he said honestly.

"I know," Trist agreed. "I will rise every morning on the way to Falais," he promised to himself as much as to Granger. "And work my cuts, my footwork. By the time we have mustered and headed south through the pass, I will be back in good shape."

John nodded. "I've thought to send Henry and Luc with you," he said, after a moment. "In all honesty, m'lord, I'd thought to go myself, but..."

"No," Trist agreed. "My father is not as young as he once was, and we need you here to command the men, to keep the village safe. To protect my wife," he added, though it felt strange and unnatural to use the phrase.

"They're good men," Granger said. "They were with you the morning you pulled De Lancey out of the water. Asked to go with you, actually, both of them."

"I remember," Trist said. "I will be happy to have them."

John Granger looked back up to the empty window. "Do you have a man to stand at your side, m'lord?"

Trist looked away. "No," he admitted. "It should have been my brother, but..."

"Allow me, then." Trist looked back to the Master at Arms, surprised at the offer. "You've been the best student I ever had," John Granger admitted, the first time Trist had ever heard him say something like that. He was normally sparing of praise. "Could tell since you were waist high," Granger joked with a laugh. "But I couldn't let it go to your head. And you've grown into a good man, despite all that's happened. I'd be proud to stand at your side, if you'd have me."

"Thank you," Trist said.

Brother Hugh performed the ceremony to wed Trist and Clarisant that evening, after leading the company in vesper prayers.

This time, the village was not invited.

They spoke their vows at the same monastery chapel where his bride had stood not a week earlier, and Trist had a hard time looking up from where his calloused hand was bound to Clarisant's. Her skin was soft and cool, and he imagined he could feel the pulse beat in her fingers. John Granger stood at Trist's side, for Trist's sword had been left in the armory. He did not want it hanging from his wall this night, did not want Acrasia in the room with Clarisant.

There was a small meal, just the two of them with his father, Granger and Brother Hugh and Brother Alberic, six places in all. Trist picked at his food, hardly eating anything, and noticed that his new bride did much the same. Afterward, Trist escorted Clarisant to his rooms. Neither of them wanted to go to where Percy had been murdered.

"Untie me?" Clarisant asked, turning her back to him and sweeping her dark hair off her neck, holding it around her front. Trist swallowed, and worked the laces of her bodice with trembling fingers that seemed too large and too clumsy. It was only now, so close to her body, that he breathed in the perfume of cedarwood that she wore. There was a hint of fruit to it that he didn't recognize, and beneath it all the scent of her body. Finally, she shrugged out of the bodice, and dropped her dress to the floor. His bride walked to his bed in only her linen shift and stockings, long hair unbound, and turned to face him.

"Trist," she said quietly. "I promise you, I've never done this before."

She had to say it, he knew, whether or not it was the truth. How many men would have refused Clarisant? A young widow, so close to her wedding night she might already be with child? "It does not matter whether you have," Trist said finally. It was the least he could do for his brother.

He stepped forward, wrapped his arms around her, and tried not to compare the taste of Clarisant's lips to Acrasia's. Being wrapped in Acrasia's arms had been like a fever-dream, a boy's fantasy of love. Clarisant, on the other hand, trembled so much that it was clear to him she was terrified. Of her first time with a man? Of whether he would reject her? Or perhaps she was simply remembering a monster crashing through the window on her last wedding night. She didn't deserve anything that had happened to her.

"All will be well," Trist murmured. "I promise."

The next morning, Trist set off through the Ardenwood for Falais.

Chapter Fifteen

A Party of Three

Da's Rabbit Stew

One Rabbit (or more), skinned and dressed

One handful Chicken of the Woods (or other mushrooms)

Splash of Wine (red or white)

One Onion or Leek, chopped

Spices as you can get them: Garlic, Parsley, Rosemary, and/or Thyme

-Henry of Camaret-à-Arden

24th Day of the Planting Moon, 297 AC

They filled Caz' saddlebags as much as they could, but a destrier wasn't a pack mule, and it would have been a disservice to treat him as one. The war horse was trained to be a weapon: to kick, and to bite, and to carry Trist along on a devastating charge into the thick of the melee. Better that Henry and Luc carry heavy packs than that they discard a living weapon during a dangerous journey.

And so, Trist rode, the haft of his lance set into his right stirrup to carry the weight. He wore his chain shirt, repaired by Hywel, over a new thick gambeson. The heavier armor pieces were packed away with the travel rations: hardtack of barley, bean flour, and rye; dried, salted beef; and a wheel of good, aged cheese made by the monks from local cow's milk. The taste of Clarisant was still on his lips, her scent in his memory; she'd urged him to try one more time to give her a child, when they woke. He knew it was out of fear, not love, but he hadn't been able to say no.

Trist and the men made certain to cross the stream where Tor De Lancey had drowned a safe distance north of the waterfall, and from there they headed west as best they could. Henry, Trist was pleased to observe, remained as skilled a woodsman as he'd been that awful morning.

"My father is a hunter," the man-at-arms explained around mid-day, in response to Trist's question. "We never had an empty table; he'd bring back nuts and berries, a stag to dress, a brace of rabbits. Mushrooms - if I see any I'll gather them up - quail." In addition to an arming sword, Henry had a longbow of Iebara wood, unstrung, and a quiver of black arrows with good steel heads.

"Useful skills to have," Trist observed. "I suspect we will be glad you came on more than one occasion."

Henry dipped his head. "Thank you, m'lord," he said, eyes never ceasing to scan the surrounding foliage.

"And you, Luc?" Trist asked.

"Da's a farmer," the burly man said. "Lots of hauling hay for me. Splitting wood, carrying stones out of the new fields. Grew me up big and strong, though."

They didn't reach the old Etalan road on the first day, nor even after the second. Both nights, they dug a fire-pit and lined it with stones, and cleared the pebbles and leaves of the forest floor away to make room for their bed-rolls. Henry had, indeed, taken two quail with his bow, during the late afternoon of their second day in the Ardenwood, and after two days of walking they were all eager enough to have a small pot boiling over the fire. Fresh rosemary and thyme, gathered along their path, went into the pot with the trimmed quail, and after everything had boiled down a bit, they dipped pieces of hardtack into the stew to soften. All in all, by the time they were ready to turn in on the second night, it was with full stomachs.

Trist snapped awake to the sound of howling wolves in the night. His first instinct was to grab for the hilt of his sword, mind too bleary to remember that would give Acrasia license to come out and speak to him.

The faerie woman's eyes sparkled with excitement, by the light of the banked embers and the bright moon. "The Horned Lord is hunting tonight," she practically cackled, and Trist felt a shock of fear run down his spine.

"Hellequin?" He asked, as Henry and Luc stirred in their bedrolls. The sound of howling was coming closer, and the wind had picked up, shaking the branches of the trees around their camp.

"The Wild Hunt?" Luc shook his head, wide eyed. "That's just a children's story, m'lord. Isn't it?" Henry, on the other hand, grabbed his bow and strung it with practiced ease.

Trist kicked his way out of his bedroll and rose, left hand holding his sword by the leather sheath, right on the hilt. He could draw in an instant, but he didn't want to present himself as an enemy until he had to. "What can you tell me of the Horned Lord," he demanded from Acrasia. "How do we protect ourselves?"

"Is he talking to his sword?" Luc asked Henry, leaning in with a furrowed brow that Trist didn't have time to deal with at the moment. Henry shushed the big man.

"The easiest way is to not stray from the road or the path you're on," Acrasia explained, perching herself on a nearby fallen log as if it was a chair. "But you lot are well and truly off any beaten path, so that's right out. If he gives you the chance to aid them in their hunt, take it, and he'll be bound to reward you. Whoever they're chasing must have really gotten Auberon angry."

Something was coming through the brush; Trist tried to swallow, and found his mouth dry. "No one attack, unless I give the word," he ordered his two men. "No matter what you see, you understand me?"

"Yes, m'lord," Henry answered, an arrow nocked but undrawn. Luc, on the other hand, had already drawn his arming sword, and settled a round Iebara wood shield on his left arm. With a crash, a great host came through the brush and into the glow of the embers.

White wolves with fiery eyes paced forward, fangs bared, growling and snarling at the three men. Each one was the size of a pony, and looked more than capable of ripping a full-grown man's arm off with a single bite. Cazador snorted and reared back, threatening the wolves with his heavy hooves. The snarling hunting pack parted, and a great black horse, fiery-eyed like the wolves, but with six legs instead of four, stepped into the ember-light. It's rider was massive and horned, carrying a hunting spear in one hand.

His elegant features, slim, pointed ears, and hairless jawline bore a striking similarity to Acrasia.

And indeed, it was to Acrasia's immaterial form, lounging on the log, that the Horned Hunter turned. "Ill met, sister," he boomed, "To see you enslaved to an unworthy mortal, bound to a dead length of metal."

Henry and Luc looked at each other, ashen-white, and the larger man-at-arms mouthed the word 'sister' in astonishment.

"Big brother!" Acrasia leapt up from her perch and pranced over to the hunter. The nightmare steed lowered its head and nuzzled against her chest, and she stroked his mane. "This is my lover, Trist," she explained, flinging an arm out in his direction. "He was only angry with me and killed me the one time, but I expect we'll be over it shortly."

The Horned Hunter turned to Trist, who offered a polite bow. "Lord Hellequin, I believe," he greeted the faerie. "I am Sir Trist du Camaret-à-Arden, and these are my men, Henry and Luc. We travel to Falais, to muster with the Crown Prince's army."

"You travel only if I do not strike you down where you stand," the Horned Lord said with a sneer, and his steed tossed its head. "For your impertinence. What hubris, for a mortal to strike a Lady of the Fae." The wolves stepped forward, low to the ground, fangs barred and growling, and Trist didn't think he could kill more than one or two before they tore him to pieces. Perhaps that would be enough time for Henry and Luc to flee; perhaps the Horned Hunter wouldn't pursue them once he had what he had come for.

"No longer entirely mortal," Acrasia pointed out to the leader of the Wild Hunt. Her brother, apparently. "Look at my lover again, Cern."

The Horned Lord frowned, and Trist felt as if his heart was being weighed on a butcher's scales. Could Acrasia's brother see the threads of his two broken Oaths? He suspected so. "Why would you tie yourself to him so, Sister?" he asked, after a moment. "The Accords..."

"The Accords permit me," the faerie maiden insisted, "To do as I have done. He will Tithe souls to the King of Shadows, and be granted Boons in return. He is a knight of our court, now, not yours to hunt for sport."

The Hunter scowled. Cern, she'd called him, Trist realized. Not the name by which the leader of the Wild Hunt was known in the stories children told on dark nights. "He is not on the path, Sister," Cern assayed. "Nor either of his very mortal servants. I could hunt them."

"Do I not have a choice?" Trist said, and Cern's eyes bored into his own. "In all of the stories, if you happen upon the Wild Hunt, you can join. And if you help bring down their prey, you are rewarded."

Acrasia chuckled. "He's got you there," she taunted her brother, who scowled at her before returning his attention to Trist.

"You would have a test, then, erstwhile Knight of the Shadow King?" Cern's steed pawed at the ground. "Mount your warhorse, then, and take up your lance, and leave your men-at-arms here. We will hunt together, you and I, and we will see whether you are worthy of your title, worthy of my sister."

Trist nodded, and turned to Henry and Luc. "When the sun rises, head west," he instructed them. "Until you reach the road. Then head south. I will find you," he promised them.

Luc looked over the snarling wolves and the Horned Lord. "Say the word, m'lord," he promised, "And I'll fight for you right now. Damn the hounds, they'll fall to a good sword."

Cern laughed, and Trist shook his head. "No," he insisted. "You are my men, and I have a duty to you. I will not have you die at the fangs of the Hunt. Do as I say." He looked to Henry. "Swear it?"

"I swear it," Henry said, "And I'll drag this oaf with me if I need to. We'll meet again on the old road, m'lord."

"Good." Trist stepped over to Cazador. The Hunt waited while he saddled the destrier and untied him. Trist pulled his shirt of rings on, buckled his sword across his waist, and swung up into the saddle. Henry passed him his lance, and he turned back to Cern. "I am ready, Horned Lord," he said, putting as much steel into his voice as he could muster.

"Then follow," the Hunter growled, wheeling his six-legged horse around. "If you fall behind, my wolves will tear you to pieces." With a kick, they were off, Trist urging Caz into a pell-mell gallop that seemed scarcely controllable. Brush and twigs whipped at them from either side, Caz taking to the air over a fallen tree while the wolves swarmed all about them, in front and behind, howling. Before Trist even had time to think, they'd gone so far into the night-shrouded Ardenwood that he doubted he would be able to find his way back to the evening's campfire. It was all he could do to stay in sight of the Horned Lord.

The night race continued, and Trist's fingers grew numb and cold from the wind of their passage. A bright crescent moon hung overhead, when he caught a glimpse of it through the foliage of the wood, and eventually Trist found there were less and less wolves running at his sides. Instead, he guessed, they would be ranging ahead, finding the scent of... whoever they all were hunting. They forded at least one stream, and it left his legs wet and cold.

He was surprised to catch the scent of the sea on the air, who knew how many hours later. When his mother had still been alive, their parents had taken he and Percy to visit Rocher de la Garde. Trist had learned later that they'd gone to finalize negotiations for Percy's betrothal to Baron Urien's daughter, but at the time he'd been fascinated by the sea. Though they hadn't stayed more than a fortnight, in his mind, the entire event was an infinite golden summer of childhood, when he'd swum naked in the sea and lay baking on the hot sand, watching ships come into the harbor over the sun-decked waves. The scent of ocean air was a scent Trist would never forget, as long as he lived.

When Cern pulled up his six-legged black horse at the top of a grassy dune, Trist brought Caz to a halt as well. The destrier was nearly blown out, and he doubted the warhorse would be able to carry him much longer. There had to be some sort of magic at play, Trist knew, or they would never have been able to reach the coast in a single night's ride.

Below them, crowded around a small bay, was a fishing town, picked out in the light of the crescent moon. The ships rocked at anchor; it was the darkest time of night, before even the faintest light of dawn, but it still wasn't early enough for the fishermen to rise from their beds and leave the harbor.

"There," the Horned Hunter said, pointing a single finger down at the sleeping town.

Chapter Sixteen

The Wild Hunt

For the crime of full thievery, by which we mean stealing something worth a silver or more, the punishment shall be hanging from a tree or a gallows, or by banishment from the city and its environs, at the choice of the lord of said city. If the stolen goods are worth less than a silver, it shall cost the thief skin, through public flogging, and one or both ears, at the lord's pleasure.
-From the Revised Legal Code of Henry the Barnlock, fourth King of Narvonne

25th Day of the Planting Moon, 297 AC

"Who are we hunting?" Trist asked softly. He doubted anyone in the town was awake, or that the wind would carry his words to someone who had not already heard the tramp of hooves or the howling of the hunting wolves. Now that they had stopped, the night was so still that it felt presumptuous to break the silence.

"A mortal," Cern the Horned Hunter answered, eyes pale and cold. "A thief who stole the Graal of the King of Shadows."

Trist frowned. He had never been good with languages - yet another way in which his brother had always surpassed him - but he knew enough to recognize that the word was Old Narvonnian. "What is that?"

"A bowl," the Horned Lord explained. "Hand turned, of fine rosewood." Trist raised his eyebrows; rosewood came to Narvonne only by ship, from far across the sea. "But the true value of Auberon's Graal is this: whenever it is set out to serve the virtuous at table, it will always be full of fresh fruits and vegetables and nuts, all good to eat. And so long as those who hunger eat from it, it shall never be empty, until they are sated. And if it is filled with water or wine, then whosoever drinks of it will be healed of all wounds or sickness that troubles them. The King had given it as a gift to a favored mortal pet, but a pack of thieves stole it three nights past when the ship Amarante stopped here to take on supplies."

Caz snorted and shook his head. Trist patted the destrier's neck, pleased to see him catching his breath again. "How do you intend to do this, Lord Hunter?" he asked the faerie.

"Simple. We ride down the bluff and burn them out of their hovels," Cern explained. "The wolves take anyone who runs, and drag them back. We take eyes and hands until we find the vermin who did this, and recover the King's Graal."

Trist's eyes widened. "You cannot do that! Most of the people in that town had nothing to do with this. They are simple fishermen and their families."

"Do not presume to tell me what I cannot do," the Horned Hunter hissed, eyes flashing cold as ice, as he leaned toward Trist. "I am finding fewer and fewer reasons not to feed you to the wolves, myself," he threatened.

Suddenly, Acrasia was seated on Caz with him, riding at the front of his saddle and leaning back into his chest. His left arm was around her body, holding the reins, and her hair tickled his chin. The faerie maiden was the perfect size to tuck her head under his jaw and nestle in.

Trist scowled. "Let me go in," he proposed. "Have your wolves surround the outskirts and capture anyone who runs. I will find the thieves and flush them out."

Cern's eyes narrowed. "Our hunt must be finished before dawn, mortal," he warned. "I will permit this, but take too long, and I will do just as I have said. And if you should happen to burn, along with the vermin, that will simplify my night a great deal."

"Understood." Trist pressed his heels to Cazador, and with Acrasia in his arms, rode down the sandy bluff into the town below.

"I assume you have a plan to find the graal?" Acrasia murmured to him, as Caz's iron-shod hooves clomped on the worn old cobblestones. Trist looked around. The town was arranged around a single main street, which looked to have been paved by the old Etalan Empire. This road curved along the line of the bay, radiating smaller lanes of crushed white sea shells out, as if someone had chopped a spoked wagon wheel roughly in half with a few axe-strokes.

"I do," Trist confirmed. "When I saw you - the real you - it was like I saw... glowing vines, or spider webs of fire, extending out into some other place. Like torchlight through the mist. And now you are connected to this sword, yes?" He reached down to pat the pommel.

"Yes," Acrasia said slowly, tilting her torso forward and turning so that she could see his eyes.

"And this graal would be connected to the King of Shadows, then," Trist explained out loud what he had been thinking in his head. "So that means you could see those fiery strands reaching out from it, back to him?"

Acrasia smiled. "Clever boy," she said, darted in to peck him on the lips. He flinched, and she settled back into his chest. "That way." She raised a delicate hand and pointed a pale finger to the south side of the bay.

Trist turned Caz's head with the reins, and they rode south along the main street, the sound of night surf gentle in his ears. Trist trusted Caz to keep himself out of the wagon ruts worn into the stone by centuries of use. He sighed in relief that his guess had been right, but her confirmation left him with questions. "Why could not your brother have done the same, then?" he asked.

"Cern and I served different purposes for the king," Acrasia explained, choosing her words carefully, as she waved him down a rather close street. Trist had a hard time seeing when the shadows of the buildings cut off much of the light of the moon, but he had no trouble at all detecting the scents of rotting garbage and refuse. "I was like a beautiful flower, meant to lure in and trap the unwary. Cern is a wolf like the rest of his hunt. For him, causing terror in the name of the king is as much the point as anything else. Everyone should fear the Wild Hunt."

"So he could have," Trist lowered his voice to a murmur, "But he did not want to."

"Yes. And now he's testing you, to see what you'll do. There." Acrasia indicated an alleyway, and they turned into a maze of dark, cramped places between the buildings. It was hard to tell at this time of night, but if he had to guess they'd entered a section of old warehouses. These alleys weren't planned: they were byproducts of haphazard construction, and then probably decayed as this neighborhood went through hard times. Poverty and a lack of maintenance put the buildings in this state. Some might even be abandoned.

They came to a length of ragged cloth strung across the alley, as a sort of curtain or wall. Trist reached out his lance to pull it to one side, and kneed Caz through. As the cloth fell behind them, the alley opened into a courtyard, no larger than a small house, where weeds grew through the bed of ground shells. Here, there was a little more light, as the moon shone down, and by the glow of banked embers he could see that a fire pit had been dug in the center of the space. All around the coals were scattered bundles of rags, huddled together. The smell of unwashed bodies hit Trist in the face hard enough to make his eyes water.

With low cries of fright, a few of the bundles began to move, scrambling back away from Caz' hooves, and Trist realized they were children. He set the lance back into his stirrup, and raised his voice.

"Children," he said, and he thanked John Granger for forcing him to practice projecting his voice so that he could be heard on a crowded field of battle. All of the bundles moved now, waking up with a shock. "I am Sir Trist du Camaret-à-Arden, and I give you my word as a knight, upon my honor, that I will allow no harm to come to you."

There was fearful whispering, but none of them had tried to bolt past him for the alley yet, so Trist kept speaking. "I have come for something that was stolen. A turned bowl of rosewood, finely crafted. Who knows where it may be?"

"This isn't going to work," Acrasia murmured to him, though he was quite certain none of the children would hear her voice regardless of how loudly she spoke. "They're terrified, Trist. Probably abused and starved, as well."

Trist on the other hand, was watching the children, and how they studiously tried to avoid looking to his left. Down, up, at him, away to the other side - anything but at where a warehouse's massive, barn-like doors were shut, under a ragged awning.

"In there?" He asked Acrasia, and she nodded. "Any of you who is still here when I return," Trist said, raising his voice again to the children, "I will do what I can to help you." He slid down off of Caz, and secured the lance in a leather loop on his saddle included for this purpose. There wasn't really anywhere good to loop the reins, however, unlike in a forest.

"Watch your horse for a coin, sir."

One of the little urchins had come forward, a child with dark hair falling in a shaggy, untrimmed and ill-kept mass past their jaw. It was hard to tell in the darkness, but Trist thought the boy might have a split lip.

"This horse is trained for war," Trist warned the urchin. "Try to steal him, or do anything he does not like, and he will kick you with those hooves." He handed over the reins, and a single silver coin from his purse. "His name is Cazador." Acrasia sat prettily atop the destrier, sidesaddle now, but of course, it was all for his benefit, as only he could see her.

"What're you lot doing out here?" a hoarse voice shouted out into the desolate courtyard, and Trist saw that one of the two doors leading into the warehouse had been opened. An unshaven man with shaggy hair, dirty clothes, and a dagger in his hand stepped out from under the awning and into the moonlight. "You be quiet till morning, or I'll cut your tongues out!"

Trist strode across the courtyard toward the man, setting himself a course around the fire-pit where the embers still glowed in the dim moonlight. "Hand over the graal," he called out, right arm across his body ready to draw his blade, "And no one need be hurt this night."

From behind him, atop the horse, Acrasia laughed, the same as she'd laughed when he'd been a child and they'd played by the river. She was looking forward to watching this, apparently.

"Who in the name of the pit are you?" the ragged man asked, with a sneer, and as Trist approached he could smell the scent of alcohol wafting off of him, mixed with piss and sweat and heaven knew what else. "What graal?" He raised his dagger, but to Trist's eye the man had never really been trained with it: he had no stance to speak of. What was more, no Knight of Thorns or animated shadow stood before him now: only a mortal man. Trist drew his sword, and raised it with both hands, above his head in High Guard, pointed to the moon.

The drunk stabbed forward with his dagger, but it was a stupid decision: Trist had more than enough reach on him. His footwork smooth from years of daily drill, the Knight slid to his right, moving off-line from the dagger thrust, and brought his blade down diagonally. His angle was good, the strike was true: blood sprayed into Trist's face as the man's arm dropped to the ground with a wet thump.

The man had time for a single scream before he hit the ground, bearing Trist's sword down with him. He placed his left boot on the dead man's chest and pulled the blade out of his torso with a heave. It was surprisingly easy, compared to his duels in the Ardenwood.

Back atop Cazador, Acrasia cheered. "That's one for the King of Shadows!"

And indeed, Trist felt the jolt of something moving through the blade and up his arm. He had the briefest glimpse of a fiery serpent, winding its way out of the corpse and up the steel. The man's soul, on its way to pay the Tithe to the faerie king?

From inside the warehouse, he could hear a commotion. The door was hanging open to the courtyard, and someone had screamed; of course all of the thieves would be awake, now. Trist had always thought gangs of brigands made their bases in forests or caves, but it seemed that a run-down part of town worked just as well for them in this case.

"Terrel?" Two men stepped out into the filthy courtyard, one carrying a shortsword and the other a crossbow, though it wasn't raised. Trist didn't wait for them to see the body: he had no desire to take a crossbow bolt to his guts. He slid forward, unleashing a rising cut, but the man with the crossbow scrambled back with a strangled cry.

There was the sound of a mechanism releasing, the twang of the crossbow string, and the whistle of a bolt skittering off along the ground, into the crushed shells. The man had panicked, off balance, and pulled his trigger while he was still stumbling backward. The second man lunged forward with his short-sword pointed at Trist, who easily set it aside with a crooked cut that took off his enemy's sword hand at the wrist. A jolt passed through Tristan's arm as the man fell, howling in pain, his lifeblood pouring out of his stump.

"That will be two," Acrasia crowed, and she was right: without a barber-surgeon, the man would bleed to death shortly.

The surviving man had set a new bolt into his crossbow, stepped on the curved wood, and was pulling back the string while screaming for help from within the warehouse. "Bron! Get out here, Bron!" he called in a panic. Trist sliced crosswise, parallel to the ground, cutting through not only the stock of the crossbow but also the man's belly, tumbling his guts out onto the ground in a stinking pile. The overpowering smell of blood, shit, oysters and wine made Trist gag.

"And the third for you!" the faerie maiden shouted from behind him. "That's your first Boon, Trist!"

Before he could respond, a massive man, ducking his head, lumbered out of the door.

"Bron, I take it?" Trist asked, with a wince.

Chapter Seventeen

JUSTICE

While it was King Aurelius who created the role of the knight, it was under the regnancy of his wife, Queen Elantia, that many of the mores of chivalry we now celebrate were formalized. The role of a squire for instance, as a knight-in-training, who would both learn and serve before growing into manhood, was her invention, and she used it well. It is said that at least one son of every major family in Narvonne spent seven years as a squire at her Court, growing up with her own son. It was these knights, when grown, who were King Laurent Aurelianus' greatest supporters.
-François du Lutetia, A History of Narvonne

25th Day of the Planting Moon, 297 AC

Trist was not a small man.

He'd always had a healthy appetite, and both his father and the Master at Arms had encouraged he and Percy, especially once they'd begun to put on muscle from their exercise in the yard around the time they needed to begin shaving, to eat as much meat and fresh produce as they could. John Granger had always said that you could tell people who'd been through a famine or a stretch of real poverty in their youth, because they didn't get their full growth. Trist had realized young that his great talent was the sword, and so he wanted every inch of height and reach, every pound of muscle that he could get. A skilled, quick, small man could beat a slow, clumsy big man; but a skilled, quick big man would beat them both. The last time he'd been measured, against the notch on the stable door, Trist had come in at five foot, nine inches, when he'd finally passed Percy.

Bron had at least a head on him, likely more. He also had a massive club, which looked to have been chopped from a tree branch, with a handle wrapped in leather and long iron nails driven through the head to poke a finger's width out the other side.

"Little man," Bron said, shaking his wild beard so that drops of ale flew in every direction, "You came to the wrong place." Like a charging bear, he lurched forward, raising the nailed club in both hands.

Trist's one saving grace was that he really was better, and he really was quicker. He dashed forward to meet the monster, ducking past Bron on the man's left, and slicing at the exposed shoulder as he went by.

Unlike the first few men, Bron simply roared, spun around, and swung the club at Trist's head. He didn't have a lot of hope in blocking the monstrous weapon, but he also didn't want to take it to the face, so Trist swung his blade up into Ox to set the blow aside. Just before the impact, his sword lit up with a fiery glow. Trist wasn't sure what was happening, but whatever it was, the sheer power behind the swing knocked him backward three steps and rang the sword like a bell. He was fairly certain that any normal sword would have simply been broken by the tree limb.

Bron was bleeding from the shoulder, though, and his left arm drooped. The big man shifted the club entirely into his right hand, which left his left side open again. Trist lunged forward, bringing his blade around in a tight arc and down at a diagonal, slicing straight through the man's bicep and into his chest.

The brute staggered, club raised, and for a long second Trist was sure it was about to come crashing down into his skull.

Then Bron swayed, dropped, and the sword pulsed a shiver of power up his arm.

"Another Tithe for the King," Acrasia said, appearing next to him, lips at his ear. "Would you accept a piece of advice from me?"

Panting, Trist couldn't quite manage a scowl. "What?" he finally said. No matter how much she disgusted him, Acrasia knew secrets that he needed to survive.

"My brother will owe you a reward once you come back to him with the graal. Wait and see what he offers before deciding what you spend your portion of the Tithe on. I can hold it for you in the blade, for now."

"Fine," he said, and staggered into the dark warehouse.

The cavernous interior was sectioned off by moth-eaten, ragged curtains, creating a series of rooms. In the center, which had been left as a kind of makeshift great hall, was a fire pit. Curious about where the smoke would go, Trist looked up, and saw stars above through a hole in the roof. He was surprised the entire warehouse hadn't caved in yet.

Too exhausted to deal with the niceties - and was the sky beginning to lighten with the promise of dawn? If so, he didn't have much time - Trist began tearing down the curtains. "Come out and surrender the graal," he called, "And you have my word as a knight I will show you mercy."

"A knight?" The voice was reedy and thin, and the man that followed it out into the dim glow of banked embers was thin, too: nearly skeletal in his arms and legs, his hair lank, skin pale. The only part of his body that disturbed the overall impression was his belly, which bulged obscenely beneath his filthy linen shirt. "This is a lawful place of business, sir," the man wheedled, sidestepping like some kind of crab. Trist remembered catching one, as a child, and watching in fascination how it moved along the tidal pools at Rocher de la Garde.

"Lawful, is it?" Trist did not lower his sword from the Plow Guard, and kept the tip in line with the man's chest. "A lawful business that deals in stolen goods? Whose men come out armed to kill at the slightest disturbance? And what of all those starving children sleeping in the courtyard?"

"War is on the horizon," the man proclaimed innocently. "Who could fault a businessman for arranging protection during such troubled times? And the urchins, I confess, an act of mercy on my part, the poor dears. I throw them what scraps I can afford, and have not the heart in me to deny them a place to sleep."

"It's over this way," Acrasia called, moving past Trist as if the gaunt man was no threat to her at all. Which, of course, Trist realized, was true, now that her physical body was the sword in his hands.

"What is your name, sir?" Trist asked.

"Monipodio," he answered, with an ingratiating smile. "A simple tradesman, Sir Knight, a purser. See, here, the oxhides of my craft?" He raised an arm to indicate a few ratty tanned hides, hanging from the rafters of the warehouses.

"Liar," a small voice said from behind Trist, and he turned to see one of the children had come in from the courtyard - the boy with the split lip. The orphan might have stood to Trist's chest, at most, and when he brushed his dark, ratty hair back from his face, it was obvious how sunken and starved his cheeks were. "You're no purser, you're a kidsman. All the purses in here are those you've had us steal for you." He stepped up to Trist's side, seemed to find his courage, and said, "He won't feed us otherwise. And his men you killed beat us every day we don't bring them something back."

Trist narrowed his eyes.

Monipodio scowled at the child, and spat his reply. "Shut your mouth, you ungrateful little bastard." He turned back to Trist, voice once again as sweet as a ripe strawberry. "One need not put too much stock in what children say, Sir Knight. Might I enquire your name?"

"Trist du Camaret-à-Arden," he answered, without putting much thought into it. "Remain where you are, sir," he ordered, and strode after Acrasia, following her behind two heavy velvet curtains - though just as ragged and dirty as the rest of the place - into a more comfortable space lit by braziers. Rugs were piled on the floor, and someone had dragged a four post bed and a desk in here. He imagined this was where Monipodio slept. On the desk, he found a rosewood turned bowl. "This is it?" he asked Acrasia, and she nodded.

"Look at it," the faerie maiden whispered, and beneath Trist's gaze, the familiar loops of fire filled his vision. Instead of red or orange or even yellow, the knotted twin threads shone white-blue, and trailed a long, braided cord out into the night. Trist's eyes fluttered, and a succession of images flitted before him, while it was all he could do to keep his balance.

A feast, attended by people both fair and tall, under the bright summer stars. The bowl full to the brim, and indeed spilling over, with nuts and berries, broken honey combs, and a score of good foods, besides.

Another flash, and a boy with the black sores of the plague which had taken his mother, exhausted head cradled by a delicate hand, sipped from the bowl. Before the vision faded from Trist's gaze, new life returned to the boy's pale face.

Trist's eyes opened again in shock, and he sucked in a breath, but he didn't let his thoughts linger on the power of the object in his hands. Gingerly, as he might handle a wild animal, he tucked the bowl under his left arm, and shoved his way back through the velvet curtains.

From the moment he stepped out into view again, Trist observed Monipodio's eyes latched onto the graal. It dispelled his last doubt as to whether the older man knew what he had. The child, on the other hand, watched Trist with a kind of awestruck worship.

"Are you a real knight, sir?" he asked. "Your horse is as big as an ox!"

"I am," Trist said. "Hold this for me, boy," he commanded, and shoved the graal into the child's hands. "In fact, take that out into the courtyard and set it down for all the children. I think you will find a bit of food inside when you do. But do not let anyone run off with it."

"Yes, Sir Trist," the boy said, and scampered off with the bowl clutched to his chest. With both hands free, Trist now was able to resume a proper grip on the hilt of his sword.

"Do we get to Tithe this one, too?" Acrasia asked, with a grin, circling Monipodio like a wolf around a wounded stag.

"Mercy, Sir Trist," Monipodio begged, raising his hands. "A man falls on hard days, and sometimes we must do distasteful things to survive. But at my core, you'll find me a virtuous man. I swear to you now, let me leave, and I shall go directly to the church, confess my sins, and live as a new man."

"Is there a lord of this town?" Trist asked.

"Sir Auron has departed for the war," Monipodio said, spreading his arms by way of apology.

"Then it falls to me to see justice done." Trist walked over to a table full of purses, which he swept aside. "Put your right hand on the table."

Monipodio hesitated.

"You asked for mercy, old man," Trist said. "Do you refuse it now? By law I should hang you. Put your hand on the table."

"As you say, Sir Knight," Monipodio finally sighed, walking over to Trist's side.

It was the scrape of blade against sheath that warned him, and Acrasia must have heard it, as well, for she shouted in warning: "Trist!"

He spun, the longsword describing a shining arc in the dim light of the warehouse, and the head of Monipodio hit the floor with a wet thump, then rolled under the table. The body collapsed, the treacherously drawn knife fell with a clang, and another fiery serpent ran up Trist's blade, shivering his arm, as a fifth Tithe was collected for the evening.

Outside in the courtyard, the children were stuffing themselves with nuts and berries of all kinds. When Trist joined them, they looked up at him, fearfully.

"Follow me," Trist ordered them. Orphans, he decided. Children of the streets. He swung up into Caz's saddle, and reached down for the graal. The same boy who'd shown the courage to enter the warehouse and speak out against their master handed it to him, and he tucked it into a saddle-bag with some difficulty; the bowl was large.

In the pre-dawn light, Trist led the whole crew to the town's church, where he banged on the door until the priest emerged.

"These children are orphans," Trist said, to the sleep-addled and befuddled man. "See them taken care of, or I will hear of it."

"And who are you, Sir Knight?" the priest asked him.

"Sir Trist du Camaret-à-Arden," he said, hoisting himself back into the saddle. As he turned to leave, though, one child ran up to the destrier and caught at a stirrup. The boy who'd followed him into the dark warehouse.

"Please sir," the boy said. "Take me with you."

Trist frowned. "What is your name, boy?"

"Yaél," the boy said, brushing back his mop of dark hair. "Of Havre de Paix. That's... that's here, Sir Trist. This town."

Trist's eyes flicked to Acrasia. It was not the sort of name peasants gave their children, and that left him with questions. But he needed to get back to the Horned Hunter before the sun broke the horizon over the sea in the east.

"I am off to war, Yaél du Havre de Paix," he said. "If you come, you come as a squire, and I will work you as a squire. It will be harder than anything you have ever done, and you may well die in battle."

"I've nothing here, sir," the boy said. "Please, take me?"

Trist reached down his hand, and pulled his squire up into the saddle; the boy was light as a bundle of rags.

Chapter Eighteen

The Hunter's Boon

Of the many curious legends told about these woods, that of the Wild Hunt must be one of the most peculiar. It is said to be a mob of ghostly hounds or wolves, running at the heels of a faerie hunter, sent by their master to drag some unfortunate soul to the faerie world. Staying on the road will protect an unwary traveler, but once off the path, there is little recourse. Any foolish enough to stand against them will be punished; but those who help the hunt are rewarded, sometimes with gold, sometimes with the leg of the prey - a gruesome prize indeed.

-François du Lutetia, A History of Narvonne

26th Day of the Planting Moon, 297 AC

The dawn sky was painted in vivid shades of red, orange, and purple by the time Cazador came to a halt at the top of the bluff, where Cern the Horned Lord, and the wolves of the wild hunt, waited.

The Horned Hunter's cold eyes flicked to the boy sharing the saddle with Trist, and he frowned. "You have the graal?"

Trist nodded, reached into his saddlebag, and removed the rosewood bowl. He extended his arm, holding Auberon's Graal out to the leader of the Wild Hunt. In truth, he was glad to have something so dangerous as far away from him as he could get it.

"A pity," Cern said, lip twisting in contempt as he accepted the bowl. "I would have preferred to kill you."

"I did as you asked," Trist said, dropping his hand back to the pommel of his sword, to be ready in case things went very, very badly. "And now I claim a Boon of you."

"Did my sister tell you to say that?" Cern scowled. "I do not understand why she still aids you."

"I don't require your understanding, Brother," Acrasia said, appearing at the side of the six-legged horse upon which the Horned Lord rode. "But you are required to follow the Accord."

"You have a Tithe for me, then, to pay the Boon?"

Trist nodded, though he wasn't certain how any of this worked. "Stored in the blade."

"I claim it, then, and grant you my Boon in return for the service you have done," the Hunter said begrudgingly. At a wave of the faerie lord's hand, Trist caught sight of a sparkling lash, burning yellow as the sun, whipping out from Cern and sinking into his chest.

Trist's body jerked, muscles spasming uncontrollably, and if Cazador had not shifted beneath him, he might have fallen out of the saddle entirely. He felt as if fire was burning from his heart out through his limbs to the tips of his fingers and toes. He was only just able to focus on Cern's parting words.

"See that we never meet again, mortal." The Hunter's horse wheeled, and the wolves sprung to follow as the Wild Hunt raced back towards the Ardenwood.

"...was that a faerie, Sir Trist?" Yaél asked from behind him.

"It was," Trist confirmed, gasping. "The Horned Lord of the Wild Hunt. Acrasia," he said, turning to where she bent to examine the bright pink flowers dotting the sea grass above the bluff, "The Boon?"

"Look at it," she said, "Just like before. I think you will be pleased, my love." He held out his own arm, and his gaze focused beneath the skin, where a red cord pulsed, and the familiar loops of fire overwhelmed Trist's view of the world around him.

His mind flashed back to the midnight ride with the Hunter: the way they had pounded through the Arden, without tiring, further and faster in only one night than any mortal could ride with an earthly steed. All in pursuit of the Hunter's prey.

Trist blinked, and the memory passed. "You knew what this would be, did you not?" he asked Acrasia. "This Boon means we can find Henry and Luc in the Ardenwood."

"Perhaps even before they reach Falais," she agreed, straightening from her inspection of the flowers. "Mallow. I think they're pretty." Acrasia ran her hands through her hair, and it turned the same shade of pink as the petals. She grinned, and turned to Trist, posing winningly. "Do you like it, my love?"

Trist grunted, focusing on his memory of Henry. There it was - almost like Abatur's north star shining at night, somewhere off to the west and a bit south, at the end of a thin red cord he could just make out.

"Sir Trist?" Yaél spoke up from behind him. "Who are you talking to?"

"My sword," he answered, and Acrasia yelped in displeasure. He ignored her, pressed his heels to Caz's flanks, and they were off. The burning line stretched out before him, drawing both Trist and Cazador on toward Henry and Luc. He knew that they could not get lost, and would not tire.

Cazador thundered through the dawn-dewed forest, leaping logs and ravines, dodging between tree trunks and stands of brush. Trist leaned forward in the saddle, rising easily in the stirrups. Man and steed moved as one, used by long hours of training to working together, and now entwined by that burning red thread, pulsing in time with their joined heartbeat. The only awkwardness was the young boy, Yaél, who Trist was now quite certain had never ridden a horse before, and bounced about behind him in all the wrong directions. Acrasia, rather than cram her illusory self into the saddle in front of him, seemed content to tease Trist with the occasional scent of her body, or the tickle of a curl of soft hair against his face.

They rode until the sun was high in the sky, beams of golden light falling down through the leafy canopy to dapple the shade of the wide boughs. Their mid-day meal was entirely fetched from Trist's saddlebags, but Yaél devoured the cheese and jerky given to him as if the boy had not eaten from the Graal just hours before. They passed the wineskin back and forth to quench their thirst while Caz pranced about, as full of energy as if the destrier had been cooped up in a stable all day, not running.

"Sore?" Trist asked, when he'd had his fill. He took his Iebara-wood calendar wheel from the leather saddle bags, and spun the outer wheel so that the carved window revealed the twenty-fifth day; soon it would be time to turn the moon wheel on the inside. Acrasia was lying on her back in the sun, flower-petal pink hair fanned out around her head, knees crooked and one leg bouncing over the other. She was singing the song about the trees again, and he tried to ignore the memories her voice conjured.

"Yes," Yaél admitted, but then gave him a fierce look. "But I've had worse, Sir Trist. Don't slow down for me."

"I will not," he promised. "We need to catch up with my two men before they reach the mountains. We have been delayed enough, already, so we are riding hard all afternoon until we reach them. Once everyone is together again, we can slow down a bit."

"Can I ask you something?" The boy enquired hesitantly, and Trist gave a grunt and a nod in assent. "Your sword. You said you were speaking to it, before? Is it... is it a magic sword? Like in the stories?"

Acrasia cut off singing, and sat up, suddenly interested in what he had to say. Trist tried to ignore her eyes on him as he answered the boy. "I do not know much about magic," he admitted. "I do not know what a wise-man would name it. But the sword is tied to the fae, and has power. It is not like in the stories, though," he said, after considering a moment. "At least, I do not think so. I would give the sword up in a heartbeat to go back to how things were before I had it."

"Oh, my love," Acrasia said, suddenly behind him, wrapping her pale arms around his neck and leaning her head down so that her perfumed hair fell about his face. "You can't ever go back. And you could never have truly loved me until you knew what I am."

He caught a glimpse of the boy's wide eyes through the curtains of her soft hair, and knew that Yaél had only heard what he wanted to hear: what fit with a boy's dreams. "You are just like a hero in the stories, then," the urchin concluded, breathlessly. "A magic sword, riding with the faeries... you swept in to save us like a hero. I'll do whatever you say, m'lord. Please, teach me to fight like you!"

Trist grimaced. "We are going off to war, boy. I told you I was going to work you hard, and I will. You will learn what every squire learns, as much as I can teach, but you will also clean my armor and take care of Caz, here. Are you certain you want all that?"

"If you teach me to fight," the boy said, nodding. "Then I won't have to let anyone hit me ever again."

Trist sighed. "That is what I will teach you, then." He rose, and Acrasia slipped off of him as gracefully as if they'd been dancing. "Find a good tree to do your business," he told his new squire, "we will not be stopping again until we hit the road, or until dark." Following his own example, he set to unlacing his breeches.

"I'll just go off in the woods a bit," Yaél said, and Trist sighed.

"Do not go too far. Plenty of wolves and bears and worse things in these woods," he grumbled. A few moments later, they were riding again.

The burning lodestar of the Hunter's Boon led them to the ancient Etalan road before they reached Henry and Luc, and it made Trist restless and worried. He wouldn't truly relax, he knew, until they'd not only found the two men-at-arms, but also gotten off the road. He couldn't see Yaél's eyes, but the tone in the boy's voice was the same as when Trist had confirmed the sword was special.

"It looks so old," the new squire said, as they paused, Caz dropping his head to graze on blades of roadside grass.

"Almost a thousand years," Trist confirmed. "Though my brother was always better with the histories than I was."

Wide enough for a horse-drawn wagon, the road was of gray granite. The pieces in the middle of the road were irregular, fitted closely together with small white stones, called Cat's Eyes, set wherever a small gap left room. At night, Trist knew from his studies, they reflected the moonlight, allowing travel even after the sun had set. The whole arrangement reminded Trist of how a wall was constructed, if a wall had been set on its side. The borders of the road were of square stone, instead, set evenly, and shallow ruts had been worn by the long passage of wheels, where the granite was grooved to the thickness of a man's finger or more.

"How is it still here?" Yaél asked. "They're always adding a new load of crushed shells to the roads in Havre de Paix, seems like every summer."

"This is not anything like your shell-streets," Trist explained. "The Etalans were famed builders. There is something like half a dozen layers to that road: lime, sand, mortar and stone going down as deep into the ground as a man stands tall. A lot of good it did them, in the end," he muttered, looking north up the road. He didn't see any daemons. Didn't see anything on the road that was living, north or south.

"They worked magic into the foundations of what they built, as well," Acrasia said, and stepped gingerly onto the ancient stones. When nothing happened, she smiled in relief. "No iron, and whatever wards were here are long since decayed. Feels like nothing more than an itch," she proclaimed.

Trist nudged Cazador onto the stones, and they set off south on the road at a trot. The wind rustled the grasses to either side, and the arched vault of tree boughs overhead shaded them from the glare of the afternoon sun. Trist felt that they were drawing closer to the two men, due to the power of the Boon he'd been granted, but it was not until the forest broke around them, revealing a lake of striking blue water, bridged by a span of ancient white stone, that the entire party was finally reunited.

Henry and Luc leaped up from the grass to the side of the road, not far from the bank of the lake, with smiles on their faces and cheers. "Sir Trist!" Luc shouted, and with a feeling of relief, Trist felt the Boon's effect fade. He drew Caz to a halt, swung down out of the saddle, and then helped the boy, Yaél, down to the ground as well. He was somewhat amused to observe that the new squire walked stiffly from the day's ride, and he was equally satisfied to see how quickly Acrasia tried to shoo him off the stones and onto the grass. Once the sword was outside the bounds of whatever spells the ancients had worked into the stone, she slumped in relief. Just a bit of an itch, indeed.

"We worried we'd never see you again," Henry admitted, as they all sat in the soft grass and took a moment to pass around a bit of food and drink. "I can't believe you rode with the Wild Hunt!"

"Not something I will ever do again, if I can help it," Trist promised, "Though I am glad that good came of the whole thing. This is Yaél du Havre de Paix," he introduced the boy, "My new squire. Yaél, this is Henry, and Luc, men-at-arms in the service of my family. They are coming with us to muster with the Crown Prince's army."

"Yes, m'lord," Yaél said, suddenly shy.

Luc regarded the boy skeptically. "A bit small for a squire," he commented, which only seemed to make Yaél shrink further.

"That's the good thing about boys," Henry said. "They grow. You'll be tall and strong in no time, I'm sure," he said, and Trist was glad that Henry at least seemed to warm to the child.

"I am glad we caught up with you before dark," Trist said, taking a sip of watered-wine and passing it on. "Surprised you stopped, though. There is still plenty of light before dusk."

"Well, that's the thing, m'lord," Luc said, looking to Henry. "We couldn't cross the bridge."

Trist frowned. "Why not? Is it falling in?" That would be the last thing they needed; he was already trying to calculate how long it would take to ride around the lake and find the road south again.

"No, m'lord," Henry said. "It's on account of the monster."

Chapter Nineteen

The Monster in the Lake

Kalends of Primus, 980th Year of the Empire
I have tasked my retainer, Marius, with assembling and compiling every scrap of intelligence we can gather on these daemons. After the debacle at Vellatesia, we cannot afford to remain in ignorance. The men name them daemons, after the old legends, and I cannot say they are wrong.
-The Campaign Journals of General Aurelius, volume III

26th Day of the Planting Moon, 297 AC

"The monster?" Trist looked to the sparkling blue surface of the lake. It seemed peaceful enough, but who could say how deep the waters were, and what might lurk down there in the dark?

"Aye, m'lord," Henry continued. "Horrible, it was, with a long snout and sharp teeth, and a wide tail like the paddle of a boat. Leapt out of the water and nearly had Luc by the leg. Armored it was, in bronze maybe, and it had a big sword, like a butcher's knife for carving."

Trist looked to the big man-at-arms for confirmation, and Luc nodded, showing everyone where the right leg of his breeches was torn. "I was lucky," he said. "Jumped back just as it came. Can't rightly say how I knew, but everything just seemed too calm. Like the whole forest was holding its breath, and I didn't like the feeling."

"Once we'd run off the bridge, it slipped back into the water," Henry recounted. "But there's no way we can pass with something like that here. We didn't know what to do; we didn't want to leave the road, because we knew that's where you'd look for us. We'd just about decided to camp here when you rode out of the woods, m'lord."

"You did the right thing." Trist looked at the lake again, then at where Acrasia stood on the bank, gazing out on the waters. "Do you know what it is?" he called over to her.

Acrasia was silent a moment, peering at the beautiful waters, and then turned back and walked over to sit at his side. "I think so," she said, leaning in. "When the Etalan Empire fell during the Cataclysm, the daemons they'd summoned rampaged across the lands. Here in the Ardenwood, all sorts of daemon-spawned monsters poured out of the old capital. King Auberon's knights were forced to fight four great battles before the forest was scoured clean of the filth. One of the daemons was driven into a lake, wounded. From what I recall, the King hoped it would wither away down there."

"...they simply took that for granted?" Trist asked in disbelief.

"No, of course not," she said, snuggling in against him. "The court wove a binding about the lake, to imprison the daemon there and let it wither to almost nothing. And the binding should have held! But that was three hundred years ago, my love. Just like the wards have faded from the road, it must have found some way to slip loose of its chains, eventually. It will be feeding on whoever it can catch, using their souls to slowly regain its power."

"...does he talk to his sword a lot?" Yaél asked Henry.

The woodsman shrugged. "The sword talked to the Horned Hunter, too," he said. "But I can't hear it."

Trist tried to ignore them. "Does this daemon have a name?" he asked Acrasia.

"Addanc," she whispered in his ear. "Best not to speak the names of daemons aloud, my love, lest you draw their attention. More dangerous for your men, than for you."

"If we could lure it out," Trist considered, "I could charge it with my lance."

The two men-at-arms and the new squire exchanged glances. "Not any of you," he assured them, with a sigh. "You are not bait for me to catch a fish."

"It wouldn't work, anyway," Acrasia chided him. "It's like me. The form mortals see is only a small piece of it. Even if you skewered that with your lance, you couldn't kill it. The only weapon you have that can really drive something like that off is the sword, because the sword is part of me, and I am part of it."

"She says only the sword can hurt it," Trist said to the other three. "Or some other weapon like the sword, I suppose."

"She?" Yaél asked.

"Acrasia. The faerie in the sword," he explained.

"The sword's a woman?" Luc asked, and Trist ignored him. "Feel like I should be on better manners, then..."

"That means I am the only one who can fight it," Trist realized, letting out a sigh as he thought things through. "I would have liked to place Henry back with his bow, taking shots at it. And without a charge on Caz... how big did you say the damned thing was?" he asked the two men-at-arms.

"Two men or more tall," Henry said, exchanging glances with Luc, who confirmed with a nod.

"At least."

"So it will have reach on me. I am not seeing a lot of advantages to us fighting it," he admitted, "Instead of just going around."

"I wouldn't normally say this, and Auberon would almost certainly disagree, but every soul it's collected," Acrasia said, "Will be ours if you kill it. A third to the King, a third to me, a third to you. This is a chance to prepare yourself for the war."

"I am not convinced that is enough of a reason to risk everyone's lives," Trist answered her.

"Do you think you're going to be the only one under the Accords?" Acrasia asked, placing one hand on his thigh. As much as he wished it didn't, her touch made him want to catch her in his arms and tumble them both onto the grass. *You have a wife, now, and perhaps a child coming, as well,* Trist reminded himself. *And she is a monster.*

"You can be certain both the Crown Prince and the Caliphate will have at least a champion each, with Angelus to guide them," the faerie maiden continued. "People who have been tithing under the Accords a lot longer than you have. You won't be able to stand up to them if you don't grow stronger, and quickly. And they're going to see you as a quick source of souls to pay their own Tithes. Kill the daemon, my love. Kill it while it's weak. Because you have much more dangerous challenges coming ahead."

Abruptly, he realized that everyone else was looking at him, waiting for his conversation with the woman in his sword to end. "Acrasia," he said slowly, "Believes I should fight the daemon. She says it will make me stronger, and that I will need that strength when we go to war."

Yaél grinned, eyes wide. "I know you can defeat it, m'lord!"

"I don't know," Luc said. "Thing was big and mean, and I thought that before we knew it was a daemon. No offense, m'lord," he apologized to Trist. "I know you're good, and you have a magic sword. But you didn't see the thing."

Henry was the last to speak. "I agree with the faerie," he said, after a moment, "If you want my opinion, m'lord. I've heard plenty of stories from men in the service of other lords. When Sir Tor came to visit, for instance, his men talked over ale. Exarchs, they call them - the church does. The men with Angelus at their backs. They say it isn't even worth fighting one if you don't have a champion of your own: they can kill a dozen men as easy as taking a breath. If we come up against something like that... you're the only one who can face them. And if she thinks this will get you ready? Might be its a risk that has to be taken."

"Sir Tor," Trist tasted the word, and let it simmer in the back of his mind. "Now there is a thought. Thank you, Henry." He stood up. "I have heard council from all of you. Yaél, time to learn the first duty of a squire. Let us get my armor unpacked."

To the pauldrons and vambraces which he'd been able to squeeze into when he went to the chapel, the adjusted greaves and cuirass had been added, and the whole set of armor packed in oil cloth. Trist was already wearing a new padded gambeson - there'd been time to make that - and Hywel had repaired the broken links in his shirt of rings. It wasn't a full set of armor, by any means, and he would have preferred to have a helm if he could get it, but Trist was grateful that this much of his brother's armor had been salvaged.

"The pauldrons before the cuirass," he corrected Yaél. "That way, the straps go under the plate."

"Yes, m'lord," the boy said, dropping the cuirass back onto the grass and scrambling for one of the shoulder plates instead. Trist tried to be patient with Yaél; he couldn't imagine the boy had ever strapped a piece of armor onto someone in his short life, so he talked his new squire through the process one step at a time. It wasn't really any easier than doing it himself, at the moment, but the boy's fingers were quick and clever, and he would learn.

Finally, Trist stood, the closest to fully armored he had ever been. He didn't count the beat up, ill-sized and padded training equipment that John Granger had scavenged from who knew where for he and Percy to use as children. For a moment, Trist wondered just what they had been planning on sending him off to war in, before Percy had been killed. Only a shirt of chain?

That was what Henry and Luc were slipping into, right now. Trist didn't plan on putting either of them at risk against the daemon, but he agreed with their prudence, and gave both men-at-arms a nod of approval.

"Yaél," he said, once the final buckle had been pulled tight, "You are to stay with Henry and Luc, and keep a good hold of Caz. He is going to want to come fight with me, because that is what he has been trained to do."

"Yes, m'lord," the boy said nervously, going to stand by the destrier. Trist rolled his head around, once to each side, to loosen his neck, and hopped from one foot to the other to let the armor settle on. Then, he drew his longsword, and cast the sheath aside. No point in bringing anything that wasn't going to be immediately useful, he resolved. It would only slow him down. He'd faced Acrasia's monsters of shadow and thorn; he could face this.

"Remind me to get a helm fitted, as soon as we get to the Crown Prince's camp," he muttered to Henry, then set out toward the bridge, walking along the old Etalan road. There was enough old magic in it to make Acrasia itch; maybe that would distract the monster.

The faerie maid fell into step beside him, her hair suddenly pale blonde again, just like it had been the day they first met, when he was a child. Trist snuck a glance at her. For just a moment, with the sun falling on her face, he could imagine he was looking at Linette again, and that he'd never lost her. They could have been making this journey together, with Percy at home with his new wife, if she'd only had the patience and faith in him not to act.

But no, he decided, that wasn't right. The Faerie King would have been pushing her for Tithes one way or the other, and the moment they got to the camp, would she really have been able to hide what she was?

"Going to fight with me?" he asked the woman he'd once loved. Trist couldn't decide whether he still did, or not.

"I'll do what I can, my love," the faerie promised. "But you know I've never been a fighter. I was always the beautiful flower, so pretty the men had to come look. I may be able to distract a daemon, but I can't defeat one. That will be up to you."

Trist smiled. "There is one thing, at least," he confided to her.

"What?" she glanced over to him. They were only steps from the bridge of white stone.

"This is the first time I have had no qualms whatsoever about killing what is in front of me," Trist said. "Killing a man is a hard thing. Killing a daemon? That is what I have been waiting to do my entire life."

Side by side, the knight and the faerie stepped out onto the bridge and walked out over the lake.

Chapter Twenty

The Addanc

The forms of the daemons that rose from the ruins of Vellatesia are as diverse as the fish of the sea and the fowl of the sky, as are the varied devices by which they tempt and corrupt men, or lay to waste the works of the Empire. Indeed, a daemon whose only hunger is for bloodshed is the very simplest evil to fight. Far more insidious and sinister are those who can turn men to their own service, twisting their form and soul alike into a grotesque mockery of man.

-The Marian Codex

26th Day of the Planting Moon, 297 AC

With every step, Trist expected a monstrous daemon to come rushing out of the lake.

He crept out onto the span of cracked and crumbling white stone, further and further away from the shore. He held his longsword in Plow, to his left side at about waist height, pointing up and in toward a prospective enemy's chest. It was a good guard to set aside an attack from, or to simply extend and allow a charging enemy to impale themselves on the point of his blade.

Nothing happened. Trist's heart pounded so that he could hear nothing else; there were no bird cries, no wind seemed to rustle the trees or send waves to lap against the shore of the lake. Next to him, Acrasia's steps were silent; she did not disturb even the broken pebbles that littered the ancient Etalan bridge, for she had no physical form. Trist truly wasn't certain how much she would be able to help him, but against a daemon he would take any aid he could get.

Trist was just thinking that it would have been convenient for the Horned Hunter to bring the Wild Hunt to find him now, instead of the night before, when a loud splash of water came from behind him. "Trist!" Acrasia shouted, and suddenly he could again see her true form: that shining, tangled skein of power stretching out from the sword in his hand to... somewhere. Wherever the fae were truly from. Lashes of burning light speared past him as he turned, raising his sword and bracing himself for the daemon's charge.

The daemon was enormous, though at first Trist had only the vaguest impression of it beyond that, as massive jaws came at him, snapping. He raised his blade, pushed off with his right foot, and slid aside. A small part of his mind thanked his Master at Arms: if John Granger hadn't drilled his footwork from the time he was seven winters old, Trist would have been snapped up in those jaws and bitten in half, and that would have been the end of the battle right there. He cut with his sword as the rush of the daemon carried it by him, but the monster was too fast, and he didn't connect.

For two breaths, Trist and the daemon faced each other across the bridge, separated by a half dozen paces - the length the monster's rushing attack had carried it past him. Trist raised his blade vertically above his head into High Guard, and swallowed against a throat gone suddenly dry.

Addanc, the daemon of the lake, was truly of immense size. Larger than the heaviest destrier, Trist guessed it must be nearly fifteen feet tall at full height, and it could clearly stand on two legs when it wished to, because it did so now. Water dripped off its scaly hide, and clumps of lake weed still clung to where its rusted armor, a kind of bronze cuirass that only covered the chest, all sharp curves and spikes, was held on by straps. It wore vambraces of a type with the cuirass, and a kind of skirt of metal plates. As Trist's men had described, it's snout was long and filled with teeth, its lashing tail flattened for propulsion through the water. There were wicked-looking black claws, too, clutching an enormous curved sword that Trist would have had to grasp in two hands - if he were able to wield it at all - while the daemon easily held the blade in one.

"Fresh meat," the daemon growled. "And what's this? The scent of delicious faerie, as well. Your souls might finally sate my hunger!"

"Sir Tor De Lancey," Trist intoned. "I call upon you. Stand with me against this foe."

The cracked white stone of the bridge frosted over in an instant as the temperature dropped.

"This," Tor De Lancey's boisterous voice echoed across the lake, "Is a battle worthy of a knight!" The Addanc must not have even seen the ghostly knight appear; Tor, fully armored in spectral plate, slammed a pale warhammer into the daemon's belly with a mighty blow, knocking it back an entire step. The daemon gasped, involuntarily hunching over, and the pain of the impact distracted it long enough for Acrasia's burning strands to lash at it, but she couldn't seem to get a grip, or to hurt it in any way.

As long as the burning red cord held: that was as long as the spirit of Tor could stay to help him, and Trist knew they had to end this soon. The longer the battle went on, the greater the chance of the Addanc wounding him, and even if it didn't kill him with a single blow, Trist knew he couldn't count on either Acrasia or Tor to end the fight. Acrasia had fully admitted she wasn't a warrior, and he didn't expect her to be much more than a distraction, whatever she was doing. And if Trist fell, Tor might well not be able to remain long enough to finish the daemon. All of which boiled down to the fact that this was the time to strike, and Trist couldn't afford to play a defensive game or try to wear the creature down over time.

Pushing off with his back foot, Trist shot forward, swinging down from above his head as he came within reach of the Addanc. The daemon, in return, lifted its sword to parry, knocking Trist back, and the two exchanged a series of thrusts, cuts and parries while Acrasia's burning strands of magic tried to wrap around the monster's limbs or spear through its flesh, occasionally shattering the stone of the bridge when they missed. The spirit of Tor fought beside Trist, but for the moment none of them were able to land a telling blow, only an occasional blade or hammer-strike skittering off rusted and wet armor plates.

Trist had little time to think: everything was action and reaction, avoiding death by inches, skittering over the wet stone, gasping for breath, all while trying to hold onto Tor. He wondered whether this battle would have been over by now if he'd only invested his single Tithed Soul into the Fae-Touched Boon. The thought was a distraction he couldn't afford, and he tried to stuff it to the back of his mind so that he could devote his entire focus to the life and death struggle on the bridge.

He was better than the daemon was.

That much was obvious to Trist even within the first exchange of blows. It was a surprise to him that Tor De Lancey wasn't, but Trist certainly was. Once he'd adapted to the daemon's massive, inhuman form, he was still able to read the movements of its feet, its hips, its shoulders, and follow the tells of where it was going to strike next. Trist's footwork was better, his cuts cleaner, his parries more precise, and if it was simply a matter of form he had no doubt that he could take the thing apart piece by piece.

The problem was, he realized, as he swung a diagonal cut to bind the Addanc's blade, that the thing was overwhelmingly stronger than him. It was a hair faster, and he could deal with that because he could predict it, but the strength! The daemon casually powered through the bind, and Trist had everything he could do to not only avoid the notched edge of its blade, but to not collapse to his knees. A swipe of its tail sent Tor flying and nearly over the edge of the bridge. They simply couldn't contain it, and something needed to change.

Scrambling for his footing, Trist fell back into a Low Guard, watching for his moment. He needed not just to draw blood, but to make a cut that was crippling, that would swing the battle in their favor. Tor rushed in with his warhammer lifted high, and swung it down with all his strength, but the daemon leapt aside, and the head of the hammer hit the bridge, sending chips of white stone flying in every direction.

Acrasia's strands of fire lashed past them both, piercing the Addanc for the first time, and the daemon let out a roar. Trist saw no blood, and no sign of any physical wound, but it was clearly hurt, and this was the opening he'd been waiting for. As the daemon threw its head back, it dropped the tip of its sword slightly, and its eyes were off him for just a moment. Trist lunged forward, and extended both arms in a thrust, piercing the daemon's throat, and sinking nearly a foot of his blade into its head. Black ichor gushed out from the wound, spilling down his blade and onto his arms, spraying into his face so that he was forced to squint his eyes and turn away. With a yank, he pulled the sword back out again, and leaped back, falling into a hasty Plow Guard to defend against whatever counterattack was coming, blade once again pointed at its chest.

With a horrible, gurgling intake of breath, the daemon collapsed, its curved sword ringing off the stone of the bridge as it fell from the Addanc's grip. The body convulsed as the daemon tried to suck in air. Did daemons need to breathe?

"Now, my love," Acrasia urged. She was next to him, suddenly. "Finish it. Tithe all of the souls it's collected." he was repulsed by how positively hungry she sounded.

Trist swallowed, gingerly stepped up to the daemon's side, and chose his spot. There. Between what passed for ribs, coming up from under it's odd cuirass that left the belly exposed. Up, and into the heart. With all his strength, he made the thrust, and the body stiffened.

A jolt traveled up his arm, as the blade jerked. Writhing snakes of fire and light shot up from the daemon's corpse, twining about the blade, some sinking into it and causing the metal to heat and vibrate, others burrowing into Trist's arm.

When it had finally stopped, and he pulled the sword back out, Trist was exhausted. He sat down on the bridge, gasping for breath. Somewhere in the midst of all this, the ghost of Tor De Lancey had vanished, and it was a great relief.

"How many?" he asked Acrasia.

"Six mortal souls, and one of his own," she told him. "You'd just paid a Tithe to the King for the leader of that gang of criminals, and then one to me for the Kidsman, so the next one is yours. Three each for you, and another two each for Auberon and I. You have three souls to trade for Boons."

"Will that be enough?" The entire process of trading in souls disgusted him, but she'd been right to say he was not yet as strong as he needed to be.

"It's never enough," she said, suddenly serious. "You defeated me, after all, without any. But you won't be quite so tempting a target, I don't think. Do you know how you're going to spend them?"

"I know the first," Trist said. The insane strength of the daemon had decided him, and he wasn't going to wait any longer: for all he knew, something else would happen, some new crisis, and he would regret not having done this when he had the chance. "Use one for Fae Touched." Acrasia grinned, and above the stinking corpse of the daemon, she sculpted loops of fire, then thrust them into his body with an outstretched hand.

Just like a few hours earlier, when the Horned Hunter had given Trist his first Boon, the burning strand dove into his heart, then grew outward, through each and every muscle. Trist fell to the bridge, curled around himself. His body twitched and ached as the fire passed in ripples of pain, as if his very muscles were tearing themselves apart, one after the other.

But when it had passed, the exhaustion faded from his muscles immediately. Instead of gasping for breath, Trist felt his heart slow. With new strength, he easily rose to his feet, and lifted his sword. It felt... lighter in his hands. Out of curiosity, Trist assayed a rising cut, and it felt quicker and smoother than any other cut he had ever made in his life: as if he had precise control of the blade, and could place it exactly where it needed to go. He looked to Acrasia.

"Daemons focus on strength," she explained. "The Addanc's Boons would have increased the power of its muscles to utterly inhuman levels. In that regard, it would outstrip even an experienced, powerful fae like my brother. But our Boons focus most on your reflexes, your agility, your hand-eye coordination. Your strength, your stamina, those things are still within the upper bounds of human limits - but you're faster than any mortal could ever be, now."

Chapter Twenty-One

DAEMON BANE

Alas, my love, you do me wrong
To cast me off discourteously
For I have loved you well so long
Delighting in your company.
-Traditional Narvonnian Ballad

26th Day of the Planting Moon, 297 AC

It was a lot to take in, so Trist walked back along the bridge in the light of the setting sun, half off balance with the capabilities of his radically altered body. Once he'd gotten back onto the shore of the lake, he walked off the path and down toward the water. He was covered in black ichor: it was hot, sticky, and it stunk.

"Squire!" he shouted, and not only Yaél, but Henry and Luc as well came running. Even Cazador, he was amused to see, followed them, having gotten free from the boy's grasp in all the excitement. The destrier ambled down to the lake's edge for a drink, while Trist held his arms out so that the men-at-arms and the boy could get his armor off.

"By the Angelus, this is disgusting," Henry commented, wringing his hand in an attempt to fling the repulsive ichor off.

Trist's mind, however, was elsewhere. "You have invested your Tithes into the blade," he murmured to Acrasia, and she nodded, confirming his guess. The faerie was ankle-deep in the water of the lake, holding her dress up to her knees as if it was still possible for it to get wet.

"I did," she confirmed. "That sword is now my only physical connection to the mortal world," she reminded Trist. "The last thing I need is for it to get destroyed, too. And with you going around letting big men hit it with spiked clubs, or trying to parry daemon-swords nearly as large as you are, my priorities are quite clear, thank you very much."

"I can see the orange strand," he said, as the last of the armor came free from his body. "You made the blade stronger, I presume?"

"I did. But it isn't unbreakable - yet - not without a greater Tithe of souls, so don't go thinking you can just do anything with it," Acrasia warned him.

"No, I will take care of it," he promised her. "Thank you," he told Henry, Luc and Yaél in a more audible voice. "I am going to try to get clean in the lake. Yaél, start scrubbing the armor with sand from the bank."

"...not water?" the young squire asked.

"That'll rust it, boy," Luc told him with a frown. "Dry sand. Here, let me show you."

Trist ignored them, stripping off his foul clothes and leaving them in a pile on the lakeshore, and then he waded into the chill water. He couldn't help but grin at the refreshing shock, after the sweat, grime, and the exertion of battle. He ran forward a few steps and dove in, letting the waters close over his head, and only surfaced when he was deep enough to tread water.

"Reminds me of the waterfall," Acrasia said, and he opened his eyes to see her swimming next to him, wearing not a scrap of clothing, her hair spreading across the water like spring lilly-pads. It seemed she no longer needed him to touch the sword in order to appear to him.

"It does," he admitted, but then forced himself to focus. "You put more than one soul into strengthening the blade."

"It was the most important thing I could do."

"I have two Tithed souls remaining," Trist pondered. "The new strand is red; I presume reinforcing the Boon with further Tithes would only increase the effect. That seems the most clearly beneficial thing to do." Focusing on understanding the magic helped him to avoid thinking about her nude body.

"There's a big difference," the faerie maiden pointed out. "Making the sword more durable doesn't really change anything about the way you fight, my love. But your whole physical body has just undergone a substantial improvement. You are stronger, yes, but your reflexes are quicker, your control of your movements more precise. You can exert yourself for longer without tiring. You need to adjust. My best advice is to spend a few days sparring, to get used to what your body is like now. If you improve yourself even further, it will actually hold you back in the short run. You'll be off balance, you won't know your own strength."

"I can see the sense in that," Trist said finally, with a sigh. "I do not like being so outmatched as against that daemon, but I can understand what you're saying. Knight of Shadows, then, and save the last."

"You have one more option." She swam up to him, and wrapped her arms around his neck. "Daemon Bane."

"Daemon Bane?" He took a step back, trying to get away from her.

"You slew a daemon," she explained, nuzzling against his neck. "So you've earned the right to it. It will help you to kill more daemons in the future. I think it will be to your taste."

"I will do that, then," Trist confirmed, and with a wave of Acrasia's hand, the whirls of light filled his vision again. It was the work of only a moment for her to invest his Tithed souls into the two Boons, winding new threads into his core, where now four red strands burned, twisting about each other in a knot.

The change to his body was not so obvious this time. Instead, one of the two new threads split, and pierced his eyes, so that he cried out from the stabbing pain, and had time only to hold his breath before his head dipped under the surface of the lake.

When his sight cleared, and the burning pain had receded, Trist looked into the shadowed depths of the lake, and found that he could see the sandy bottom clearly. He picked out swimming carp in the darkness by their golden scales. After a moment, he cupped his hands and swam back to the surface.

Trist blinked the water out of his eyes, trying to take it all in. He didn't object to having an easier time killing daemons in the future, but it wasn't immediately obvious to him how the Daemon Bane boon would help him do that. The Knight of Shadows Boon, on the other hand, he was less excited about: the only reason he'd invested in it was to be able to see better at night. The harrowing ride through the Ardenwood with the Wild Hunt had given him enough trouble for one lifetime, and if he ever did anything like it again, he wanted to actually be able to see where he was going.

He realized that while he'd been distracted, Acrasia had wrapped her legs around his hips and that, whether her body was illusion or not, she certainly felt very real, and very naked. The memory of what they'd done beneath the hill flooded him with excitement, and he put his hands on her shoulders. He was now a married man, now. And she had murdered his brother.

"No," Trist said, shoving her off and paddling back toward shore.

"Why not?" the faerie whined, simply appearing next to him, floating.

"Acrasia," he said, more bite to the words than he'd meant to put in it. "I understand that Percy did not matter to you, but he was my brother. If you had the patience to wait, to trust me, we could have been together. But you did not. You have lied to me about what you were since the day we met, and then you killed my brother. This all seems to be a game to you. You certainly do not seem to care about most people, and I do not know why I am different. But if you expect me to put aside what you did like it never happened, you are going to be disappointed."

He dove under the water, pulled hard for shore, and she didn't follow.

Cleaning the armor continued around the campfire that night, and it kept all of them up until the moon had risen high, the stars were out, and the cook-pot scoured clean. Finally, they wrapped the pieces of plate in oiled cloth again and packed them away to continue the journey in the morning. His wet clothes, washed in the lake, they hung over a low hanging branch.

No Wild Hunt came in the night; no wolves, Knights of Thorns, or daemons of the lake. Trist slept through the night, better than he'd slept since before Percy's wedding feast, and when he woke in the morning, he felt full of life and energy.

Acrasia was wrapped around him, and though he didn't really know how much a faerie without a body needed sleep, she seemed at least unaware of what was happening near her. Carefully, he extricated himself. How to stop her from crawling into his bedroll in the night was a problem for later, Trist decided, and walked down to the lake to splash water in his face. Then, he found a good, shady spot by the bridge, leaned out over the water, and put his hands in. By the time Henry had risen and stirred the embers of the campfire into life, Trist had tickled two trout out of hiding, caught them, and tossed them onto the grass. When he brought them over to clean by the fire, Yaél gave him a look like he'd just done magic.

"How did you do that? Without a line or a hook?" the boy asked, rubbing his hands by the fire. The morning was cool.

"Our lord grew up on the banks of the Rea," Henry explained, with a laugh. "He's been tickling fish out of water since he was knee-high, him and his brother. We all did."

"I would teach you," Trist said, putting neatly fileted slices of fish onto a woven lattice of sticks to hold them over the fire, "But we will not have time this morning."

"Indeed, my love, you're quite talented with your fingers," Acrasia giggled as she watched him work.

He ignored her. "We need to press on south and catch up with the army. We've spent enough time wandering around the Arden already."

And push hard they did.

Acrasia complained about the itch of the Etalan road, but the group stuck to it anyway, trusting in the old stones to guide them where they needed to go. Trist gave Yaél lessons every morning before they set out, and every evening while Henry got dinner going in the pot - the woodsman was far and away their best cook.

He taught his new squire how to stand, and how to step. They practiced set-asides, Yaél borrowing Henry's arming sword. Trist drilled the boy in the basic guards: Plow, Ox, Low, High, and how to cut from each. There would be time to get more complicated, later, but the earliest days needed to be simple. He often thought back to how John Granger had trained him, and he heard the old Master-of-Arms' words coming out of his mouth.

"In combat, we descend to the level of our training," Trist emphasized, over and over again. "Your body must cut a thousand times, a thousand thousand, before it truly knows how to move. Again!"

Sometimes, Trist rode, but most of the time, they simply walked. Yaél was the one who would tire first, which surprised none of them: the boy was small, unused to such exercise, and had probably never before eaten so well in his life as he did now on the road with them. When Trist judged it necessary, they put Yaél up in the saddle to ride Caz, which was its own lesson. Even Acrasia, perhaps chastened by his words to her at the lake, did not do anything to disturb the calm of the journey, though Trist went to sleep alone every night, and woke with her head on his chest every morning. He suspected that Clarisant would not be pleased, but he didn't know what to do about it.

Finally, a week after they'd set out from Camaret-à-Arden, they left the Ardenwood for blooming fields of lavender and saw the purple mountains of the Hauteurs Massif rising above them to the south, impossibly high. The old Etalan road gave way - or at least was covered by - something far more modern, and the small group walked toward the village of Falais, at the foot of the pass through the mountains, where the army of the Crown Prince was mustered to defend the Kingdom from the Caliphate.

Chapter Twenty-Two

CLARISANT

There is much speculation as to the incredible effectiveness of iron against all manner of faerie creatures. The native Narvonnians would have you believe that iron, produced as it is through a process of smelting and forging, is somehow unnatural, and thus a symbol of humanity's dominion over the natural world. Thus, faeries, presenting themselves as creatures of nature, in the forest and under the hill, cannot stand against it. And yet, copper or bronze have no such effect. Moreover, it is said that even sprinkling a circle of iron shavings or dust is sufficient protection to hedge out one of these creatures. There must be something unique to the metal itself, therefore, though we cannot as yet describe what.

-The Marian Codex

27th Day of the Planting Moon, 297 AC

It was the third morning since her new husband - her second husband, so strange to think - had departed, and Clarisant du Camaret-à-Arden, formerly of Rocher de la Garde, rose as soon as morning sunlight from the east window fell into her eyes. The monastery bells had a different tone than the cathedral she'd lived near for years at Rocher de la Garde, and she'd not yet become accustomed to the jarring sound. Once again, Claire found her arms wrapped around the second pillow when she woke, squeezing it to her chest.

She set the pillow aside, and rolled out of the bed she'd shared with Trist for a single night. His bed, really, and it still smelled of her new husband. It was most certainly still his room, as well, with an armor stand to one side of the bed and little in the way of decoration. Claire had been a little surprised to find a small bookshelf against the other wall, with a pile of worn fencing manuals the only occupants. La Fleur de Bataille, or the Flower of Battle, one of them was called, somewhat fancifully, and she'd leafed through it before going to sleep the night before. It was full of careful drawings of human figures in contorted positions, armed with swords, daggers, and all manner of other weapons. She could imagine a much younger Trist pouring over the manual in his free time, and the thought brought a smile to her face.

Claire pressed her right hand to her belly, underneath her linen shift. She wondered if she would feel anything, yet, if there was a child inside her. It had only been three days, so she doubted it, but her mother had always claimed she'd known right away whenever she'd gotten with child. Perhaps if Baroness Blasine had been there, she would have told her daughter what to look for.

A gentle knock came from the sitting room, and Clarisant said, "Come." Her maid from home, Anais, entered and shut the door behind her.

"Good morning, m'lady," the girl said, with a curtsy. Anais was only fourteen years old, ten years younger than her, and so tiny that she reminded Claire of a mouse, or perhaps a delicate bird, the kind that could easily be crushed in the hand.

"Good morning, Anais," she said, sitting down on the same chair they'd had brought into the room while Trist had been recovering from his wounds. Now, her maid stood behind the chair to brush out Claire's long, dark hair with a wooden comb.

"Did you sleep well, m'lady? I have an awful time myself," Anais admitted. "Can't quite get used to all these forest sounds. What I wouldn't do for the proper sound of the ocean to put me to sleep."

"Both of us need to get used to it," Clair pointed out. "This is our home now. If we go back to Rocher de la Garde, it will only be for a short visit."

"If it's our home," Anais asked, gently working out a knot, "How come this room don't feel like you at all? Not like your rooms back-"

"At my father's keep?" Claire considered. "I hardly know my husband at all. This room, the way he left it, I feel like it helps me to learn about him, some small amount." But her maid's words set her mind turning, all through the brushing of her hair, and the washing of her skin, and the smallest dabs of perfume from the sea-side market at Rocher de la Garde. She let Anais rub her face with cream, and do her cheeks with a bit of blush, while she made up her mind.

"An overskirt and my doublet, today," she told Anais, who paused for a moment.

"Going hunting, m'lady?" her maid asked.

"Something like that," Claire answered vaguely, and let Anais lay out her clothing. While the girl pulled piece after piece from her traveling trunks, then laid them out on the bed, Claire stood and pulled her own shift over her head, folding it in half and setting it aside over the back of the chair. She shivered in the cool spring morning, her skin pebbling with goosebumps, but her mind was already skipping forward while the girl dressed her. Linen smock, stays, a new kirtle in green to match the heraldry of her new family. Over those, a black overskirt and black lady's doublet, with matching sleeves laced on. A belt in green silk and silver, with her sheathed dagger at her hip. A silver circlet about her forehead, then a white veil pinned in place over it. Black was not appropriate for a new bride. Fur lined riding boots of brown leather, turned down just under her knee.

"Thank you, Anais," Clarisant said, now that she was put together. "I will be riding out after breakfast. Could you see that Tystie is saddled and ready for me?"

"Of course, m'lady," Anais agreed, giving one last curtsy as Claire left the room and headed downstairs to the hall. Her father in law was already seated at the head of the long table, speaking with the man who had stood for Trist during their wedding three days past. The Master at Arms, if she remembered correctly from her past visits. When Claire entered the hall, both men rose and bowed.

"Join us, Lady Clarisant," Rience du Camaret-à-Arden greeted her. "I hope that your night was restful."

"It was," she assured him, and the two men sat when she took her own chair, one of the footmen pushing it in for her as she sat. He poured her a goblet of watered wine, then began to serve her a plate. There was fresh bread, cheese, and cold cuts of last night's roast boar. "That will be more than enough, thank you," she stopped him when it was only half full. She could already hear her mother's haranguing that there was too much.

"M'lady appears dressed for riding," the Master at Arms observed, sitting back down. Claire noticed both men were drinking beer, rather than wine.

"That is so," she said, taking a sip to wash down her first slice of boar. It was well seasoned with cider, sage and juniper berries. "Master at Arms," she asked. "Do you know where the ruined chapel in the Ardenwood is located?"

"Aye," the man said. "I suppose that I do."

"I would like you to take me there," Claire said, after trying the cheese. "Tomorrow, perhaps, or the day after. I will know after I speak with the blacksmith."

Sir Rience and his man exchanged glances.

"May I ask m'lady's intentions?" the Master at Arms inquired. Claire decided that she would have to learn his name.

"I intend to be absolutely certain that nothing can ever come from that place to hurt my family," Claire told the two men. "Ever again."

The smith's name, it turned out, was Hywel.

"You know your husband asked me for something like this," the broad shouldered man told her, "Before he went there, too. Only in Sir Trist's case, it was a single dagger. What you want, m'lady, will take me longer."

"I understand that." Claire sat her palfrey sidesaddle, as a lady should. The Master at Arms, whose name she had learned was John Granger, had sent two armed men to protect her on her day's outing. "How long will it take you?"

"Two dozen of em?" He scratched his jaw as he thought about it. "Say the rest of the day today and tomorrow as well. Come by the morning after that, at terce, and they'll be ready for you, m'lady."

"Excellent." Claire smiled, and passed a handful of silver coins to Hywel. "That should be enough to get you started. Send your final price up to the manor and I will see the difference paid." The smith bowed - not a proper court bow, but the kind a peasant gave who'd never been taught any better. She simply inclined her head and turned Tystie's head up the road to the Monastery of Saint Kadosh.

She'd been there to bury her first husband, and then for her second wedding, and today Claire needed to speak to the monks. Her guards followed along on foot, and she didn't let the palfrey go faster than a walk, so that they wouldn't be left behind. When she arrived, there were several monks working in their garden, and quickly enough she found herself inside, sipping a goblet of wine, opposite the head of the monastery, and one of his brothers.

"We have not done anything like what you ask in a very long time," the Abbot, Brother Hugh, said slowly, glancing over to the other man. Brother Alberic, he had introduced himself as.

"I did have the relevant manuscripts out just the other day for your husband," Alberic said, after a moment's thought. "It would not be too much trouble to pull them out again, now that I know where they are stored in the library, and which tomes we would need."

"The accounts of Brother Accolon and Sir Baylin?" The Abbot ventured.

"Yes," Brother Alberic confirmed. "Those accounts should contain records of the original prayers."

"Excellent." Claire set her goblet down and rose, ending the conversation and forcing the two monks to rise with her. "The morning after tomorrow, then. I will meet you at the blacksmith's shop at terce, with the Master at Arms."

Both men frowned, but she had not really left them any room to refuse.

When Clarisant arrived to pick up her order from Hywel the smith two mornings later, just as the monastery bells finished ringing the hour, she wore red, as close to the shade of blood as she owned. She didn't know whether anyone who saw her would understand; she did it for herself. Perhaps if she dressed bravely, she would feel brave.

"Two dozen," Hywel said, as the men John Granger had brought with them loaded the long, wrapped bundles onto a small wagon. "Just as you ordered, m'lady."

"Thank you, master smith," Claire said from atop Tystie, with a nod. "You do good work, and quick. I shall have no hesitation to place further orders with you. I believe you have my husband's measurements, yes?"

"I do," he agreed.

"Then we will speak further, I think, another day. Ah, here come the brothers." Abbot Hugh and Brother Alberic were in sight, walking toward them.

"My Lady," the Abbot said, slightly out of breath, once he'd gotten close enough for a conversation. "Are you certain about this?"

"You have brought all the necessities?" She responded with a question of her own. Never allow your lessers to question you, her father had taught her.

"We have."

"Good. Perhaps you would prefer to ride in the wagon," she offered, and the old man took her up on it, at least as far as they could proceed along the woodsman's path.

"We go on foot from here," Granger said, and his men unloaded the wagon quickly, then followed him into the Ardenwood. A flick of Claire's reins sent her palfrey after them, and it was not so long before the small party arrived at the ruins of the Chapelle de Camiel. She tried to picture Trist climbing the steps with his sword out, all in armor. The idea seemed more dream than reality, but he had done it. He was brave, after all, and he had been kind and gentle with her.

"I had imagined it," Lady Clarisant remarked, "As something from a nightmare. Dark and twisted, or stained with blood. But it is only an old pile of stones."

"Aye," the Master at Arms said. "Your command, m'lady?" The two monks had already begun their prayers, waving smoking thuribles from long chains, trailing streams of sweet-smelling incense.

"Begin." At Clarisant's word, the men drove spikes of cold iron, two dozen of them, into the soil in a circle around the hilltop, enclosing the ruins and the old tree within. Let the faeries try to pass that, she told herself, with satisfaction.

Chapter Twenty-Three

The Muster

Without the bureaucracy of the Etalan Empire to support his new holdings, and with the destruction of the provincial capital at Vellatesia taking with it nearly the entirety of the province's trained civil servants, General Aurelius needed a new solution. From his core of knights, he chose four of his most loyal and named them barons, setting one over the southeastern coast, one to hold the southern mountain passes, one the western coast, and one to control the extensive breadbasket north of the Arden. Each Baron was given the right to divy up their lands among their own knights, so long as they remained loyal to Aurelius and came when he called them to war. There was a brief attempt, a century later, to install a fifth baron to control the Ardenwood, which failed utterly, but the other four baronies dating from the founding still exist today.
-François du Lutetia, A History of Narvonne

3rd Day of the Flower Moon, 297 AC

What grass might once have grown outside the village of Falais must have died within a day of the army making camp. Cazador's hooves sent up puffs of dust with every step the destrier took down the dirt paths that wound between rows of tents, and Yaél went into fits of coughing until Trist decided it would be easier to simply let the young squire ride. It was afternoon, but until he heard the bells, Trist wouldn't know the precise hour.

"Keep your eye out for a black tree on green," Trist commanded his three companions. "With white flowers, like on my armor. That will be my cousin, Lucan. Failing that, look for a white sea shell on blue."

"Baron Urien," Yaél blurted, and Trist turned to look up at the mounted squire. "I've seen it when his men came through to speak to Sir Auron."

"Just so," Trist confirmed. "My new father-in-law should be expecting us, though I cannot say how well received we will be," he admitted.

"Father in law?" Yaél muttered.

"M'lord married the baron's youngest daughter just over a week ago," Luc explained to the boy, but Trist found himself distracted by Acrasia, who appeared at his side and caught his arm in hers.

"Be careful, my love," she hissed, though he had no idea who in the camp could possibly overhear her besides him. "I can sense the presence of the Angelus. And if one of them is here with their Exarch, they will be able to sense me, as well."

"There, Sir Trist," Henry broke in, pointing over the rows of pavilions and clusters of smaller tents to where a banner hung dead in the heat: as Trist had described a moment before, a white shell on blue. The small party turned toward the camp of the Baron of Rocher de la Garde, but the twisting paths of the encampment made it difficult to judge where they were going. Rounding a stand of tents, Trist found himself face to face with a line of tied warhorses, where men were shoveling manure onto a cart, and he and his companions were forced to double back and search for another way.

Finally, the small party was able to get themselves onto a broader track of packed dirt and dead grass, where the dust was not so thick or cloying. Trist could actually see two men at arms standing guard outside the entrance to the baron's pavilion, now, and he picked up his steps. It had been a long journey.

"Trist," Acrasia squeaked, clinging to him, "He's here!" The faerie shot a fearful glance back over her shoulder, and Trist followed her eyes to a group of soldiers, armed and armored, clustered around a rider atop a white destrier. The pursuing group surged forward, towards them, pushing people out of their path as they came.

"Clear the way!" one of the men at arms shouted, and people began scrambling to the sides to make an open space.

"Damn it," Trist swore. They were almost to the baron's tent, but he didn't think they would make it before their pursuers caught up with them. "Take the boy and get to the baron's men," he ordered Henry, passing Caz' reins to the hunter. "Tell them who we are. Make sure they know that we are Baron Urien's liegemen."

Henry nodded, and Trist turned to face the group of armed men, stepping to the center of the beaten track, where he rested his left hand on the pommel of his longsword. Acrasia was practically hiding behind him, now.

"Stop those men," a strong voice rang out from the center of the knot of soldiers. Now that they had caught up, Trist was able to get a good look at the man on the white destrier, whom he took to be the leader.

The knight was older than Trist, though that was no surprise. The rider wore no helm, and his head was shaved clean, save that he wore a bushy, wiry red beard streaked with gray and white. His armor was full plate, a matched set, and polished to a shine. From his lance hung streamers of white and gold, and matching gold filigree glinted on his armor, picked out by the sunlight. The kite shield on his left side was emblazoned with golden wings on a white field, and below it a sword crossed with what looked like a lash. When their eyes met, Trist caught a glimpse of something much like Acrasia: a pulsing cloud of burning lines and whirls, attached to the man. The Exarch, Trist realized. This would be the first time he met someone else bound by the Accords.

"Well met, Sir Knight," Trist called across the dusty path. Everyone but he and the armed men had pulled back, now, forming a kind of ring to observe what might happen next. "I am Sir Trist du Camaret-à-Arden," he introduced himself, "sworn man to Baron Urien du Rocher de la Garde. I regret we have not yet been introduced. Might I have the honor of your name?" Despite his courteous words, Trist made certain his stance was balanced, ready to draw steel at a moment's notice.

"I am Sir Bors du Chêne Fendu, Exarch of Masheth, Champion of the Crown Prince Lionel Aurelianus," the older man proclaimed, voice booming to fill the area. "And whoever you may be, boy, you will surrender yourself to me now, as you fear the Angelus, or I will crush you under my boot heel like an adder."

"I do not believe my family has any quarrel with you, Sir Bors," Trist replied with an even eye and as steady a voice as he could manage. Whispers were spreading like fire after a summer drought all through the crowd. "And so I can think of no cause for you to make such a request. In any event, having just arrived, my first obligation is to present myself to my liege lord. I beg of you to postpone this matter, whatever it may be, until that duty has been fulfilled."

"Do not speak to me of duty," the exarch roared, face flushing red with wroth, "When you have so clearly abandoned your duty to the Angelus. Do you think I cannot see that monster hiding behind you? Have you no shame, to stand here and boldly claim we have no cause for quarrel, when you have sold your soul so cheaply? Your sins demand punishment, boy, and I am the lash come to reckon them at last."

At Bors' words, light exploded from him. Trist recognized the fiery whips and tendrils, nearly identical to how Acrasia had fought the daemon at the lake. The people around them cried out and scrambled back; some, he could hear praying for the forgiveness of the Angelus.

What Trist could see, that he suspected they all could not, was the source of the burning lines and whirls: a shining man all in white, eyes burning, wings spread.

"Turn the sword over, mortal," the Angelus commanded. "And you may yet find me merciful."

"He's mine, you stilted ass," Acrasia cried, stepping out from behind Trist. "You can't have him!" Whips of fire and shining loops of light whirled out from her, now, coiled like serpents about to strike the older knight. The crowd around them verged on full blown panic, and Trist realized they could see enough to understand both immortal beings were prepared to battle it out, right here and right now.

This was the second time that the faerie maiden had put herself in danger to protect him since being bound to his sword, and Trist wasn't certain how to feel about it. He decided there would be time to sort it out in his mind if they both survived this.

"We need not draw steel on each other this day," Trist called to Bors over the cries of the crowd. The other knight scowled, and Trist knew the next words out of the man's mouth would touch off a battle between them. His fingers twitched, and he prepared to unsheathe his blade.

"What is the meaning of this? Knights, stay your hands!" A middle aged man in rich clothes of blue and white, worked with sea shell buttons, shoved his way through the crowd and stormed out into the empty space between the two swordsmen. Ranging after him came two hunting hounds, unleashed but with leather collars.

"Baron Urien," Bors said evenly, and Trist felt a surge of hope. This confrontation would not end in bloodshed, after all - surely the Exarch would not dare defy a baron as powerful as the ruler of Rocher de la Garde.

Yaél dogged Baron Urien's heels, and Trist's cousin Lucan was with them, a step back; Henry's bow was strung, Trist saw, and Luc looked ready to fight, as well. The boy had done well. The entire scene seemed to hold a breath in a long drawn moment of silence, as everyone waited for Sir Bors to withdraw.

"You are a man worthy of respect," Bors said, finally. "But we are not in your city, Baron Urien, and the laws of the Angelus are higher than the laws of men. Stand aside, and let me do their work on this earth."

"You will stand down, Sir Bors!" Urien shouted angrily. Trist could hardly believe the other knight's behavior.

"Move aside," Bors repeated, "Or may what follows be on your head." The exarch drew his sword from its sheath with a rasp, and his men followed his actions, readying their own weapons. At the movement, Urien's hounds stepped forward and began to growl. With a grimace, Trist drew his blade, and settled into the Plow Guard, the hilt held to his left, even with his waist, and the point in line with Bors' body. He caught a glimpse of Henry nocking an arrow to the string of his Iebara-wood bow. Trist wondered whether he would leave a child behind, like his father had wanted, or whether their line would end with him, in this place, on this day.

"What madness is this!" A new voice broke upon the scene with an unmistakable air of command, and to Trist's surprise, the people who had crowded around to watch fell to their knees as one.

"Put up your blades," Baron Urien commanded, "And kneel before your Prince!"

Chapter Twenty-Four

Lionel Aurelianus

The Exarchs of Narvonne are little more than puppets, their strings tied to the idolatrous throne of their so-called king, and loath the monarchs of that land have been to let their toys venture far from court. What use are heroes at the gluttonous feast, or lost in lust at their balls, when they should be hunting the daemons that escaped the Cataclysm? The Narvonnians claim it is all to protect their earthly monarch, but I think it is just as much this: an Exarch in the service of their Angelus naturally becomes a leader of men - and that is a political threat.

-The Commentaries of Aram ibn Bashear

3rd Day of the Flower Moon, 297 AC

At his father-in-law's words, Trist immediately shifted his grip and turned his long sword point down, grounding the tip in the dry earth, then dropped to one knee, and bowed his head. The Crown Prince! While the lonely village of Camaret-à-Arden had long sent Iebara wood to the capital city of Lutetia, and to the king's castle of Cheverny, he had never made the journey with the wagon loads of lumber. And while the fine wood they sent was, he knew, well regarded and prized throughout the entire Kingdom of Narvonne, never in Trist's life had the King - or any of the royal family - deigned to visit the manor of the humble knight who protected the edge of the Ardenwood from which the lumber came.

Trist couldn't see what Sir Bors was doing, with his own eyes on the parched ground, but the utter silence of the crowded camp, save for the occasional snort of a horse, and the lack of a blade cutting his head from his shoulders, led him to the optimistic conclusion that a duel had been averted for the moment.

"Sir Bors I recognize," a voice stirred the silence. It was the gentle, melodious voice of a man who expected to be obeyed, Trist thought, filled with the quiet confidence of a lifetime of authority. Footsteps sent puffs of dirt into the air, and the dusty leather toes of a pair of boots entered Trist's vision. "Is that an Iebara tree worked into your arms, Sir?"

Trist found his throat suddenly parched, and swallowed once before he could find a tongue to speak with. "It is, your Royal Highness," he answered.

"The arms of Sir Rience du Camaret-à-Arden, I believe," the Crown Prince observed.

"Indeed, your Royal Highness. Sir Rience is my father," Trist explained. "I am Trist du Camaret-à-Arden, at your service."

"Rise, sir, so that I may look upon your face," the Prince said, and so Trist rose, though he kept the tip of his longsword planted in the beaten dirt of the camp road. He found the Crown Prince dark of eye, a broad man who seemed exceptionally solid, with the tan coloring of Etalan descent, and sun-worn skin that spoke of a lifetime in the field. Trist guessed the Crown Prince to be about a decade older than him, with short cropped dark hair, a few day's growth of stubble, and field clothing that was well made, but plain. This man needed no badge of office or heraldry to be recognized, nor to command respect. Trist was shocked when the prince offered his hand.

"Lionel Aurelianus," he said, and when after a moment Trist reached out to take the offered hand in his own, he found the grip firm, even when matched with the strength Trist had gained from his Boons. "I expect you already knew that, Sir Trist. My father speaks well of yours. I recall hearing the tale, when I was a child, of how Sir Rience and his boon-companion Sir Tor were ordered to hold the line with the rear guard, against the

Caliphate van, and how they fought for an entire day through the storm and the mud, until the southerners had bled out all their will to fight upon the field."

"Thank you, your Royal Highness," Trist said, for he had heard portions of the same story. He put his right hand back to rest on the pommel of his longsword when Prince Aurelianus released him.

"I am glad to have his son come to fight for me," the Crown Prince said, and turned to Sir Bors. "Exarch," he raised his voice. "How did there come to be strife between two such honorable knights in my service?"

"That is no true knight," Sir Bors fumed, "But a power-hungry boy who sold his soul to the faeries."

Prince Aurelianus turned back to Trist, eyes suddenly sharp and probing. "Is it true, Sir Trist? Are you an Exarch?"

"I do not know if I have any right to the title," Trist admitted, truthfully, aware of every eye in the crowd upon him. "But yes, your Royal Highness, I have an Accord with the faerie Lady Acrasia, who is sister to the Horned Hunter, and in the service of the King of Shadows." With those words, he placed his fate entirely in the Crown Prince's hands: if Trist had doomed himself with this admission, there was no one higher in this army he could appeal to. For a long moment, the Prince's face was unreadable, and then he broke into a broad, kind smile.

"What excellent news!" Prince Aurelianus raised his voice again, so that the entire crowd might hear his words clearly. "The Angelus favor our cause! They have sent a second Exarch to stand with us against the Caliphate! Three cheers for Sir Trist, Exarch of the Lady Acrasia!"

The first cheer was somewhat ragged, but Baron Urien's voice rang out a clear 'huzzah,' and Yaél with him, and Henry and Luc, and then the second cheer, to Acrasia's clear delight, was strong. The faerie-maid beamed at the crowd, though they could not see her, puffed up in the moment like a rooster in the barnyard, and she soaked in the third cheer as her personal due.

"Back to your business," Baron Urien called out gruffly. "And take heart! We have two champions!"

"Sir Trist," the Crown Prince said, lowering his voice and stepping close so that Trist could hear. "Speak with me a moment." He turned to the Baron du Rocher de la Garde. "May we step into your tent, Baron Urien?"

"Of course, your Royal Highness," Trist's father-in-law said, lowering his gaze and extending his arm toward the pavilion.

"Sir Lucan! Show Sir Trist's companions where they may make camp," Prince Lionel said. Only then did Trist recall his cousin, who caught his eyes for a moment, then led Yaél, Henry and Luc away. A well-dressed young woman emerged from the crowd and slipped her arm around the Prince's, and the entire group proceeded into the pavilion, where Baron Urien's men at arms closed the canvas over the entrance after the last of the party had passed through.

The pavilion was larger than any of the other tents around it, though once he'd stepped inside Trist could see that portions of it were closed off into separate rooms by hanging flaps of canvas. The entire thing must have been at least thirty feet long, and nearly as wide, and the middle portion had been turned into a sitting area, with straw on the ground, folding camp chairs, low iron braziers, and even a table. Prince Lionel led the woman on his arm to a chair first, and only once she had taken a seat did he follow suit, and then Baron Urien next to them, on the other side of the prince. The two hounds paced protectively, then laid down at Urien's feet when he snapped his fingers.

"You will not, I imagine, have had a chance to meet Lady Valeria yet," the Crown Prince began. "Lady Valeria, Sir Trist is the sworn man of Baron Urien, and his father did good service to mine during the last war against the Caliphate. Sir Trist, please allow me to introduce the Lady Valeria du Champs d'Or, daughter and heir to Baron Maël du Champs d'Or."

The lady in question was roughly Trist's age, he guessed, with striking auburn hair that tumbled about her shoulders unbound, like a war-horse's wind-tossed mane. Her skin was pale as cream, with a blush in her cheeks, and lively hazel eyes, and she was dressed in the yellow and green of her father's heraldry. She raised her hand, offering it to him, and Trist accepted, bowing over it.

"It is a great honor to make your acquaintance, Lady Valeria," Trist said, before releasing her hand and rising back to his full height. "I am told an armed camp such as this can be a rough place for a lady such as yourself. If there is ever anything that I can do to secure your comfort or safety, you have only to send for me, and so long as my liege has no need of my service, I will be yours to command."

Valeria raised her elegant brows and smirked. "I may well call upon you, Sir Trist, if I find myself in need of an Exarch. I already find you more courteous, as a true knight should be, than our own Sir Bors."

Urien coughed. "Now that we've made introductions," he began, "I find myself with no few questions. Sir Trist, I sent my daughter Claire to wed your older brother not a turning of the moon past, and just days ago I had word by pigeon that not only was Percival du Camaret-à-Arden dead, but that you would be fulfilling the marriage contract in his stead, before coming to muster with us here at Falais. And now you arrive an Exarch to a faerie, and immediately have a grudge against Sir Bors, the lynchpin of our forces. Tell us what has passed, and do not leave us wanting for detail."

Trist nodded, swallowing the dust of the journey. "It will be a long story, and thirsty work, my lord," he ventured to Urien. "Perhaps I could sit while I tell it, and have a cup of wine to wet my throat?"

"Of course," the Crown Prince said, and made a motion to one of Urien's servants. A camp chair quickly appeared for Trist, and a goblet of watered wine. Trist couldn't help a sigh when he settled into the chair, at finally getting the weight off his back, and swirled a deep gulp of red wine around his mouth before swallowing it.

"The night of the wedding," he began, "I escorted the newlywed couple to their rooms, and then descended to the hall to speak with my father. Suddenly, we heard a woman scream..."

By the time Trist had finished his tale, the sun had set, and the only light in the tent was cast by the two braziers. Distant bells from Falais had rung out twice, for both nones and for vespers. Outside, somewhere in the night, an owl hooted. The Baron's servants had long since come and gone, bringing out a small meal of goat meat stewed in red wine gravy, served over roasted onions and potatoes, topped with a scattering of parsley, thyme, rosemary and marjoram. There was nothing left in the bowls but a few smears of gravy, and even those vanished once Baron Urien placed them on the floor to be licked clean by the two hounds, who set to with great eagerness.

"...and from the lake, it was only a few days to the camp here," Trist came to the end. "We set about to look for my lord the Baron's tent, and were accosted by Sir Bors, for our part in which, your Royal Highness, my lord, my lady, you all have my deepest apologies."

The story ended, Trist found himself still the focus of attention in the tent, but now with no clear idea what he should be doing or saying. He reached for his goblet, took another sip of watered wine, and realized he was down to the dregs.

"By the Angelus, I don't even know where to begin," Urien admitted, with a scowl. "You were deceived by this faerie murderess for years! Years, she played you for a fool, and now you still aren't rid of her! There is no justice. Your family has been entrusted with a key strategic resource for the entire Kingdom of Narvonne, and now, on the brink of war, all of the plans your father and I made to ensure stability have been thrown into chaos!" As the Baron continued, his face grew red, though Trist could not tell whether it was from the wine, or from anger. Perhaps both. "You are not the husband I chose for my daughter," the older man's voice began to rise in volume.

"I do not believe that Sir Trist bears fault for what happened," the Crown Prince interrupted, and the Baron of Rocher de la Garde settled, clearly unwilling to countermand his future king. "This is clearly a shock, especially to you, Urien, my friend. You spent years securing your beloved daughter's future, and shepherding the affairs of your barony, as befits a good lord." He raised his voice, looking around the tent to meet everyone's eyes one at a time. "I lay no blame at Baron Urien's feet, whatsoever, for these tragedies that have occurred. Let that be clear. And I know my father will agree."

"Now," Lionel continued, turning to pin Trist with his gaze. "I would like to speak with your faerie lady."

Chapter Twenty-Five

A Grudging Oath

Of faerie Exarchs, in the history of Narvonne, we have only a single known example: Sir Maddoc of the Wood, who made an Accord with the King of Shadows when King Luther the Unready attempted to install a Baron in the Ardenwood. It is said that Sir Maddoc wielded a blade of glass, sharp enough that when he cut an apple, he could put it back together after, as if it had never been cut at all. It also, coincidentally, cut the neck of the only ever Baron of the Ardenwood.
-François du Lutetia, A History of Narvonne

3rd Day of the Flower Moon, 297 AC

Trist blinked, and suddenly Acrasia was sitting in his lap, her skirts falling about his legs, her head leaned back so that she could nestle into him. Only the knowledge that his liege lord and future king couldn't see her prevented him from shoving her away in a blind panic.

"Can you speak to them?" he asked the faerie.

"It would be a lot easier if you hadn't shoved an iron dagger into my chest," she groused, in much the same tone as his father had taken with him as a boy when he'd done something naughty. "But I should be able to speak to anyone who touches the sword. I would suggest placing it on the table."

Trist looked back to Prince Lionel and Baron Urien, who had been watching him closely this entire time. "She says that she can speak to anyone touching my sword," he explained. "May I set it on the table?"

"Please do." The Crown Prince motioned with one hand, and servants scurried to clear dirty dishes away and make room. Trist stood, Acrasia alighting on the edge of the table, instead of his lap. He drew his longsword, and set it down lengthwise on the wooden camp table, hilt toward the Baron and the Prince, tip toward himself. Once he'd sat back down, he placed a hand on the tip of the blade. In the back of his mind, Trist noted that he would need to oil the blade well before going to sleep tonight.

Urien stared at the sword, hand half upraised in hesitation, but Lionel Aurelianus simply reached out and took the leather wrapped hilt in his fingers. The Baron frowned, but found a place on the pommel to set his hand. The moment each man touched the sword, they blinked as if waking from a dream, and focused their eyes on where the faerie woman sat.

Acrasia's hair hung loose about her shoulders, long and pale, with streaks of soft pink the shade of those woodland flowers she'd enjoyed. On top of the white shift she often seemed so fond of wearing by itself, she had conjured the appearance of a sleeveless overdress in pale blue silk. It brought out her eyes, a distant part of him observed.

"Lady Acrasia, I presume?" Lionel asked, voice calm and steady as if he met immortal faerie creatures every day for breakfast.

"I am," his former lover declared, imperiously, looking down at the Crown Prince and Baron from where she perched on the side of the table. "As my love has said, I am sister to Cern, the Horned Hunter, whom mortals sometimes name Hellequin; and my liege is Auberon, the King of Shadows."

"I am Lionel Aurelianus, Crown Prince of Narvonne, and this is Baron Urien du Rocher de la Garde, liege lord of Sir Trist. With us is the Lady Valeria du Champs d'Or." Lionel's eyes measured and weighed her with the same look he'd given Trist himself. "You have empowered Sir Trist as your Exarch in keeping with the Accord?"

"I have," Acrasia said, meeting the man's gaze without fear. "He is mine."

"Sir Trist has many obligations," Lionel continued. "He owes familial duty to his father, and in time will take up his father's place. Therefore, he owes service to his liege lord, and protection to the people who live within his Knight's Fee. He owes the duties of a husband to Lady Clarisant, and the duties of a Knight of this Kingdom to me - such as mustering when called, in time of war. Will you support him in these duties and obligations?"

"He owes Tithes to the King of Shadows." Acrasia's eyes sparked like winter sun on ice.

"So he does," Lionel agreed, "And he will have ample opportunity to collect those Tithes in battle. But by the Accords, what he owes the King of Shadows comes only after his other commitments. I ask you again, Lady Acrasia, will you support Sir Trist in his duties and obligations?"

"I have already fought beside him against the daemon of the lake," Acrasia replied. "And other foes besides. You need have no concern I will abandon him during this war of yours."

"And what of his lady wife?" Lionel leaned back in his camp chair, and Trist watched the Baron's face harden. Lady Valeria, whose hands remained folded in her lap, also looked interested, though he remembered that she would only be able to hear half the conversation.

"What of her?" Acrasia shot back haughtily. "She is of no more concern to me than those hounds that cleaned the plates."

"Watch your tongue, faerie," Clarisant's father growled. "That is my daughter you speak of."

"Your daughter should keep herself out of my knight's bed," Acrasia taunted the older man.

"Acrasia," Trist broke in. "You cannot speak of my wife that way. I have a duty to defend her honor, and Clarisant is a good woman besides. I would be neglecting my duty as her husband to not give her children. She did not ask for what happened, she carries no fault or blame. I will not see her suffer any more for the choices you made."

Acrasia turned back to him, eyes wide, sputtering.

"I do not like it," Baron Urien said, with a note of finality. "How can I know my daughter will be safe? This faerie has already murdered one good man. What is to stop her from killing my innocent daughter in a fit of jealousy?"

"She has no physical form," Trist pointed out.

"Not now," the Crown Prince said. "And not for some while. The Lady Acrasia has been sorely wounded, but it is a wound that can be healed, in time. That is correct, yes, Lady Acrasia?"

The faerie frowned. "It is true," she admitted, and turned to Trist. "But not quickly, and not easily. I would have told you, when it came time."

"You would have told him just in time for my daughter to die of an accident, and for you to fall into his grieving arms," Urien grumbled.

"I must have an Oath from you, Lady Acrasia," Lionel said. "An Oath that you will not allow the Lady Clarisant, or her children, to come to harm, whether through your own action, or through your inaction when given the opportunity to protect her from others."

"Finely worded. You have been well schooled in the Accords, mortal prince," Acrasia hissed.

"My father has kept at least four Exarchs at Court for as long as I can remember," the Crown Prince admitted. "And I have been tutored in the Court customs of King of Shadows, including Oathcraft. You have something to gain from such a burden."

"Oh, yes, power to be used in protection of my rival!" Acrasia shook her head. "Not enough. Not fit compensation. I will not endure the cruelty of being enslaved to the woman who steals my bed! To serving her brats when Trist could give me children of my own!"

"I was not finished," Prince Lionel said, calmly, his voice somehow cutting through the faerie's complaints without being raised in the slightest. "In exchange for this Oath, I will not only affirm Sir Trist's right to inherit his father's lands, and Lady Clarisant's rights as his widow, in the event he falls in battle. I will confirm his position as Exarch, recognize it by royal decree, so that no man - not even Sir Bors - may question it. You must know, Lady Acrasia, that never before has an Exarch bound by Accord to the Court of Shadows been endorsed by the Kingdom of Narvonne. Protection and immunity from the Church of the Angelus. They will not like it, for the divide between Angelus and faerie is old and bitter, but in this Kingdom they will not go against my word."

"All of that helps Trist," Acrasia fought back. "But what of me?"

"If you truly love Sir Trist - and I say truly, not simply playing a faerie game - protecting him will be enough," Lionel said simply. "If it is not, that tells me all that I need to comprehend your heart, Acrasia of the Court of Shadows. You are now reaping the seeds you have sown with your own hand, and that it is a bitter harvest is the fault of no one but yourself. What say you? An Oath, in exchange for Royal protection of the knight you love?"

"I have no choice, do I?" Acrasia said, after a long moment, her voice so quiet that Trist could barely hear it at all. She swallowed, despite her lack of a physical body, and he allowed himself to wonder for a moment if it was entirely artifice, meant to evoke sympathy, or if she had formed the habit over years with a physical form.

"I swear that I will not knowingly allow harm to befall the Lady Clarisant, nor her children," the faerie said, her voice gaining strength as she went. "Nor will I knowingly allow harm to befall them through my own inaction. I make this Oath willingly, and may the King of Shadows strike me down if I betray it. There," she snarled at the Crown Prince. "Does it please you?"

As Trist watched, he caught a glimpse of the lines of fire extending back from the sword, from the image of Acrasia, and perceived a new knot being tied in the strands that were the faerie's true form. It shone brightly for a moment, and when he blinked, the sight was gone. Had she shown it to him deliberately? Or was he getting better at perceiving things of the faerie world?

"Yes, it pleases me," Prince Lionel said. He glanced to Baron Urien. "And you, my lord? Are you satisfied with your new son-in-law?"

"We shall see," Urien said, after considering a moment. "I am not best pleased with this beginning. But my daughter, in her letter, has begged me to accept him. Which reminds me." He reached into the leather pouch that hung at his waist, and removed a small roll of parchment. "Two pigeons, she sent to us here at Falais. One for me, and one for her new husband." The Baron extended his hand toward Trist, and he accepted the rolled scroll. It was hardly the size of his middle finger, and tied tightly with ribbon.

"Read it later," Lionel Aurelianus said, and though the tone was gentle, it was clearly a command. "You are new to your role as Exarch. Tomorrow we will test your capabilities, but for now, let me explain your place in this host. You have not been to war, Sir Trist."

"No, your Royal Highness," Trist confirmed.

"I know it," Lionel said with a smile, "For the Kingdom of Narvonne has not been at war in your lifetime. A few skirmishes against gangs of brigands, but otherwise, peace for twenty-four years."

"The Vultures had near two thousand men before you crushed them," Lady Valeria spoke, breaking her silence for the first time in quite a while. "I suspect my father might take issue with your characterization of that as 'peace.'" She placed her fingers lightly on

Lionel's arm, and her smile seemed very familiar to Trist, but it was no business of his what was between them.

"As you say, my lady," Lionel conceded the point gracefully. "What I am saying, Sir Trist, is this: as an Exarch, your place in this army is special. You are no mere soldier, nor even like other knights in the retinue of your liege. You are a weapon of last resort, to take the field at my explicit order, and mine alone. The only counter for an Exarch is another Exarch, and our enemies in the Caliphate of Maʿīn will not come to this war without their own champions."

Trist frowned. "Forgive me, your Royal Highness," he said, trying to wrap his head around this. "But are you saying I am not permitted to fight? How can I pay the Tithe if I cannot fight? Why am I even here?"

Chapter Twenty-Six

An Exarch at War

...and to Saint Masheth the Destroyer, we offer our prayers for holy vengeance: that the Angelus reach down their smiting hand to punish those who have committed the most abominable sins. His are the murderers, the men who beat their wives and children, fallen knights who ravage innocent women, and all who fall victim to the sin of wrath.
-Father Kramer's Sermon on the Feast of Saint Masheth, 291 AC

3rd Day of the Flower Moon, 297 AC

"You aren't going to need to worry about paying your Tithe," Crown Prince Lionel Aurelianus assured Trist, from his seat at the end of the camp table. The heir to the throne of the Kingdom of Narvonne kept his hand on the hilt of Trist's longsword, where it lay on the table, which meant that he could still perceive Acrasia, who was regarding the prince with skepticism and more than a hint of resentment. Trist knew her well enough to be certain that she had not appreciated being forced to swear an Oath, and that she wasn't going to forgive his Royal Highness easily.

"I trust your word, your Royal Highness," Trist said carefully, "But I admit that I am having a hard time understanding how all of this is going to work."

"I imagine," Lionel began, wetting his throat with a sip of wine, "That your father told you as many stories of the last war against the Caliphate as my father told me. I am afraid you are going to have to forget most of what Sir Rience told you. He was in a fundamentally different position, when he fought for us, than you are now, and as a result, I will use you entirely differently than my father used yours."

"Because I am an Exarch," Trist confirmed.

"Yes. Have you fought anyone yet? Since Lady Acrasia came to an Accord with you? Wait," the Prince said before Trist could speak up. "Those men in Havre de Paix. The ones keeping all those street children. You mentioned you fought them, yes?"

"I did," Trist confirmed. They had been the first men he'd ever killed. Terrel, with the hoarse voice, reeking of alcohol, who'd stumbled out into the yard. The two after him, with crossbow and blade, whose names Trist had never even learned, before killing them or since. The giant with the club, Bron. Monipodio, the kidsman who lied with every word that he spoke.

Lionel nodded. "How many were there? How were they armed?"

"Four fighters," Trist elaborated. "But no true knights, nor even well trained soldiers, among them. The first had a knife, then one with a crossbow, one with an arming sword, and the last with a club. They had all been drinking."

"Four armed men." The Prince laughed. "Did your master-at-arms not teach you to run from four men?"

Trist shrugged awkwardly. "Well, it was not four at once. And I did not know there were four," he made excuses. "They only came out a few at a time."

"Most men in your shoes would have been dead, boy," Baron Urien pointed out.

"Especially from that crossbow," Lady Valeria added. "I saw plenty of good men die with a crossbow bolt in their guts when the Vultures were put down. It punches through armor like a needle through wool."

"And that was before he'd even harvested any Tithes," Acrasia bragged shamelessly. "You should have seen him when he fought the daemon of the lake."

"The point is," Lionel said, "You were already a talented swordsman. Your father wrote of that when he sent word to Baron Urien. Becoming an Exarch will quickly make you a warrior beyond the ability of any mortal man to match. We will take your full measure tomorrow, but I have no doubt that you will be able to scythe through men on the battlefield as if they were wheat. But take heed, for the next part is what is important. The moment we send you to do that, our enemies will send out their own champions, their own Exarchs, to stop you."

"And their men will be fresh," Urien pointed out. He long since taken his hand off the sword, and now refilled his own goblet with the last of the bottle of red. "Fresh, and more experienced than you are. You've only just made your Accord, boy, and you're green as summer grass."

"You will be tired from hewing your way through dozens of men," the Crown Prince picked up the thread, "And they will hit you with no mercy. When you fall, that leaves the enemy Exarch free to wreak havoc on our forces, because we have no threat held in reserve, no one to replace you."

"You have Sir Bors," Tristan said. "And what if I do not lose? What if I beat their Exarch?"

"You are a strategic resource, now," Lionel explained. "As important as our supply lines, or this castle town defending the pass. We can't gamble you away lightly. When we draw out an enemy Exarch? Then into the fray you go - you or Sir Bors, depending on my judgment. If its a young Exarch, come recently to the Accords like yourself, then yes, I'll blood you against them. It will give you experience, help you to grow stronger. If I judge the foe is beyond you? You hold back. And remember, we don't know how many champions they have. What if they drop a second onto our flank while Sir Bors is dueling an enemy Exarch, holding the center? You are then our only option. I hope you see how much it changes things for us to have you here. My father would not send more than one Exarch; if we use you well, you have brought as much to our cause as a thousand infantry. But the key is that you must let me use you. You must trust in my decisions. And that means you won't just be another knight in the charge."

After a long moment, Trist nodded. "It is not precisely what I thought it would be," he admitted. "And I am not certain I understand everything. In fact, I am sure I will think of a dozen questions as soon as you are not here to answer them, your Royal Highness. But I came here to fight for you. I will do that in whatever manner you think best."

"Good. That is all I ask." Lionel Aurelianus stood. "I think we should let you clean off the dust of the road and get some rest, Sir Trist. Come to my pavilion tomorrow morning just after dawn - Baron Urien can have someone show you where. Bring your arms and armor and your squire to help you. I mean to test you hard." Lady Valeria rose and slipped her arm through the prince's, but Urien remained seated.

Trist stood, and bowed; he knew a dismissal when he saw it. "As you wish." He paused. "My Lord, I feel obligated to seek out Sir Auron and inform him of my actions within his lands."

"Don't worry about that, lad," Urien said, gruffly. "I'll speak to him myself." At Baron Urien's nod of permission, he sheathed his longsword, retreated three steps, then turned and left the tent, stepping out into the crowded evening.

Once he'd passed the guards who flanked the entrance to the Baron's tent, and took a few steps out onto the dusty beaten path that served as a camp road, Trist paused, looked around, and realized that he had no idea where his men had been quartered. Cook-fires burned in every direction, carrying the smells of stew and woodsmoke. Lines of tied horses let out the occasional whinny, and he even heard a few voices raised in song in the distance, but none of it gave him a clue where he was supposed to be until he felt a tug on his sleeve.

"Took you long enough in there," Yaél muttered, having appeared at his side as if some phantom or faerie with the power to befuddle the mind. More likely, Trist knew, it was the expertise of a boy who'd grown up starving on the street. Not being noticed had likely been his new squire's best defense. "Once we had Caz tied, Henry sent me to wait for you," the squire explained.

"Good thinking on Henry's part," Trist acknowledged with a smile. "Can you show me where we are to make camp?"

"This way! I'm starving," Yaél exclaimed, setting off at a brisk pace. "I hope they've saved enough stew for us. Did you really spend that whole time talking to the Prince? What's he like?"

"One question at a time," Trist pleaded as he followed. "Yes, we spoke, and he seems... like a prince."

"That's no answer," Yaél shot back, turning to glare at him, then ducking around a man leading a laden mule.

"I do not know how to explain it better," Trist said. "When he is speaking to you, you feel like you have his full attention, like there is nothing more important in all the world than what he is asking you. You could not even think to do anything but what he tells you. And he knows things, all manner of things I did not think anyone could know. About the Accords, and Oaths, and strategy."

They rounded a corner, and Trist paused. The largest tent he'd yet seen lay ahead, surrounded by a near complete circle of other tents around an open area that had been left clear. There were lines of horses, fine destriers all, and a man in a chain hauberk dropped a halberd across their path as they approached. He wore the royal heraldry of a golden lion on a field of black, marking him as the Prince's man.

"State your name and business," the man said sternly.

"This is Sir Trist," Yaél proclaimed proudly, "The new Exarch! I'm his squire. The Prince's men told us to camp here."

"Exarch," the man said, withdrawing his halberd, and bowing his head in deference. The peasants back in Camaret-à-Arden had treated his family that way, but he hadn't expected it from the Crown Prince's guards. "Good to have you with us, m'lord," the man continued. "All the lads are talking about you."

Trist blinked. "Thank you," he said after a moment. "Your name?"

"Bill, m'lord," the man answered, with a grin. "William, if you want the name me Ma gave me, but it's been Bill of Bankside so long no one calls me anything else."

Trist extended his hand, and the soldier shifted his halberd to his left hand to return the grip. "It is an honor to meet you, Bill of Bankside," he said, with as warm a smile as he could manage. He was exhausted. "I admit I do not know the camp yet, Bill," he continued. "I might need to ask you for directions, tomorrow."

"Of course!" Bill nodded.

"And if you have no duty tomorrow morning," Trist continued, leaning in and lowering his voice, "I am told his Royal Highness means to put me through my paces on the practice yard. Feel free to come by at prime; a friendly face would be a comfort."

"You may have more than a few friendly faces," Bill said, with a twinkle in his eye. "Your men have set up inside. Last tent on the left, you see?" He pointed to one end of the near-circle surrounding the yard, and Trist recognized Luc's massive silhouette in front of the fire.

"Thank you, again," Trist said, and he and Yaél set off across the yard. Trist wasn't hungry, after eating in Baron Urien's tent, but he was eager to finally get his boots off and relax after the tension of the day. He had gone from one crisis to another, between the confrontation upon arriving at the encampment, and then having to withstand the scrutiny of not only his liege lord, but the Crown Prince of the Kingdom, as well. He sped up as they neared his men's cookfire, and he raised a hand in greeting when Henry and Luc looked up.

Both men's eyes widened, and Henry called a warning. "My lord!" Trist recalled every way he'd watched his own death, in Acrasia's visions, cut down from behind each time.

It was all the notice Trist had before a hand clamped down on his shoulder from behind, arresting his movement and spinning him around. Reflexes trained since childhood took over, and his right hand dropped to the hilt of his longsword, at his waist, ready to draw.

Glaring at Trist, an arm's length away, was the Exarch of Masheth, Sir Bors.

Chapter Twenty-Seven

A Letter From Home

We call them carrier pigeons now, but our ancestors who first trained them called them rock doves. They built nests all around the shores of Etalus, and legend has it that Emperor Haetianus was the one who first used them as war pigeons. Damndest thing; cage them and take them as far away as you like, they will always find their way back to where they were raised. Of course, it means we have to cart wagons full of cages around with us in our baggage train...

-The Campaign Journals of General Aurelius, volume I

3rd Day of the Flower Moon, 297 AC

A cold iron spike of fear shot through Trist's heart, as the visions of the curse Acrasia had shown him filled his mind. Bors could have cut him down from behind, just now, and he would never have known until he was dead. The thought was enough to nearly drive him into a full-blown panic.

The older knight's eyes dropped to Trist's hand, where it grasped his longsword, and the man's lips curled in a scowl of disgust beneath his red beard. "Go ahead, boy. Draw steel on an unarmed man. Show everyone exactly what metal you are made of."

Trist took a deep breath. Now that he had time to take in what was happening, he observed that the other Exarch was no longer wearing armor - only a belted tunic, with his arming sword sheathed. Cautiously, he removed his hand from his own weapon, straightened his back, and offered the older man a bow. "Good evening to you, Sir Bors," he said, keeping his tone even. "I admit I did not hear you coming; I beg you, forgive my surprise." From his peripheral vision, he saw his men come up at his sides, grouping around him in common cause.

Bors leaned in, lowering his voice to a growl. The man's breath stank of onions and ale, and Trist had difficulty not flinching from it. "The Crown Prince is young," he said, too low for anyone but Trist and his men to hear. "The young trust too easily, sometimes. As his champion, it is my duty to be there when his trust is betrayed. You understand me, faerie knight?"

"You may take comfort, Sir Bors," Trist said. "I will not betray Prince Lionel's trust."

"Pretty words," Bors grunted. "It's easy for a man to speak pretty words. But what you do, on the field of battle, is what defines you. Your father knew that. I will be watching you, boy."

"A true knight is courteous," Trist shot back. "Even to their enemies. To be less than courteous is to lower ourselves, and prove unworthy of our oath."

"You're young, too," Bors observed, and took a step back. The movement reminded Trist of a stalking wildcat. "See how those pretty words serve you when your boots are slipping in a man's spilled guts, and the stench of blood and shit and piss fills your every breath." Finally, the older knight turned and stalked back across the yard to his own tent.

"He's bad one," Yaël said.

"He's a knight," Henry responded.

"I've seen lots of bad men on the streets," Trist's squire replied. "Men who like to hurt people. You get to know em when you see em, if you want to stay safe. And that's one."

"Smart boy," Acrasia murmured in Trist's ear.

"Come along," Trist said, turning back toward their fire. "Let us get the boy something to eat."

Trist rose before the dawn. He had to piss, and the scent of cooking bacon wafted in from someone's cook fire. The tent he'd been given wasn't as large as what Baron Urien had, nor nearly as impressive as the central tent that had to be the Crown Prince's pavilion, but it was more than he'd expected as a poor knight from a minor family. There was clean straw over the packed earth, and a flap of canvas to give him a private place to sleep, while his squire made do next to the entrance, cramped among all of their supplies.

The boy wasn't awake, and Trist didn't have the heart to rouse him yet. In sleep, something of the sharpness, the wariness usually present in Yaél's face was eased, and he looked like any other boy. Trist wondered if Clarisant was with child yet, and whether their son might look so peaceful. The thought reminded him that he'd been given a message from her, and after he'd relieved himself he found a seat on a worn log next to last night's fire. Once he'd stirred the coals a bit and fed it with new wood, Trist carefully held the tightly rolled parchment in both hands, squinting. His new wife had written in very small letters, cramped to fill every inch of the parchment, and it was difficult to read.

My lord husband,
I pray to the Angelus you are safely arrived. Your lord father sends his earnest wishes for your continued safety, and for your victory in battle. Brother Hugh offers prayers for you daily, and Brother Alberic speaks of you often when we work in your father's study.
Your father is not well. The loss of your brother has turned him into an old man. I try to take what burdens from him I can, and so Alberic and I handle the numbers: such and such taxes to be collected, so much grain needed to last through winter, the cost of repairs to the roof of the south wing. I know you would hate it: your brother often told me how you would rather be in the practice yard than working at a multiplication table.
The war is far from us, here, and we are safe. It is too soon to know whether I will give you a child, but for this, too, we offer prayers daily.I have a small number of pigeons from my father,

raised in Falais, and I will write to you so long
as they last.
Your loyal wife,
Clarisant

Once he had finished reading, Trist released the bottom of the parchment with his right hand and let it roll back up. He put it in his coin-purse, for safekeeping, and fed another piece of wood to the fire. They would want a good bed of coals to cook on.

"News from home?" Henry sat down next to him on the log. "If m'lord forgives my asking."

"It is," Trist confirmed. "My lady wife writes that my father is not well. Old before his time, she says."

"Aye," Henry said with a sigh. "Losing a son will do that to a man."

"At least she didn't try to say she loved you," Acrasia cut in, twirling around on the other side of the firepit so that her skirts lifted in the air. Trist looked away from the flash of her pale legs. Of course she looked beautiful: the faerie maid looked like whatever she wanted to look like.

"His Royal Highness means to put me through my paces, this morning," Trist told Henry. "Let us cook a bit to eat, and get the others up."

"We've got our share of rations from the supply train," Henry said, rising. "Bread's not too old, yet, and we've good grain for pottage. With your leave, m'lord, I'll get the pot and start it cooking." Trist nodded, and let the hunter get to work.

By the time the bells from Falais woke the others, the meal was cooking nicely over the coals. Yaél was the last to rise, which earned the boy some friendly jibes from Luc. "It is fine for today," Trist said, "But from now on I will be waking you up if the bells do not. We train every morning at prime, just like on the road."

The three men and the boy scraped the pot clean to fill their bowls, and then scraped their bowls clean again with hunks of black bread to get every last bit of their food. "One thing," Yaél said around a mouthful of pottage, "About being a squire. Haven't ever eaten this well ever."

"It will not be this good once we are away from the town," Trist warned him. "Carrots, turnips, eggs... are these chunks of rabbit, Henry?"

"Got em this morning," the hunter said with a nod. "Fresh."

"A full belly every day's better than on the streets," Yaél insisted, but still looked mournfully at his own wooden bowl, and then the pot, just to see if there was anything left over.

"Alright," Trist said, rising, and putting his bowl aside. "Help me get the armor on. You still need the practice, if nothing else."

By the time Trist was buckled into the steel cuirass, vambraces, pauldrons and greaves, a crowd had begun to gather around the cleared field in the middle of the semi-circle of tents which made up the Crown Prince's encampment. Those of higher rank had brought out camp chairs or stools from their tents, as word seemed to have gotten around. Trist spotted Baron Urien with his dogs at hand, and a knight at his side Trist took to be Sir Auron. There was Lady Valeria, with a knight he didn't recognize at her side, and even Sir Bors, who glared at him. Thankfully, Trist's cousin Lucan walked over, carrying a helmet under one arm, a pair of gauntlets, and a training sword.

"It is good to see you, cousin," Trist said, with a smile, extending his arm for Lucan to clasp. "I regret I did not have time to greet you properly last evening."

"Trist, always in trouble of some kind," Lucan said, shaking his head with a grin. "You haven't changed at all, have you?"

"How is Miriam?" Trist asked.

"She's well. Home in Roche de la Garde with our youngest," Lucan assured him.

"What's wrong with that sword?" Yaél asked, leaning in to peer at the blade Lucan held in his left hand.

"This is my squire, Yaél," Trist introduced the boy, elbowing him gently. "A knight is courteous. Introduce yourself before you just start jawing at people."

"Yes sir," Yaél said with a grin. "But it is an odd sword, isn't it?"

"It's a feather-sword," Lucan explained, holding it up so that Yaél could look. "See? A smith grinds down the edges of an old blade, until there's just this bit in the middle, no wider than a big man's thumb. Makes it nice and flexible, blunt. And then they grind down the tip and cap it with leather."

"Why not use wood?" Yaél asked.

"Feels all wrong," Trist explained. "And you are more liable to break a bone with wood than with this. Always wear your gauntlets, though. I watched Percy's finger pop like an overstuffed sausage once when he did not."

"Angelus, I remember that," Lucan said, with a sad smile. "He screamed fit to wake all the daemons of Vellatesia." Trist's cousin looked away. "I miss him already."

"I do, too." Trist coughed. "Let me try that helmet and see if it fits."

It fit well enough, and Trist took it off again after making sure of it, tucked the helmet under his left arm, and accepted the feather-sword from Lucan. "You hold this," he told Yaél, and handed the boy his sheathed longsword. "Behave," he whispered to Acrasia. "Do not torment the boy."

Then, he and Lucan stepped out into the middle of the yard. By this point, even men-at-arms and servants had gathered around, including Bill of Bankside, sitting on the trampled grass and dirt.

"Sir Trist!" Crown Prince Lionel Aurelianus called from his camp chair, between Baron Urien and Lady Valeria. There was a fourth person as richly dressed as those three, and from the heraldry of a black mountain on red, Trist guessed her the Baroness of Falais. "We mean to take your measure as an Exarch this morning. Are you prepared?" Three knights in full armor waited near the Prince.

"I am," Trist called back, donning the helmet and then offering a bow. "Which of these gentlemen am I to fight first?"

The row of powerful nobles chuckled together, as if at a joke.

"You are to fight them all at once!" Prince Lionel responded. "Now, begin!" At his word, all three knights strode forward, weapons in hand, and began to spread out to encircle Trist.

Chapter Twenty-Eight

THE TEST

The leannán sídhe is one of the more peculiar legends of our ancestors; one of the faerie people who live under the hills, she is a beautiful woman who takes a mortal lover, driving a man to a brief, but glorious life. A man who once accepts her love finds that even death is no escape from her, for she collects the souls of her lovers and keeps them as her phantom slaves.
-François du Lutetia, A History of Narvonne

4th Day of the Flower Moon, 297 AC

Trist had killed two half-drunk thugs in the dead of night, but fighting three trained knights at the same time was an entirely different thing, and he knew it. The only way to win was to take out one of his opponents immediately, before they could group up on him. As soon as the Crown Prince shouted the word 'begin,' he lunged forward at the knight on his left, a man wielding a longsword just like himself. Years of footwork practice helped him to cover more ground than most people would expect in an instant as his feather-sword rose and fell in a diagonal cut.

It only took a single pass to know that his swordplay was better than this man. Their thinned, flexible practice swords met with a clang, hard, and Trist let the other man lean into the bind for a split second before lifting his own sword. The other man's blade passed by Trist harmlessly before he could pull it back, and then, inside the knight's guard, Trist walloped him on his right arm. That earned him a satisfying grunt, and Trist knew his opponent would have a colorful bruise to show for it, despite his mail and the padded gambeson beneath it. Immediately after scoring a hit, Trist pulled back and settled into a Plow Guard, smoothly sliding back along the beaten earth in an attempt to keep all three of them from coming at once.

The three knights were well trained enough not to be shaken, though Trist heard the one with an arming sword and a shield remark, "Bastard's fast as a wildcat." In truth, to him, they almost seemed to be fighting at half speed, and it was only now that Trist truly began to appreciate the speed and reaction time he'd gained since the fight at the lake. A crimson thread of power vibrated within him, in time with the beating of his heart. The man he'd bruised lunged forward, the leather-padded tip of his longsword extended in a thrust, and Trist casually set it aside with a crooked cut, knocking the other man's feather-blade down almost into the dirt. That was all he had time for before the other two men were on him.

Each was using a shorter arming sword in their right hand; the one in the center had a dagger for parrying in the left, while the last knight was carrying a kite shield kept high and in position. Trist set aside the first man's cut at his head, but as he brought his sword back around to defend against the final knight, the man took him by surprise. Instead of following through on a cut with his arming sword, the last knight suddenly lunged forward to bash his kite shield into Trist's loaned helm. The blow rocked him back, and he bit his lip, tasting the hot coppery tang of his own blood. Cheers rang up from around the crowd.

Trist shook himself, swallowing blood. However much faster he'd gotten - and he had gotten faster, the sensation was almost giddy - he wasn't quick enough to beat three armed and armored men working together. Whatever the Crown Prince said about Exarchs carving through mortal men like butter, Trist clearly wasn't at that point yet.

"Yaél!" Trist shouted, backing toward the edge of the field to put some space between himself and his three opponents. "Throw me my sword!"

"This is a sparring match!" Baron Urien shouted. "No sharp blades."

"Your Royal Highness," Trist called, turning to the Prince. His three opponents, in the meantime, were hesitating, and had not closed the gap. "You want to see what I can do? Let me hold my sword for but a moment. I swear to you I will not swing it at these knights."

Lionel Aurelianus considered for only half a moment. "Give him his sword, squire," he called to Yaél. The boy ran forward, and Trist shifted the feather-sword to his left hand so that he could reach out and lay his right on the hilt of his longsword.

"Are you doing it?" Acrasia asked with a grin.

"Tor De Lancey," Trist intoned, loud enough for the entire crowd to hear him, and with his mind grasped hold of a single red thread. "I summon you to battle." A frost spread out from where he stood, coating the trampled earth as if on a winter's morning, just after sunrise. Pale in the sunlight, not quite opaque, Sir Tor coalesced at Trist's side. The crowd gasped at the appearance of a fully armed and armored knight, and the Baron's hounds roused themselves and set to howling.

"By the Angelus," Baron Urien gasped. "It cannot be. De Lancey?"

Tor's helm swiveled as he looked over the three knights facing them across the field. "Three against one, is that the way of it?" the dead man asked.

"So it is," Trist answered, handing his own sword back to Yaél and bringing his right hand around to grasp the hilt of his feather-sword. He lifted it over his head in High Guard.

"Hardly seems fair, does it, lad?" the old knight asked. "Why don't we see how they are against the two of us, then." With a laugh, the ghostly knight charged, and Trist sprang forward to keep up. The three knights they faced, on the other hand, had dropped the tips of their weapons, no longer in line with Trist's torso, and in their shock seemed unable to decide what to do.

Trist did not have long to even the odds; even now, he could feel the thread that held Tor De Lancey straining. If it had been a real fight, with sharp blades, he would have been more confident. It only took one severe injury to cripple a man and take him out of the fight. With a ground down, dulled old blade and a leather-capped tip, however, he was only landing touches to keep score. Even bruising his opponents wouldn't really put them out of the fight. Old blade... something about that tickled at the back of his mind, and Trist smiled.

Once again, Trist's advantage in speed and agility was overwhelming. Fueled by an inexhaustible red haze of vigor, he lunged ahead of Sir Tor, and before any of the other four men on the field could react, swung a rising cut at the man he'd hit once before. Instead of a feint, he put all his muscle into the cut, hoping to draw out the parry.

The impact of steel on steel rang out across the practice yard, and half the length of a feather-sword went spinning off to the side, where it skidded across the dirt in a puff of dust before coming to a rest. Trist's opponent stared down at his broken blade, then took a knee. Before Trist could get more than a glimpse of Tor De Lancey's spectral form dueling the knight with a shield, roaring with laughter all the while, his third opponent came in, parrying dagger held in one hand and arming sword in the other, and cut at Trist's head.

If he hadn't been an Exarch, Trist realized, he would never have been able to stop that blow. As it was, he barely got his sparring sword up into Ox, sending the arming sword off target by a bare few inches with a clang. Trist whipped his feather sword around into a diagonal cut, deliberately keeping the motion just slow enough for the other knight to parry, and then levered the crossbar of his sword around, taking one hand off his hilt in a well practiced disarming maneuver. By the time Trist had pulled back, footwork smooth, he held an arming sword in one hand and his own feather-sword in the other.

"Yield?" he asked the other knight.

"Yield," the man agreed, panting for breath, and dropped his parrying dagger before reaching up to pull his helm off. Trist glanced over to see that Tor De Lancey had shattered the shield of the third knight with his warhammer, then knocked him to the ground, and was standing over the fallen man, hammer raised.

"Hold!" the Crown Prince called, raising his voice to cut over the murmuring of the crowd. "I believe we have seen sufficient demonstration of Sir Trist's abilities, and I venture that no man here would deny his right to be addressed as Exarch."

Tor, in the meantime, turned, and knelt, burying the head of his warhammer in the dirt. The dead knight nodded in the direction of the Crown Prince and his former liege, Baron Urien, before dissolving into sparks of light that just as quickly burned away in the morning sun. Baron Urien's face, Trist noted, had the pallor of a man taken ill, and only now did his dogs settle.

"Three cheers for our Exarch!" Lionel Aurelianus raised his goblet. "Huzzah!"

"Huzzah!" the crowd of knights and squires, men at arms and servants, roared back, and then slowly began to disperse as it became clear that the spectacle had come to an end. Trist dropped both practice swords to the earth, pulled the helm he had been lent off, tucked it under his arm, and offered his hand to the sweating knight who had just yielded to him.

"Well fought, Sir Knight," Trist said.

"Sir Divdan du Falais," the knight, a man with close cropped hair and a few day's stubble on his chin, introduced himself. "And the Angelus willing, that will be the last time I ever wield a blade against you, Sir Trist. I'd much rather be by your side than facing you." His eyes twinkled with good humor, and his easy smile caused Trist to instantly take a liking to him. When Sir Divdan extended a gauntleted hand, Trist returned the grasp.

Before either man could say more, the Crown Prince approached. "I crave your pardon, Sir Divdan," he said, then turned to address Trist. "We must, I am afraid, compel our newest Exarch's presence at our war council. It should have been last evening," Lionel admitted to Trist, with a smile. "But your arrival threw everything into a bit of chaos, I am afraid."

"You have my deepest apologies, your Royal Highness," Trist said, lowering his eyes. The Prince, however, waved him off.

"What you bring to us, Sir Trist, is worth a short delay. Tell me, how many Tithes have you taken, for your part?"

"Four," Trist admitted. Sir Divdan, in the meanwhile, took three steps back, so as not to intrude; in the meanwhile, the other two knights he'd fought had removed their helms and taken up guard near Lady Valeria. "I must confess, most of them are not the sort of thing to use on a training field. I strike more true against daemons, my Prince, having slain one; as Lady Acrasia serves the King of Shadows, I can see as well by starlight as at noon; and for riding with the Horned Lord, I can trace my target unerringly in a hunt, and ride without tiring until dawn."

"All useful things," Lionel agreed, "And, as you say, not easy to demonstrate against these worthy knights here today. But now that I have a gauge for your skills, I can plan for how to make best use of you. I suspect, Sir Trist, we may send you with a scouting detachment, ahead of the main force. It seems suited to your Boons."

"Whatever duty you have for me." Trist gave a shallow bow.

"Take some time to visit my armorer, and have your horse seen to, as well," Lionel said, after a moment. "Bring your squire to be fitted for armor - unless I am mistaken? I did not take note of any packed on your single horse for him."

"No, your Royal Highness," Trist confirmed.

"Get the boy geared up, then, and send him off with the other squires. He'll serve you during the council. My own lad, Kay, can take him in hand. Any questions?"

"None," Trist responded, and was a bit surprised when the Prince clapped him on the shoulder.

"Good. Get moving then, and I will see you at midday in my pavilion." Lionel Aurelianus turned and walked away: as soon as he'd gone a few steps, a crowd of people gathered about him, like fallen leaves pulled by a river current.

"Amazing, isn't it?" Divdan observed, stepping back up to Trist's side. "I don't think he even knows he does it. But it's like he's the center of the world... the warm fire everyone gathers around on a winter night. As long as we have the Prince, I truly believe we can defeat any foe. Come!" He shook himself. "I'll lead you to the Prince's armorer, and show you around a bit."

"My thanks," Trist said, but for a moment, the bright sunlight seemed to dim under the shadow of a passing cloud.

Chapter Twenty-Nine

FALAIS

The General did send to the other provinces! Of course he did - we needed reinforcements, as quick as we could get them. But with the senate gone and the Emperor dead, there was no one could tell the generals of the other legions what to do. That bastard Scipio just holed up south of the mountains and fortified all the passes, and refused to even send supplies north, leaving us to starve.

-The Life and Times of Legionary Titus Nasica

4th Day of the Flower Moon, 297 AC

"This is heavy!" Yaél exclaimed in surprise as the shirt of rings fell down to hang about his thighs. Trist nodded, examining the fit as the Crown Prince's armorer, Clovis, double wrapped a long leather belt around the squire's waist. Sir Divdan watched with only half his attention, leaning against the wooden counter near the smith's forge, cutting chunks out of an apple with his dagger and eating them one by one.

"A bit long, I think," Trist decided, after a moment. "If we were not about to march, I would say he would grow into it in a few moons, but..."

"It's as you say, Exarch," Clovis said, tugging at the rings and then counting up from the bottom of the shirt. "I will take off... half a dozen rows. It won't take long at all. A helm should be no problem; there's enough squires running around the camp, we keep a few in the right sizes. What will take the most work is to get a pair of gauntlets fitted." The smith was a well built man in his middle years, with broad shoulders and arms that looked like they could lift a cow. "If I had more time, I'd like to fit you both out better," he admitted. "And do a bit of barding for your destrier, as well. An Exarch should have only the best. But with only an afternoon to work..."

"We understand," Trist said, laying a hand on the smith's shoulder. "Whatever you can get together in that time to keep my squire alive is all we ask. Anything is better than bringing him out in a linen shirt."

"I think I can send him out with more than 'anything,' the smith grumbled. "Here, boy, let me try this on you." He brought over what must have been the smallest set of gauntlets he had on hand: not with articulated fingers, like the ones Trist had back at their tent, but a sort of overlapping mittens of steel plates, over soft leather.

"I can't get my fingers all the way in," Yaél said.

"Aye, they aren't long enough," Clovis said, pinching to find just where the boy's fingers ended, leaving empty leather. "I'll take off one piece of steel, cut the leather and have it sewed back into place shorter. Don't worry, lad, we'll have you kitted out by nightfall. Alright, take it all off."

He stood up and faced Trist. "Send him back tonight, before he has his supper, to pick it all up."

"You have our thanks," Trist said, clasping hands with the smith. Yaél, in the meantime, was bent forward, trying to worm his way out of a chain shirt that was now bunched up around his head and shoulders.

"Ow! My hair's stuck!" The boy complained, and Trist lent a hand. Finally, the mail flopped down onto the packed earth with a metallic shimmer, like tiny clinking keys or chimes.

"Then we need to get your hair trimmed by the barber-surgeon, as well," Trist declared. "This is why we keep our hair short. But for now, you are due for your appointment with the Crown Prince's squire." Divdan tossed aside his apple core, and the three were off.

Trist left Yaél with a troop of young men in a practice ring, sectioned off by short wooden fences. Sir Divdan led he and Cazador to where another smith was shoeing horses. What luxury and wealth, Trist thought, that the Crown Prince had his own smith entirely dedicated to making armor. Here, for the rest of the army, half a dozen more plied their trade, not only shoeing horses, but repairing mail, adjusting barding, sharpening daggers, and all manner of other tasks that an encamped army might require. He even saw an apprentice barely older than Yaél turning out spikes for tents and pavilions.

"Don't worry, m'lord," the apprentice of the smith working on horse shoes assured Trist. "We'll have this big boy seen to by terce, if not sooner, and delivered back to His Highnesses' encampment."

"You know how to handle a war-trained destrier?" Trist felt obligated to check: Caz was perfectly capable of caving a man's head in with a single kick. He'd been taught to do it since he was a yearling, after all.

"Handle em day in and out, m'lord," the boy promised, and with only a slight degree of apprehension Trist handed the lead over.

"Be good," he warned Caz, and the destrier gave a mischievous snort. "None of that. I know you," Trist said, then turned to follow Divdan back into the maze of beaten tracks that ran throughout the army's encampment.

"I think I should have armor," Acrasia said, clutching his left arm and leaning into him as they walked. "For the next time we fight a daemon."

In spite of himself, Trist looked down at the faerie maid, instead of shaking her off his arm. Thank the Angelus no one could see her: the last thing he needed was his new father-in-law hearing tales of pretty young women who weren't his wife clinging to him. "How would that even work?" he asked her. "You do not have a body."

Divdan shot him a look under furrowed brows. "Is that your faerie lady you're speaking to?" the other knight asked.

"It is. Sir Divdan, I know you cannot see her, but this is Lady Acrasia walking beside us. Lady Acrasia, Sir Divdan, in service to..." Trist grappled for it. "My apologies, Sir Divdan. I do not think I actually asked after your liege."

"Not your fault, Trist," Divdan said. "I didn't mention. I'm the sworn man of Lady Arnive, Baroness du Hauteurs Massif," he explained. "Not one of her landed knights, of course, I don't hold one of the three towers, I serve at her side. You might have caught a glance of her watching you this morning."

"The black mountain on red?" Trist asked, recalling the heraldry.

"That's right," Divdan said with a nod. Both of them stepped around a cart of turnips making its way through the camp. "Lady Arnive's a hard one, but she needed to be after the old Baron died."

"A widow, then," Trist said. Like Clarisant.

"Aye. I've served her and her husband before her. There was talk of a knight's fee, a few years back, but she wanted me to take a wife."

Trist raised his eyebrows. "And you would not?"

"Never!" Divdan said, with a grin. "Bullocks to that. Women make you dumb. No offense, Lady Acrasia, but men and boys both do all manner of silly things for love - or lust. Throw money away, fight duels, betray their lieges... I'm figure I'm better off alone. That way I can keep my head about me."

The faerie glared at him, though he couldn't see it. Trist half expected Sir Divdan's shadow to rise and thump him over the head. For his own part, rather than risk angering her more, Trist decided to maneuver the conversation onto less dangerous terrain. "You mentioned three towers?" he asked Sir Divdan.

"Never been to the mountains before, have you?" Divdan chuckled. "Here, we have an hour or so yet before we're due at the council. Let me show you a bit of the town."

They turned left down a beaten-dirt track that seemed, to Tristan, much like any other in the army's encampment, but Sir Divdan moved with the confidence of someone who knew exactly where he was going. As the two knights and the phantasmal faerie left the encampment, Trist recognized the air: Divdan moved, here, with the lifetime of familiarity that Trist felt back in Camaret-à-Arden.

"The River Durentia," Divdan explained as they walked, "Cuts through the stone of the mountains here. That's why you see cliffs on both sides." He waved his hand, and Trist indeed could see cliffs rising up above Falais, higher than any building. He guessed that even if you stacked three of the local Church of the Angelus on top of each other - the tallest building in the village, at its spire - you still wouldn't match the height of the cliffs that rose on the other side of the river. The rock was a mix of gray stone, on the one hand, and then of a pale, sandy color, warm as the beaches at Rocher de la Garde. Perhaps when the war was over, he would take Clarisant and their child to the sea of her home, and lie on the sand like he'd done as a boy. He imagined she would like that.

"It looks like the cliffs come right down to the river on the other side," Trist said, craning his neck.

"They do," Divdan agreed. "About the only thing that's over there is the anchor ring for a great chain, drilled into the stone of the cliffs. If anyone tries to come north by riverboat, we can raise the chain with a winch from this side, and stop them from getting through."

Their steps took them into the town proper which, from Trist's view, was laid out very oddly - nothing at all like the village he'd grown up in. There seemed to be only two or three long streets, including the old Etalan road as a main concourse, following the course of the river, in roughly parallel but winding paths, each higher than the last, between the bank and the sheer cliffs, all of which didn't cover very much distance at all. There appeared to be cross streets that connected them, and these were short and steep. In fact, they turned right onto one, and Trist saw that large sections of it were actually a staircase. All of this resulted in a village that was three or four times as long as it was wide, in an irregular strip.

"Where are we going?" Trist huffed, as they climbed up the stairs. Divdan bounded up them with all the energy Trist imagined a mountain goat would show.

"The Church of Saint Abatur," the other knight answered, not even out of breath, and paused at the top of the stair to wait for Trist. "There." He lifted a hand and pointed at the church Trist had glimpsed from a distance. It was built into the very side of the cliff, of the same sandy-stone formed into bricks. The facade, above the entranceway and the steps, rose to a tower and then a spire that stretched up to the blue mountain sky. "Best view in the village!"

"I do not like going into churches," Acrasia whined. "They feel itchy."

"I could leave the sword here, leaning up against a wall," Trist offered.

"And let anyone who comes by run off with it?" The faerie rolled her eyes, then bustled up the stairs past Divdan. "I'll survive." Trist followed the two of them into the Nave, which he found quite cool compared to the streets outside.

"This entire thing is built into a cliff?" He shook his head in wonder. Where other churches might have dozens of stained glass windows depicting the Angelus descending to aid humanity against the daemons, the Church of Saint Abatur instead made do with frescos. The only windows were in the facade, jutting out from the cliff as it did.

"Welcome, Sir Divdan," a man's voice echoed throughout the nave, and Trist spied a priest approaching down the aisle. "I trust the Baroness remains well? Her donations to the orphans are always appreciated, and I can assure you that we make good use of them."

"Aye, she's well enough, Father Kramer," Divdan answered. "I've come to give my friend here a good look at the town and the pass. It's his first time in Falais."

"Certainly!" The man slowed his steps as he reached them, and turned to address Trist. His gray hair was thinning, but his steps were still spry. "A friend of Sir Divdan is always welcome here, and a Knight of the Kingdom doubly so. May I..."

The priest's voice trailed off and, following his gaze, Trist realized the man was staring directly at Acrasia.

Chapter Thirty

The Church of Saint Abatur

The Etalans carved Velatessia out of the Ardenwood with iron and blood, but the land was never theirs, and it is not now the property of any King of Narvonne, nor any man he is foolish enough to name a Baron. The forest has reclaimed its own; do not look to steal from the King of Shadows a second time, lest you taste my blade, as well.
-Sir Maddoc's letter to King Luther the Unready

4th Day of the Flower Moon, 297 AC

"This holy church is the tomb of Saint Abatur," Father Kramer pronounced gravely, eyes still fixed upon where now Acrasia leaned into Trist's side. "Did you truly think, Forsaken One, that even in your exile, you could step onto consecrated ground and not be discovered?"

"Still your tongue, mortal," Acrasia hissed, and her voice sounded to Trist just the same as he remembered from the night of his brother's death. His skin pricked with goosebumps, and his hair stood so stiffly that a gust of breeze from the church doorway hurt his scalp when it ruffled the strands.

The faerie maid stepped out from him, pressing toward the priest, and her shoulders were set, her head lowered as if preparing for a charge, but her eyes met Kramer's so that neither of them seemed willing to look away, or to admit weakness. Lashes of fire, to Trist's sight, uncoiled from her true form, which he could still only catch a glimpse of.

"Acrasia!" Trist called, but she seemed not to hear him.

"Do you know what sort of creature you have brought here?" Father Kramer continued. "Something in the manner of a cur. A dog that simpers at the feet of her master, eats from the master's hand, and then, at need, lazes away by the fire, unwilling to bestir herself in her master's defense."

"Your soul would make a good Tithe to my king," Acrasia taunted, and her burning whips flexed and writhed, edging closer to the priest.

"Sir Trist," Divdan broke in, hand on the hilt of his sword. "Put a stop to this, man. We cannot permit violence in a tomb of the Angelus!"

"Acrasia! Linette!" Trist shouted, and at the sound of the name he'd loved her by, she finally turned. A small part of his mind wondered that her illusion was so real: her blonde tresses spun in the air at her motion, then settled, just as when the two of them had leapt and climbed among the rocks and the cascades so many years ago. He choked back a sob.

The faerie's eyes were wide, the eyes of an animal caught between flying from the hunter, or turning to make her final stand against his baying hounds. Trist reached out a hand: he wasn't certain it would work, that he would be able to touch her, but the illusion, at least, of contact was there. He took her by the shoulders, gently, and the burning lashes of her soul were like venomous snakes that paused in their anger, settling. "Not here," he urged her. "You want me to forgive you? I do not know if I can, but I know this: you cannot kill another innocent person, if you want me to try. If you ever want a chance."

"You'll forgive me? You'll love me again?" she asked, looking as if she might weep.

"I do not know if I can," Trist admitted. "I will try, but you have to try, as well. Be guided by me, in this, please. Let him live."

Trist's eyes flicked to the priest's face, and what he saw there gave him pause. Though the older man's face was pale with fear, his eyes did not waver. No, his gaze burned with a violent hate only barely kept in check.

"Perhaps we should leave," Divdan suggested, and began to back toward the doorway of the church. The other knight's hand never left the pommel of his sword, and as much as Trist liked the man, he was not certain who would be struck if Sir Divdan drew.

"Come," Trist urged Acrasia, pulling her toward the door with him by one delicate hand, and she let him. At the very threshold, however, she paused, and looked back at the priest.

"Keep your tomb," the faerie spat. "Worship the chains of your master, if you like, but you are ever a slave." With a final tug, Trist got her out the door, and Divdan slammed it shut behind them, putting good, solid wood between Acrasia and the priest. Even then, it was only halfway down the stairs to the next street that either of the knights relaxed.

"Well, that was not what I expected of my morning," Divdan admitted, with a grin, and Trist couldn't help but let a single bark of laughter out.

In the end, they decided that it would be safer to get a look at the village and the pass from the walls of Baroness Arnive's castle, though they were not as high as the spire of the church. The tomb, Trist mentally corrected himself. He had known, indeed Brother Alberic had taught him, that some of the Angelus had died fighting against the daemons during the Great Cataclysm, but to actually be in a church built above the corpse of one...

South of the long village, the River Durentia continued to cut a gorge through the Hauteurs Massif, and there was enough space between the cliff and the water on this bank for the old Etalan road to continue south and out of sight. To the south, the town was protected by a stone wall with a stout gate, the final line of defense against any army trying to come north into the Kingdom of Narvonne. Up on the parapet of the keep, to either side of them, catapults stood ready to hurl stones over the town wall and into a besieging army.

"So," Sir Divdan asked, arms crossed over the stone of a crenelation, looking south through the Passe de Mûre, "Lady Acrasia, is it? What was all that about."

"He won't be able to hear me even if I answer him," Acrasia grumped. She perched atop the stone, the wind ruffling her hair and tossing it artfully about her face. If she'd still had a physical form, Trist would have worried about her falling. As it was, his heart still jumped, despite himself, when he caught a glimpse of her framed against the great blue sky and the buildings below.

"I will pass along what you say," Trist promised.

"Fine." She rolled her eyes. "Tell him... the Angelus have never quite gotten over that we didn't just fall in line against the daemons."

Divdan frowned when Trist communicated her words, and he had questions of his own. "But I know your people fought the daemons," Trist said. "Like the one at the lake. Addanc. You said the faeries bound it there."

"We did," Acrasia confirmed. "Cern led the hunt, driving it into the water, where the King of Shadows bound it. But that was because it came into our woods. If it hadn't entered the Arden, we would never have gone out to fight it."

"This is the one you slew, Sir Trist?" Divdan asked, and he nodded.

"Yes. With quite a bit of help from Acrasia," he said. "And the ghost of Sir Tor De Lancey."

Divdan shuddered. "No offense intended, my friend, but that gives me a bit of a chill. The thought of a dead man coming to answer your call. The way the frost spread out on the ground..."

"It won't only be one forever," Acrasia pointed out. "Send a few more Tithes my way, Trist, and you'll have a whole fist of Restless Knights fighting at your side."

"That actually brings me to a question," Trist said. "Something that has been at the back of my mind since I accepted the Horned Hunter's Boon. Can we get them horses, Acrasia?"

"...you want ghostly horses, now?" Divdan asked incredulously. "A few ghasts of your own aren't enough for you, now you're asking for cavalry?"

"That is exactly what I want," Trist said, with a nod. "Knights are best used mounted. A charge of heavy cavalry to break enemy lines. On foot we are somewhat wasted."

Acrasia cocked her head to one side, considering. "Well," she said, after a moment. "There's no reason that we couldn't bind the soul of a horse to the sword. You're going to have to use the sword to kill it, though."

"That will not be a problem, once the fighting starts," Trist observed grimly. "After the first battle, there will be plenty of dying horses needing a bit of mercy."

Sir Divdan coughed. "On that pleasant note, the sun seems to be climbing high in the sky, and the bells rang terce on our way to the castle. Shall we tend our steps back toward the Crown Prince's pavilion?"

"I think that is a good idea." Trist nodded, and without thinking about it, offered a hand to help Acrasia down from where she sat on the wall. It wasn't until after she'd accepted it and hopped down that he remembered that she could have just appeared next to him.

Divdan led them down from the wall, and it was clear that he was well known and respected here, for guardsmen and servants alike greeted him as they passed. When they reached the gatehouse, they found a small bustle of activity where a carriage had been hitched to two horses, and was waiting to depart.

"That will be the Baroness' carriage," Divdan explained to Trist. He glanced around and, surely enough, Arnive of Falais was just emerging from the keep, surrounded by servants, maids and squires who were all wearing her livery.

"Sir Divdan!" The Baroness called. "Is that Exarch Trist du Camaret-à-Arden with you?"

Divdan bowed. "He is, my Lady," the knight answered his liege.

"Excellent." The Baroness looked Trist up and down, her eyes pausing on his sword for a mere heartbeat. "Into the carriage then, the both of you."

"My lady?" Trist asked.

"You are wanted at His Royal Highness' war council," Arnive reminded him. "As am I." She turned to the carriage, and Divdan hurried to offer her a hand in. "There is no good reason for you to walk when I am already taking a carriage to the camp," she called out to Trist. "Besides, I wish to speak to you. Come along now."

Trist frowned. The tone in the Baroness' voice reminded him of when his mother had scolded him for stealing apple tarts out of the kitchens as a young boy. However, he remembered his courtesies as a knight. "Thank you for the invitation, then, my lady," he said, evenly, and followed her out of the bright sunlight and into the carriage.

"You as well, Divdan," Arnive snapped, and her knight scrambled in to take a seat next to her. Which was just as well, Trist reflected, since Acrasia had appeared at his side, facing the Baroness. He didn't need to watch someone sit on her and force her to dissolve the illusion.

A footman closed the door of the carriage, and with a jolt, it rolled into motion, wheels rumbling across the ancient stone of the Etalan road. Around them, people scrambled out of the way, then lingered by the side of the road to call to the Baroness and wave to her as the carriage passed. Arnive fixed a serene smile to her face and raised a single hand to wave back, which gave Trist a chance to study her.

Arnive, Baroness du Hauteurs Massif, was at least ten years older than Trist, but younger than his father. He guessed her to be in her mid-thirties, and quite a striking woman, with a sharp face only slightly softened with the passing of her youth. She was small, as well, shorter than either Clarisant or Acrasia, and he suspected Lady Valeria, the daughter of the Baron du Champs d'Or, as well. She wore a dress of rich red velvet, with a veil over most of her hair, both trimmed in matching black lace. If her hair had been merely a dark shade of brown, that lace would have pointed it out: but no, it was black as night, as well, with not even a hint of gray, yet. After considering it for a moment, Trist concluded that she must have to beat suitors off with a sword. She looked young enough to have another child, if not for too many more years yet, and since the untimely death of her husband she was now one of the five wealthiest nobles in the Kingdom.

After a few waves, the Baroness pulled the curtains of the carriage shut and turned to face him. "I have a son who is just twelve years of age this past winter," Arnive began. "And I am well used to the trouble he causes. Tell me, Exarch Trist, why today's trouble comes from a man full-grown, and a knight, at that."

Chapter Thirty-One

Baroness Arnive

...but when the herdsman entered the cave, he recognized King Aurelius of old, with his white beard grown long with age.

"Do the eagles still circle the mountaintop?" The King under the Mountain asked, and when the herdsman replied in the affirmative, Aurelius continued: "Then you must leave, for my time to wake has not yet come."

From 'The Mountain King,' traditional Narvonnian folk tale

4th Day of the Flower Moon, 297 AC

Acrasia wrinkled her nose and pouted. "She powders herself with too much clove and lemon," the faerie observed, while Trist tried to keep a straight face. "I can't believe I'm saying anything to praise that woman, but I prefer what Clarisant wears."

Trist couldn't help but shoot a look to the faerie at his side.

"What? I caught the scent of her perfume when she picked the sword up," Acrasia grumbled. "At least Clarisant is subtle. This is just too strong."

"I assume that's the faerie speaking to you," Baroness Arnive interrupted, and when Trist turned back to face her, he saw the older woman's eyes were narrowed.

"Yes, my lady," Trist said, considering his phrasing carefully. "Lady Acrasia was commenting on your choice of clove and lemon," he finished.

"Good. Then she can listen to what I have to say, as well." Arnive raised her hand into the middle of the carriage, between all four passengers, and then extended a single, well-manicured finger. "First, neither you, nor the faerie, nor both of you together, are to enter the Church of Saint Abatur. You've upset Father Kramer quite enough already, and I don't have the time to smooth his ruffled feathers when war is coming to our doorstep. Is that understood?"

"It is, my lady," Trist acknowledged, bowing his head. "Quite clearly."

"Secondly," the Baroness continued. "When the Crown Prince sends you into the mountains, I need you to take Sir Divdan with you."

On the carriage bench next to her, Divdan stirred. "I had thought to remain with you, my lady," he said cautiously, "And with the young Lord. Where I can be certain to keep you both safe."

"We will be safe enough behind the walls," Arnive assured him. "Despite Lord Isdern's intentions otherwise, I will not allow my only son and heir anywhere near the fighting. But most importantly, Sir Divdan, I need you to take the Exarch to check on the bindings."

It was as if all of the sound and motion had gone out of the carriage at once. "Bindings?" Trist repeated, feeling a stone settle in his belly.

"Oh no," Acrasia murmured.

"Are you certain?" Divdan asked Arnive, slumping back on the bench.

"You are the only one I can send," the Baroness stated flatly. "You were there. You can lead the Exarch. Is there someone else you would trust more than yourself to see this done, Sir Divdan?"

"No," Divdan exhaled in defeat. "I will do it, my lady."

Arnive wheeled from her own knight to face Trist again. "This is not to be spoken of at the war council," she commanded him. "The Crown Prince is aware, and has made his plans accordingly, but what I am about to tell you now does not leave this carriage. If I could trust less people with this knowledge, I would. Four and a faerie is already too many."

"I wonder which one it is," Acrasia said, with a sigh. "Get ready for a truly awful mess, my love."

"You will have my utmost discretion," Trist said, doing his best to ignore the faerie. "You have my word as a knight."

"Very good." Arnive fell back into her seat, and her eyes focused on something no one else could see. "When I wed my late husband, Owain, he shared with me the secret of the Mountain King."

"I know the story," Trist said, thinking back to his childhood. "The first King of Narvonne, Aurelius. He was wounded fighting the Caliphate in the Hauteurs Massif. Before he could die, the Angelus took him under the mountains, where he sleeps until the day the kingdom needs him most."

"Like most stories, there is a grain of truth at the center," Arnive said, with a nod. "King Aurelius was wounded fighting in the mountains. But the battle against the Caliphate forces was interrupted by the attack of a daemon. I will not say its name aloud, for it is dangerous to do so."

"Well, at least she knows that much," Acrasia grumbled.

Instead, the Baroness removed a small, folded slip of paper, not vellum, but the kind used in the Caliphate. Trist recognized the material from one of Brother Alberic's most prized tomes, imported from the south by way of the port at Rocher de la Garde. Arnive unfolded the slip of paper and held it so that Trist could see. On the paper was only a single word.

Adrammelech.

From beside Trist, Acrasia sucked in a breath so quickly it made almost a hiss. "No, Trist," she said. "You aren't ready for this. Let the angry man and his stupid Angelus fight this one."

"I confess I do not recognize the name," Trist said slowly, chewing over his former lover's words. "Lady Acrasia, however, does, and wonders if it might not be a battle more suited for Exarch Bors."

"We do not want you to fight it," Arnive said. She rolled the piece of paper up and popped it in her mouth, then chewed for a moment, swallowed, and made a face. "The binding was tied to the corpse of the Angelus Abatur, to anchor the working. So my late husband said, at any rate. The church was built over the corpse to conceal it and protect it. The slow dwindling of the corpse gives us warning of the declining strength of the binding. Three years ago, Father Kramer begged an audience of my husband to tell him the corpse was nearly entirely gone. Owain took five men to investigate the site of the binding. Sir Divdan was the only one to return alive."

"The worst day of my life," Divdan muttered, his eyes hollow. "My lord led us to a cavern, high in the mountains. We had to leave the horses tied up outside. Everything around had died," he said, sitting back up and leaning forward, elbows on his knees, forehead cupped in his hands. "Nothing but dead grass, rotting wood. There were stairs leading down."

"You never told me that," Arnive broke in.

"I don't like to think about it," Divdan said, after a moment. "Two hundred steps, carved into the rock. Baron Owain didn't know who'd carved them. Said there were no records of it in the books kept by his ancestors."

"No one carved them," Acrasia said softly. "The daemon simply wanted to make it easier for mortals to find their way to him."

"It opened up, finally. The cavern was immense." Divdan was silent for a moment. Around the carriage, Trist could hear the sounds of soldiers in the encampment, now. They'd almost reached their destination. "It looked like the rock had melted and dripped down, like candle wax. And then in other places, risen up from the floor, like the way a wolf's fangs come together from the top and bottom of its jaw. And there was writing on the rock. A pool," he said. "It should have been dark, but it was lit from underneath the water. Glowed like... fireflies, maybe, beneath it."

"What happened?" Trist asked.

"What happened is I carried my liege across my shoulders, up two hundred stairs and then down a mountainside," Divdan said, sitting up, but not meeting Trist's eyes. "He was still breathing when I started up the steps. By the time we got to the nearest farm, I was soaked in his blood, and he was cold." The knight swallowed, and raised a hand to his eyes. "I apologize," he said hoarsely. "I need a moment."

"Three years since that day," Arnive said, as if chipping ice with every word. "What we need, Exarch, is to be certain the daemon won't slip its bindings and strike our forces from behind. We need to know if the bindings will hold long enough to defeat the Caliphate. We don't want you to fight it. Go and look. Let your faerie lady look on the magic there. She will be able to tell you the state of it."

Trist turned to Acrasia. "Will you? Be able to?"

Acrasia reached for his hand. "If you get me to the water? Yes," she said, after a moment. "I might even be able to reinforce the working. But if it gets loose, Trist... none of us will survive."

Trist looked back to the Baroness, meeting her eyes. "This is the order of my Prince?" was the only thing he asked.

"It is," Baroness Arnive du Hauteurs Massif said.

"Then I will do it." Angelus help me.

The war council took place in Crown Prince Lionel's pavilion, which was even larger than Baron Urien's. Trist had difficulty imagining just how many servants it must have taken to raise the thing, and he was equally impressed by the table that had been arranged as the centerpiece for the army's leaders to gather around. There were camp chairs, and smaller camp tables to hold plates of cheese, fruit, and other finger foods, but the table commanded the eye.

It was all of oak, longer than the height of two men stacked head to toe, and wider than a longsword from tip to pommel. A cloth map, cut to fit and fastened tight along the top of the table, had been carefully painted to represent the Hauteurs Massif range, the River Durentia that had carved the pass south, and the Ardenwood to the north. Carved wooden towers were scattered across the mountains, while models of both the southern wall of Falais and the keep were set in place. A tray of carved and painted miniatures rested off to one side on a separate table: knights, archers, catapults, infantry, all the great variety of arms that could be mustered on the field.

"Excellent!" Crown Prince Lionel said, rising with a smile at the group's entrance. To Sir Divdan's obvious discomfort, he had been admitted along with Trist and the Baroness. To their number was added the group which had already gathered and awaited them: the Crown Prince himself, Lady Valeria, Baron Urien and his two hounds, and Exarch Bors; and also four knights who bowed to Lady Arnive. In addition to these eleven, there were half a dozen squires to serve, among them, whom Trist had not seen all morning, Yaél.

"I believe most of us are already acquainted," Lionel continued. "Exarch Trist, these are Sir Kahedrin, who holds command of the Tour de Roche Rouge; Sir Madoc, of the Flèche de L'aube, and Dame Chantal, who commands the Tour de Larmes." He motioned to the three tower pieces set on the map, and Trist clasped the hand of each knight in turn. "Finally, leading the troops from the Rive Ouest, in the name of Baron Everard, comes Sir Florent." The last was a grizzled veteran with a close cropped white beard and a grip of iron.

"Now that is out of the way," his Royal Highness said, circling the map-table. "Let us begin with Dame Chantal's report. Dame Chantal, I believe your scouts have caught sight of the Caliphate army?"

"They have, your Royal Highness." Dame Chantal was a woman of middle age, with iron gray hair clipped short and a scar running down the left side of her face that just missed her eye. "And they have identified the enemy commander. We face Shadi ibn Yusuf, the most recent Exarch of Jibrīl - the same Angelus we faced twenty-four years past, when they brought down the Tower of Tears."

"Jibrīl," Trist repeated the name, tasting it. "I feel I have heard that name before."

"You should have," Lionel told him. "It was your father that killed the last Exarch of Jibrīl, all those years gone by."

Chapter Thirty-Two

A Royal Command

The Massacre of the Hauteurs Massif was the work of a true villain, a bloodthirsty northerner whose name is reviled throughout the Caliphate. It has been customary for generations of skirmishing in the mountains that high ranking men are captured and ransomed, not cut down after they've already been wounded.

-The Commentaries of Aram ibn Bashear

4th Day of the Flower Moon, 297 AC

"Battle isn't like the stories they tell. It's mud and piss and the smell of someone's guts falling out of their belly onto the ground. It's the scream of horses dying, and rolling around in the shit until you can jam a dagger into some poor boy's neck, because if you don't, he'll do it to you," Rience du Camaret-à-Arden had told Trist just under two weeks before.

Looking down at the Crown Prince's map, now, where the carved wooden piece representing the Tower of Tears rested, Trist wondered just how his father had left an Exarch dead in the mud of the Passe de Mûre. Exarchs weren't invulnerable: Trist could speak to that. He'd almost been killed by the daemon Addanc, and if it weren't for his ability to call the spirit of Tor De Lancey to his side, he probably would have lost to Sir Divdan and the other two knights that morning. Three on one odds wasn't yet the sort of thing he could overcome, it seemed. But as Acrasia had explained it to him, he was also very young for an Exarch. Whoever had fought with the Caliphate army at the head of an invasion twenty-four years ago would have been someone like Sir Bors, wouldn't they? A simple knight, no matter how good, shouldn't have been able to defeat that.

"He never told me that story," Trist said, after a moment with his thoughts.

"No?" Crown Prince Lionel asked, frowning. "I would have thought that he would make certain his sons knew that."

"Not Rience," Baron Urien said. "He never saw it as a glory, just something he had to do. I sometimes thought he was ashamed of it. No, the only thing that came of that war he ever cherished was Lady Cecilia."

"We've gone a bit far afield," Lady Valeria pointed out.

"Of course," Lionel said. "Quite right. Dame Chantal, were you able to discover how many Exarchs they brought, in total?"

The older woman nodded. "They didn't make a secret of it. One other Exarch, and the soldiers knew her name. Seemed quite taken with her, actually, so it was easy to overhear around the campfires. Ismet ibnah Salah, Exarch of Epinoia. They call her the Red Knight."

The Prince looked around the room, but everyone shook their heads.

"She must be new under the Accords," Baroness Arnive said. "Keeping the Kingdom's southern border, I make it my business to know all of the Caliphate Exarchs. If she'd been an Exarch longer than, say, the last six months, my spies would have heard of her."

"Somewhat in the same position as our young Trist, then," Lionel observed.

"Lure her out," Exarch Bors rumbled, speaking up for the first time. "Get her away from Shadi, and I'll crush her. Then we have two to their one."

Trist recoiled. "That is... not chivalrous," he pointed out, and Bors scowled at him.

"Chivalry doesn't win battles, boy. We send you out to duel her, we take an even chance on who comes back. Better this way. More certain."

"I do not think we have reached that point yet," Lionel said. "Numbers, Dame Chantal?"

"Two hundred lancers," the gray-haired knight began her list somberly. "A roughly equal number of horse archers and foot archers - less than a thousand, total. Say about four hundred each. At least five hundred infantry. And our scouts counted about twenty-five hundred in levies. Call it a bit over four thousand, all told."

"Damn them all," Baron Urien growled. "That's more than double our strength. Perhaps three times."

"And yet," Crown Prince Lionel observed, "We have the advantage of fortifications, and of terrain. As we did twenty-four years ago."

"With all respect, your Royal Highness," Urien said, "You weren't there all those years ago. I was. It was a near thing, and it will not happen again. Wrong season, for one. This new Exarch learned from last time: he came later in the year, after the spring rains were already done."

Trist frowned, but didn't want to speak up to ask questions.

"True. And I suspect he will be slow to advance..." Lionel stood, reached into the tray of carved figures, and began selecting handfuls, which he set up on the map table in rapid succession. In spite of himself, and though he felt he had nothing of note to contribute, Trist stepped forward so that he could have a better view.

"They cannot leave the Tower of Tears behind them," the Prince pointed out. "Even if they reduced the wall or brought down the gate to use the road through the pass. Our men there would harry their supply lines and bleed them daily. They have to take it. After what happened last time, I think this Shadi ibn Yusuf will be cautious. Their mistake was charging forward to seize an opening, overextending their lines, and they paid for it in blood."

"I feel a bit late to the ball," Lady Valeria commented, lifting her goblet of wine to take a laconic sip, "As if I've missed the first dance. That battle was a generation ago, and I believe I was still being nursed, at the time. Military history was not deemed a suitable subject to be included in my education."

"My apologies," Baron Urien said. "It was like this, my lady. The Caliphate is dry, most of it. Arid. Deserts to the south, and even the north, near the pass, doesn't get much rain. As if the clouds get caught up in the mountains. In any event, they must not have given thought to how much rain we get in the spring, in Narvonne. By the time they were sieging the tower, there, at the southern end of the pass, it was raining for a week straight. So our boys are putting up a good fight of it, but it's clear they can't hold much longer, and I'll never forget it. Rience - your father," he nodded to Trist, "Rience says, 'They want the pass so badly? Let's drown them in it!"

The Prince took up the explanation. "They began pulling back in the night," he said. "In the meantime, at Sir Rience's direction, the men took axes to every barrel of water or ale they had. Even the casks of wine. They added it all to the mud the rains had left, right behind the gate in the wall across the pass. Then, they got the oil, too, and dumped that. By the time the sun came up, my father said you couldn't walk within a hundred yards of that gate without losing your boot in the sucking mud."

"And in the meanwhile," Urien continued. "They put all the archers, all the crossbowmen, up on the heights. Had em climbing rocks like they were Falaisian goats. Begging your pardon, Baroness," he said, dipping his head to Lady Arnive.

The Baroness raised her eyebrows. "Our goats are one of our greatest economic strengths," she responded, with a grin. "And yes, they can climb quite well. I will not be offended, Baron Urien, unless you speak a bad word about the cheese they produce, which I am quite partial to."

"In any event," Lionel finished, with a grim smile. "The Caliphate army takes the gate down, finally. Maybe a hundred men sacrifice themselves manning the walls, to put up a show. But when those fine lancers, and horse archers, and infantry come through the gate and start running into the pass, they get stuck in the mud. Clumped up. The entire van slogs to a halt in the muck. That's when the arrows start coming down from the heights."

"We held the knights in reserve," Urien said. "They'd just about broken from the mud and the archers, and out comes this Exarch, sword raised high in the dawn sun, shouting to rally them. And that's when we make the charge. By the time we got to them, the Exarch already had three arrows in his chest, but he hadn't fallen. Bastards are hard to kill. Tor's hammer knocked him ass over tits, and then your father's lance took him in the throat. That was the end of that."

"Thank you, Baron," Lady Valeria's lips quirked in a smile. "Such colorful language you have."

Trist tried to imagine his father lancing an Exarch through the throat, or gathered around a table just like this one, only with the king himself, and Urien and Tor, all of them so much younger than they were now. It was a surreal feeling. "But they will have learned from last time, and not make the same mistakes," he repeated, after a moment.

"Aye," Urien said. "So, then. If you were going to take this pass, Sir Trist, what would you do?"

Acrasia appeared to lay a hand on his arm, but Trist ignored her and scanned the map on the table. "The pass is the strong point," he said, after some consideration. "We not only have a tower at the southern end, and Falais at the northern end, but the chain over the river and the wall across the pass, gated. Trying to hit us where we are strong is just asking to bleed their way through the mountains. We only have two towers in the mountains, with no wall between them."

"You can't move a large group of soldiers through the mountains," Baroness Arnive said confidently. "It's all hardscrabble and goat paths and crumbling slopes. They'd get lost, or stuck, and our watchers in the towers, or our scouts, would find them."

"Not an army, then," Trist said slowly. "But what about a few men, under cover of night? Either in the mountains, or swimming the river, to come around behind and unlock the gate. Or to hit our archers on the heights from behind. They must know that we will put bowman there, again."

"The guards on the gates?" the Crown Prince asked Dame Chantal.

"Already doubled, Your Royal Highness," she said confidently.

"And once we move up more troops to reinforce the tower, it will be more. No, slipping a few men upriver at night might get past us, but they won't be enough to unlock the gate," Lionel said, still considering.

"Through the hills to the archers, though," Bors said gruffly, clearly unhappy to give Trist credit for anything. "Boy has a good thought, there. Archers won't stand up to a few good men once they get into their ranks. The bowman will panic and run. Wouldn't even take very many, if they have the right kind of men."

"Sir Trist," Lionel Aurelianus said, coming to a decision. "While we move troops up to reinforce the Tower of Tears, I want you to take a small group up into the mountains and look around."

Baroness Arnive shot him a look, and Trist understood that this was what she had been speaking about in the carriage. "The Baroness was kind enough to tell me a bit about the mountains on our way here this evening," he said. "She mentioned that Sir Divdan knew the area well. Might I take him with us?"

"I'm glad to hear that she had time to speak to you," the Crown Prince said deliberately. "Yes. Take your own men, and Sir Divdan. Be on the lookout for any Caliphate skirmishers who have been sent up into the heights. Deal with whatever you find. The

Baroness and Sir Divdan know the best routes for you to take, I believe. You may depart to make your preparations."

Trist bowed. "As you command, your Royal Highness," he said. "Baron Urien, I believe you have some small number of pigeons for Camaret-à-Arden? May I have the use of one, so as to send a response to my wife?"

"Have your squire bring the letter and I'll see it sent," Urien said, already focusing back on the map. Trist backed up three steps, bowed to the Crown Prince again, and left his tent, with Sir Divdan, Yaél, and Acrasia following him.

It was time to find the daemon in the mountains.

Chapter Thirty-Three

REMEMBRANCE

There have been five plagues since the Cataclysm, during which the first is said by contemporary records to have taken fully a third of the population of Narvonne. The second plague took a king, and the fifth a princess. Without fail, each has marked a time of turmoil and change. May we not see another in our lifetimes.

-François du Lutetia, A History of Narvonne

4th Day of the Flower Moon, 297 AC

They found Henry and Luc sitting around the cookfire outside Trist's new tent, spooning pottage out of their bowls with hunks of fresh bread for their supper. "Yaél, get a full belly and then run to pick up your new armor from the smith," Trist said, then turned to Divdan, having made a decision. "We need a horse for the boy."

Sir Divdan looked the squire's skinny arms over, and nodded. "I can bring one from the Baroness' stables. A gelding, nice and gentle. We use him to teach her son." Unspoken between the two knights was the understanding that Yaél would never be able to keep up with the grown men if left to manage on foot.

"Where we off to, then?" Luc asked, around a mouthful of bread.

Henry elbowed him. "Chew before you talk, you big ox. Your pardon, Sir Knight," he apologized to Divdan, who waved it off.

"I'll give you my pardon if you give me a bowl," he said, finding a seat. "We can request supplies from the Prince's men, but we'll be eating rations for the next few days."

"Up into the mountains," Trist answered Luc's question.

"We'll manage on foot, then," Henry said, with a nod. "Hunting southerners?"

"We are," Trist confirmed. He wouldn't tell them the rest of it until they were actually up in the high paths, away from prying ears.

"A daemon like Adrammelech will eat them up like a hawk swooping down on a field mouse," Acrasia warned him, pacing nervously. "And I won't be much help either, my love. I'm still weak."

"I know," he said, with a sigh. "We will speak more of this in the mountains. Henry, we brought a few small rolls of vellum for sending messages, did we not? And a pot of ink and a quill?"

"That we did, m'lord," Henry said, setting his bowl aside and heading into Trist's tent.

"We will load supplies up onto the gelding," Trist continued, thinking out loud. "Leave the destriers free for a charge."

"Liable to break a leg on a charge up in the heights," Divdan cautioned him.

"Yes. Better to have the option, however," Trist said, still ruminating. When Henry returned, he handed Trist the writing supplies. Trist found a seat on one of the logs his men had dragged over, and sat it sideways, so he could use the wooden surface to write on. For a moment, Acrasia paused, and he thought she might sit with him, but then her face turned stony and she vanished. It took Trist long enough to write that Yaél had finished eating and run off to get his armor by the time he was done. The sight of his own chicken-scratches only reminded Trist of how elegant Clarisant's handwriting was, but there was nothing for it now. He looked over his letter one last time.

My lady wife,

I received your letter from your father. Both he and I are well. The Crown Prince is sending me out from the camp tomorrow morning, and I do not know how long it will be before I return. If you do not hear from me for some time, do not think the worst.

I pray that my father recovers his strength. Tell him I have had the story of his victory at the pass from your father and I wish he had told it to me sooner.

I have taken a squire; an orphan boy from Havre de Paix I encountered in my travels.

I pray also for your well-being, and if you are with child, the well being of our son or daughter.

I had a thought that, after the war is won, we might make a trip to Rocher de la Garde, and bathe in the sea there, and sleep on the sand. I remember loving that as a boy, when we visited.

Your loyal husband,

Trist

It seemed to him entirely unsatisfying, reading the message over, but neither could Trist decide what he might add to the letter to improve it. With a sigh, he blew on it gently to help dry the ink, then held it open to the air until Yaél came trudging back, laboring under the weight of his new chain, helm, and gauntlets. The boy had an arming sword strapped to his waist, and was wearing a black padded gambeson that was only a little large on him. Trist almost felt sorry for the squire when, after he finally dropped all of his new things and collapsed onto a log, Trist reached out a hand to offer him the letter.

"Run this over to Baron Urien's tent, then. That is a good lad."

Yaél looked at him with wide-imploring eyes, red in the cheeks and huffing. "You couldn't have sent Henry or Luc?"

"Henry and Luc do not need the exercise," Trist explained, with a smile. "I told you this would be hard. If you think you are tired tonight, wait until after you have ridden all day in armor tomorrow. Off with you, now, and then you can go to bed." The other men around the cook-fire chuckled fondly.

"You're lucky Sir Trist doesn't have a stable," Sir Divdan prodded the boy. "When I was a squire, they made us shovel out the stalls everyday. 'Isn't this what we have stable boys for,' I made the mistake of asking Sir Gaheris once. 'Stable boys don't need enough muscle to cut a man's arm off,' he says to me. 'And just for talking back, go to the blacksmith and help pump the bellows until supper." Divdan shook his head. "I was a right little shit, I was." Everyone laughed again, and this time even Yaél joined in.

Once the boy had gone, Henry said, "He's a good lad. Wasn't sure when you brought him out of the forest, but he does work hard."

"He does," Trist agreed. "He is not the only one who should get a good night's sleep, however."

"Right you are." Sir Divdan rose. "Thank you for the meal, gentlemen. I'll be off to the castle, to pack my things and get one last night on a real mattress." The two knights waved goodbye to each other, and Trist found himself staring into the fire while Henry and Luc cleaned up. The coals and flames blazed with the same colors he could see in glimpses of Acrasia's true form: red and orange and yellow, and sometimes almost white where it burnt the very hottest.

Trist was still sitting there on the log when the moon had risen high above, and the cookfire had died down to glowing coals. He was a bit surprised that Acrasia had not appeared since he had finished writing the letter, and he wondered if he might get a night of sleep alone, after all. An owl cried out somewhere nearby; it must have had good hunting, he thought, with all the mice that would try to get into the grain stores.

"I see that you cannot find sleep, either," Crown Prince Lionel Aurelianus observed, striding out of the gloom.

Trist rose to make a bow, but the Prince waved him back down with one hand. "Your Royal Highness," he said. "I did not expect you this evening. I apologize, but we do not have anything better than a few logs to sit on and a skin of wine."

"That will do well enough," Lionel said, sitting down on the log opposite from where Trist settled back down. "I wanted to tell you that you did well today. First, to hold what Baroness Arnive told you close to the chest, and then to take the lead I gave you, and propose a reason to go into the mountains. I know that I have thrown you into deep waters, and for that I apologize. But I said it before, and I meant it: I will use you as I must for the good of this kingdom."

Trist exhaled, gathering his thoughts. "I cannot truly object," he said, after a moment. "Especially after how you spoke for me in spite of Sir Bors. If you had not, I believe that I would be a dead man already."

"I couldn't let that young wife of yours be widowed twice over, could I?" Lionel said with a grin, and Trist let an answering smile come to his face. "Exarch Bors is a fearsome fighter, but he lacks the sort of graces that are required at court. Disdains them, actually, which is why father sent him with me. No one wants him around back at Cheverny, I am afraid. Speaking of your wife - you wrote her, I hope?"

"I did." Trist nodded. "Had my squire run the letter over to Baron Urien before I sent him to bed. I imagine the pigeon is well on its way to Camaret-à-Arden."

"Good." The Prince stared into the coals, which cast his face in shadow. "Take a piece of advice from me, Trist. You will never understand how much you truly have until it is taken from you. Hold her close while you can, for nothing in this world is forever."

Trist thought of Percy, and of Clarisant's words about his father's failing health. "You sound as if you have personal experience of loss," he ventured after a moment.

The Prince was silent a moment. "You lived through the plague, thirteen years ago," he observed. "What would you have been? Ten? Twelve?"

"Nine," Trist said, without hesitation. As if he could ever forget.

"By the Angelus, you are young." Lionel shook his head. "I was eighteen, and just married. Gwen and I were hoping for our first child, but it was too soon to be certain. We'd had reports of plague in Champs d'Or, but no one realized that it had spread to Lutetia yet. A dozen people took sick that day, I learned later, but the only one I cared about was Gwen. I woke in our bed to find her hot and soaked in sweat. At first, I hoped it was something else."

"And then the boils start to swell up," Trist said softly.

"Aye." The Prince looked up from the fire, to Trist's face. "Who was it for you?"

"My mother," Trist admitted, swallowing back a sudden urge to weep. Not in front of the Prince, he promised himself.

"Lady Cecilia." Lionel sighed. "I knew that she'd passed at some point since the war, but I hadn't realized it was from the plague that year. My apologies, Trist."

"No need, Your Royal Highness," Trist said, shaking his head. "I was just a boy. The years... they've dulled it, somewhat. You lost your wife." He didn't have to ask: it was clear from the Prince's voice.

"I did," he admitted. "My father has been after me to wed ever since, and I fear I cannot put him off much longer."

"It seems to me," Trist said cautiously, "That the Lady Valeria would be amenable."

"Aye," Lionel confirmed. "That she would. And Valeria may well get what she wants." He shook himself, and rose. "But that is a matter for another day. I wanted to wish you well, if I do not see you off tomorrow morning. By the time you make it back to us, it may be that you need to make use of your own best judgment. I cannot say what state the battle will be in by then. You have good instincts: use them."

"Thank you, your Royal Highness," Trist said, rising. The Crown Prince took two steps around the embers of the cookfire, and offered his hand. Trist took it, and for a moment they clasped hands alone in the night.

"Until next we meet," Lionel Aurelianus said.

"Angelus be with you," Trist responded, and then they parted ways, each to find what sleep they could before dawn.

Chapter Thirty-Four

The Hauteurs Massif

Nor was it only by making Accord with Exarchs that the Angelus aided us against the daemons of the Cataclysm. They taught men to be their priests: to raise churches to them, to see the daemons who were not always visible to mortal men, and to bind our adversaries with prayer. Those days were the beginning of the Church of the Angelus.
-François du Lutetia, A History of Narvonne

5th Day of the Flower Moon, 297 AC

Trist tugged on Yaél's sword belt, then nodded in satisfaction. "Good. How does the mail feel?"

The squire shifted in the dim light just before dawn. "Heavy?"

"You'll feel it in your back by the time night comes," Sir Divdan said with a smile. It was clear that he was the sort of knight who was entertained by watching a young squire go through the same harsh training he'd endured - a rite of passage.

Trist looked around. "Everyone is ready?" he asked. He'd checked the saddlebags himself: they had cheese, salted meat, and hardtack, enough to last for days, mostly loaded onto the gelding from the Baroness' stables. He was counting on Henry taking a rabbit or quail here or there with his bow, as well. In turn, the men and the boy nodded. Trist and Divdan each placed a boot in the stirrup of their respective destriers and swung up into the saddle; they both were wearing only a shirt of rings, with the rest of their armor packed. Yaél got a boost from Luc. Bill, the gelding, accepted a rider with the placid calm of an animal who'd been carrying children around in circles for years.

Sir Divdan turned his destrier - Charger - about and led the procession west out of the camp, pointed in the direction of the stars with the light of dawn at their backs. Most of the camp was still asleep, but the guards set to watch the perimeter and the horse lines gave them all salutes and nods as they passed.

"Good hunting, Exarch!" one guard called, and Trist gave a wave.

"I will never get used to this," he confessed to Divdan once they had passed and were safely out of earshot. The two knights rode abreast at the front, now they were out of the camp, with Yaél on Bill behind them, and Henry and Luc bringing up the rear on foot. They kept the horses to a walk.

"You will," Divdan assured him. "That's the thing about being human. We can get used to anything, given time. Imagine how they felt after the fall of the Old Empire, and the Cataclysm? All you've got to put up with is a bit of renown and people knowing your name."

"Small in comparison," Trist agreed.

Sir Divdan led them past a handful of farms and to one of the streams that tumbled down out of the mountains to feed into the Durentia, the river that cut its way through the Hauteurs Massif, forming the Passe de Mûre. There was a path along the edge of the stream where lavender grew wild among the brush, and here they had to proceed in a line, single file, because there was no room for more. The land rose, and the stream tumbled down over rocky falls into occasional pools or wide, stony beds. There were trees to either side: oak and olive and bay, and even the occasional pine or maple. Once, Trist rounded the bend of the trail to come face to face with a great eagle-owl, watching him as he passed.

By the time the sun was up, they were well and truly climbing, up into the hills, where they saw small clusters of white sheet and goats cropping the grass of the heights. When they stopped for dinner just around mid-day, Trist judged they were now far enough away from the camp, the village, and anyone who might overhear that he could share the truth of their mission.

They'd tied the horses' reins to a low hanging oak branch, and sat on a rocky outcropping that leaned out twenty feet or more above the stream. The hot sun warmed the rock, and made for a pleasant place to cut into the first wheel of cheese, and pair it with a bit of salted goat meat.

"This is northern cheese," Sir Divdan sighed. "Not our local stuff."

"What's the difference?" asked Yaél. At least he was learning to swallow before talking, Trist reflected.

"Goat cheese is soft," Divdan explained. "You get your dagger, see? And you spread it over the hardtack. This is all hard and crumbly. Nice and sharp, though," he admitted.

Trist took a swallow of watered wine from his flask to wet his throat. "Now we are away from camp," he began, raising his voice slightly to catch everyone's attention, "I can tell you the rest of what the Prince has sent us to do."

"There's more than hunting southerners?" Luc asked, frowning, and Henry elbowed him for the interruption.

"There is," Trist said. "The Prince and the Baroness want us to check on something. A binding," he said, and noticed that for the first time since the evening before, Acrasia was now visible, sitting at the edge of the rock where she could dangle her feet and kick them in the air. The sunlight through her blonde tresses made her hair light up, and he had to blink and look away to pull his thoughts back together. "I am told it is not wise to say the name of the daemon very often," he said, and glanced back between Divdan and Acrasia for help.

"He's also been called the Prince of Plagues," Acrasia said, and Trist thought that enough to work with.

"The Prince of Plagues, then," he said, nodding to the fairie maid. "Bound here in the mountains since the time of King Aurelius."

Divdan looked over Trist's men. "You pledged your secrecy," he reminded Trist.

"Aye, my discretion," Trist confirmed. "Look around, Sir Divdan. These are the men we have. They need to know what we are facing. What they will be facing. Either of us could fall along the way, and the knowledge die with us."

The local knight chewed on it a moment, then nodded. "I suppose it is only right you all know the manner of evil you face. It has been the duty, ever since the fall of the first King of Narvonne, for the Barons of the Hauteurs Massif to protect the binding, and guard against the daemon waking," Sir Divdan said, all traces of his normal humor gone. "Three years past, I accompanied my liege with a small group to check the bindings. I am the only one who survived that journey."

"They were all killed by the daemon?" Yaél's eyes were wide.

"I never saw the daemon," Divdan admitted, after a moment, staring down at the bare rock they were all sitting on. Trist saw that Acrasia was now standing above the other knight, staring down at him as if she were a hawk and Divdan a mouse.

"We followed the stairs down under the mountain," Divdan said, and Trist recalled this part of the story from their ride in the Baroness' carriage. "Steps carved into the rock."

"You said everything around it was dead," Trist prodded him. "All the trees, the grass."

"Yes." Divdan nodded. "Two hundred steps. We'll have to leave the horses at the top of the stair. I brought an iron spike to drive into the earth; I don't trust those dead trees. When I came three years ago, we tied our horses to a branch, and they were all gone when I got back. The branch had broken. If I'd had a horse, Baron Owain might have survived."

"We drive the spike, tie the horses, and go down the stairs," Trist confirmed, nodding. "You said there was a lake at the bottom."

Divdan coughed, and Henry passed him a flask of watered-wine. Once the knight had gulped down a mouthful, he was able to speak again, though he did not raise his eyes. "A lake with lights in it. Like fireflies. When we stepped closer, some of the lights rose up out of the water, and floated in the air. We didn't know what they were."

Trist glanced up to where Acrasia was standing. Whatever else was between them, he needed her knowledge of the daemonic if they were all to survive this quest. "I need to see it," she said, meeting his eyes. "It could be a lot of things. My guess is that the lights were the physical manifestation of Adrammelech's power, reaching up out of the bindings."

"What happened next?" Yaél asked, hanging on the tale as if it was a fireside ghost story instead of their very near future.

"One of the lights touched Aglovale," Divdan said. "Sir Aglovale of Dawn Spire. He screamed, like he'd been run through with a blade, and fell to the cavern floor. Baron Owain ran over to help him, and... his armor was falling off. Not just the armor," he explained, finally raising his eyes to look around at the men and the boy who were listening to his tale. "But the flesh beneath, too. Like a snake shedding its skin. Or like... an overripe fruit bursting. Angelus above, the screaming just went on and on, while the rest of us tried to avoid the lights. When it was done, there was just a pile of meat, and pus, and armor, with something stirring beneath."

"It shook itself like a duck shaking off water on the river," Divdan recalled, and from his eyes Trist thought he was no longer aware of where he was, or who was with him. The older knight was lost in the horror he'd experienced three years ago. "Blood and pus and black… stuff, I don't know what it was, flew everywhere. The smell - like an open latrine. And then it spread its wings. Like a great hawk, but with the long neck of a serpent. It leapt at Brutus, and ripped his throat out in a single move. It must have had teeth, instead of a beak, but I couldn't get a good look. Baron Owain drew his blade and swung at it, and then it was on him, ripping with its talons. I'm ashamed to say I didn't jump in until that moment." Sir Divdan laughed. "I'd pissed myself, though, I remember that."

"Did steel hurt it?" Acrasia asked Trist. "We need to know."

"Your blades," Trist asked Divdan. "Did they draw blood?"

"They drew something," the older knight said. "I do not know if I would call that mess blood. But we killed it, yes, the two of us. Not before my liege was torn half to pieces. You know the rest," he said to Trist. "I carried him up the stairs, and down the mountain again. He did not survive."

"That's good," Acrasia said. "The others can keep the birds off you, if it comes to that."

"Better if there are no birds," Trist told her. "We go in fully armored," he said, making up his mind. "If you do not have a gorget," he looked at Yaél, Henry and Luc, "We are going to make one for you out of leather. Pieces of saddle or belt. Whatever we have. We start tonight when we make camp. No one is getting their throat ripped out."

Henry nodded. "I think we can make that happen. We brought a few tools to repair a girth strap or a stirrup if we needed to."

"We know to look out for the lights," Trist continued. "No one lets a light touch you. All we have to do is confirm that the daemon is still held, not free. Either way, we look, and then we leave. If the bindings hold, we go back and tell the Baroness and the Crown Prince."

"If the daemon is free, we run like we're on fire, and pray to the Angelus," Divdan muttered.

The rest of the men nodded, even Yaél, but Trist remained silent. He looked down at his sword, remembering the fight against the daemon Addanc at the lake. When he looked up, Acrasia's eyes were hard as steel.

"Do not fight it, Trist," she begged, but he couldn't bring himself to make a promise he was not certain he could keep.

Chapter Thirty-Five

The Red Veil

It is said, among the wise, that like daemons the ghūls were once Angelus. They did not betray their purpose entirely, as the daemons did, but instead grew too greedy. They wanted only Tithes of souls, but did not care for the war between daemon and Angelus, saying that it was no concern of theirs. They were exiled to our world as punishment, when the Cataclysm was over, and any who sought to leave struck down by comets. Now, they haunt the wasted places of the world, shape-changers and tempters who lure the foolish and the unwary into misfortune...
-The Commentaries of Aram ibn Bashear

5th Day of the Flower Moon, 297 AC

The Narvonnian scout died on his knees, coughing up blood, and Ismet ibnah Salah shook his corpse off her spear, letting it fall to the ground. An appropriate posture for a man who licked the boot of a mortal king, instead of honoring the Angelus. A rush of power flowed through her, and she could hear the beat of wings in the back of her mind as Epinoia took the Tithe. "Did any escape?" Ismet asked, raising her voice to the lancers who had accompanied her into a grove of olive trees just south of the Tower of Tears.

"All are accounted for, Exarch," Fazil ibn Asad assured her. He was young, her second, as young as her, and the son of the chief of an important oasis town far to the south of here. His older brother had already taken a team of scouts ahead into the mountains, she knew, and the General had asked her to look out for him.

"Well done," she praised her lancers. "Now, with me. I want a look at the pass."

"May I remind the Exarch that Narvonnian longbows are notorious for their range," Fazil said, quietly, spurring his mare to ride level with her.

"I recall," Ismet said. "We will not close the distance. I only want to see it for myself, before we lay siege to it. The General has been here before; I have not."

They turned their horses out of the grove, back onto the northward road, and shortly after around a rocky outcropping as tall as a building. There, Ismet reined Layla in. Like Fazil, she rode a mare: one of the desert breed, not as large as a Narvonnian knight's destrier would be, but quick on her feet, intelligent, and loyal as a hound.

"There it is," Fazil said quietly, shaking his head. "To think of how many good men died trying to take that pass... I only pray to the Angelus it is not haunted."

"Mortal men do not become ghūls." Ismet narrowed her eyes, examining the fortification carefully, looking for anything that would help her when it came time to seize the pass. The Tower of Tears was built of the same stone as the wall across the pass: sandstone, like so many of the rock faces in this area. While the wall was only perhaps twenty feet high, with a crenelated parapet for the northern archers to shoot from, the tower was much higher. It rose from the end of the wall opposite the River Durentia, round and not square, the better to withstand stones from a siege engine. She estimated it must be nearly a hundred yards high, with thin windows in the stone only toward the top. Above the windows, the tower flared outward to a crenelated crown, from which Ismet guessed the commander of the garrison would observe the forthcoming battle. A great chain stretched across the river from the end of the wall, and past all the fortifications Ismet could see the heights, where archers had shot down from the cliffs twenty-four years ago and slaughtered an army.

"Can we take it, Exarch?" Fazil asked her. Ismet noticed, not for the first time, how thin his beard was.

"Of course," she answered. "They are only Narvonnian, Fazil ibn Asad. They turned away from the true way of the Angelus long ago. A generation past, they won through trickery and a lack of honor. That will not see the northerners through a second time."

The pounding of hooves up the road caught Ismet's ear, and she turned Layla about. A messenger, wearing no armor and riding at a gallop. Ismet waited for the man to pull up.

"Ismet ibnah Salah, Exarch of Epinoia?" the messenger asked. His horse was nearly blown out; he must have ridden all up and down the line of march, searching for her.

"You have my attention, messenger," she said simply.

"The general must speak with you," the man said. "He requests you return to the column immediately."

"Then I shall do so." Ismet raised her lance, and Layla pawed at the dirt of the road. "Back!" she cried to her men. "Back to the army! We have killed enough northerners for today!" The men cheered, and when she kicked Layla to a gallop, they followed her south down the road.

General Shadi ibn Yusuf, Exarch of Jibrīl, rode at the center of the van, just behind the outriders. His guard of Mamluks, trained from birth to be his family's personal protectors, made way for Ismet. If the two Exarchs fought each other - not that either would dare defy the will of the Angelus in such a way - no mortal would be able to stop either of them, in any event.

"General," Ismet greeted him as she guided Layla to walk abreast of his horse. "We destroyed another unit of northern scouts. I am told you requested my presence?"

"Just so," Shadi said, greeting her with a smile. "More Tithes for the Angelus, is it? Good. We need you well and truly blooded before we attack the wall."

"I caught sight of it," she admitted. "The army should reach it by nightfall, I would judge."

Shadi nodded. "As we have planned. And yet, complications and obstacles are placed in our path. Nothing can ever be simple."

"The Narvonnians seem content to hide behind their walls," she said. "Aside from scouts. I have not found any of their knights in our path."

"I do not speak of knights." The general glanced to their right, then to their left, and then lowered his voice so that Ismet had to ride a step closer, their horses nearly touching, in order to hear his words clearly. "Do you remember our reason for coming north, Exarch? This is no mere war of conquest."

"I remember your words in the garden," Ismet assured him. "You told me that what was once bound, is now stirring. That daemons wake, and the northerners are blind to it."

"I feel them, now," Shadi ibn Yusuf told her. "Jibrīl whispers in my ear, but even without an Angelus to tell me, I think I would know it. There." He pointed not in the direction of the Tower of Tears or the pass, but up into the mountains. "Something ancient and evil is rising there. I can see it, like the glow of the rising sun, or a great fire at night, just over the horizon - the camps of an army, burning. Can you see it, yet?"

Ismet squinted at the mountains. "I see nothing but trees on the heights," she admitted. "Snow on some of the higher peaks, I think."

"You are still young, and new to such things. It is not a failing," the general assured her. "In time, you will grow used to seeing as I do. The Angelus will help you learn. For now, it seems, you will have to rely upon Epinoia to guide you."

"Into the mountains?" Ismet frowned. "Would I not be of more use to you taking the pass?"

"A siege is no quick thing," General Shadi pointed out. "We will still be here by the time you return; if not at the southern end of the pass, at the northern end. Do not forget we must take the town of Falais, as well, and the castle there. Only after we take both ends of the pass will the way into Narvonne be open to us."

"As you say, General." Ismet inclined her head. He had much more experience than she did, after all.

"You will take your men," Shadi ibn Yusuf explained, "Through the foothills and up into the heights. You have my permission to strike enemy troops you find at your discretion. I trust your judgment, and you have given me no reason to doubt you thus far. But that is not your true purpose."

"No," he continued. "Above all, you must follow the guidance of the Angelus. Find whatever is rising in those mountains. If you can destroy it yourself, then do so, and return to us. If it is beyond you, then you must come and tell me what you have learned. If need be you and I will face this threat together, after we have secured the pass. Do you understand?"

"I do." Ismet bowed her head again, thankful that the red veil hid her grin. Finally! A chance to strike a blow against the daemonic itself.

General Shadi frowned. "I must urge you to use caution, Exarch," he said, quietly. "I recall all too well the confidence of youth. The last thing I need is you dead up in those hills, leaving me blind and deaf to whatever struck you down."

"I understand," she assured him. "If I can handle the threat safely, I will. But first I will send a messenger back to you. If we are outmatched, we will retreat. You have my promise that I will not disappoint you, General."

The older man held her eyes for a long moment, then nodded. "Good. Hone your weapons now, Exarch. Collect your Tithes. I need you the best you can be for the campaigns to come. Rest your horses, pack your supplies, and leave at first light."

Ismet pulled Layla's head away, and wheeled back to ride alongside the column of troops. She found Fazil and the rest of her riders where they'd fallen in, just behind the van. "Good news!" She greeted her lancers. "The General has orders for us. Take the rest of the ride to catch your breath. Tonight, pack your saddlebags with as much food as you can carry. Tomorrow at dawn, we go up into the mountains."

"Good girl," Ismet crooned to Layla. The eastern sky was light, but she could not yet see the sun. She was already wearing her armor and her red veil, and the mare was just eating oats from her hand. She ran her hand over Laya's soft nose.

"The men are ready," Fazil ibn Asad reported, leading his own horse over to her. Ismet looked back, counting the men who'd gathered to ride with her. Twenty, in total, all with lances, shields, bows, and either axes or scimitars. Her men. Ismet patted Layla one last time, brushed the remains of the oats off her palm, stepped a boot into one stirrup, and hauled herself up into the saddle.

"Today," she addressed her men, "We ride into the heights. We ride at the call of the Angelus. Our mission is from the General himself, under the guidance of the Angelus Jibrīl! Will you fail them?"

"No!" the men cried, Fazil grinning over that barely-grown beard.

"Come then!" She urged Layla on, and the mare tore off away from the camp, toward the heights of the Hauteurs Massif.

Whatever it was up there in the mountains, she was going to kill it. Ismet ibnah Salah was an Exarch of the Angelus, and nothing could stand in her way.

Chapter Thirty-Six

SINS OF THE FATHER

...and furthermore, funds from the royal treasury to be allocated for the raising of three towers in the Hauteurs Massif, so as to secure the mountains against attack from the south. These to be raised of local stone, and wages fairly paid to the workers of the Barony, at the generosity of the crown.
-Royal Order of King Aurelius of Narvonne, 14 AC

7th Day of the Flower Moon, 297 AC

On their third day into the mountains, Trist and his companions found a group of Caliphate scouts.

As near as he could tell, Sir Divdan had been leading the group west by southwest, through the foothills and then up into the heights. They'd followed the stream for all of the first day, and then forded it mid-morning on the second before cutting further south, in the general direction of Dawn Spire.

"Why's it called Dawn Spire," Yaél had asked as they left the sound of the stream behind, "If it's the middle tower? Sun rises in the east, so wouldn't you name the eastern tower that?"

"Dawn Spire is the highest tower," Divdan explained. "Not that it's any taller than the rest, but it's built at the highest elevation. They say you can see the first rays of the sun come over the horizon there, before anywhere else in the Barony."

"I'd like to see that," Luc said, and everyone turned. The big man was usually the quietest member of the party, and he flushed at the attention. "I mean, it just seems it would be something. To stand at the top of the tower, at the top of a mountain, with the stars above you and the land dark beneath, and see the very first light..."

"Perhaps we will stop to resupply there, if our mission takes us close enough," Trist offered, and they continued on.

It was Yaél who caught sight of the enemy first; the boy had been clambering up and down the rocky heights as if he was a goat himself, poking into everything that caught his interest. They were following a game trail along the crest of a great ridge, that dropped off a cliff to their right, with wildflowers growing scattered all around, when he hissed. "Trist! Trist!" the squire jabbed a finger down, and when Trist brought a hand up to shield his eyes from the sun, and followed the gesture, he saw a mounted party riding far below.

"Good eyes, Yaél," he praised the boy, when they'd all reined in and looked down. "How many can you make out?"

Yaél slid down a treacherous slope of loose earth and crept to the edge of the cliff. Trist was surprised to feel a sudden jab of panic in his belly, but Henry half followed the squire and grabbed a hold of his sword belt from the back, and the trunk of a sapling with his other hand. "I've got him, m'lord," he assured Trist.

"Five, I think," Yaél said, after a moment. "I don't think they've seen us, neither."

"Let us keep it that way," Trist said. "Come on back from the edge to be certain." He was able to breathe easier once Henry judged it safe enough to let go his hold of the boy's belt. "Sir Divdan," Trist turned to the knight, who alone among them knew the highlands well. "Can you tell where they are headed? Can we intercept them?"

"I'll be damned if I see how they got past the three towers," Divdan said with a scowl. "I'll give those garrison boys a piece of my mind next time I see them. Anyway, the southerners look to be cutting back east. Trying to find a route to the heights above the pass, like you thought."

"Is there a place we can bar their path?" Trist asked, again.

"Well," Divdan said, considering. "If they keep on like they are, they'll end up in the ravine that leads to Leatherman's Cave."

"Can you get us there before them?" Trist asked. A ravine would be good; five on horse outnumbered their group, and Trist had only recently been taught a lesson about just how difficult it could be, even for an Exarch, to deal with superior numbers.

"Aye," Divdan said, after a moment. "Tie your horses up, and follow me, then." Trist and Yaél looped their reins around the branches of a convenient maple, and the party took just long enough to get Divdan and Trist armored. The young squire was starting to get a better feel for how to strap Trist into his plate, and Henry gave Sir Divdan a hand. The two knights went with only pieces, instead of donning their full set: cuirasses, pauldrons and vambraces, over the chain shirts they'd already been wearing, but they left off their greaves and helms for the run through the wooded heights. The other three all tied on their new-made leather neck-stocks in place of gorgets.

"We'll be splashing through a stream or two," Divdan shouted as he took off, leading the way down slope away from where the ridge fell away to the land below in a sheer cliff. Trist batted branches away from his face, skidding through thick drifts of dead leaves as he careened downhill, grabbing the trunk of a sapling to help him turn in Sir Divdan's wake. Behind him, Henry moved like a wildcat, bow held in his left hand, as if this run was the most natural thing in the world. He shortly passed Trist, in fact, as they swung left.

Trist didn't mind that, so much; as long as he could keep sight of either Henry or Divdan, he wouldn't get lost. He was more worried about leaving Yaél or Luc behind. The young squire had begun at a sprint, a wide grin on his face, and even passed Trist with Henry for a short while, but he still wasn't used to extended exertions, and shortly was falling behind again, red-faced and panting.

"Breathe like this," Trist called to him as he came up even with the boy. He huffed out twice with his steps, then stuck in. "Out, out, in." Yaél nodded, but Trist didn't want to risk losing the boy, so he slowed his steps.

Luc, on the other hand, never once got out in front of him. The big man's long stride might have helped him were they running on a flat road, but skidding through the leaves downhill past trees and brambles on every side, the man was like a lumbering, half-dead bear. He swayed back and forth, when Trist risked a glimpse behind to check on him, as if drunk and wildly off balance. Once, he slammed into a tree, shook himself, and kept going.

"Stream!" Henry called back. Trist couldn't even hear Divdan, now, but with the warning he saw it in time: a cut through the earth, grassy on either bank, perhaps a foot or a foot and a half down, and maybe two across. Trist planted his right boot a few inches back from the edge and pushed off without slowing, vaulting the stream and landing easily on the other side. Next to him, Yaél landed too close to the edge of the bank, and it crumbled beneath his weight. The boy's arms windmilled for balance, and Trist grabbed his arm without thinking, yanking him forward.

"You alright?" Trist panted, and at Yaél's pale nod, they took off again. Behind them, he heard splashing and a curse from Luc, and ahead he could barely see Henry. They followed the hunter down a terrace of alternating rocky outcroppings, and thinly soiled, mossy patches of ground with the occasional skinny tree, clutching the rock with a knot of roots like an old man's gnarled hand.

Trist was moving like he never had before, the red threads laced through his body pulsing and beating with power. Even in armor, he was breathing hard but not out of breath, and his boots fell exactly where he meant them to. He leapt down three feet of rock, caught the trunk of a sapling in his left hand, and pushed off again before the moss could tear under his weight. Finally, he skidded to a halt at the bottom of a ravine, to find Henry and Sir Devan bent double, both heaving for breath. With a yelp, Yaél tumbled down after them, landing on his side. Thankfully, Trist observed, not the left side, on which the boy wore his arming sword. The young squire gave a moan, and Trist let him lay there for a moment.

"Henry," he said, and the hunter looked up, red in the face. "Find yourself a perch. Cover us, but do not take a shot unless they attempt something unchivalrous." Henry nodded, sucked a mouthful of watered wine from his flask, and then made his way over to the edge of the ravine, where he began climbing. Trist risked a glance up the way they'd come, and saw Luc carefully lumbering his way down. The big man turned around, as he watched, and dangled his legs over a stretch of sheer rock, scooting backwards until most of his body was over the edge, then finally letting himself fall the last foot or so.

"Which way will they be coming from?" Trist asked Sir Divdan, who pointed down the slope of the ravine. Trist nodded, took a drink from his own flask, and then picked his spot. He found a patch of good ground: bare dirt, and mostly smooth, without much in the way of roots or stones. There, Trist rolled his head a few times, stretched his back until it popped, and shook his shoulders out. He should be exhausted after a run like that, but he wasn't.

"The Fae Touched Boon," Acrasia reminded him, having found a place to perch in the curve of a low hanging oak bough. Her bare feet swung beneath her, and he looked away from the smooth, pale skin of her calves where her dress had bunched up. "You can feel it? It lets you run like the stag, or the wolf, swift and tireless."

"The moment I have enough Tithes," Trist commented to her. "I will strengthen it." Then, he drew his longsword and planted it before him, tip down in the earth, with one hand on the leather-wrapped hilt and the other on the pommel.

That was how he was standing when five Caliphate lancers rounded the curve of the ravine, coming uphill toward him. They all wore caps that reminded him of onions, with scarves of various colors. Their hauberks were not any type of mail common in the Kingdom of Narvonne, he observed, but of the kind his father had referred to as lamellar: they looked like someone had cut small, uniform rectangles of metal and laid them against each other. More of the same hung down their thighs, attached at the waist he guessed, but overall they were more lightly armored than he would have expected. Certainly not as heavily armored as a Narvonnian knight in full plate. They carried lances, but also a quiver of arrows each on their backs and a horse bow, and Trist saw that they also had round shields and curved swords.

"Hold!" Trist called out to them, as their horses drew closer. The breed was smaller than the destiers he was used to, and he doubted they would match up to a charge of fully armored knights. "You have come armed for war into the Kingdom of Narvonne. Turn back and return to your home in peace, I beg you."

Now was the test, he knew. If the southerners kicked their horses and charged forward, Trist was going to have to dive aside for his life. Things would go badly, then. Instead, the lancers drew rein, and their horses stopped perhaps twenty feet from Trist.

"And who is it that stands in our way?" the leader said, riding another step forward, just enough to be in front of the pack. Trist was glad enough that the man spoke Narvonnian, and more impressed that his accent was mild.

"I am Sir Trist du Camaret-à-Arden," he called, raising his voice, "Sworn man of the Baron of Rocher de la Garde, and here on the order of Lionel Aurelianus, Crown Prince of Narvonne. I have the honor to be the Exarch of the Lady Acrasia, of the Court of Shadows."

A second man spurred forward. "You say you come from Camaret-à-Arden?" he called forth, words heavily accented. "Do you know Sir Rience, the Butcher of the Pass?"

That was the first time Trist had ever heard that phrase. He wondered if his father was even aware of it. "Sir Rience du Camaret-à-Arden is my father," he said simply. "And a good and honorable man."

"Then I am for you, sir," the second man shouted, jerking the head of his mount around in anger. "I am Alī ibn Yaqūt, and my father died in the mud beneath the Tower of Tears. This day, I will avenge him."

Chapter Thirty-Seven

A Tithe for the Shadow King

Exarchs: 8,000 pieces of silver
Priests: 2,000 pieces of silver
Barons: 500 pieces of silver
Knights: Between 50 and 500 pieces of silver
Squires and other valuable servants: up to 50 pieces of silver
-From a list of recommended ransoms published by the Church of the Angelus, 214 AC

7th Day of the Flower Moon, 297 AC

"Are you certain?" Trist called in response. He had not expected his father's name to cause trouble on the Prince's mission. The southerner dismounted and handed the reins of his horse to one of his companions. "Whatever passed between our fathers, there is no shame if you turn aside from facing an Exarch, Alī ibn Yaqūt."

"Just kill him already," Acrasia said, with a pout. "You're going to need every Tithe you can get before we go mucking about with Adramelech."

Alī shrugged out of his quiver, and handed over both that and his horse bow to another of the Caliphate soldiers. "There may be no shame," he said, "But there is also much glory in slaying an Exarch of the Narvonnians. How many lives will be lost if I allow the son of a butcher to walk away from this place?" He settled his round shield onto his left arm, and drew his curved sword; neither were the sort of thing Trist was practiced at facing. "If you have a shield, Sir Trist, lift it now," the southerner warned him.

"No shield," Trist said, lifting his longsword up and spinning it until he held the weapon above his head, tip pointed to the sky, in High Guard. "I salute your courage, Alī ibn Yaqūt."

For a moment, there was no sound but the wind rustling the leaves of the oaks above, then his sweaty hair; no feeling but the hot sun in Trist's face, the pulsing of his own blood shooting through his body; no taste, but the fresh mountain air he sucked in with each breath.

Alī ibn Yaqūt slid forward, boots scuffing the bare earth of the pass, shield high with his scimitar held out to his right side. Trist waited for him, judging the distance. The moment the southerner moved into his range, Trist lunged forward, his own footwork instinctual after years upon years of drilling in the practice yard under Master of Arms Granger. Alī's eyes widened; he had underestimated how far and how fast Trist could move, and, off balance, he tried to backpedal. But to Trist's enhanced reflexes, the other man seemed to be moving as slowly as a leaf drifting down the River Rea.

Trist watched Alī begin to lift his shield up and to his left, to protect his head from the descending cut he anticipated that Trist would make. Instead, Trist dashed low and wide beneath the shield, slicing an arc that cut the back of the man's thigh with the last inch of his blade. Trist spun: he had plenty of time to parry the southerner's return stroke with a crooked cut, knocking the scimitar's tip down almost into the dirt with a sharp clang of impact.

With the scimitar out of line and the other man off balance, the only thing in Trist's way was the round wooden shield, which Alī had allowed to drop a bit as he made his cut. Faster than anyone but an Exarch could react to, Trist spun his sword up, almost passing through High Guard for a split second, then cut down again. His longsword clove the top two inches of the wooden shield off, throwing splinters in every direction, and continued on into Alī's upper bicep.

It was a perfect cut: Trist could feel the edge align with the angle of the swing, and his hands moved on the hilt of his sword to drive the last few inches of his blade to maximum speed. He knew what was going to happen before it did. It was just like practicing on a slaughtered pig in the yard back at home.

The tip of his blade, the length of a man's hand, sliced through the laminate hauberk as if it wasn't even there, continued through Alī's skin and muscle, and then through the bone itself.

The arm and the shield fell to the dirt, blood spraying from the ragged stump left attached to the southerner's torso. Trist's training had him drawing the blade back and taking a step away from Alī, before he'd even finished processing what had just happened. The Caliphate soldier staggered for just a moment, color draining from his face, then fell, his scimitar dropping from limp fingers. Trist thrust his sword into the ground and left it wavering there, standing up from the dirt, while he rushed to the fallen man's side.

"You fought bravely, Alī ibn Yaqūt," Trist said, cradling the man's head. There was no way the man would survive a wound like that, up here in the mountains. There was no one to treat him; perhaps if they'd had a fire already built, they could have closed the stump with a hot iron, but there was no time. Alī's blood continued to spurt from the wound, soaking the ground.

"First your father killed mine," Alī muttered. "Fitting... Angelus take me." Trist guessed the man was about the same age as Percy had been. He wondered whether there was a wife or a sister, somewhere south of the mountains, to weep over him.

Trist swallowed, and bowed his head as the light left the southerner's eyes. He felt the jolt of Alī ibn Yaqūt's soul leaving his body, now a Tithe.

"This one is the King's," Acrasia said, suddenly beside him, her cool hand on the back of his neck. Trist wanted to bury his face in her hair. He wanted to scream. This man hadn't been a criminal, preying on orphans. He wasn't a daemon. He was just a soldier trying to do right by his homeland, by his dead father, and by the Angelus. It seemed so stupid a reason to be killed.

"I can see that your words were truly spoken," the leader of the four remaining lancers said, gravely. "Trist, Exarch of Acrasia, Knight of Narvonne. It is clear that mortal men such as we cannot stand against you. You have our surrender, and I ask your mercy for my men." He kneeled, turned his scimitar around, and offered it to Trist.

"Shhh, my love," Acrasia murmured, wrapping her arms around him. Sir Divdan stepped forward.

"Your name, Sir," he asked the Caliphate commander.

" I am Shīrkūh ibn Asad," the man said, keeping his head lowered. Voiceless and feeling sick, Trist watched Divdan accept the scimitar by the hilt.

"We accept this blade in token of your surrender, Shīrkūh ibn Asad," Divdan said, pronouncing the strange sounds with more ease than Trist would have managed. "Now, we must trust in your honor. With your surrender, you are Exarch Trist's prisoners, until you are ransomed by your families. We will have your oath, by the Angelus, that you will not seek to escape."

"And you have it," Shīrkūh said, waving for his men to dismount. "I am grateful for your mercy."

"We cannot take you with us," Trist said finally, shrugging Acrasia off of him and rising. "We have a greater quest to complete, which I am sworn not to speak of unless in the most dire need. You will descend out of the mountains and go to the Crown Prince's encampment at Falais. There, you will surrender yourselves as prisoners. You will inform them who it was captured you, and that you have comported yourselves as honorable men, and may be ransomed as such."

"As you say." Shīrkūh bin Asad looked down at the body of his former companion. "And the remains of Alī ibn Yaqūt?"

"Take him with you," Trist decided. "On his horse. And give him what burial and funeral rights you think best."

Shīrkūh bowed once more. "Exarch Trist du Camaret-à-Arden," he repeated. "I do not think we will forget this name." He cocked his head to one side. "There are not many of our men in these hills."

"Our quest is not to hunt your men," Trist said, "Unless we come upon you by chance."

"Then whatever you hunt," Shīrkūh said, rising, "I pray the Angelus grant you their favor. We will care for our companion from here."

They watched as Alī was wrapped in a horse-blanket, then slung across the back of his steed. Shīrkūh took the reins in hand, and Sir Divdan gave him direction on the best way down from the foothills and to the camp outside Falais. Then, the four men and the boy watched the southerners ride off.

"And that's really it?" Yaél asked. "What if they lied? What if they just go right back to fighting our people?"

"Then they would be men without honor," Trist said, suddenly exhausted.

"This is the courtesy between knights," Sir Divdan explained. "A surrender is honored with mercy. Mercy is honored with surrender. We are not animals, my lad. None of us want to kill more than we have to."

Acrasia blew out a breath, grumping. "That is four Tithes you're letting walk away, my love," she complained. "Two for me, and one for you. We are going to miss them if we're forced to fight Adramelech. I hope you do not have cause to regret your mercy and your courtesy then."

"Come along," Trist said, after taking a gulp from his wineskin. "We have to walk all the way back up to the ridge, now." Yaél groaned.

By the time they'd retraced their steps on foot, the sun was setting over the mountains to the west. Instead of pushing on, they made camp by mutual agreement, all too exhausted to go any further even if they'd had the daylight remaining to try it.

Henry had a cook-fire going and pottage started soon enough, and Trist sat cross legged, talking Yaél through how to properly clean the longsword and oil it. "This is not a normal sword," he explained, and noticed that not only was the squire paying attention to his words, but all of the other men, as well.

"The Lady Acrasia is a part of it, now," Trist continued. "And her power makes it stronger."

"So it's a magic sword," Yaél said gleefully, as he rubbed an oiled cloth along the blade.

"Something like that," Trist confirmed, with a tired grin. "Part of that is being more durable than any normal blade. But it can still break, so we need to take care of it, just like any other sword, lest it fail when we most need it."

"If you'd gotten me another Tithe," Acrasia complained, "You wouldn't have to worry about that so much, now would you?"

"How much farther do we need to go?" Luc asked. "Before we get to the daemon cave, and all."

"We're headed between those two peaks," Sir Divdan explained, pointing into the sunset. And indeed, Trist could see a kind of notch between two mountains of the range: one uneven, not symmetrical, but with a long sloping ridge leading up to a peak that dropped off quickly into the notch. The second mountain was smaller, snugged right up against the first. "We call them the two brothers. The older brother, and the younger. A day to get there, I would say. Then we'll camp in the notch before heading down into the valley. We don't want to spend a night there if we don't have to."

"Good idea," Yaél said, nodding and eying the pot like a wolf sneaking up on a herd of sheep. "Not sleeping where the daemon can get us in our dreams, I mean."

"Daemons can't get you in your dreams," Henry scoffed.

Trist wasn't so certain. "Can they?" he asked Acrasia.

"Some of them," she said.

"...what did she say?" Divdan asked.

"She said some can," Trist said, but then added, "But I do not think this one is one of them." All around him, faces relaxed.

"I never said that," Acrasia murmured, with raised eyebrows. The sun was nearly entirely down now, but he could see her by the firelight.

An owl hooted nearby, and Trist turned just in time to catch it flapping away. "Never seen so many owls as in these mountains," he remarked, glancing at the pot to see if their meal was ready.

"Wait. How many owls have you seen?" Acrasia demanded, grabbing him by the shoulder.

"One just now," Trist said, trying to think back. "One a few days ago, I think. But I hear them at night nearly all the time. Why?"

"Owls." Acrasia frowned. "They aren't our allies, Trist. The Etalans knew that, before the end. If you see another one, have Henry shoot it."

That night, for the first time, the hooting of the owls did not help Trist sleep.

Chapter Thirty-Eight

THREE PLAGUES

The General - the King, by then - had asked me to lead a patrol to where the mountains meet the western sea on the coast. Half a dozen fishing villages, you see, hadn't been heard from in a month, and merchant traders had been reported missing. So I took a dozen lads and set off. It was the damned birds we saw first, circling up above. That's when I knew everything had gone to shit.

-The Life and Times of Legionary Titus Nasica

7th Day of the Flower Moon, 297 AC

For the first time in days, Trist woke to Acrasia's hair in his face. She was nestled against his chest, eyes closed. He wondered, sometimes, just how much beings like her really slept. They certainly didn't operate by the same rules that mortals did, but she'd also been distracted enough that he was able to catch her in a vulnerable moment, under the Chapelle de Camiel.

Not for the first time, he mourned what she'd done, and what they'd lost. If Acrasia had never acted on that wedding night, perhaps she would be with him in body, right now, his Linette, who he'd loved since they were children. He might not be an Exarch, of course, but would it really be so bad to be a simple knight, sharing a tent with his wife back at the encampment? Even after what she'd done to Percy, there remained a piece of him that wanted nothing more than to forget about it, to pretend that it hadn't happened, and go back to the way things were before. The memory was like a freshly scabbed wound, and he couldn't stop picking at it.

But she'd killed his brother, and Trist couldn't forget that. Carefully, he dislodged the faerie maiden and got to his feet. Today they would cover the last leg of the journey. Tonight, they would camp just outside the valley where Adramelech was bound. Tomorrow, they would descend the cursed stair into the roots of the mountains. Rather than wake anyone else with his restlessness, Trist gathered a bit of kindling and set to blowing on last night's embers to get a cookfire going.

By the time Henry rose, Trist had their breakfast started in the pot. "I can do that, m'lord," Henry murmured, coming over to join him in front of the fire.

"I could not sleep any longer," Trist admitted. "So I thought I should spend my time on something useful. You are the better cook, though," he admitted to the hunter, with a smile.

"I have to be better at something," Henry shot back with a grin, digging through the saddlebags and pulling out some of their supplies.

"You are also better with a bow," Trist pointed out. "At skinning game. Tracking. In fact, now that I consider it, what am I better at, again?"

"Oh, just sword and lance and riding," Henry replied, coming back over to the pot with his findings. "All those knightly sorts of things." By the time their meal was ready, the others had risen, as well, and save for Acrasia, who watched with an odd look in her eye, the group devoured their pottage quickly.

"We go to the valley today, right?" Yaél asked, looking between Trist and Sir Divdan.

"As long as you can keep up we do," Divdan teased the young squire back with a grin. "But yes. I'll set a hard pace, and we should be at the notch with time to spare before sundown. Be good to have a pair of rabbit for a stew tonight," he suggested to Henry.

"If I can get em, I will," the hunter promised.

"Acrasia," Trist said aloud, turning to the silent faerie. "You recognized the name of the daemon. Would you be willing to tell us what you know of it, today?"

"I never fought him myself," Acrasia said, shaking herself and tilting her head to meet Trist's eyes. "All I have is hearsay, and what I can piece together from your guide's story."

"Anything you can tell us is better than going in blind," Trist pressed her gently.

"As you wish, my love," she said, with a sigh. "Let me ride with you, and I will tell you what I can, and you can give my words to your men."

"What did she say?" Divdan asked.

"While we ride," Trist told the other knight. "The Lady Acrasia has never faced this foe herself, but she will tell us what she knows." Divdan nodded, and Yaél as well, though Trist suspected the boy was simply trying to fit in.

By the time the sun was well and truly up, the party had cleaned their bowls, packed their saddlebags, and set off. Acrasia was, of course, invisible and silent so far as the rest of the group was concerned, but to Trist, her presence was so perfect an illusion he could almost believe her real. She sat in front of him on the saddle, her white skirts bunched up higher than any well born lady would ever permit, because the faerie wouldn't ride side-saddle. Trist was almost completely certain it was not because she was incapable, but because Acrasia preferred to back herself into his body and enjoy the physical contact. Or, perhaps she was amused by how he squirmed, with her curves pressed against him. His cheeks burned at the thought of it.

"The first thing your men need to understand," Acrasia said, nestled in his arms atop Caz, "Is that they can't actually kill him. Adrammelech. You understand why, my love?"

"I do," Trist said. "He is like you, and like Addanc at the lake. But I thought we were not to say his name aloud?"

"I am not mortal, Trist," Acrasia said, and he could picture her smile from her tone of voice. "You are in more danger from him than I am. And your men, more danger than you."

Trist frowned, but he did his best to explain. "This first piece, I can put words to myself, I think," he said, slowly. Thankfully, Sir Divdan had the lead of the party, and Caz could be trusted to do most of the work of following the other knight's destrier. "Understand that creatures like the Prince of Plagues - and like the daemon at the lake - are similar to a rock in a stream."

"What do you mean?" Yaél asked, from his seat on the gelding just behind Trist. The early morning sun streamed down gold through the foliage overhead.

"You only see the tip of the rock," Trist answered. "Most of it is underwater. I will admit I only have experience of a few fae, a minor daemon, and a glimpse of an Angelus, but they all seem to follow this rule. Mortals cannot see most of such immortal creatures." Except for the priest, he remembered. "And your weapons cannot kill them."

"But men are said to have slain daemons before," Sir Divdan argued.

"You may be able to defeat the corporeal body they use," Trist admitted. "But that is only the part of the rock above the surface of the river. Even if a strong man chipped that part of the rock away with a pick, the rest of the rock would still be waiting beneath the water."

"Can't say I understand, m'lord," Luc said, after chewing on that for a moment. "But if we can't kill it, what good are the rest of us?"

"The first part of the answer is that if all goes well we will not be fighting it; it will remain bound," Trist explained. "But if we do have to fight? Hurting the portion you can see still does wound it. And if we kill that physical body, it is... limited."

"Annoyingly so," Acrasia complained. "Good explanation, Trist. Next. The Prince of Plagues was known to us, during the Cataclysm, for the threefold plagues he brought down upon Etalan cities with his presence. First, as your friend described, the Ornes - the terrible birds of whom Adramelech is the lord and master. In numbers, they will swarm the countryside, come down from the mountains, and destroy all the crops, the fruit trees like those olives over there, everything. Left to their own devices, they will cause a famine. To say nothing," she continued, "Of all the people they will kill. Their beaks and wings are hard as metal, and they will drag people to their nest, where they lay their eggs in the intestines. I have heard it said it takes only a moment for the eggs to hatch, and birth more. With Adrammelech bound, they were all hunted down and destroyed: but he can turn any mortal into one with a touch. And once he has a handful, they will breed again. Rapidly."

Trist passed on Acrasia's words, and Divdan, though he looked pale at the memory, nodded. "Yes," he said. "Their beaks tore out throats as easily as the edge of a dagger. What Lady Acrasia says fits my memories."

"The second plague," Acrasia continued, "Was that of a horrible, haunting wailing. A great cacophony, that stirred fear in the hearts of even the strongest warriors, and made it so that no one could sleep but they would suffer the most terrifying nightmares. A few days of it would drive weaker men mad. Adrammelech would delight in using these sounds to soften an army or a city before the assault by his flock of Ornes."

"Well that sounds pleasant," Divdan groaned, once Trist had relayed the faerie's words.

"We should stop our ears with wax," Yaél suggested, and everyone turned their heads to look at the boy. "What? None of you ever heard the stories of sirens what lured men to drown with their songs? You plug your ears up and sail right by."

"Would it work?" Trist asked Acrasia.

"It might," she said, after thinking a moment. "My worry is that the sounds may only be an outward manifestation of an attack directly on your souls... but I suppose that it can't hurt to try."

"We have sealing wax in the supplies," Henry said, though Trist gave him a surprised look. "I thought you might need to seal and send a message back, depending on what happened, m'lord," he explained.

"Very well," Trist said. "Tonight when we make camp we split the sealing wax into smaller pieces. Tomorrow morning we warm it up by the fire to get it soft, and plug our ears."

"The final plague is this," Acrasia said, as their horses crested a ridge. Ahead of them, loomed the notch between the mountains, with a vast stretch of forested slope obscuring the route they would follow for the rest of the day. "Adrammelech is a master of what the Angelus would call 'Sacred Geometry."

"I have no comprehension of what you mean by that," Trist said, with a sigh.

"Simply this," Acrasia explained. "The art of arranging the physical world to control the energy that flows through it, and turn that energy to a purpose. Churches, for example, are built in certain shapes and proportions. They are designed with the guidance of the Angelus to sanctify the ground they are built on. It's why I cannot enter them without feeling uncomfortable. The old Etalan roads, as well."

Trist conveyed what she'd said to the rest of the group, and then he asked, "So this daemon can design a church that would be sacred ground?"

"No," Sir Divdan said, shaking his head. "I understand. Trist, if you learn your guards and cuts properly, you also know how to defend against them, yes? Or how to break an enemy's guard?"

"Exactly," Acrasia said, with a nod. "Adramelech won't use his knowledge to build a church on sanctified ground. He'll use his knowledge to corrupt that ground. To turn it from a place aligned to the Angelus, to one aligned to daemonic power. During the Cataclysm, his forces would make surgical strikes: poison a well in one place, burn a sacred grove in another, dig up the graves in a bone yard. Burn a building."

"Anyone who does not have the same knowledge base," Trist decided, after thinking for a moment, "Would not be able to identify these things accurately. One might be a feint, another a true attack - but it is not like our own bodies. We know our throats are a vital area to protect - but no one knows which of the Prince of Plague's targets are vital."

"Good," Acrasia praised him. "Not without someone like an Angelus equally skilled in the arts of sacred geometry, at least. Which left Adrammelech, much of the time, with easy targets to strike, defended by people who didn't understand his aims until too late. Not to bring down a church, but to corrupt, to twist it to his own ends and his own benefit. Something I believe he's spent the last three centuries slowly doing. The cavern we're going to is less a prison, every year that passes, and more his center of power."

Chapter Thirty-Nine

A Stair into Darkness

The daemon had devoured the villages - every single one. We couldn't find so much as a stray chicken left alive, but the Ornes were everywhere, and I lost two men to them. We near ran out of arrows by the time we pulled back, and it was clear nothing short of an army was going to be able to clear the things out.

We never saw the daemon. If I'd known it was there, I would have argued harder when the King said he'd take command himself.

-The Life and Times of Legionary Titus Nasica

7th Day of the Flower Moon, 297 AC

The two knights and their companions stopped to make camp when they found the first dead trees.

"This is further out than when I came here three years ago," Sir Divdan observed, swinging down from the saddle of his destrier. The sun hadn't even touched the peaks on the western horizon, yet.

Trist frowned, riding over to look at one of the dead trees more closely. All of the oak's branches remained, but there were no leaves at all. What he did see, in unusual abundance, were several varieties of fungus.

"Oyster mushrooms," Henry said confidently, reaching out to begin pulling white, scalloped caps that reminded Trist of sea shells on the beach at Rocher de la Garde. "See how the gills run down into the stem, m'lord? These will go well in the pot."

"What are those shaggy ones," Trist asked, pointing.

"Lion's Mane," Henry answered. "Good for the wits. Get ready for a nice mushroom stew tonight."

"Well, I suppose someone should be happy about this wasteland," Sir Divdan grumbled as Trist got down off of Caz. "I find it oppressive." He waved his hand at the forested slopes ahead of them, leading the last stretch up to the notch between the two mountains. The further Trist looked, the more dead trees he saw, and the less green.

"Are they really going to be safe to eat?" Trist asked Acrasia, who was still up in the saddle, as he tied Caz's reins to the branch of a living tree.

The faerie considered it a moment. "I suspect so," she said eventually. "We are right on the edge of Adrammelech's influence. Most of the trees here are still healthy. Those mushrooms are just doing what they do naturally - growing on a dead oak. But I don't think Henry should do any harvesting further in."

Trist passed along the warning, and then they all settled in to make their last camp before descending beneath the mountains.

Breaking camp the next morning was a somber affair.

No one had the heart to make jokes, or to poke fun at each other's foibles. Instead, they helped each other into their armor. Trist and Sir Divdan wore every piece they had, with the exception of their helms, which they secured to their saddlebags, waiting for when they drew closer to the long stair into the cavern. They helped Yaél, who'd was so nervous he'd thrown up his breakfast, wriggle into his new shirt of rings. Henry double checked his arrows and his bow, but otherwise wore only his chain shirt and a leather stock about his neck. Luc had picked up an old and ratty padded gambeson, a size too small, somewhere around the encampment outside of Falais, and now the big man pulled it out of a saddlebag and forced his way into it, to pad his own shirt of rings. Then, they set off.

They fed the horses with oats not only in the morning, but also when they finally stopped to tie them up at the top of the stairs. The entire valley was a sight of desolation: not a single living tree remained, and most of their branches had long been broken off by the wind and storm. Now, pale, bare trunks stabbed at the sky like needles, hundreds of them in every direction. Rather than trust the trees, they drove the metal spike they'd brought into the ground and secured the horses to that.

"Leave anything that is not of use in a fight," Trist warned everyone, as they made final adjustments to their gear. A cold wind screamed through the dead trees, with nothing in the way of foliage to shelter them from its bite.

Sir Divdan led the way down a hardscrabble slope of loose rock to where the steps began. Skidding to a halt, dust rising around him and pebbles rattling down the stairs, Trist tried to get a glimpse into the darkness; the Shadow King's Boon stirred to life behind his eyes, and everything came into focus.

"It's like the sun came here to die," Henry muttered, from just behind Trist's shoulder, peering into the darkness. "Can you see anything, m'lord?"

"The stairs curve," Trist answered. "It is gradual, but enough that I cannot see to the bottom."

Divdan lit up a torch. They'd brought rags and a flask of oil, so it burned well, and drove the shadows before it. Trist stepped down onto the first stair. "Let me go ahead a ways," he said. "I can see just as well without the torch, and the shadows will hide me."

The other knight swallowed. "Exarch," was all he muttered, and Trist went down with no one but Acrasia to accompany him.

"Trist," she said, once the gentle curve of the stair had taken them out of the torchlight. "A moment, my love."

Trist paused, and turned to the fairie, who stood up on her tiptoes and pressed her lips to his before he could stop her. There was no sign or clue that she was anything but real, and Acrasia opened her mouth, her tongue flicking out to search for his.

"No," Trist gasped, breaking away. "I have a wife, Linette. I will not betray her."

"Is it such a crime to want one last kiss before we go down there?" Acrasia's eyes flickered blue in the dark. "Come along then. I won't leave you to do this alone."

Two hundred steps down, Sir Divdan had told them. Trist counted as they descended, into the depths, into the dark. He'd thought them beyond the flickering light of the torch when they rounded the curve out of sight, but when he looked back, some time later, he could still see the dim light above.

And yet, Trist could see clearly. He wondered if this was what the predators of the night saw: wolves and wildcats and owls. The owls are not our allies, Acrasia had told him, but he couldn't ask her about it now, because he didn't want to make a sound more than necessary. At the hundred and sixtieth step, he thought he saw dim light from below, and at the hundred and eightieth, he was certain.

The stone stairs opened out onto a vast cavern, just as Sir Divdan had described: stone dripped from the ceiling and rose from the floor in irregular, pointed formations like melted candles. Strange writing and symbols adorned the rough walls, and even parts of the floor. In the center, under a vaulted ceiling, a pool, perfectly still, reflected the rock above. It glowed, and in the depths, Trist saw the firefly lights the older knight had described.

"Look at it the way you look at me," Acrasia murmured in his ear, and he would have cautioned her about speaking if he did not know that he was the only one who could hear her. "See the threads." Trist sought for it: the way of seeing that had let him glimpse her true form, the whirls and coils of fire, glowing bright as her eyes. It did not come slowly, but all at once, like the snapping of a buckle into place.

A creature nested beneath the water: coils of light, red as blood and yellow as the sunlight on an autumn afternoon. Each firefly was the tip of a long, floating tendril, thin as fine hair. He'd found one of Clarisant's long dark hairs on his white linen undershirt, the second day of the journey through the forest. A single hair, just like this.

The writing on the walls, the symbols, all glowed a dull red, just barely giving off light, and his eyes fixed on those. From each symbol extended a burning chain, down to the creature below. But to Trist's eye, the chains looked cracked and pitted, as if rusted over many years. Were the creature below to truly wake, he doubted the chains would hold it down.

Trist was just about to turn and ascend the staircase; he had done what the Prince had asked him to do. The bindings were still there, but they had no longer any strength to hold the daemon. Just as his foot found the first step, a shout came from above, and then a dark shape flew right at him. Wings fluttered in his face, and Trist swung an arm to knock aside whatever had come down the stairs.

He felt an impact, and then it was past him, settled onto one of the stone teeth rising up from the floor. An owl. Trist could see it clearly, with the Boon of the King of Shadows on his eyes.

The owl was a knot of red and orange threads.

"What is it?" Trist hissed to Acrasia.

"No!" She cried. The owl's eyes were locked on the two of them, but whips of dull fire lashed out from it toward the symbols on the walls, where the chains that held the daemon were anchored.

Someone was shouting up above, but Trist couldn't pay the words any mind. He couldn't allow the owl to break the chains. Trist's sword cleared his scabbard with a ring, and he lunged forward, sweeping a rising cut through one of the lashes before it could reach the wall of the cavern. "Stop it!" He shouted to Acrasia, and she exploded outward, her own burning whips meeting and wrestling with those that came from the owl.

"Agrat," Acrasia spat, her eyes fierce, her fists clenched. "Chosen a new Exarch, have you?"

Trist kept moving forward, cutting through the daemonic owl's tendrils as fast as he could, but not quickly enough. Steps pounded down the stairs, and he looked just long enough to see torchlight, and Yaél bounding ahead of the rest, arming sword in hand.

"We're here, m'lord!" the boy shouted, sword raised, and skidded to a halt on the damp stone, seeing only an owl, and Trist cutting the darkness with his sword.

"Go!" Trist yelled to his companions. "It's breaking the chains! Run!"

"Angelus save us," Divdan moaned. "It's happening all over again." The knight's hand clutched at the hilt of his sword, but the tremor in his fingers stopped him from getting a good grip. Henry had his bow out and strung, and as Trist spun through the loops of fire, the hunter loosed an arrow at the owl.

Agrat, for so Acrasia had named the beast, and Trist trusted her judgment in this, rose in a flutter of wings. The loosed arrow skidded across stone off into the darkness, and the daemonic owl pulled its remaining loops of fire back into its core, winging up into the darkness of the stairs.

"Is it gone?" Yaél asked, burning with excitement. "What was it?"

"A daemon," Acrasia responded, and to Trist's surprise, the squire's head whipped around toward her.

"Lady Acrasia?" Yaél murmured, but Trist didn't have time to dwell on it, because now he saw what Sir Divdan had seen first. The lights, like fireflies, were rising from the depths of the cavern pool, and each one was only the tip of a bright, burning yellow tendril. The lines crept out of the water into the cavern, seeking their prey.

"Get back!" Trist shouted, scrambling over the rocks toward the stairs. "Acrasia!"

"I'll hold off what I can," the faerie shouted, sweeping her own burning whips across the chamber between the pool and the stairs, knocking aside half a dozen of the lights.

"I can see her," Yaél cried in awe. The boy's mouth hung open, and his eyes were wide as the full moon. "She's beautiful."

Trist had finally gotten to the boy. He left the hilt of his sword in his right hand and grabbed Yaél's shoulder with his left, turning the squire back to the stairs. "Go!" he shouted. "Before they touch you!"

"No!" Henry shouted, and then Luc screamed. Trist turned to the big man in horror. There, not three steps from the base of the stairs, Luc had fallen, frozen, eyes wide in horror, with a tendril of fire connecting the daemon at the bottom of the pool to his heart.

Chapter Forty

Adrammelech

Ornes - The name given to the daemon birds that ravaged the countryside of Narvonne after the summonings at Vellatesia, after an old Etalan myth. Their feathers, claws and teeth are hard as steel, able to turn aside an arrow or tear out a man's chest with equal ease. Worse, they infect those they have killed, twisting the slain into their own monstrous form, adding to their flock with every kill they make. Some men speak of them laying eggs in the corpses, but the truth is far worse: they infect the soul itself, corrupting it in a matter of moments.
-The Marian Codex

8th Day of the Flower Moon, 297 AC

"He's lost, Trist," Acrasia shouted, as she backed towards the steps.

Henry grabbed Luc under the armpits and began to drag him onto the first stair. "Help me carry him," the hunter gasped to Sir Divdan. Instead of reaching for Luc's legs, however, the knight from Falais drew his dagger.

"We have to kill him now," Divdan said. "Before it hatches."

"No!" Henry screamed, whipping his Iebara wood longbow at Divdan like a staff. The knight was forced to back off a step, and Luc fell onto the stone. There, at Henry's feet, the big man's skin pulsed outward grotesquely. He swelled, like a sausage packed in its casing, and then screamed as his skin burst in a dozen places. The too-small padded gambeson ripped with an audible tearing sound, throwing steel rings in every direction, and the stink of blood and pus swept out from the base of the steps like a cloud of dust, causing everyone to retch and cough.

It was just like Sir Divdan had described. "Angelus forgive me," Trist said, closing his eyes for a moment, then striding forward, blade in hand. "Back off the both of you," he ordered.

"But m'lord," Henry pleaded. "He's one of ours. Help him."

"This is the only way I can help him," Trist said, gritted his teeth, and plunged the tip of his sword into Luc's heart. A shiver of power rushed up his blade as he collected the Tithe. Acrasia laughed, and for a moment the Tithe seemed to give her enough strength to push back the whips of light lashing out from the underground lake. Then, the mountains began to shake.

"Go, all of you!" Trist shouted, shoving Henry up the stairs. Dust and pebbles began to fall from the ceiling, and Trist could see chains of binding snapping left and right as cracks shot through the symbols adorning the walls of the cavern.

Divdan didn't wait a moment longer: the older knight grabbed Yaél by the hand and ran, dragging the boy behind him up the stairs. Their torch burned, forgotten, on the floor of the cavern, but Trist wasn't worried about anyone getting lost: there was only one way to go, and that was up. Henry tore himself away from Luc's desecrated corpse with a strangled cry of frustration, and scrambled up the steps after them, leaving only Trist and Acrasia.

The surface of the pool at the center of the cavern began to bubble, like a pot of soup over the cookfire, and the whips of light that Acrasia had been fighting suddenly pulled back into the water, fast as snapped ropes through a pulley. "Now!" Trist cried, grabbing Acrasia by the hand and yanking her along with him as he ran for the stairs.

Water exploded up and out from the pool, drenching Trist and slicking the steps beneath his boots. With his left hand, he caught at the rough stone to his side, and glanced back.

The daemon beat its wings, then touched its foot down on the slick, wet rock just past the pool. The wings were feathered the colors of a dying sun: red and orange and purple.

Adrammelech's body was smaller and slimmer than that of the Addanc, not counting the wingspan. It was all tight, corded muscle, wiry, with not an ounce of fat, skin the color of the eerie blue depths of the lit pool, stretched taught over the muscles and bones. The head was surmounted by four twisted horns like those of a ram, curling back and out to the sides, and the daemon's eyes were embers in the darkness. When it flexed its long fingers, Trist saw claws like those of a wildcat. The monster opened its mouth, and screamed.

To Trist's eyes, which somehow remained opened to the world of daemons and faeries, even through all this, the knot of red and orange and yellow behind the corporeal form of Adrammelech vibrated, like the plucked string of a lute, and then a wave of power in the same colors swept out from it, battering into both Trist and, her hand clutched in his, Acrasia. He heard the faerie scream in pain beside him, heard a man's voice shouting, and realized it was his. Trist pulled Acrasia up the stairs, to get her behind him, and then let go of her hand so that he could pull two small pieces of wax out of his belt pouch.

"I can't stand against that monster," Acrasia cried. "Another assault like that will destroy me for true. I'm sorry, Trist." Her whirls of fiery red and orange poured into his longsword, wound up tight as a spool of thread. The illusion of her physical form vanished.

The wax jammed into his ears, Trist lifted his longsword into the Ox Guard: hilt by his right ear, blade nearly parallel with the cavern floor, tip pointed directly at the daemon's chest. "Come on, then," Trist shouted to Adrammelech. With a broken oath hanging around his neck, there was no way that Trist was going to let the monster have an open shot at his back. The Prince of Plagues shrieked again, and the wave of sound ripped across the cavern toward Trist.

When it reached his ears, the sound was dull, muffled. Trist felt a slight throbbing in his temple, a building headache, but nothing more. He grinned, and spared half a thought to hope that Henry, Sir Divdan and Yaél had gotten their wax plugs in. With a shout, Trist lunged forward, whipping his blade around in a diagonal arc to cut at the daemon. He swung with all the speed and power he could muster, and the burning red cord of his Boon made it more than any mortal man could have done.

With a beat of his wings, and the speed of a snake, the daemon leapt backward just far enough to be out of Trist's reach. The creature spoke, then, and Trist saw its mouth was more of a snout, long and thin like that of a goat or sheep, the tongue curling around its sharp teeth. The words, he guessed, might be Old Etalan: no language that he'd ever mastered. Quick as a forest fire, the monster shot forward again, one arm extended, claws flexed, and Trist had half a heartbeat to realize that if he didn't get out of the way, or at least avoid the worst of it, those claws were going to rip out his stomach. The daemon's raw speed and power gave him no confidence that either his steel plate cuirass, nor the rings of mail beneath, would be enough to save him. Trist threw himself back wildly, stumbling over the wet stones, and for just a moment thought he'd been able to move fast enough.

Then, the daemon's claws punched through his cuirass and into his right side, just beneath the ribs. Trist gasped from the pain, sucking in air as his knees buckled. He felt very far from his body, far from the monster's reeking breath as it dropped him onto the stone. Trist closed his eyes, just for a moment, just to catch his breath and to rest.

"Wake up!" Acrasia shook him, and Trist's eyes snapped open again.

"Adrammelech," he coughed, and tasted blood.

"Flew up the stairs," Acrasia said. "Come on. You need to move, my love."

"Just a moment," Trist said, his eyes fluttering closed again. A slap on his cheek woke him up.

"If you don't get up those stairs, you die!" Acrasia screamed at him. "And I can't carry you. Now move, Trist! Crawl, if you have to!"

Would it truly be so bad to die? Trist wondered. Every breath sent a stab of pain through his body, down where his lifeblood was leaking out from five holes punched through his cuirass. If he closed his eyes one more time, he could rest. Adrammelech, the war with the Caliphate, the incessant need to collect Tithes for the faerie king, all of it would be someone else's problem. The Crown Prince didn't need him: Bors was twice the knight Trist was. If the older Exarch had been here instead of Trist, the daemon would already be defeated. Did anyone really need him to stay alive?

Acrasia didn't. Oh, she'd be sad for a while, Trist knew. But she was immortal, and she would go back to her brother Cern and her King of Shadows, and in a hundred years, or in two hundred, Acrasia would still be haunting the forests, and his memory would be forgotten. Percy was already dead, and Trist had failed his duty to protect his brother. His mother had been taken by the plague years ago. Who was left? His father?

Rience du Camaret-à-Arden always had a favored son, and as far back as Trist could remember, his father hadn't been subtle about showing it. All the hopes of the family depended on Percy, and Trist was just there: good with a sword, but otherwise unremarkable in every way, if not downright troublesome.

Yaél would be sad, he thought. But Divdan could take the boy as a squire, and train him just as well. Better, probably, with the resources of the Baroness behind him. Yaél would become a knight of the mountains - maybe he would even command one of the three towers, when he'd grown. It wasn't a bad life.

Trist's eyes closed, and the dark was warm and peaceful.

"Untie me?" Clarisant asked, turning her back to him and sweeping her dark hair off her neck, holding it around her front. Trist swallowed, and worked the laces of her stays with trembling fingers that seemed too large and too clumsy. Finally, she shrugged out of the bodice, and dropped her dress to the floor. His bride walked to his bed in only her linen shift and stockings, long hair unbound, and turned to face him.

"Trist," she said quietly. "I promise you, I've never done this before."

Clarisant. What would become of her, if he died down here under the mountains? Twice widowed, and the marriage certainly consummated the second time. No one would want her. She would be alone, and his father would send her back to Rocher de la Garde unless she was carrying a child.

His child.

A son or a daughter, growing up without their father. Trist thought back to the day they'd entombed his mother in the crypt behind the monastery. At least he'd known her, at least he could remember being cradled in his mother's arms as a boy. Trist's own child wouldn't know him at all; his father would be dead before he drew his first breath.

Trist sucked in a breath, opened his eyes, and reached a hand out for the hilt of his sword. It was a struggle, but he got it into the leather sheath. Then, heaving great breaths between coughing up thick gobs of blood, Trist grabbed a stone stair and pulled himself up.

Trist went on his hands and knees, a step at a time, counting the entire way. At fifty, he knew he wouldn't make it, but thought he might as well try for fifty one. At eighty, he thought this was the most pain he had ever been in, but by one hundred he knew he'd been wrong. At a hundred and twenty he nearly passed out and fell, and the thought of rolling down all those stairs to break his head on the stones at the bottom sounded better than the idea of continuing.

At a hundred and eighty, he heard the screaming. Somehow, he pulled himself up to his feet and stumbled out into the cool mountain air. With a shriek, a daemonic bird flew down at him, wings outstretched, beak coming for his face. Trist fumbled for his sword, but his fingers were numb, his body clumsy, and there was no way he could draw in time.

A lance erupted from the bird's chest. Blood spurted, splashing Trist in the face, and he fell to his knees. Above him, a woman in Caliphate armor, her head wrapped in a red scarf and veil, lowered her lance and shook the corpse of the bird off it.

"Surrender," she commanded, her words accented.

Trist fell to the side, and knew nothing but darkness.

Chapter Forty-One

A Feast in the Mountains

One of the things that continually frustrated King Luther about Maddoc was the way he and the faerie court could disappear into the Arden without a trace. Beneath every hill, within every ancient oak, a faerie might lurk. Step into the wrong circle of mushrooms, and a knight might find himself at the feet of the King of Shadows himself, in some faerie glen otherwise undetectable to mortal man.
-François du Lutetia, A History of Narvonne

8th Day of the Flower Moon, 297 AC

"See, he's awake!"

Trist coughed and sputtered out a mouthful of watered wine, raising his hand to bat away the wineskin being held to his mouth. He needed air. "I thought it was cool in the mountains," he gasped, and opened his eyes.

Sir Divdan pulled the wineskin back. The knight had a strip of cloth tied around his forehead as a bandage, and it was stained with blood. Yaél was on the other side, and the boy looked to be in one piece. Around them, Trist saw dead trees grasping up toward a dark, star-spattered sky. Off to one side was the flickering, warm glow of a fire, and the scent of smoke. A woman with her head and face wrapped in red stepped into his view.

"Be ready to move with the dawn, northerner," she said, her voice pleasant to the ear, but hard as the rock of the mountains. "If you cannot keep up, I will leave you behind." It took a moment, but her face and tone brought back the memory: a lance through one of Adrammelech's daemon birds.

"You were at the top of the steps," Trist said, the words thick in his mouth. A shiver ran through his body, and he wished he had a blanket.

"And you are my captive. I trust the much vaunted honor of the northern knights will keep you from fleeing?" She raised dark eyebrows, arched and fine as an artist's brush. His father and mother had a portrait done that summer in Rocher de la Garde, and he remembered watching the painter make magic on canvas.

"I do not recall being captured," Trist said, after a moment. He tried to sit up, but hot, burning pain stabbed through his abdominal muscles, and he fell back with a wince.

"You could not fight a newborn babe as you are now," the woman in red said. "I am Ismet ibnah Salah, Exarch of Epinoia, and even if you were healthy, you would have no chance of defeating me. Accept your situation with grace. We are merciful, as the Angelus teach us."

Trist chuckled. He'd been on the other side of this conversation only a few days ago. "Will you allow us to send a messenger to our Prince?" he asked. "It is urgent that he know what has happened here. Sir Divdan can go, he knows the way. And I am certain he would honor his parole."

Ismet shook her head. "We return to General Shadi. You will accompany us as prisoners, and you will give your report to the General. You will explain all that has happened here."

Trist shook his head, but the motion made his stomach revolt, and he retched, barely keeping whatever was left of his breakfast from coming up.

"I've bandaged you, but your wound is not good," Divdan told him, once it had passed. "The punctures are red, and they smell of pus. Was it one of the birds?"

"It was the daemon," Trist answered, shivering again. "I need a blanket."

"This is a waste of time," the Caliphate Exarch said, above him. "He will be dead by morning." Her scarlet veil fluttered as she turned and walked away.

It was Yaél who brought him the blanket; from the smell, Trist recognized it as the one he used beneath Cazador's saddle. Trist clutched it around his body in relief, desperate for warmth. "You've got a fever, m'lord," the boy told him. "The red lady, she was waiting for us with all her knights when we got to the top of the stair. But when the daemon came out, she lost half her men turned to birds, and most of the rest killed. But she's an Exarch, right enough. Divdan tried to fight her, and she knocked him out with one punch from the hilt of that curved sword she carries."

"Good boy," Trist gasped. "I need... need to talk to Acrasia. Fetch me my sword."

"She's got it," Yaél murmured. "She's got all our weapons, over by her horse, all wrapped up and tied in a bundle." The boy dragged over Trist's cuirass, turned it over, and examined the holes punched through it. Trist had a glimpse of ragged, sharp pieces of metal pointed inward, around the edges of the holes. "Need to get rid of those," Yaél sighed. "I hate to say it, m'lord, but I think you're gonna need a new breastplate. Let's see what we can do to keep these from hurting you, though." Yaél grabbed a rock from the ground and began to rub it over the rough holes, to wear down the sharp steel.

Trist opened his eyes some time later to find that he'd thrown off the horse-blanket, and that Henry was kneeling next to him, holding a bowl of pottage. Trist swallowed once; his throat was dry. "I wanted to tell you that I am sorry," Trist said. "For what happened to Luc."

Henry looked down at the bowl, spooned up a good dollop of what was inside, and put the spoon to Trist's mouth. "I've had a few hours to think it over, m'lord," he said finally. "I wish we could've saved him, but looking back? I can't see how." He gave a sigh, and once Trist had swallowed prepared another spoonful. "You did what was right. And you did what a Lord has to do - what needs to be done, to save as many as can be. I'm not a soldier, not really. I guess I don't have the instincts for it," he admitted. "Anyway, there's not much in there but salt meat and the barley we brought, but once we get down the mountain a bit, I'll shoot you a nice fat hare for the stew. That'll put you right soon enough."

"I feel like I just got out of a sickbed," Trist said, with a sad grin.

"Your lordship just needs to stop letting strange monsters poke holes in you," Henry joked. In the end, Trist managed to eat half of the bowl, and once Henry had walked away to clean it, he turned back to where Yaél was struggling with his cuirass.

Trist reached out a hand and took hold of the boy's arm. "Later," he murmured. "When everyone is asleep. I need you to bring me the sword."

"Are we going to escape?" Yaél hissed with excitement.

Trist shook his head. "I need to talk to Acrasia."

"I saw her, you know. Just for a moment," Yaél confessed. "Down in the cave. A woman with blonde hair, in a white dress. Ears, like," he flicked a finger up from the top of his own ears to indicate a pointed tip. "I thought only you could see her."

Trist let his thoughts drift for a moment. "Used to be, anyone could," he said finally. "It may be she is regaining her strength." Through the Tithes I give to her, no doubt. He released Yaél's arm. "Tonight."

The boy nodded, and Trist, cold, wrapped the blanket back around his body before closing his eyes.

"M'lord!"

Trist jolted awake. He was drenched in sweat, and must have thrown off the blanket again in the night. For a moment, he didn't know where he was. Why was his bed so hard? No, he was outside, a fat moon hung overhead, yellow against the dark sky.

"I've got it!" Yaél, the boy, shoved the hilt of a sword into Trist's fingers, and then Acrasia was there, stroking his forehead with the back of her hand.

"You have a fever," she murmured. "Yaél, pull the bandages down so that I can see the wound."

But Yaél couldn't see or hear Acrasia, could he? Trist closed his eyes again; it was just too difficult keeping them open. The bandages were suddenly peeled away from his side, and a rank stench hit his nose.

"Good. Keep your hand on the sword so that I can speak to you." Acrasia poked at his wounds, and Trist gasped at the pain, his eyes open again.

"Will he live, m'lady?" Yaél asked the faerie.

"Hard to say. Oh, my love. I told you not to fight him..." Acrasia's soft, cool fingers stroked Trist's wet hair back from his forehead. It felt nice. Was she going to stitch him up, this time? Wasn't that Clarisant's job? But she wasn't here...

"We need to get him up," Acrasia said. "I'm not strong enough to lift him. Help me."

Yaél shoved at him with both hands, then turned, placed his back against Trist's side, and pushed with his legs. That was enough to roll Trist over, and he grumbled. "Up, m'lord," Yaél whispered. "I can't lift you myself, but you can lean on me. You have to get up."

"Up, my love," Acrasia urged him. "Follow me." She seemed to shine under the light of the moon and the stars, and beneath the surface Trist could make out the beautiful, terrifying loops and whirls of fire that were her true form. He lurched to his feet and fell toward her, and Yaél came up under his arm, the sword clutched between them.

"Follow me," the faerie repeated, backing away from the fire and into the darkness between the trees. The knight and the squire stumbled after her, falling forward more than walking, down into a ravine that had the feel of a stream gone dry. Uphill they went now, along the rocky bottom of the ravine, toward a dark face of rock ahead: little more than a shadow in the moonlight. Trist's mind slipped around what was happening like a leaf in the rapids, but he noticed enough to be aware of a cleft in the rock, and it was into that the three of them passed.

Light and sound spilled out from the cleft: voices, laughter, the soft strumming of notes from the strings of a harp, perhaps, or a lyre. Once through the rock, Trist saw a bonfire at the center of a natural amphitheater, throwing sparks up to the sky. This place, the corruption of the daemon Adramelech appeared not to have touched: Trist could see scrub and brush along the edges, trees, even, and there was soft, dew-touched grass under his boots.

The company feasting in the mountains turned to examine them, and the volume of conversation fell. There was a great long table laid out with all manner of food: cuts of roast meat, sliced wheels of cheese, trays of fruits, carafes of wine. To either side of the long table, in finely carved wooden chairs, were men and women of surpassing beauty.

Pale and tall, each and every one of them, with fine, sharp-featured faces, glittering eyes, and rich, fanciful clothing. At the head of the table was a great throne of wood, carved in the shape of trees and leaves and vines, and the man who lounged in that throne was the first to call out to them.

"Is that the Lady Acrasia I see come before us?" he spoke, passing off his goblet to a servant at his side. "Maimed as you are, yet still beautiful to our eye. Long has it been since you graced our feasting, my lady."

Acrasia swept forward across the grass, her white dress trailing behind her, blonde tresses lit by the moon, and she curtsied before the man in the throne. "My king," she said, "I have come to beg your help."

"Oh? And do you bring these mortals in trade? The one looks rather close to death," the man in the throne said, "But as to the other, you know me well. I always have a place for a child at my court."

"Acrasia," Trist said, with a cough. "What is this?"

"What is this?" The man rose, and his eyes were like stars, and his hair was black as death. "Mortal, do you not know? You have come to the court of Auberon, King of Shadows. Whether you ever leave remains to be seen."

Chapter Forty-Two

Auberon

"This Maddoc of the Wood has bedeviled us since the time of my grandfather. I know not how he remains young after so many years, even secluded in some faerie glade, but I say this now: the knight who brings me his head shall be rewarded with a castle, lands, a wife if he have none, and his weight in silver."

-King Luther II, as recorded by his court scribe

8th Day of the Flower Moon, 297 AC

Auberon, the Faerie King, burned white and pale blue to Trist's sight, a cloud of a million fine threads waving in the night breeze, extending back to a brightness that was blinding. Next to him, Acrasia was a candle. He was like the high noon sun, through a thin linen curtain, his outer form completely unable to contain the radiance beneath. The colors of the Faerie King were somehow brighter than anything else around him, with the effect that the edges of his form were picked out in sharp contrast to the foliage of the glade, the goblet in his hand, and even the throne in which he sat.

"Cern," the King of Shadows called, and the Horned Hunter stepped out of the night, a sentinel two steps behind Auberon's left shoulder. "Come greet your sister." His voice filled Trist's ears to the point of pain, and vibrated in his bones.

"My sister I greet warmly," Cern said. "But you, mortal. I warned you against ever coming before me again." He thumped the butt of his hunting spear into the ground, and thunder rumbled in the sky overhead.

"My king," Acrasia began. "He is one of yours. We have an Accord, that he serve as your Knight of Shadows."

"An Accord?" Aubreron scowled. "We have not made an accord in centuries. We are not the Angelus or the daemons. We stand aside, Lady Acrasia, or have you forgotten that? I see now where the bounty of Tithes you send has come from. Not reaping them yourself, no. You are using this mortal to do it for you."

Trist took a knee, as much because he could hardly remain standing as to show respect. "Your Majesty," he addressed the dark faerie, "I beg your mercy and forgiveness for any offense I have caused by coming here today. So too, Lord Cern," he continued, inclining his head to the Horned Hunter, "Do I beg your leave. Dire events drove us to this pass, and Lady Acrasia has done as she thought best." There was the murmur of voices and the clink of goblets from the host at the banquet; elegant ladies, pale and beautiful, whispered behind their delicate hands.

After a long moment, the faerie king sat back down in his throne, and sipped from his goblet. "Very well, my unwitting Knight of Shadows," Auberon drawled. "Your liege commands you. Inform my court of what 'dire events' have brought you to our revels this eve."

Trist closed his eyes, took a long breath in, then back out, and began. The shock of their arrival at the court of the Faerie King seemed to have broken through his fevered mind for the moment, and he needed to use this gasp of clarity before it was lost to him.

"We entered the Hauteurs Massif on a mission from Lionel Aurelianus, Crown Prince of Narvonne," Trist began, marshaling his thoughts. His words might well be soldiers on the field, and if they did not win the battle and sway Auberon, he doubted he would ever leave this place. "Three centuries past, at the end of the Cataclysm, the first King of Narvonne fell in these mountains, sealing away the daemon Adramelech, called the Prince of Plagues. Our task was to assess whether the bindings still held, before the armies of Narvonne and the Caliphate of Ma'īn clashed - or whether they had broken, freeing Adrammelech as Addanc of the lake had been freed before."

"Addanc was bound by our Court long ago," Cern the Hunter intoned. "And if it was free in our forest, it is I who would have been sent to hunt that daemon, so that it could be bound once again."

"Indeed," Trist said. Acrasia took a knee beside him, and Yaél on the other side, each pressed up against his shoulders. The pressure to right and left kept him from swaying, and Acrasia grabbed his hand to squeeze in her own. "And I have no doubt the Wild Hunt would easily have defeated the daemon, and bound him. Yet as luck would have it, we came upon the lake not long after the Addanc had slipped its bindings, and could not cross the bridge without confronting it. And so the Addanc was slain soon after freeing itself; it is understandable its escape had not yet been noticed."

Cern took two steps forward. "You claim to have slain the Addanc. You, a mortal more dead than alive?"

"Look at him, brother," Acrasia begged. "Look at the threads. The proof of it is there. A Boon won by his own hand, and anchored by a Tithe taken."

"He is indeed a daemon slayer," King Auberon said, eyes narrowed. "It is as the beautiful Acrasia says. When we finish here, Cern, you will ride to the lake, but I believe I already know what you will find there. Based on the state of you," he continued, addressing Trist, "I judge that Adramelech has also slipped his chains. Is this so?"

"It is, Your Majesty," Trist confirmed. "I bear the wounds of his claws now. The injury is killing me, I think." Acrasia squeezed his hand so hard it hurt.

Auberon took another sip from his goblet, and then drummed the fingers of his other hand on the arm of his throne. "And what would you have of me, Lady Accrasia and her Exarch? It seems obvious, but perhaps you will surprise me."

"Save him!" Acrasia begged. "Purge the infection from his body. Heal his wounds. Please, my king."

The dark faerie's eyes flicked from Acrasia to Trist. "Lead your court against Adrammelech," Trist asked, and he heard Acrasia gasp beside him. "I have already failed to stop the daemon once, your majesty. One more sword would make little difference. But the power you have mustered here could save many lives."

Auberon threw back his head and laughed. "I had near forgot how entertaining mortals can be," he remarked. "For that, Acrasia, you have my thanks, if for nothing else. We do not take sides, boy," he said. "We did not take sides during the Cataclysm, and we will not take sides now."

"But... but you bound the Addanc," Trist protested.

"Aye, for it came into our Ardenwood," Cern answered. "We do not brook our demesne to be violated lightly, and we will teach that lesson a thousand times over if need be."

A dog, Father Kramer had called Acrasia, unwilling to bestir herself in her master's defense. Was this what the man had been speaking of, Trist wondered? That the faeries would not stand against the daemons, even if all the world was burning? In his despair, he felt the last of his strength flee, and with a groan, Trist fell forward onto his hands, face inches above the ground, where he coughed up a phlegmy mass of blood.

"It is for the best, sister," Cern said. "Let him pass from this world, and you linger with us. We will even keep the child, for your entertainment."

"...and yet," the Faerie King said. "You may still be of some use to me. He leaned forward. "Squire."

"Yes?" Yaél squeaked.

"Will you undertake a task for me, child?" Auberon asked. "One thing, that if you swear to see it done, I will heal both these two of their grievous wounds."

Trist tried to raise his head, to warn the boy, to stop him from speaking, but all his strength was gone.

"I will," Yaél promised. "One task for you. What is it then?"

"You will take my ring," Auberon said, though to Trist's ears his voice was now growing quite dim. "You will take it with you back to Falais, to the Church of Saint Abatur. You will do this alone, without your knight or any other Exarch, and you will place the ring on the sarcophagus at the heart of the tomb. Are we agreed, then? Do we have a bargain?"

"Yes," Trist heard Yaél say.

"Then come to me and take the ring," the King of Shadows bid the boy. Trist collapsed into the thick, lush grass that carpeted the hollow in the mountain, and closed his eyes. The wound beneath his ribs was hot now, like a pot that had been cooking over a fire, and he was so very tired.

Something cool touched his lips, and Trist's mouth filled with a liquid both cold and sweet. It tasted something of honey, and something of the purest dew left on a fresh green leaf at dawn. The pain from where the daemon had punctured his body faded and cooled, and Trist gasped for breath.

"Drink, my love," Acrasia murmured to him, and Trist realized she was cradling his head in her lap. Auberon's Graal, the very same bowl he had retrieved from the town of Havre de Paix, the night of the Wild Hunt, when Yaél had joined him, was at his lips. But in this moment it was not full of nuts or berries, but of a cold drink that quenched his thirst more thoroughly than the finest wine he'd ever tasted, like a plunge into the cold water of the Rea after a morning's sweat in the practice yard.

The faerie maid held the bowl to Trist's lips, pouring more and more long after he'd drunk as much as he could, and finally, Trist coughed and sputtered. Acrasia took the bowl away. "Is it enough?" She asked, and he felt fingers at his bandages, pulling them aside.

"It's like he was never hurt," Yaél gasped in awe.

"Such is the power of Auberon's Graal," Acrasia said, with a touch of awe herself. Trist took a deep breath, and looked around. The world seemed more clear, more comprehensible. "Even his fever is gone," the faerie said, stroking back Trist's sweat-drenched hair from his forehead. He looked down at his side, and saw fresh, pink skin, three small circles of it where the wounds from Adrammelech's claws had once been.

Before Yaél could pull his hand back, Trist grabbed him by the wrist. There, glinting in the light of the bonfire, was a silver ring set with a moonstone. To Trist's eye, it was a knot of blue and white fire, just like the Faerie King. He winced, and let himself release the squire's wrist. There was no help for it now.

"Our part in this bargain is fulfilled," Auberon's voice drifted down from his throne of carved wood. Trist sat up, for he was strong enough now, and both Yaél and Acrasia helped him to his feet. "You may depart."

"As you command, my King," Acrasia said, bowing her head and lowering her eyes. She carried the graal forward and placed it on the long banquet table, then took three steps back to rejoin Trist and Yaél. "We leave now," she whispered, grabbing each of them by the hand and tugging them along with her. "Do not turn your back on him."

Trist had trained to back away from a monarch since he was six years old, but Yaél had difficulty not stumbling over the uneven grass. Between the three of them, they managed it, and as they retreated into the cleft of rock that marked the entrance to the amphitheater, the sounds of laughter, music, and the clinking of plates and goblets resumed. Once the rock was between them and the faerie court, they turned and proceeded down the dry stream bed until they found a place they could climb out of the ravine and onto the bank. Trist went first, then pulled Yaél after him, rejoicing in the renewed strength of his arm. He was about to turn away when Acrasia held up her arm, as well. Trist frowned, but helped her up anyway.

"I do not have a clear memory of how we came to the ravine," Trist admitted. "Can either of you get us back to where the rest are camped?"

"The sky's light over there," Yaél said, pointing with his finger. "So that's east. I can get us there."

Trist followed the boy through the wooded mountain slopes. If he hadn't been able to see clearly in the dark, he would have tripped and fallen a dozen times, but thanks to the Boon of the Faerie King it was as easy as walking during the daylight.

He considered, as they moved through the woods, the difference in power between Auberon and himself, or even Acrasia. The might Trist had gained from his Accord with Acrasia had been enough to completely upend his life these past weeks, and yet the King of Shadows hardly seemed to have even noticed the new Tithes he was being sent. And his colors were so different from how Acrasia looked...

"M'lord?" Ahead, Yaél had stopped, and now called back to them.

"What is it?" Trist asked, moving up to the squire's side.

"The camp," Yaél said, pointing at a ring of stones. "No one's here."

Trist frowned. By the look of that firepit, no one had cooked here for days.

Chapter Forty-Three

A Ransom

I do not know that it is truly possible for a mortal, no matter how empowered, to comprehend the workings of an Accord. The Priests of the Angelus, and Exarchs such as myself, may make a study of matters spiritual, but we are in the end as nothing more than children. I can tell you this: every Boon we have, we earn, through our own deeds. But without a Tithe to anchor a Boon, to bind it to our very souls, to empower it, those deeds earn us nothing more than potential. Power itself comes only with sacrifice.
-The Testament of Sir Baylin, Exarch of Kadosh

Date Unknown

Yaél poked at the ashes of the firepit with his index finger. "Cold," he confirmed, though Trist had known it just from a glance. In the meanwhile, he'd been wandering the edges of the campsite, looking for tracks. But the truth was, Henry was better at this than he was. Thankfully, Trist had a Boon to take care of this - earned during the course of one wild night ride, and with the advice of Acrasia, without whom he would never have known to ask. The scarlet thread pawed at the back of his mind like a restless steed, eager to be given its head and allowed to run. Silently, he decided that he was hunting Henry, and permitted a single burning cord to unspool from his body, leading off down the mountain slope.

"You should get back in the sword," Trist told Acrasia, who grinned. "Is it close enough for that?"

"Good to see you thinking, my love," she said, and disappeared. Close enough, then, that this should not take long.

"Yaél," Trist said, "Climb up on my back and hold tight." He squatted down, but the boy hesitated.

"I can keep up," his squire protested.

Trist shook his head. "If you could, I would not be asking this," he said. "I am going to use the Boon granted to me by the Horned Hunter, Yaél. It will carry me through the forest faster than you would ever be able to match, even if you were grown. There is no shame in this. Get on."

With a grimace, Yaél stepped up to Trist's back. Trist reached down to get his arms under Yaél's legs, and hoisted the boy up with him as he rose. "Just be sure you do not choke me," he warned, and the squire adjusted his arms so that he was more hugging Trist from behind than strangling him.

Trist took a deep breath, released it, focused on the red line of power leading down the slope of the mountain, and lurched forward. Once he'd got going, and built up momentum, it got easier, even with a squire hanging like an awkward sack of vegetables off his back. Trist focused on his breathing: out, out, in, and the pounding of his boots against the earth. There were rocks to step around, branches to duck, and sections of slope that veered sharply downward, threatening to unbalance him and to send them both careening down in an uncontrolled fall. In short, there was plenty to occupy Trist's attention, and if it wasn't for the fiery red thread of the Hunter's Boon, he would never have been able to run and track their quarry at the same time.

He was dimly aware that no mortal men should have been able to run through the forested mountain slopes of the Hauteurs Massif at this speed. It was not easy, but neither did Trist collapse in exhaustion. He wondered if this was what some large hunting animal, like a wildcat, felt like, moving through the wood as if born to it. Trist did not know how fast he was running, but he knew that it was faster than he had ever run before, even during that rush to ambush the Caliphate lancers only a few days prior. Now, the hunt itself leant him speed: the very thought of coming over the next ridge and finding his quarry filled him with a burst of energy and enthusiasm, like a wolf sighting wounded prey.

Trist ran so quickly that it was difficult for him to judge how far they had come when he first caught sight of the party in the distance, following a deer-path around the base of a rock face. It was so far that he might have missed them, if not for the burning red line leading him on, like a rope tied onto the back of a wagon, dragging him after. He thought he saw horses, and riders, but the numbers escaped him before their chosen trail took them out of sight.

Hours of running should have tired Trist, but now he knew what Cazador must have felt like during that whole long night running with Cern and his hunters. His legs should have burned, but instead they felt strong. His heart pounded, true, with the exertion, but never once did Trist feel he was running out of breath. The whole state seemed so miraculous and precarious that even when his stomach began to growl at him, he did not stop for a meal. Only after he'd made the decision, and then run on, did it occur to him that his saddlebags and supplies were with the targets of his pursuit, anyway.

The sun was high in the sky when he first caught sight of their quarry, and it had dipped halfway to the treeline by the time they raced along the same deer-path. How much time had he made up? Trist couldn't be certain, but he kept going.

As the sun burnt the clouds red like the thread of power he followed, Trist continued, the falling dark not even slowing him. Now, Auberon's Boon came into play, as well: the shadows were his friends, the falling night as clear to him as the brightest day.

"How can you see?" Yaél called to him, and Trist huffed out a response.

"I am a Knight of Shadows," he exhaled, sucked in two breaths, continued. "Of Auberon." He knew Yaél didn't have the context to understand, but they could talk about it once they'd caught back up to Henry, Cazador, and their supplies. Would he have to fight the woman in red when they met? Trist would prefer not to, but it wasn't entirely under his control.

It might have been instinct that brought him to a halt, finally; it might have been the excited thrumming of the red line, or it might have been that his nose caught the smell of woodsmoke on the mountain breeze.

"Get down," Trist murmured to Yaél, and the boy clambered off his back. Trist waited for a moment to see whether he would be hit by a sudden wave of fatigue; the only other times he had used the Hunter's Boon, he'd been riding Cazador the whole way. To his surprise, he felt loose, like he'd warmed up in the practice yard and was ready to spar.

"Are we taking them by surprise?" Yaél hissed eagerly.

"No." Trist shook his head. "A knight conducts themselves with honor, even against their opponents. Stay behind me a step."

Before he could think better of it, Trist straightened and strode forward, through a screen of juniper, open hands held out to his sides to show he had no weapon, and called out, "Red Lady! I come unarmed."

Regardless, his appearance had everyone around the fire scrambling to their feet as Trist and Yaél entered the firelight. Now that he could look them over without fever clouding his mind, Trist saw that the southern Exarch and her lancers had been ill used by the attacks of Adrammelech's horrid birds. Claws had left gouges in the brigandine armor of the Caliphate soldiers, and two of the surviving four had wounds wrapped in bloody bandages.

The Exarch herself - Ismet, he recalled her name - had drawn her curved blade with a ring of steel on leather, and held it in line with his chest using an unfamiliar guard. "First you flee," she chastised him, "And then you return by cover of darkness to ambush us? Truly you northerners have no honor."

"I come not to fight you," Trist said, stepping fully into the firelight with both hands still raised. "Truly, how could I? Look at me. I wear no armor and carry no sword. You have both of those things still, unless you have thrown them aside along your march. Nor did I seek to flee; we returned as soon as we were able, though it appears the stories of time spent among the faerie courts are true enough."

"M'lord," Henry said, stepping forward. "Is it truly you? But you were on the brink of death three nights past!"

"It's us!" Yaél said, eyes shining wide in the firelight. "We went to a faerie feast, and King Auberon healed Trist, and gave me a ring, and then when we came back to the fire you were all gone, and for us it was only a single night! You say it's been three days?"

"Aye," Sir Divdan said. "We searched for you the first day, but your tracks stopped at a ravine. Lady Ismet thought you'd used the rushing water to cover your tracks, so her men searched downstream, and then up as far as the waterfall, but none of us - not even Henry - ever found where you came out of the stream."

"Water?" Yaél frowned. "I know the ravine - but when we went into it, it was dry!"

"Enough!" Ismet shouted them all down. "No man true of faith to the Angelus would go crawling to the faeries for his life."

"I did not ask for my life," Trist admitted. At that, Acrasia appeared to his eyes, standing just behind the southern woman. The faerie's arms were crossed over her chest, and she scowled at the Caliphate Exarch.

"She would not dare speak in such a manner in the presence of my king," Acrasia grumbled.

"I asked," Trist continued, "for King Auberon to ride out against the Prince of Plagues. He refused, but healed me instead. I do not know what any one man can do against such an evil, but now that I have the chance I must try. I ask you, Lady Ismet, to lend me my sword and armor and horse, so that I can face the daemon."

"You have a ransom for me, then, hidden perhaps in your boots?" The other Exarch arched her eyebrows, but the point of her blade did not waver.

"I do not," Trist admitted. "And so I can only appeal to your honor as an Exarch, and to your duty to the Angelus you serve. Adrammelech, daemon Prince of Plagues, is free. The monster will fall upon one or both of our armies, and begin slaughtering our countrymen just as he slaughtered your men at the top of the stairs," he pleaded with her, voice rising in volume despite himself as he went.

"Every man or woman killed becomes a foul, demonic bird, with feathers hard as iron and a beak that can rend a man's throat. That is the first plague," Trist explained. "A flock of those creatures will fall upon the fields and the orchards and pick them bare, and the entire region will starve. Those that survive, at any rate. But my lady, it will not end there."

Ismet ibnah Salah had not yet cut him down, so Trist pushed ahead with the only weapon he had: his words. "The second plague is the screams, the wailing of the daemon. It makes you bleed from the ears and drives you to madness with the pain. We survived only because of my squire Yaél's quick thinking - with plugs of wax in our ears. But the third is the worst. The daemon's evil has already spread to encompass the entire cavern where it was bound; now it will look to corrupt other lands, as well. It will strike holy places, and despoil them until they reek of evil. The choice you have, Lady Ismet," he appealed, "is nothing more or less than this: will you help me fight this evil, or will you stand aside and allow it to happen?"

"I am the Exarch of Epinoia," the southern woman hissed, her eyes fierce, putting Trist in mind of nothing more than a wildcat. "The entire reason I came to these lands is to fight daemons."

Trist spread his arms. "Then your choice must be clear, is it not, my lady? Stand with me. Perhaps two Exarchs have a chance to succeed where one failed."

Ismet ibnah Salah lowered her sword.

Chapter Forty-Four

An Alliance

The Narvonnian way of handling Exarchs is every bit as ridiculous as the rest of their backwards kingdom. Whatever Exarchs they happen to end up with waste most of their time protecting a mortal king, rather than doing the work of the Angelus. At the University of Ma'īn, we train the best and the brightest of the entire Caliphate, to give the Angelus the pick of our top students.

-The Commentaries of Aram ibn Bashear

11th Day of the Flower Moon, 297 AC

"Here, eat something other than faerie food, m'lord," Henry said, offering Trist a bowl. The entire group, allies now of necessity, sat around the cookfire. "Our, um, friends here brought good turnips, and something they call 'chard.' I managed to bag a brace of coneys as the sun was going down."

"In truth, they offered us nothing to eat," Trist admitted, accepting the bowl gratefully and savoring a mouthful of what turned out to be a hearty rabbit stew. It was only after swallowing that he realized how hollow and empty his stomach was.

"Good," Acrasia murmured, sitting at his side. "The healing will have taken a lot out of your body, Trist. Eating will help to restore your strength."

"Do you have a plan?" Ismet asked. Because she couldn't hear Acrasia, her words tumbled over the end of what the faerie maid was saying, and it took Trist's ear a moment to sort it out.

"I have a Boon," Trist explained, "From Cern the Hunter. It allows me to track my quarry, regardless of where they go, and lends speed and endurance to both myself and to my steed. If I had been able to Tithe more souls into the Boon, I might have been able to use it to aid all of us, like the Horned Hunter can, but I am not capable of that yet. No matter," he decided. "It is the tracking that is most important. So long as we hunt the Prince of Plagues, I can lead us to the daemon."

"What do we do when we find it?" Sir Divdan asked, leaning forward into the firelight.

"You stay back," Ismet said firmly. "Such a creature cannot be slain by mortal men - only by Exarchs."

"What all of you can do," Trist said, "Is to try to keep the birds off us. Once we get a look at where the daemon is, we will have a better idea; but you may be able to clear us a path, or to protect our flank." He turned to Ismet. "Have you ever slain a daemon before?" He asked her.

After a moment, the southern Exarch shook her head. "I have not," Ismet admitted.

Trist's heart sank. He had been hoping that she would have the Daemon Bane Boon, already. They would have to do without it. "Can you see," he asked, "Their true form? The lashes of fire?"

"...extending out behind them, like a knot of threads?" Ismet asked. "I have seen that when I look at Epinoia, occasionally," she murmured. "In glimpses."

"If Epinoia is willing," Trist said cautiously, "She and Acrasia can attack that. It is part of the true body of the daemon; what most people can see is only a small portion, and the less vital, I believe." For just an instant, Trist heard the flutter of wings in his ears, and he caught a glimpse of spools winding back from Ismet's body, burning red.

"The Angelus will aid us," was all that the Caliphate knight said.

"Good," Trist said. He considered whether they should ride right then, as soon as everyone had finished eating their evening meal. He could see just as well in the dark as during the day, after all, due to Auberon's Boon, and tracking the daemon would work either way, since he'd be following a thread of fire. The fear of what the Prince of Plagues might already be doing, down at the pass, spurred him on; but he also knew that if one of the horses broke a leg in the dark, it would only slow them down more. In the end, he decided it was better to take a measured pace than to rush ahead.

"You know you aren't any more powerful now than you were under the mountain," Acrasia warned him as he settled into his bedroll to sleep. When they all rose in the morning, Trist would have to thank Henry for making sure that none of his saddlebags had been discarded. Acrasia, or at least the illusion of her, lay on the ground next to him, her head supported in one hand, her blonde hair tumbling about her arm like a waterfall.

"I know," Trist murmured. "But this time we will not be alone. We have a second Exarch to ride with us, and with luck, we may even be able to meet up with Sir Bors, or the leader of the Caliphate army. If we can arrange it so that all four of us fight the thing..."

"That might be enough," Acrasia agreed hesitantly. "But promise me this, Trist. We're going to find the aftermath of whatever Adrammelech has been doing, as we come down out of the mountains. Don't be stubborn about Tithing from what you find."

"I will not kill innocent people," Trist protested.

"Not even out of mercy?" Acrasia glared at him. "You've seen where those birds come from, and what they can do. If you find people in the midst of turning, you had better put them out of their misery and use them to prepare yourself. They will be dead either way, and a lot harder to kill once they have wings."

Trist sighed. "I know you speak sense," he admitted, after a long moment. "If the only thing I can do for someone is to give them a quick and merciful death, then I will do it. Not for my own power, but to ease their suffering."

"My sweet love," Acrasia said, and the words made Trist flinch. "You are too innocent for all of this. I've loved you for it, but I fear that unless you harden yourself, your ideals will get you killed."

He rolled onto his side, away from her, and did his best to sleep.

The mixed group of southerners and northerners rose with the first light of dawn, broke their fast on cheese and dried meat, and armed themselves beneath the orange and pink stained clouds that spread overhead.

"You did good smoothing the metal out," Trist complimented Yaél, as the squire helped strap on his cuirass. "And Henry, thank you for making certain they did not throw aside any of my things," he remembered to tell the hunter, with a smile.

"Do we have a chance at beating it?" Yaél asked, rising to fetch his own shirt of steel rings.

"'Course we do," Henry said, checking over the fletching on his remaining arrows. "We might as well be living a legend, lad. Faerie kings and daemons under the mountain, our lord coming back from the edge of death..."

"It is like a story," Yaél admitted, wriggling into the mass of chain mail down over his head until it fell about his body.

"Here, let me help you belt that," Trist said. "You still do not pull it tight enough." He made certain that Yaél's leather scabbard would hang right over his left hip, and that the belt wouldn't loosen.

"Exarch," a woman's voice called, and Trist turned to see Ismet ibnah Salah approaching, his sheathed longsword held in her hands. "I believe you will need this, before we are finished." She was fully armored, now, in brigandine and a steel cap that sat over her long red veil.

"Thank you," Trist said, accepting the sword. "For trusting me."

"Trust is earned," the southern woman said, after a moment. "You earned some coming back, when you could have fled. Earn the rest today."

"As you say." Trist buckled his own sword belt on, then strode over to Cazador. "You ready, Caz?" He asked, taking a moment to pet the destrier's soft nose. Caz sniffed around his hand, and Trist fed him a handful of oats. One of their last handfuls; they'd been up in the mountains long enough to be nearly out of supplies, despite all they'd brought with them from Falais. "Good boy," he murmured, then brushed the last of the oats off from his hand when Caz had finished. Trist placed one boot in his stirrup, and swung himself up into his saddle. It would have been good, he thought, to have a lance for charging, but Sir Divdan had been correct that lances would be too unwieldy in the wooded slopes. Trist looked around. The entire group was mounted, even Henry, on a small southern mare who must have lost her rider to Adrammelech's escape from the stairs. The hunter sat his saddle like a sack of moldy turnips, but Trist guessed he would be better able to keep up this way than on foot.

"Adramelech isn't like anyone you've ever used your Boon on before," Acrasia warned him, appearing in her preferred spot just in front of him. "He will feel it, Trist, and he'll be able to see your thread coming. You won't take him by surprise."

"Good," Trist said, with a grunt. "Let the daemon feel what it is like to be the prey, just for once. To be hunted, instead of the hunter." With that, he invoked the Hunter's Boon, casting out a thread of fire such a dark red it reminded him of wine. Trist felt the burning thread latch onto something, down below the foothills, south and east of where they were.

"I have it," he called to the group. "Follow me!" And then Trist urged Caz into the woods - though in truth the destrier needed little urging. He was as full of vigor as a colt, and did not flag once on the ride. Trist had to hold Cazador back, for the benefit of the other horses, and it put into plain contrast just how much the Boon lent strength to his steed. He itched to give Caz his head and leave everyone else behind, and to let him run like they had with the Wild Hunt.

Henry had said this was like a story, and Trist supposed that it might sound that way to someone who wasn't actually in the middle of it. What would a troubadour have said, he wondered, of that ride down out of the Hauteurs Massif? Would their words have lingered on the glint of morning sunlight off steel? The pounding of hooves? The southern and northern knights riding together, putting aside their differences to fight a greater evil? It was all there, but it came along with a rumbling, hollow belly, a sore ass from riding, and a persistent doubt: a fear that he was leading all of these people to their deaths, just like he'd led Luc down under the mountain.

The big man hadn't deserved what he'd gotten. If there was any justice in the world, Trist thought, it would have been him that died, instead. With a sword in the daemon, perhaps, giving up his life to save the rest of them. But there hadn't been time for much of a noble sacrifice: one moment Luc had been fine, and the next, he was convulsing on the ground and there was nothing that Trist could do to help.

Trist thought of the farms in the foothills, and wondered how many other people had been touched by those lights like fireflies and fallen, wracked with horrific pain, only to rise again on metal wings in the service of the Prince of Plagues. They wouldn't even know what the lights were, because there was no one to warn them.

When they stopped to eat the last of their food, it was atop a high bluff from which they could see the city of Falais, and the point just north of the city where the Narvonnian army had been encamped only a week before. The army was gone, Trist saw, at a glance. He washed a bite of cheese down with a gulp from his flask, which was long since more stream-water than wine.

"They will have marched south, I should think," Sir Divdan said, following Trist's gaze.

"By now," Imset said, coming up beside them, "General Shadi will have invested the Tower of Tears at the southern end of the pass. He was just making camp south of the wall when I rode out."

"What was your mission?" Trist asked her, and the southern woman shot him a look. "To take the archers above the pass? I am simply trying to understand," he assured her. "Whatever you were going to do, surely it does not matter now?"

"Archers if we happened upon them," she answered after a moment, with a sigh. "But no. The General could feel something waking in the heights. He did not know what, but it must have been the Prince of Plagues. He sent us to find what it was, and defeat it."

"We both had the same mission, then," Trist said quietly, watching as a vast flock of black birds rose above the pass. "And now we must see it done. Whatever stands in our way."

Chapter Forty-Five

The Battle of Falais I: The Tower of Tears

Three towers, the northerners built to bar our passage through the Hauteurs Massif: to the west, on the cliffs above the sea, the Tour de Roche Rouge, or Red Rocks Tower, named for the way the sunset paints the stone. In the center of the mountain range, the Flèche de L'aube, which men call Dawn Spire, the tip of which is said to be the first and last place lit by the sun. And the Tour de Larmes, which would better have been named the Tower of Blood.

-The Commentaries of Aram ibn Bashear

12th Day of the Flower Moon, 297 AC

"Six days of this weighs on the nerves," Lady Valeria du Champs d'Or observed, coming up behind Lionel as he looked down from the ramparts of the Tower of Tears, upon the encampment of the Caliphate army. The southern soldiers were stirring in the light of early dawn, just out of bowshot. "I can feel it in your muscles," she continued, running her fingers over his neck and upper back. "The tension."

For a moment, Lionel allowed his eyes to half-close under the pressure of her strong fingers, in equal parts pain and relief. It had been a dozen years since Gwen had touched him like this, and no other woman since her death. It was clear to him what Valeria and her father, Baron Maël, had set as their prize: Valeria wed to Lionel, Crown Princess of Narvonne, and future Queen. With his daughter the mother of the dynasty's next generation, the wealthy Baron would wield a great deal of influence.

That it was clear did not particularly argue against allowing it to happen, however. Lionel would have been more reticent if their aims were concealed, but sending Valeria south with her father's troops had been as clear a signal as anyone could expect. And, to her credit, the young woman had been both attentive and dutiful, molding herself to Lionel's day to day routines as if to say: 'look, see how useful I would be as your wife. How will you make do without me?' She mended his stockings and shirts before he even noticed they were worn, organized the piles of papers that threatened to overwhelm him with matters of logistics, and made certain he ate even when he was lost in his work.

Nor were there any particularly better matches, he had to admit. Should he send to the Grand Duchy of Kimmeria, perhaps, or the March of Scandia, for a foreign princess? Why go to the trouble when there was an intelligent, beautiful woman of his own country right here, standing at his side even during war against the Caliphate? Valeria had made it plain that he could take her to his bed whenever he wanted, so long as he was willing to pay the price: a simple announcement of their betrothal, with a wedding ceremony to follow after the war was won.

"Thank you," Lionel said, shrugging away from Valeria's grasp. "Your hands do me a world of good, Lady Valeria, but I need to arm myself, and get down to the wall," he told her. "Kay," he called, and his squire stepped forward, ready to help him.

The young man was quick and efficient, well practiced at the task. Kay had served Lionel for six years now, and in truth, it was nearly time for Lionel to knight the lad and find a replacement. Kay secured plates of blackened steel to the Prince's body, enameled in gold, with delicately carved roaring lion heads carved into the pauldrons, the caps of the knees and elbows, the borders of the vambraces, and even the helm. They left the helm off for the moment, but his squire did firmly buckle a sheathed arming sword at Lionel's waist. He did not intend to throw himself into the thick of the fighting: that was not the place of a commander. If something did happen, Lionel knew Kay would have what he needed close at hand.

"Have you been able to find a few moments with your father?" Lionel asked his squire. A few paces to the left, Lady Valeria poured herself a goblet of wine.

"Here and there," Kay assured him. "He is well. Troubled a bit by matters concerning my sister."

Kay's father was Urien, Baron du Rocher de la Garde. "Had a chance to form a judgment of your new brother in law?" Lionel asked quietly.

"His squire's an enthusiastic lad," Kay said, after a moment. "Knows practically nothing, but loyal. It seems the Exarch rescued him from a life on the streets of Havre de Paix."

"Fishing town," Lionel recalled.

"Yes, Your Highness," Kay answered. Lionel clapped him on the shoulder, and headed for the stairwell.

By the time Lionel and Kay had joined Dame Chantal on the parapet of the wall, the Caliphate army was preparing their siege engines. "They work faster than we predicted, Your Highness," the older woman commented. "Four trebuchets in three days, and I count seven in working order this morning."

"They will have brought the pieces from Maʿīn in their baggage train," Lionel observed. "Shadi learned as much from what happened twenty-four years ago as we did. And there will be plenty of stone in the foothills. They have more engines here, now, than we have at Falais."

"So they do," Chantal agreed, and beckoned over one of the boys who ran messages for them. "Tell the scorpion crews to target the men working the enemy trebuchets," she ordered.

With a deafening impact, the first rock of the morning hit the wall. A moment later, all of the trebuchets were letting fly with their loads of stone, adding to the scars of three days of impacts on the wall across the pass. The scorpions, gigantic crossbows which launched bolts the size of a lance, began to fire at Dame Chantal's command, and Lionel observed a bolt impale one southerner, continue on from the overwhelming force of the siege engine, and pierce the body of a second man, driving them both to the ground like two spitted rabbits ready to be roasted over a fire.

Somewhere off to their right, over the cliffs which loomed above the Passe de Mûre, unexpected movement caught the Crown Prince's eye. He turned, to see a massive flock of birds winging southeast, down out of the mountains. For a moment, the significance of the sight didn't register with him.

The scream came from somewhere atop the cliffs above: an unearthly, inhuman wailing that made Lionel's teeth ache. All around him, men stopped what they were doing to grab their ears in their hands, desperate to get away from the sound. The Prince was no different, but he had enough presence of mind to look down at the enemy encampment and siege engine crews. There, men were also crying out in pain, trying to shield their own ears.

The swarm of birds descended on the southern troops. Before Lionel's eyes, one bird tore out a man's throat with its beak, shaking the corpse once and leaving it on the ground at the base of the center trebuchet. Before it could lift off again, one of the other Caliphate soldiers rushed forward and cut at the bird with his scimitar, but the curved blade glanced off the feathers of the bird's wings as if they were armored. The bird's neck lashed out, long and sinuous like a snake, and the second man screamed in pain, clutching at his eye.

But what the Crown Prince could not look away from was the corpse. It bulged and shook, as if it were an egg just beginning to hatch. In a sudden spray of blood and ichor, the corpse burst open. A second bird shook its wings, spraying gore in every direction.

The savage call of an inhuman thing sounded from Lionel's left, and he spun to see a fluttering of wings as another of the monsters descended on his own men. In an instant of clarity, the Prince knew he could not allow it to kill even a single one of the soldiers on the parapet. One bird would turn into two, and before long they would be overwhelmed by a swarm of the things.

"To me!" Lionel called, drawing his arming sword from its sheath and raising it high for a second before rushing the creature. He was dimly aware of Dame Chantal and Kay following him, but he could not wait.

Rather than the wings, the Prince swung for the monster's neck. There were not so many feathers there, he could see, and his blade bit into the serpentine length about halfway between the shoulders and the back of the head. The terrible bird reared back from its unfinished prey with a shriek, and then Chantal was beside him, plunging her own blade into its eye socket, while Kay swung at its legs. The three of them hacked at the beast long after it had stopped moving, until they were sure it was dead, then turned to a fallen soldier.

"Will he live?" Lionel asked Chantal.

"He'll lose the arm," the commander of the tower said, "But I think the surgeons can save him." Lionel nodded, and stepped back to let her handle it. Men rushed in at Dame Chantal's orders to carry the wounded man off.

Kay was at his side, holding out Lionel's helm, but he waited a moment, scanning the battlefield on both sides of the wall. The helm would protect him from the birds, but it also constricted his view, and the Prince needed at least one good look to get an unobstructed glance at what was happening.

The flock of monstrous birds had fallen upon both his men, and the men of the Caliphate. Everywhere he looked, Lionel could see soldiers fighting and dying against the monsters; and everywhere a man died, another bird rose in his place. The math was not difficult.

"Forget the southerners," Lionel told Dame Chantal, accepting his helm from Kay, now, and settling it on his head. "Our enemy is the birds. Get our infantry into formation to protect our archers, and have the archers focus on bringing those birds down. And send someone to get Lady Valeria out of here. Send her north to Falais with a small guard and the fastest horses we have. This is no place for her, now." His squire handed him his shield, and the Prince settled it on his left arm. "And tell Exarch Bors to prepare himself."

With half a dozen other men, they formed up around the trebuchet: archers on the inside, Lionel, Chantal, Kay and the rest around the outside. The battle descended into a hacking chaos: a bird would come at them, and they would close shields. Its beak either got to someone or it didn't, but either way, they stabbed with their arming swords until it fell. In the meanwhile, the archers behind them nocked, drew, and loosed their arrows over and over again. The strong, Iebara wood longbows drove the arrows through even the armored wings of these horrors, and Lionel wondered whether Sir Trist was alive. He guessed not, given the monsters that were hammering the army.

A note changed in his ear, and Lionel craned his neck to get a look over the wall. Out of the mass of screams and battle cries a cheer was rising from the Caliphate camp.

"General Shadi!" the southerners shouted in jubilation. "General Shadi and Jibrīl!"

A light broke upon the battlefield like the sun rising in the east, and Lionel heard the fluttering of wings somewhere nearby. "Two Exarchs," he shouted, gritting his teeth. "Hold strong! We have two Exarchs on the field, now!" It was strange to hear his own men cheering a general who had been their enemy an hour ago, but if it got them through this disaster the prince would take it.

Then, another ear-splitting, stomach clenching shriek rent the sky above the battlefield. Lionel looked up, and a cold stone settled deep at the bottom of his stomach.

The daemon in the sky had wings feathered red and orange and purple. Its body was all muscle, with unearthly blue skin stretched so tightly it looked apt to tear at any moment. The head had horns like those of a ram, and it extended its arms out to both sides, head thrown back to utter its horrifying cry.

"Adrammelech," Lionel groaned.

The Prince of Plagues dropped out of the sky like a hawk, plunging toward General Shadi ibn Yusuf.

Chapter Forty-Six

The Battle of Falais II: Into the Pass

The part of the Cataclysm I won't ever forget - no one who lived through it will - is the hunger. If you've only ever missed a meal, or fasted for a day, you don't understand. When farms burn, when whole villages are wiped out by the Queen of Plagues, when those damned daemon birds come down out of the sky and eat an entire field of crops, well, all of that food was meant to go somewhere. And now that food is gone. I figure we lost as many from famine as from the damned plague.
-The Life and Times of Legionary Titus Nasica

12th Day of the Flower Moon, 297 AC

They found a farm picked clean, as they rode down out of the foothills under the golden hot afternoon sun, in sight now of Falais perched between the high cliffs and the tumbling River Durentia. The fields were empty of wheat, and there were no chickens, goats, or pigs in sight, nor any sign of the peasants who should have been working the land.

"This would have been an herb garden," Sir Divdan said, from where he'd reined up next to a wooden fence. "Nothing but dirt left now."

"And bones," Yaél pointed out with one raised hand.

"A cow, I think," Trist said, walking Caz over to the fresh carcass, stripped of fat and muscle but with a bit of wet gristle left on yellow ribs that had not yet been baked dry.

"Adrammelech's birds," Acrasia confirmed, from where she nestled back into his arms. "This is why they called him the Prince of Plagues," she reminded Trist.

"Can you tell where the daemon is?" Ismet asked him, looking away from the corpse in distaste. At a motion from her hand, her remaining lancers circled around, keeping watch for any threats. Trist saw that Henry kept his bow of Iebara wood in hand, even though a longbow was not truly suited to use from horseback.

Trist looked up, letting his eyes follow the uncoiled line of dim red that traced a path directly through the town, and then into the pass. "South," he said, with complete confidence. "Somewhere through the Passe de Mûre. Perhaps at the Tour de Larmes," he guessed, "Though I cannot tell from here."

Ismet frowned. "If the monster has gone that far south... he will be facing General Shadi and Jibrīl."

"That's a good thing, right?" Yaél asked. "The Exarch'll stop the monster before it hurts anyone! Or Sir Bors will!"

"How powerful is the General? Has he faced a daemon before?" Trist asked. He wasn't as confident as his squire.

"Not a year past, he defeated Agares the Eld," the southern woman answered. "In the Maghreb Wastes. He is stronger than either of us."

Trist looked to Acrasia, who shook her head. "Agares is a minor daemon," the faerie said simply. "If I was at my full strength, I could defeat him myself."

"We need to ride," Trist said. "Better for all the Exarchs to face this monster at once, rather than let him defeat us in detail." He pressed his boots into Cazador's flank, turned the destrier's head, and led the group off at a trot.

Now that they were down out of the foothills, with roads to use, the horses made better time. Not an hour later, they thundered into Falais, with Sir Divdan shouting to the guards as they passed.

"Make way!" The other knight bellowed. "Make way for the Exarch!" People dived out of their path as they trotted down the main thoroughfare of the town, the river on their left, the cliffs looming overhead on their right. Trist spared a glance for the Church of Saint Abatur. Father Kramer had said it was built over the corpse of an Angelus, but if there was any way to use that against the enemy they faced, Trist didn't know it. Not for the first time, he felt like a green boy again, thrown onto the training yard with no idea how to fight. The truth was that he didn't know everything an Exarch should know, and was not ready to face Adramelech again.

As they came to the southern wall of Falais, Trist could see soldiers pouring back through the gate from the pass. Everywhere he looked, men were bleeding and wounded, but when they saw him coming, they cheered.

"The Exarch!" men shouted. He didn't know how they'd come to recognize his face so quickly - he'd only been in the camp for a few days. A wave of relief seemed to pass through the wounded soldiers, and they spread to either side, making way for Trist and his companions to pass.

"Trist du Camaret-à-Arden!" a woman's voice shouted from the parapet of the city wall, and Trist reined Caz in. Craning his neck to look above, he picked out the banner of the Baroness, a black mountain on red. Lady Arnive was leaning down from the parapet.

"We cannot stay here," Trist called up to her. "There is no time! The Prince of Plagues is loose."

Arnive's skin paled, but her face was set with determination. "The main part of his flock has fallen upon both armies," she said. "The Prince is still there, and the damned birds are harrying our men the length of the pass. Urien's knights are in no position to relieve them. Can you help?"

"Lances, and shields!" Trist called, and men rushed to obey. "We will do what we can, Baroness!" Divdan and he settled shields onto their left arms with the ease of long practice, while Ismet pulled her own round shield off her back. Her riders followed suit without needing to be told. When the lances came, the two knights took them in their right hands and held them upright, resting the butts on top of their boots. "Do not try," he advised Yaél, turning to face the boy when he saw someone making to hand the squire a lance. Henry, at least, knew himself well enough to wave the offer of weapons off. "You have not trained for it. Take the shield, follow behind us, and use your sword."

Yaél nodded quickly. From the cast of his face, Trist gave it even odds the boy would empty his stomach soon.

"Angelus guide you!" Arnive shouted after them as they rode through the gate, out onto the beaten earth road that stretched the length of the Passe de Mûre.

"How far to the southern end of the pass?" Trist called to Sir Divdan as they rode. The groups of fleeing, wounded men did not lessen as they moved away from the town.

"Ten miles," the older knight replied. "It winds a bit," he warned them.

"We set a steady pace, then," Ismet recommended, and Trist agreed with her.

"Aye," he said. Divdan rode at his left, the southern knight at his right, and her lancers to either side, the group of them forming a tight wedge that protected both Henry and Yaél from not only the front, but from the sides as well. At a trot, they might be able to make the wall and the tower in an hour, if they did not have to stop to fight. They might have done it in half the time at a gallop, but they'd blow the horses out completely. It had already been a long day coming down out of the hills, and even breaking to water their mounts, none of them were truly fresh.

It might have been a quarter of an hour later that they rounded an outcropping of rock where the road and the pass followed a turn of the river; time seemed to distort strangely for Trist. He was at once impatient to get where they could finally do some good, but also, he could admit to himself, terrified of what was to come. And then the enemy was in front of them, and there was no more time for fear, or for anticipation.

A small group of riders was galloping north up the pass, straight for them: a woman surrounded by three horsemen, all but her armed and wearing the prince's colors: a golden lion on black. Above, a fragment of the great flock wheeled, and two of Adrammelech's horrid birds swooped down before there was any hope that Trist and his companions could possibly close the distance. One dived and banked, straight into the flank of the horse of the rearmost rider, knocking the courser to the ground with the rider still in the saddle. The man and horse landed heavily, and Trist winced as the man screamed.

"Go on!" the guard's shout made its way to them over the cries of the birds. "Get her away!" The second diving bird hit him then, came down right atop the man's chest where he was pinned beneath the thrashing horse, and its beak shot down at the man's face.

"Lances!" Trist cried, and next to him Ismet echoed him in the tongue of the southerners. As one, seven lances descended, and the riders picked up speed. Bird after horrid bird was swooping down out of the sky now, and one picked a rider out of his saddle like a child plucking berries off a bush.

Ismet called out in the language of the south, beside him, and her men cheered.

"For Falais!" Sir Divdan cried. The birds were nearly on the woman, her guards dying around her, giving their lives for hers.

"And Narvonne!" Trist shouted with him.

They crashed against the birds like water tumbling from atop the falls down onto the rocks below, and the birds broke. Trist aimed his lance like he had a thousand times in the practice yard, under the watchful gaze of his father and John Granger. The bird in front of him pulled its head up on its long, serpentine neck, ripping an eye from the socket of the man beneath, and then Trist's lance pierced it through the chest. Cazador carried him past, and the lance took the impaled bird with them. He wasn't able to Tithe the monster, but there was plenty of that to come. Trist dropped the lance and the dying bird and drew his longsword.

The wedge of riders had all come through their charge: the birds had been focused on their victims, and only now that half a dozen of them were dying did they see the danger. Trist led them in a wheel almost to the bank of the river, then back to where dead men and dying horses had fallen. The Ornes they hadn't got the first time through flapped their great wings, desperate to take flight, but they weren't fast enough. Trist and his companions rode through them on a second pass, this time with swords flashing under the hot sun, and the foul blood of Adrammelech's birds painted the rocks around them.

Overhead, dozens more of the monsters circled. The muscles in Trist's arms clenched as a Tithe surged up his blade, and this one was for him, finally. "Henry," he said, looking up at the birds crying out in the sky, "Are they in bowshot? I mislike leaving them to simply dive at us whenever they wish." His broken oath weighed on his mind; it would be all too easy for one of the Ornes to swoop down at his back.

"I should think they are," Henry said, sliding down off his horse and nocking an arrow. Trist dismounted, as well, in front of the single horse which had fallen but not risen. Divdan began going from man to man, killing the new-formed birds growing within them with a single stroke each.

"A broken leg," Trist said, and plunged the point of his sword into the poor beast's heart. "Were you able to get it?" He asked Acrasia.

"I think so," the faerie said, appearing next to him. "But Trist..." Her brow furrowed. "Something is odd, here."

"I owe you my life, Exarch," a woman's voice broke across the pass, and Trist turned, recognizing at last the rider these men had died to protect.

"Lady Valeria," he said, surprised. "It is good to see you unharmed. You were at the southern end of the pass? How fares our Prince?"

The wind tussled Valeria's auburn hair as she guided her palfrey close enough to him to speak without shouting. "Not well, I fear," she said. "The birds grow in number whenever they kill. Both Exarchs are locked in battle with the Prince of Plagues, but I do not know if they will be enough, even fighting together."

Trist's brow furrowed. "Did the Prince tell you of our mission?" he asked.

"Trist!" Acrasia screamed, and he threw an arm up in time to keep the diving owl from his eyes.

Chapter Forty-Seven

The Battle of Falais III: Agrat

The Queen of Plagues, as she calls herself, was never one to participate in direct combat. Instead, Agrat the Dancer's presence could be felt in the waves of sickness that began at Velatessia, and then were carried by Aurelius' army to every corner of Narvonne.
-The Marian Codex

12th Day of the Flower Moon, 297 AC

The owl was a knot of dull fire, just as it had been under the mountain, and a coil of orange wrapped around Trist's forearm, even as it banked to his right and swooped back up out of reach.

"Agrat," he hissed, as the metal of his left vambrace heated up. Rather than chance the awkward cut, he yanked the daemonic owl towards him with his left arm, then swung his longsword in an arc to intercept its physical body. Its wings were an unnatural, deep purple-red, its eyes crusted and leaking black filth. To his surprise, the monster was forced to release its hold on him, uncoiling the tendril, to flutter back out of reach and escape the counterstroke. Even with his increased strength, Trist doubted a ploy like that would have worked on the Addanc.

Next to him, Acrasia shrieked in anger, unspooling her own fiery threads, but she lashed out at Lady Valeria instead of the owl.

"What are you doing?" Trist shouted as the noble woman yanked her palfrey's head around by the reins.

"Look at her, Trist! Look!" Acrasia screamed, and he did, narrowing his eyes as if he was trying to look into the sun. There was - something. The air around Valeria du Champs d'Or wavered under his regard, and it reminded him of the air shimmering over a hot rock at the height of summer, one that had been baking under the sun all day. Something in his eyes snapped into place, or perhaps something broke about the noblewoman he was staring at, and suddenly he could see it: the threads of red and orange fire running throughout her body, the knot at her heart, and the tether connecting her to the owl. Connecting her to the daemon Agrat.

"It is you," Trist exhaled. He wasn't the quickest mind around, but once he saw, and understood, it was impossible to be mistaken about this. "She is a daemonic Exarch!" he shouted, to warn the others, then raised his sword into High Guard, and lunged forward, swinging his blade down and around into a horizontal slice at the legs of the palfrey, to cut the horse out from beneath Valeria and prevent her from riding away.

Before his sword could connect, something dove out of the sky, crashed into him, and knocked Trist aside, bearing him to the ground. He had a brief impression of leathery wings, soft curls of hair, a warm body, and he thrust it aside, spinning to reorient himself and withdrawing back a step, giving himself space to get his blade up in front of him, extended straight out to create distance in the guard sometimes dubbed 'unicorn.'

The daemon Agrat stood between Valeria and Trist, now revealed in her true form. She took the shape of a woman, as Acrasia did, but her skin was sallow: pale, with a faint yellow-ish cast, and a feverish sheen of sweat. Wine dark hair the same color as her wings hung in moist curls around her shoulders and collarbone, and her eyes were wine-red as well, dripping dark, crusted tears like the dregs at the bottom of a goblet. Four horns rose from her head: two from the hair above her eyes, and two from the sides, just behind her ears, all curved backward to elegant points. Her delicate fingers ended in wicked claws.

Ismet stepped up beside him, curved sword in her hand. "Four against two, daemon," the southern knight spat. "A poor choice to face us here and now."

Valeria pouted, as Trist had seen her do while clinging to the arm of the Crown Prince. "I admit, I had not intended to be discovered so soon," she said, the palfrey pacing. Sir Divdan, Ismet's men, and even Yaél had all moved to circle her, cutting off any avenue of escape. Trist couldn't see Henry, but he was certain the hunter had an arrow nocked to his Iebara-wood longbow.

"Not 'till after you'd wed the Crown Prince, I wager," Divdan said with a scowl. Trist's eyes widened. Of course! He could see the outlines of a stratagem taking shape, though still indistinct in his mind. She would wed Lionel Aurelianus; the king would be disposed of somehow or other, and after she'd given birth to a son, her husband would be disposable. As the mother of the future monarch, her own father a wealthy Baron, she would rule as regent - and the entire Kingdom of Narvonne would be under the sway of the daemons.

"Clever boy," Valeria said. "Of course, I cannot allow any of you to live, knowing what you know. If you told my dearest intended, you would ruin everything." Agrat flexed her wings and hissed, the mere threat of the monster driving Ismet's lancers back a step. Out of all of them, Trist was the only one who had ever actually killed a daemon; in fact, most of them were no threat to this creature whatsoever.

Trist frowned. So why hadn't Agrat attacked yet? A sudden rush at either Trist, or perhaps Ismet, could reduce this to a one-on-one fight. If that happened, the daemoness' victory was much more likely. Instead, the pair seemed to be waiting for Trist and his companions to make the first move. But it didn't make any sense...

"This is a diversion," Trist realized. "The longer we stay here, the longer Adramelech has to defeat Bors and Shadi. She wants to keep us from rallying together."

Valeria scowled, and it made her beautiful face ugly. "Oh, Trist," she taunted. "Don't try to think too hard. You're more enjoyable as simply a pretty face. I even thought there might be a place for you in my bedchamber before this is all done. After we've torn your faerie-wench into a thousand pieces and scattered her threads from here to Skandia, of course."

"Leave the daemon to Ismet and I," Trist commanded, through gritted teeth. "Everyone else take Valeria."

Ismet was on his right, so Trist moved forward and cut at Agrat from the left, intending to force the daemon to throw herself away from his blade and right into the southern Exarch's assault. Instead, however, the daemoness jumped forward, inside his guard, and caught his wrist in both of her hands. The claws scraped against the metal of Trist's vambrace, making a horrible screech. The daemon's strength belied her sickly looks: now that she was not the size of an owl, she was able to hold his arm in place, though not as easily as the Addanc or Adramelech could have. He had half a heartbeat to wonder how many souls he would need to Tithe before all of these daemons were no longer stronger than him, and then he recoiled as Agrat lunged her head forward, as if she were trying to kiss him. Instead, she blew out a reeking breath, and he coughed at the smell. Could daemons rot? If so, this one must be decayed already, from the inside like a dead oak.

Trist tried to shove her back, but the daemon only laughed at him, until Ismet came in from the other side, cutting not at Agrat's body, but slicing instead between her and Trist, aiming for the delicate forearms that somehow were strong enough to hold Trist in place. Rather than risk losing a limb, Agrat let go of Trist and fluttered back in the same kind of quick retreat that Adramelech had made under the mountain. There was a pattern there, with the way daemons used their wings, but Trist didn't have the time to figure out how to take advantage of it at the moment.

Trist heard the twang of a bowstring, and a woman's cry. He had a vague awareness of his companions rushing past where he was fighting, in the direction of Valeria on her palfrey, but he didn't have any spare attention to pay to that now.

Acrasia's lashes whipped by Trist's head, drawing a line of black ichor, instead of blood, across Agrat's chest, just beneath her collarbone. It looked exactly like what had seeped from the wounds of the Addanc, on the bridge over the lake. He saw Epinoia, then, fly past them on white wings, hair dark as the spaces between the stars streaming behind her, the Angelus' skin so pale that it glowed like a full moon hanging low over the horizon. A skein of threads burst from her, like a net, to tangle Agrat, and the daemon snarled, wings encumbered by the attack.

Trist's head throbbed, and he felt short of breath, sweating under his armor with the exertion of combat, but he pushed past the feeling to swing low at the daemon's feet. He didn't want to risk cutting the net that was slowing her. Agrat jumped back, instinctively, but her wings weren't available to lift her with a backstroke, and she tumbled down to the ground.

"Now!" Ismet cried, lifting her curved sword above her head and leaping forward to bring it down on the daemon with all her strength. Agrat raised her arms, crossed, between her face and the descending sword, catching the blade on her forearms, which were pushed back nearly to her nose. More black ichor sprayed, but whatever passed for the bones of a daemon held without breaking, and the scimitar did not reach anything vital.

"Back!" Trist heard Epinoia call, and it was the first time he'd heard the Angelus speak, in a voice like the ringing of bells, deep and sonorous. She yanked her own Exarch a dozen feet away, just in time to avoid a phlegmy gob of black blood, hacked up by Agrat and spit right at where Ismet's face had just been. With a cry, the daemon flexed her arms and her wings, and with a mighty effort tore asunder the shining net that had bound her.

"Acrasia!" Trist shouted, and pressed the attack, lunging forward with a thrust that forced Agrat, who was just scrambling to her feet, to twist out of the way to his left. It was smart of the daemon to try to put Trist between her body and Ismet, but she had to use her left forearm to deflect his blade, which left her with another deep cut. This was the problem with using claws instead of an actual weapon, as Addanc had used its massive chopping sword. Trist didn't try to fight the momentum she imparted to his blade, instead sweeping it up and around over his head to make a diagonal cut down from his left to his right, aimed precisely at where the monster's slim neck connected her head to her torso. She tried the wing trick again, but the faerie must have understood Trist's intent, for a single loop of fire had closed around the daemon's right foot, and arrested her backward motion.

Wine-red eyes wide, Agrat leaned backward, her spine bending so far that he couldn't believe she didn't fall, her torso going parallel with the ground, her knees bent, one hand down to the packed earth of the pass to keep herself from collapsing.

She couldn't entirely get out of the way of his sword, however, and it cut a gash along the left side of her torso, above the ribcage, sending a spray of black ichor out. Before Trist could press the attack, he was overcome by a coughing fit that ruined his stance. Both he and Agrat scrambled backward, putting distance between them.

"Good, you feel it now," the daemon half-purred, half-hissed. "And the fever is coming."

Ismet yelled something in the southern tongue, and though Trist couldn't understand the words, the hate in them came across plain. She took Trist's place, pressing the attack with fast, shallow cuts of her curved blade, giving him a chance to catch his breath.

"Fever?" Trist swayed, arms trembling with exhaustion. How had this fight tired him out so much? He'd run through the forest with Yaél on his back!

"Cecilia gave up too much to have you," Agrat sneered, sending Ismet flying with a slash of claws to the southern knight's back. "A mewling babe, and for what? To die the same way she did?"

Trist coughed again, a wet, hacking sound, and he saw it: his mother in bed, coughing up blood into a cloth, face pale and sweaty, the horrid pustules rising all across her skin.

"Did you not know?" the daemon taunted him. "I am Agrat, Daemon Queen of Plagues."

Chapter Forty-Eight

The Battle of Falais IV: A Parting

Reliable accounts place the development of the plague as nearly instant, when Agrat herself is the vector; but when it passes from person to person, between two and eight days. The afflicted develop fever, headache, chills, and weakness and muscle aches; and some number of swollen pustules, sometimes as large as chicken eggs, in the groin, armpit, and neck. Some die in as little as two days, and it can destroy an entire town in only two weeks.

-The Marian Codex

17th Day of High Summer Moon, 284 AC

"My sweet boys," Cecilia du Camaret-à-Arden had sighed, as if even three words was more effort than her plague-wracked body could endure. Her neck was swollen with pus filled sacs of skin. Her black hands reached out, and Trist would have grasped one in his own, but Brother Alberic caught him and held him back.

"You can't touch her, my boy," their tutor said. "You shouldn't even be in the room." The smoke of burning rosemary filling the bed chamber couldn't cover the stench of the dying woman's breath, or the smell of rot wafting from her body.

As always, Percy came to his defense. "It's my responsibility," Trist's older brother said, from the other side of the bed. And if we take sick, I will answer to father. But he deserves to say farewell to her."

Percy had been right; it was the last time that Trist ever saw his mother alive.

12th Day of the Flower Moon, 297 AC

Trist gritted his teeth, hacked up a gob of phlegm and spit it aside, then tossed back his sweat drenched hair. "Keep my mother's name out of your mouth," he snarled at the plague-daemon, and launched himself forward with every bit of speed he could muster. He could almost see the air pulsing in a red haze around him, the same low burn as the threads woven through his body by the Tithes he had made.

With no thought of defense, Trist pressed the attack, swing after swing, a thrust that Agrat deflected to her thigh followed by a steel-capped forearm to her face. Where he struck her, plague pale skin reddened, steamed, then blackened as if torched by fire, the Boon he'd earned form killing Addanc of the lake being put to full effect. It reminded him of how Acrasia's body had reacted to the touch of iron. Agrat's claws rent his mail, sending broken steel rings flying, then scored his breastplate, but unlike Adramelech, she didn't seem to have the raw strength to punch directly through the metal. The world swayed around him, and it was a near thing to keep his balance, but Trist could see victory just a few moves ahead. If not this feint, than the next: Agrat, Queen of Plagues, was slowing down, overcome by her own wounds and the exhaustion of the fight. Her sickness might be a terror upon the world, but it was clear that she was not a trained warrior.

"Not enough," Trist gasped, darkness eating the edges of his vision. "You are not enough, monster." Ismet rejoined him, and they attacked from alternate sides, working together as if they'd practiced every day in the yard for years. Her scimitar sliced a cut along the daemon's right cheek, and while it didn't blacken and burn like Trist's strokes did, the wound seeped that disgusting dark ichor he'd come to recognize. And now he could see it: the fear in the daemon's eyes. An all too human expression on an inhuman face.

"Agrat!" Trist's eyes flicked to the Lady Valeria. She was standing over her dead horse, and the bodies of two lancers besides. At a glance, Trist recognized the blackened skin, the swollen pustules rising, and knew they'd been felled by the plague. He imagined the only thing keeping him standing was the burning red thread of the Boons that filled his body with vigor. The daemonic Exarch thrust a finger to the sky, scrambling back from Sir Divdan, Yaél, and the final two southern lancers. A shadow passed over them, as when storm clouds obscure the sun, and Trist could not help but look up to see what new danger was coming for them.

At first, his mind could not comprehend the sheer size of the monster: bat-like wings spread wide, serpentine neck and tail, dark scales, and four horns, just like Adramelech and Agrat. The creature was flying south along the pass, from Falais to the Tower of Tears, moving more rapidly than a fast horse could gallop, and a single beat of its wings stirred the dust of the road around them into clouds.

"Sammā'ēl," Ismet's Angelus breathed, and then before anyone could stop her, Epinoia, with a mighty downbeat of her wings, leapt skyward, like an ember from a bonfire. Agrat used the distraction to change her shape into that of a gigantic owl, and by the time Trist looked back down to her, the daemon was already flying to her Exarch. Agrat snatched up Valeria in her oversized talons, just as if she'd hunted a particularly tasty mouse, and then, carrying the Exarch, flew up above the pass. Trist sank to one knee, panting and coughing.

"She should be going south," he managed, between hacking breaths. "Three daemons against two Exarchs, while we are delayed here."

Sir Divdan raised his hand to shield his eyes, gazing northward. "I see smoke over the city," he said, after a moment. "Do you see smoke over the city, Trist?"

Ismet, in the meantime, had dropped her sword and drawn her horsebow, and was firing arrow after arrow at the massive form of Sammā'ēl. Trist didn't see how she could possibly be missing an enemy so enormous, but she might as well have been for all the reaction her arrows seemed to get out of the daemon. Suddenly, the Caliphate knight gave a strangled sob, and Trist could just see something fall out of the sky perhaps half a mile further down the pass. Epinoia, he guessed. Before anyone could stop her, Ismet rushed over to her desert horse, swung up into the saddle, and rode south. Her two remaining lancers delayed only long enough to get into their own saddles before galloping after her.

"I still do not understand," Trist said, falling back to sit on the ground. He left his sword on the earth beside him, and used one hand to cover his mouth while he coughed. "My wineskin," he called to Yaél, and the squire ran over to Cazador to get it.

"Remember," Acrasia said, pulling back her burning loops and whirls to her center, like winding a ball of yarn. "Adramelech was known for three plagues, Trist."

"And we have seen all three," he said, accepting the wineskin from Yaél. A great gulp of warm, watered wine was enough to let him speak more easily. "Those monstrous birds - the Ornes, you called them. By now they likely have nearly destroyed both armies. The horrid wailing and shrieking. And then the way he can corrupt places, like underneath the mountain."

"But she said," Sir Divdan mused, "That during the Cataclysm, hardly anyone could predict where Adramelech was going to strike next, and that hasn't been true here. Our first thought was that the daemon would hit the armies, and he has done just that. Now they've revealed a third piece on the board, and from the look of it set Falais ablaze. But why, when the Exarchs they need to defeat are all south of the city?"

"Because they want us all to be south of the city," Trist said, puzzling it over slowly. "They have maneuvered us away from Falais. Even this fight just now was a delaying action, to bog us down on the road. But I do not see the end goal. If the Prince of Plagues means to corrupt the tower at the south end of the pass... he would want all of the Exarchs somewhere else."

"Then his goal cannot be south of us," Acrasia repeated.

"I... m'lord, I think I know," Yaél said, raising a hand. Surprised, Trist blinked, then motioned for the squire to continue while he took another drink. "Well, the faerie king asked me to do that thing for him, right?"

Trist felt as if he'd swallowed a stone, ice-cold from the river in winter.

"What is this?" Sir Divdan asked, looking back and forth between Trist and his squire. Henry, in the meantime, ever practical, had begun collecting what arrows he could, to see whether they might be used again.

"It was the price," Trist explained, unable to lift his eyes from the beaten earth of the pass. "For my healing. I wish you had not agreed, Yaél," he said quietly.

"If I hadn't done, none of us would be here now with a chance to stop all this," Yaél pointed out. "So anyway, Auberon, the faerie-king that is, he says I need to take this ring for him, and put it in the church up in Falais." He held his hand up, and sunlight glinted on a bit of metal around his finger.

"Why," Sir Divdan said, casting about for Acrasia, whom he could of course not see, "Does your king want a ring brought to the Tomb of Saint Abatur? Answer me, faerie maid," he demanded.

Acrasia sighed. "Tell him, Trist, that my king is no more likely to explain his commands to me, than his is to him," she said, with a roll of her eyes.

"We do not know," Trist said, diplomatically. "But if the King of Shadows sees something of importance in that church..."

"Then the Prince of Plagues might, too!" Yaél finished the thought, with a grin. Trist swayed, and for a moment it did not seem like it would be so bad to simply lie down and sleep, and let the plague take him like it had his mother.

"Will he live?" Sir Divdan asked, but the words seemed far away.

"You aren't dead yet," Acrasia said, putting a cool hand to his forehead. "Which makes me guess you will survive, my love. One thing is certain: Auberon will not be healing you a second time."

Trist counted three deep breaths, finished his wineskin, and tossed it aside. "We part ways here," he decided. "Help me to my feet." He reached for the hilt of his longsword.

Yaél came without hesitation, and Divdan did after a moment, as well. "I'm like to die one way or another today," the older knight decided. "It might as well be plague as torn apart by a daemon. Lift, lad."

"Get me over to Caz," Trist told them, and somehow, between all three of them, he was hoisted into the saddle and got reins in hand. "Good. The three of you ride back to Falais. You are not there to fight Agrat, you understand? You ride straight for the church, and you put the ring there like Auberon wanted. And then you get out."

"Aye," Divdan acknowledged, climbing up into his own saddle. "I'll get the boy there, you have my word on that. Come on up, lad," he said, extending a hand, but Yaél ran over to the first bird that Trist had killed. He set his foot on the daemon corpse, grabbed the lance with both hands, and pulled until it came out of the body. Then, he ran it over to Trist.

"You'll need this, m'lord," Yaél said, and Trist smiled.

"Thank you. Take care of yourselves, both of you," he said, and used his reins to turn Cazador's head south.

"I see you aren't coming with us," Divdan called after him. Henry, in the meanwhile, had scrambled up into the saddle of the horse he'd inherited over the course of the journey.

"No," Trist said, doing his best not to cough. "I ride south. If I can meet up with Dame Ismet, I will. Perhaps four Exarchs will be enough to turn aside that monster that flew overhead."

"Angelus give you strength, then," Sir Divdan said solemnly. "And better you than me. Ha!" He turned his destrier north, Yaél seated on the saddle behind him, and kicked the horse into a full gallop.

"Just you and I, then," Acrasia said, appearing in the saddle, between Trist's arms. "Just like when you were a child."

"It will never be like that again," Trist coughed, pressing with his knees to urge Caz to a trot. "But at least I am not alone."

The faerie and the knight rode south through the Passe de Mûre, toward the battle.

Chapter Forty-Nine

The Battle of Falais V: Lances

We called the damned beast the Great Cataclysm before the historians ever set pen to page, that's for certain. "The Cataclysm hit Skandia and slaughtered half the Fifth Legion," that's how you'd hear it, and we all knew what that meant. I think they named the age after it because of what it did to Rumen. They say it roosted in the capital of Etalus for an entire moon, like the ruins were its nest.

-The Life and Times of Legionary Titus Nasica

12th Day of the Flower Moon, 297 AC

Trist found Ismet and her two remaining lancers around the last curve of the pass, just in sight of the battle raging on both sides of the wall that extended from the Tower of Tears down to the River Durentia.

"Epinoia?" He asked her, calling across a distance of fifteen or twenty feet, rather than chance getting close enough to infect the Caliphate warriors.

"Taken shelter in me," Ismet ibnah Salah answered. "The daemon hurt her gravely." Her red veil, caught by a breeze, fluttered out like a pennant. "I was just debating whether to ride back for you. I doubt the Narvonnians would allow my men and I to pass without you in our company."

"I share your doubts." Trist coughed. "Where is Sammā'ēl?"

"The Great Cataclysm itself," Ismet said, with a shake of her head. "When I came north, never did I think that was what we would be hunting." She extended her hand and pointed one pale finger. "It's been making great circles over the battlefield. That monster should be coming out from behind the cliffs just about... now."

The space of three heartbeats later, the massive, winged serpent indeed glided above the rocks and then down over the wall, stooping like an enormous hawk only to rise again with men clutched in its talons. Even from here, Trist could hear the screams, and Sammā'ēl rose again, soaring on its great wings, only to drop the doomed soldiers among the mountain crags west of the pass.

"By all the Angelus," one of her lancers moaned, "How do we fight something like that?"

"It dives to strike," Trist said, grimly. "We charge it when it comes down." He kneed Caz into motion, and the other three formed up with him. He was grateful that he didn't need to do any of this on foot: in truth, he wasn't certain he would be able to get down out of the destrier's saddle without falling on his face.

They rode for the wall, Ismet and her two lancers using their horsebows to great effect as they came. Now that they knew to avoid the tough wings, even the two men who lacked the power of an Exarch were skilled enough to put an arrow through the eye of Adrammelech's Ornes, while the birds feasted on corpses. It was nowhere near enough to stem the tide of the daemon birds' swelling numbers, but Trist resolved that every dead monster was a step in the right direction.

For himself, Trist shifted his lance to his left side, rested it on top of his boot and in the crook of his arm, and drew his longsword in his right hand. The blade was not even slightly meant to be wielded with a single hand, and from what he could tell the curved, one-handed scimitars carried by Ismet and her men were far better suited for what he was about to do, but he trusted that Cazador's momentum would help to make up for it. Trist took the lead of the small group, steering the destrier to pass any Ornes in their way by the left, so that he could lean over and slice their scraggly, serpentine necks on the way past. Acrasia, nestled in front of him, counted gleefully as they made their way through the chaos to the gate of the wall.

"One for you, my love," she murmured, and he could picture the grin on her lovely porcelain face as he lopped the head off a monstrous bird that had once been a man.

"Not enough," Trist grunted, steering for another bird. "I need at least two Tithes of my own before we meet the daemons." He nearly lost his balance as he swung Cazador past an Ornes just emerging from a corpse, but the destrier had been his since coming to Camaret-à-Arden as a yearling, and Caz was doing his best to compensate for his rider's condition. "Good boy," Trist told the horse. "He won't let me fall."

"Daemon Bane? Or Fae Touched?" Acrasia asked, as Trist picked out another target. He hoped that Ismet was able to Tithe the monsters with her arrows, and blamed himself for being too fogged by fever to ask her.

"Make way!" Trist shouted, riding into the mass of Narvonnian soldiers pressed around the gate. He could see it was open, now, not broken, and could only guess that the Crown Prince had ordered that once the flock of daemon birds had descended. Men dove aside, as much to avoid being crushed by four charging horses as out of any recognition of who Trist was. As long as no one shot a crossbow at Ismet or her men, he would take it. There were no birds to kill for a moment, and then they were out from under the wall and onto the battlefield where the Caliphate army clashed with Adramelech and his flock.

Trist had known that the Ornes would grow in number rapidly, but actually seeing it was another thing altogether. They darkened the sky in every direction, moving in great waves, and his mind searched for something to compare it to, in order to understand. Finally, he seized on a memory from the beach at Rocher de la Garde: schools of tiny fish in the shallows, gleaming in the sunlight. They had been made up of dozens of individual creatures, yet somehow instinctually turned as one. The Ornes moved like that, and though volley after volley of arrows and crossbow bolts rose from the Narvonnian soldiers manning the ramparts of the wall, nothing seemed to kill enough of the creatures to make a difference.

Over Trist's head and behind him, the sound of a scorpion letting loose, and the shriek of the massive bolt spinning through the air, caused him to flinch. He followed the flight of the projectile with his eye, and it led him directly to where he needed to go.

Corpses were piled up where they'd been flung in a great, irregular ring surrounding the battle between Adrammelech, Sir Bors, and a man armored in the Caliphate fashion, who Trist guessed must be the general that Ismet had spoken of. As Trist watched, the scorpion bolt forced a swooping Sammā'ēl to turn aside; instead of striking the monster itself, the siege weapon plowed through Ornes birds and soldiers alike. Someone up on the wall had decided the scorpions were better used against the Great Cataclysm than individual birds, and Trist couldn't help but agree.

"We ride there!" Trist shouted to his three remaining companions, pointing with his longsword. Their route would take them straight through the thick of the battle, where the southern men were doing their best to maintain some kind of ordered formation against the flocking birds. Trist had to give them credit, though only days before he would have considered the Caliphate men enemies: he didn't know whether the Narvonnians could have maintained their discipline in the face of such horror.

"Agreed!" Ismet shouted back, slinging her bow across her back and drawing her scimitar. Her men did the same, but just as they were about to charge across the battlefield, the shadow of Sammā'ēl passed overhead.

"The scorpions," one of Ismet's lancers shouted, and Trist saw what he meant.

"Away from the wall!" he called, but it was too late.

Sammā'ēl did not stoop to lift men in its claws, or even to pick up the scorpions and throw them. Instead, the massive daemon crashed into the top of the wall, at the center of where the siege engines were mounted, with its great bulk, armored in scales. The top of the wall burst, showering blocks of stone in every direction. Men fell screaming, and were crushed by the debris. The entire gate collapsed, the wall falling away from it bit by bit until the daemon crouched in the rubble, the siege engines destroyed.

Trist had been the furthest from the wall, and the first to react; Cazador might not have been as fast as the southern desert steeds, but this was enough to get the destrier and his two riders out of everything but the great cloud of dust that billowed up from where Sammā'ēl had landed.

"Ismet!" he shouted, coughing as much from the dust as from the plague, now, but he couldn't find her.

A scream echoed across the battlefield, and Trist turned to see the Caliphate general seized in the claws of Adrammelech. Torn between where he could be of more use, Trist was too far away to do anything as the poor man was ripped limb from limb, leaving only Sir Bors to face the daemon.

"This is getting worse and worse!" Acrasia shouted over the din of the carnage.

"Bors cannot beat it alone," Trist decided, and turned Caz' head for the pile of corpses at the center of the battlefield. It was a relief to have made up his mind; it meant that he didn't have to think, only to do what he'd been trained to do. Trist veered left and right, swinging past two more opportunities to behead the monstrous Orners birds.

"One for you," he counted, as the head of the first went flying, splattering blood in every direction. Cazador's hooves bounded over packed earth and men's corpses alike. The last bird he missed a clean swing at the neck, and cut the actual head in half instead, but it was enough. The power of the Tithed soul surged up his arm, combining with the Tithe he'd saved from the other side of the wall.

"Fae Touched!" he shouted to Acrasia as Caz' pounding hooves ate up the distance between them and where Sir Bors struggled against the Prince of Plagues. She touched his chest, and Trist felt a fire inside him stoked by the Tithes: a single one of his threads burned orange now, instead of red. Renewed strength surged through his tired muscles, and even the fever of the plague seemed to recede from his mind.

Ahead, Sir Bors was not using a sword, but instead a great spiked ball on the end of a chain, with a half broken and rent shield on his left arm. Masheth blazed at his side, while the Angelus that had been bound to the Caliphate general screamed in pain and loss. Trist sheathed his sword, the motion easier now, as the Exarch of Masheth slammed his flail into Adrammelech with enough force to fling the daemon prince back. Rather than fall, however, the monster extended its wings to catch the air, rising up ten feet or more from the corpse-strewn field. As Trist urged Caz into a full gallop, he saw the Prince of Plagues pause there, extend each clawed hand to the side, and prepare to swoop down at Bors.

This was the third time Trist had fought a winged daemon, now, and the third time he'd seen that technique for dealing with being thrown back, or used to retreat in the face of a blow. He could see exactly the path the Adrammelech would take as it charged Bors. Settling his lance in his right hand, Trist leaned forward in the saddle, his head over Acrasia's shoulder, and steered his charging mount not to where the daemon was, but to where it would be.

"Tor De Lancey, I need you now," Trist breathed, the words stirring Acrasia's blonde tresses. A burning red thread unspooled from his blade.

"What a battle!" the ghostly knight's voice rung from where he coalesced at Trist's side, the two of them riding together. Tor had no lance, only his warhammer, but he rode upon the horse that Trist had put down that very same day. The experiment had worked exactly how Trist had hoped it would, and without needing to be told, Tor fell back just behind Trist as they rode together into the duel.

Adrammelech shot forward along the precise path Trist had predicted, its attention utterly consumed by the old Exarch it was about to kill. The daemon didn't even realize Trist was there until his lance took it in the chest.

Chapter Fifty

The Battle of Falais VI: The Great Cataclysm

Avitus must've had balls of solid granite, I'll tell you that. You know I saw it at Vellatesia? It was there with all the rest of them, the Prince of Plagues, the Scarlet Duke, the Plague Queen, the Serpent of Gates and all the rest of them, but there was nothing worse than that monster Sammā'ēl. What possessed the governor to make an Accord with something like that, I'll never understand. It's more like an eclipse or an earthquake than a living creature. We never did beat it, you know. It just disappeared.
-The Life and Times of Legionary Titus Nasica

12th Day of the Flower Moon, 297 AC

Crown Prince Lionel Aurelianus set a boot to the head of the daemonic bird that was still twitching on the stone of the parapet, then yanked hard to pull six inches of his blade out of the thing's brain. Black ichor sprayed in every direction, but he'd long since passed the point of giving the disgusting stuff much thought, and his armor was covered in it.

"Still with me?" he asked Dame Chantal, turning to look her over. The older woman was sitting against one of the crenellations meant to protect archers atop the wall, letting one of the army's barber-surgeons tie a bandage tightly diagonally across her face, to cover her left eye.

"You won't be rid of me yet, Your Highness," the knight said, and accepted his hand back up to her feet.

"She's lost the eye," the barber said. "She should really be sent back to Falais to recover." The bandage was already beginning to soak through with blood.

"See who else you can save," the Prince said, before Chantal could let loose a string of curses at the poor man who'd bandaged her up. "You are doing good work, and we will not forget it." He turned to scan the battlefield beneath them as the healer scurried toward the stairs. The Exarch, Sir Bors, had ridden out to join the battle against the Prince of Plagues perhaps a quarter hour before, and Lionel could make out glimpses of what was happening. Even with two Exarchs against a single daemon, it didn't seem to him that things had been going well; and since Sammā'ēl came winging down over the cliffs for the first time, the slaughter had only gotten worse.

"Swing this scorpion around and get it reloaded!" he shouted, and men leaped to obey.

"You're going to try to shoot the damned thing down, aren't you?" Chantal asked him with a grin, putting her back into moving the siege engine, right along with her men. "You know that's the Cataclysm of the Old Empire itself?"

"I know it," Lionel said. "Hold. Right there. Load!" Two soldiers ran over with a new bolt, protected by half a dozen more men who fought off any birds that swooped too close to them. "You have a better plan, Dame Chantal?"

"I like your plan just fine," she said, with a grunt, as the scorpion settled into place. Straightening up from her task, the knight grabbed a swig from her wineskin, then tossed it aside, presumably empty. "If I'd known you were this kind of crazy, your Highness, I would have come north to fight for you a long time ago." She laughed, and he couldn't help but join her for a moment.

"Loaded!" one of the engineers called, and Lionel got a hold of himself.

"Alright, men!" he called. "Hold until it swoops down. We're only going to get one shot at this monster, so make it count. Everyone who is not manning the scorpion, you are on bird duty. Whatever happens, you cannot let them interrupt our engineers! Now, let us kill this beast once and for all!" The scorpion crew and the soldiers gathered to protect them let out a ragged cheer when Lionel finished. Every man's eye was fastened on the monstrous daemon as it dropped still-screaming soldiers from a great height onto the rocks below, circled, and began flying for the ongoing battle between the two Exarchs and the daemon Adramelech.

"Hold," Lionel cautioned the engineers, as Sammā'ēl bore down on the two champions. "Hold... loose!" The mechanism of the scorpion released, the hum of the great string of twisted sinew vibrating and filling the air for long seconds after the bolt was launched. Again, every soldier's gaze followed the path of the bolt, directly toward the massive daemon. Lionel held his breath; it was going to hit!

With preternatural agility and far greater speed than a monster of that size should possess, Sammā'ēl turned aside just in time for the bolt to skim past its belly and plow into the mass of soldiers behind and beneath the daemon.

"Reload!" Dame Chantal shouted. "We turned it aside! We can keep it off the Exarchs!"

The men scrambled to obey their commander, but Lionel kept the daemon in his sights. It did not veer to one side in order to loop back around toward the center of the battle, nor did it stoop to lift more helpless soldiers into the sky. No, with each beat of its wings, it drove forward, directly at the wall that closed the pass.

Directly at them.

"Get down!" Lionel shouted, grabbing his battered kite shield back up from the ground and settling it on his left arm. "It comes for us now!"

Forever after, he would remember the sight of the engineers. They must have been just as terrified as he was, as anyone else atop the wall. They had no shields to protect themselves, and no more armor than a leather jerkin, but they continued in their duty, slotting the next bolt into place and cranking back the siege engine to get it ready to fire, even as the Great Cataclysm itself bore down on them all.

Everything happened at once, and he lost all sense of where he was.

The scorpion loosed just before Sammā'ēl hit the wall, or perhaps just after. It didn't matter, because the impact of Sammā'ēl's mass against the stone shattered everything.

Men and stone and wood went flying in every direction. Something battered Lionel's shield as the world fell out from under him, and had just time to suck in a lungful of choking dust before he hit the ground at the foot of the wall, driving all the breath back out of his lungs with a horrible pain in his back.

He lay there, sucking for air that wouldn't come, unable to see through the cloud of dust. No matter how expertly forged and fitted, his plate armor was designed to deflect spearheads and sword thrusts, not to safeguard him at the hard end of a long fall. Lionel pictured sharp stones beneath him: falling down onto rubble from such a height would be like being struck by a warhammer, the kind of impact that could easily cave in the steel. Perhaps his back was broken even now, and that was why he couldn't breath.

Gradually, the pain receded, and the Prince finally got half a lungful of air. Not enough to move, but enough to quell his rising panic, and to push back the dark, fuzzy edges of his vision. A few moments later, he was able to turn himself over, and crawl. Around him, concealed by the dust, men screamed and died, and Lionel might as well have been blind. Had the monster moved on? Was it still here?

An echoing roar, loud enough to make him clutch his ears between his gauntleted hands, answered that question. Sammā'ēl was somewhere nearby, the cause of the constant screams of pain. Lionel cast about for his arming sword; his shield was still buckled to his left arm, but he must have lost his blade in the fall.

Suddenly, a massive shape emerged from the dust. Dark and scaled, larger than any creature had the right to be. Something whistled over the Prince's head as the daemon turned: a great wing, beating aside the dust until he could finally start to see the wreckage of the collapsed wall.

Men lay broken everywhere: half buried by fallen stones, pinned by wooden support beams, or screaming under the tender mercies of the daemonic birds which had swooped in to take advantage of the carnage, like carrion crows. The bulk of Sammā'ēl shifted, a clawed foot as large as a wagon lifted and came down again, grinding a soldier beneath it as easily as a man might pulp a lemon.

Lionel scrambled back, drawing his belt knife in his right hand. It was a tiny weapon, pathetic and useless against the raw immensity of the monster he was faced with. The only reason that he was still alive was that it hadn't noticed him yet. If he could get back far enough, the dust cloud might hide him...no. It was thinning with every breeze that blew across the battlefield. Somewhere behind him, then, was the River Durentia. If he could get back there, leave his armor behind, he might be able to swim upriver to Falais, and rally what troops remained there. It was clear that the Tower of Tears was lost, and the southern end of the pass with it, but Urien might still have his knights in the mountains.

Sammā'ēl swung round again, and this time that massive, lizard-like head on the long neck of a snake came toward him. Lionel's fingers tightened around the hilt of his dagger. If it saw him, he resolved, he would wait until the last moment, until it had snatched him up in its jaws if necessary, and stab it. Perhaps he would be able to reach the eye. He was so close to the daemon now that he could see the color of its scales: a purple so deep and dark it was nearly black.

Hot, rank breath blew over him, and a great eye blinked, bloodshot and yellow, and utterly inhuman. It saw him, and the head moved forward faster than the Prince could scramble away. Lionel had long enough to hope that Lady Valeria had made it safely north to Falais. He had long enough to regret that he hadn't remarried sooner: if he had listened to his father, and not allowed himself to wallow in grief for so many years, there might be an heir safe at Cheverny Castle now, secure under the protection of the King's Exarchs. Instead, the royal line would fail here, today. There was nothing he could do about it now.

"Come on then!" Lionel Aurelianus screamed at the daemon. He managed to get one foot under him, and his shield out in front, as the head came in, jaws open as wide and high as a castle gate. There would only be one chance to strike, and he must make it count.

"Die, beast!" A light shone through the settling dust, and a red veil snapped in the breeze like a banner. The massive head of Sammā'ēl recoiled from the force of a glittering slash, the ring of steel against scale, and somehow, Lionel saw thick black blood leak from a wound on the monster's snout. A Caliphate knight was in front of him, round shield high, curved sword catching the light of the sun.

"Get up!" the red knight shouted, and Lionel realized it was a woman's voice, choked raw by dust and the use of battle. He staggered to his feet. "It will be back again," the southern woman gasped. "Can you take its blow on your shield? If you can, I will strike."

"I can do that much," Lionel promised them both, accepted her offered gauntlet, and felt himself yanked to his feet with surprising strength. "Who are you?" he asked.

"The shield!" she shouted, dropping her own, and he saw that Sammā'ēl's head was coming back again. Lionel dropped his knife, braced his shield with both hands, and set himself a wide stance. When the head came in, and the jaws tried to close about him, he wedged the shield in between, slipped his arm out of the leather straps, and scrambled back just before the wooden shield splintered.

The woman in the red veil leapt atop Sammāʾēl's snout and ran forward as if she was not wearing heavy brigandine armor, but a light linen chemise. Before Lionel could comprehend what he was seeing, she had dashed up to the monster's eye and thrust her scimitar in up to the hilt. The daemon shrieked, beat its wings, and tossed her off with a single shake of the head as it retreated back up into the sky.

Lionel, for his part, crawled over to where his rescuer lay among the debris. Her eyes opened, she gave a groan, and he collapsed next to her in relief.

"Ismet," she said, after catching her breath. "Ismet ibnah Salah, Exarch of Epinoia."

"Well met," the Prince said, deciding that the ground next to her was very comfortable indeed. "Well met, Ismet ibnah Salah of Maʿīn."

Chapter Fifty-One

The Battle of Falais VII: Pursuit

There is reason to speculate that, toward the end of the Cataclysm, certain of the more powerful daemons developed a means to obscure themselves from the notice of Angelus, Exarch and priest alike. That the Angelus were able to teach priests to see the monsters implies that they, in turn, could have learned to hide, somehow. The most compelling evidence for this theory is that neither Sammā'ēl, nor Agrat, were ever bound or destroyed, despite being hunted across every province of the old Empire.
-The Marian Codex

12th Day of the Flower Moon, 297 AC

Henry clung to the neck of the southern horse with his right hand, his black longbow held in his left, and winced everytime he slammed back down into the saddle after being bounced up into the air. If he never rode a horse again after all of this, he would be a happy man.

Ahead, that mountain knight, Sir Divdan, spurred his destrier on toward the next turn of the pass. Henry couldn't get a good look at his lord's squire, in the front of the saddle, but trusted that he would have noticed if the poor boy had fallen off somewhere along the way. If not from the shouting, than from the cursed birds.

The daemon birds - Ornes, Sir Trist had called them at one point - had been following the riders ever since they rode north back toward Falais. As the horses rounded a great, jutting cliff of rock on their left, the walls of Falais could be seen ahead of them, at the end of the pass, and the monsters must have known they were running out of chances. Sir Divdan rode with his shield slung across his back, and his arming sword in his right hand, and Henry had watched the knight cut down no less than two of the daemon birds during their headlong rush north. Now, however, three broke off from the flock and dove from above.

"Three's too many," Henry groaned. He reached back to his quiver for an arrow, and nearly fell off the horse. He was forced to grab at the beast's mane again, abandoning the arrow, which clattered to the rocky ground of the path beneath the desert steed's hooves. "Don't bounce me so much!" he complained to the animal. Maybe if he squeezed tighter with his legs, he could keep his balance long enough; he didn't know how those Caliphate horse bowmen did it.

Perhaps three horse-lengths ahead, Divdan cut down the first bird that dove for him, but the second latched onto his left pauldron, then ducked its beak forward, that long neck lashing like an adder, and tried to get in under the steel helm.

"It's up to you, Henry," he told himself. "Come on. Just like yer Da taught you." Before he could think better of it, he squeezed his legs around the horse's flanks, reached back and drew an arrow. He turned the longbow sideways, nocked, and loosed just in time to grab onto the horse's mane again. His arrow took the bird in the throat, carrying it off Sir Divdan, who cut the third and last bird down easily enough once he was no longer being harassed.

Which was fortunate, Henry reflected, because for some reason the cursed beast he was riding sped up, sprinting past Divdan and Yaél on the destrier, and barrelling toward the city gates so fast the wind brought tears to his eyes.

"Stop!" he shouted, pulling back on the beast's mane. "Slow down!" It all would have been easier if he hadn't dropped the reins long since, and it took him to the gate itself before the horse finally stopped. Even then, Henry wasn't certain if it was him, or the crowded mass of wounded soldiers retreating up the pass to take shelter in the city that convinced the horse to slow.

"Good shot, Henry!" Yaél called to him as they caught up.

"It was," Sir Divdan agreed, "But if any of us survive this, we need to give you some riding lessons!" The knight laughed, then called to the gate. "Make way! Make way in the name of the Baroness!" The guards must have recognized the knight, for they quickly began clearing a path, and ushered both horses and their riders through. Past the gate, Henry gasped. In every direction, laid out on the cobblestones of the main street of Falais, and then on the side streets climbing up toward the cliffs on the left, and even on the bank of the River Durentia, lay wounded men and women. Soldiers, mostly, with the townsfolk of Falais pressed into service to bandage them as best could be managed, or to bring a flask of watered wine to their lips. Henry didn't even try to count them all; it was more than his fingers and his toes, that was for certain. He'd never seen so much blood, never heard such a pitiful moaning and screaming, in all his life. Above it all, smoke rose from burning buildings.

"There must be more wounded than everyone in all of Camaret-à-Arden," he muttered, unable to pull his eyes away from the sight.

"Sir Divdan!" A woman's voice called, and Henry recognized a handsome noblewoman, skirts in her hands, descending from the parapet toward them. He thought she was the same one Sir Trist had spoken to on their way through the gate just hours before.

"Baroness!" Divdan responded, spinning his destrier about. "My liege, did the Lady Valeria come this way?"

"Not a quarter of an hour past, not even," the Baroness responded, handing her knight up a flask to drink from. "You may be assured she is safe; I sent two of our men with her to the church, to safeguard her from the rioters."

Divdan took a single gulp, then handed the flask back. "Then we must be after her. She has betrayed us, and Angelus only know what she wants in that holy place."

"Betrayed us?" the Baroness gasped, and Henry wondered whether she would offer him a drink, as well. He could certainly use it.

"She has made an Accord with a daemon," Divdan explained, turning to look over the smoke-darkened skyline of the town to the steeple of the church at the base of the cliff.

"She fought Exarchs Trist and Ismet, and us as well. I recommend you order her killed on sight. Come, Henry," he said, and Henry knew he wasn't getting a drink.

Divdan kicked his destrier, now foaming at the mouth, back into motion, and Henry followed. The three companions raced through the streets of Falais, with the knight shouting "Make way! Make way!" They tore through narrow alleys, and even rode the horses up stone steps with houses so close to either side Henry could only throw both arms around the neck of his beast and hold on, closing his eyes in fear.

Finally, the horses clattered to a halt on the cobblestones in front of the Church of Saint Abatur, and Henry was able to open his eyes. He found, when he did, that Sir Divdan had caught the reins of his southern horse, and that was how they'd managed to stop. Yaél slid down out of the destrier's saddle easily enough; Sir Trist had been teaching the boy to ride, after all, as a squire should. Henry, however, couldn't make his aching legs move, and he merely clung to his horse's body, trembling in agony and exhaustion.

"We need you Henry," Sir Divdan murmured, reaching up to help him down. "We need your bow to cover us. Look - she's here already, and her work has begun."

Once Henry got his feet under him, he followed the knight's pointing finger to where two men at arms, in the colors of Falais, were slumped on the steps of the church. Neither moved, and Henry nearly puked when he saw what had been done to them.

The men's bellies had been opened, and their intestines strung out to drape the open doors of the church. Their blood had been used like paint, and strange symbols, still wet, dripped on the outer walls of the facade, the open doors, even the cobblestones.

"Angelus protect us," Henry said, clutching his hand over his mouth and nose to block the smell.

"She'll be inside," Divdan said. "Come." He settled his shield on his left arm, raised his blade in his right hand, and led the way into the desecrated church. In spite of himself, Henry drew an arrow, fitted it to his bowstring, and followed.

"Stay behind me, lad," he murmured to Yaél.

Inside, the entire nave was painted in red light. Henry looked back over his shoulder, up at the stained glass above the entrance, and saw that the formerly beautiful images had been covered in red. More blood, he knew, and the light of the sun filtered through the gore.

"Look!" Yaél cried, and Henry turned back to see Sir Divdan and the lad approaching the altar. There, a priest lay, disemboweled, with his entrails spread across the entire area. The horror of the scene only deepened when the man coughed.

"How can he still be alive?" Henry gasped.

"Father Kramer!" Sir Divdan rushed forward, bounding up the stone steps to the altar, where he cradled the dying priest's head.

"Divdan," Kramer gasped. Henry approached warily, and reached out a hand to hold Yaél back a step. No need for the boy to see this.

"The Lady Valeria?" Divdan asked.

"She's a monster..." Kramer hacked up blood. "She and her daemon."

"Where are they?"

"Below... to the Crypt of Saint Abatur..." The dying man clutched at the knight's hand with his last strength. "You must stop her."

"I swear that we will," Sir Divdan promised. "Upon the Angelus and my faith. Rest, now." The priest's hand fell, and with a last, rattling gasp of breath, the life left his body.

"Where is the tomb?" Yaél asked.

"Below. Follow me." Divdan led them to the left of the altar, through a set of doors, and then down a spiral stair of stone, deep under the mountainside. Torches guttered along the walls as they passed, and echoes came up to them from below.

"Women's voices," Henry murmured, as the three descended.

Indeed, as they made the last turn of the staircase, they not only say the crypt laid out before them, but its horrible occupants, as well. The room chiseled deep beneath the roots of the mountain first presented them with a sort of small antechamber or gallery. Beyond it, framed by symmetrical pillars of the same orange-brown rock as the cliffs over their heads, was the tomb itself. It was sunken down half a dozen broad steps, and rectangular in shape, with a sarcophagus of stone occupying the place of honor in the center. Before it were perhaps a dozen stone benches, split six on either side of a wide aisle, which Henry guessed were meant for priests, exarchs, or whoever else might have been given the honor of entering the tomb.

Valeria and her daemon stood on either side of the sarcophagus, arms extended over the stone to meet in the center, hand in hand. Both were soaked to the elbow in blood, and the daemon Agrat's wine-red wings flared behind her and out to the sides. Together, the two figures were singing a song, but in no tongue Henry had ever heard before. It seemed to him that the daemon led the melody, with the Exarch providing harmony, and it reminded him of his mother and sisters singing together at festival times.

"Lady Valeria," Sir Divdan called into the tomb, striding forward with his shield raised and his sword in hand. "Surrender to me now. Break your Accord with this daemon, and it may be that his Royal Highness finds it in his heart to treat your betrayal with some degree of mercy."

As one, both women's heads cocked toward the approaching party of three. The daemon Agrat hissed, revealing a mouth of fangs beneath her otherwise beautiful lips.

"Bold of you to offer terms so close to the precipice of your own defeat," Valeria responded with a smile. "Let me make a counteroffer. Whichever of you falls to your knees this instant and pledges to serve at my feet, I shall reward. They will die quickly and painlessly, and I will not use their blood to desecrate this tomb."

Chapter Fifty-Two

The Battle of Falais VIII: Strike

It would be the work of a dozen lifetimes to study and record the differences between the three immortal races that walk our world; but some observations are immediately useful to the student of such matters. While all seem to need some sort of anchor in this physical world for their spiritual essence, the type of anchor differs. Angelus make Accords with mortal men and women, tying themselves to a perishable, mortal person. When they lose their anchor, they must find another. Faeries, on the other hand, tie themselves to a place, and defend it with great fervor.
Daemons tie themselves to concepts - such as plague, storm, or the Cataclysm.
-The Marian Codex

12th Day of the Flower Moon, 297 AC

The lance pierced Adrammelech's chest at the side. Cazador's weight and momentum, a destrier at full gallop carrying an armed and armored knight, drove the daemon before them like a dam burst by rain-swelled torrents. The lance splintered and broke at the force of it, leaving two feet of solid wood protruding from the gaunt, inhuman chest of the monsters. Trist and Caz swept by and began their turn, but before the Prince of Plagues could do more than fall to the ground, screaming in that horrid wail, the spirit of Sir Tor De Lancey, astride a spectral steed, followed in Trist's wake with a rising blow. His warhammer connected with the daemon's chin, lifting its entire body up off the ground with a crack.

Trist, in the meantime, had drawn his longsword and lifted it in his right hand, extended out and somewhat behind his body. A single cut, when the daemon rose, to sever the head, and this would all be over. The Ornes would cause no end of trouble before they were hunted down, it was true, but they still had two Exarchs to do it, at the least, and he was not going to count Ismet dead until he'd seen her body. An orange cord hummed in his body, and even the plague was not enough to stop him from fighting.

"Get off the horse, boy!" Sir Bors yelled, regaining his feet and spitting a gob of blood off to one side. He shook the useless remnants of his shield off his left arm, and grasped the hilt of his massive flail in both hands.

Trist wasn't sure why Bors would say that, but there also wasn't time to consider it. He rode in just as Adramelech was getting back to his feet again, and swung his blade in a shining arc straight at its neck.

With savage speed, Adrammelech tucked its wings and leaped forward, horizontally, straight over Caz' extended head and at Trist. Acrasia blinked out of existence, withdrawing to his sword, and the daemon barrelled into Trist. He saw it coming, and for a moment everything around him seemed to slow. The daemon was like a leaf caught in the wind, drifting slowly and without hurry. There was no way to turn Caz aside from the tackle, and now Trist understood what Bors had meant: when the daemon was not being taken by surprise, it simply moved and reacted too fast for a horse to be useful. Since he couldn't avoid what was coming, Trist unhooked his feet from his stirrups, released the reins in his left hand, and pulled his sword in, keeping the tip in line with the daemon's body.

The shock of the impact took him straight out of the saddle. Cazador continued on, and Trist was carried back, with the daemon on top of him, until they hit the ground. His head slammed onto the earth, and if he'd been able to think straight he ought to have been grateful he didn't come down on something hard enough to crack his skull wide open, like a rock or a piece of metal armor. Trist blinked, trying to get his vision into focus. A cough of rank breath in his face made him gag involuntarily, and black ichor splattered across his skin.

"You again," Adrammelech coughed, and Trist was surprised to find it could speak Narvonnian. The daemon's weight was atop him, pinning Trist to the ground. His hand, on the hilt of his longsword, was trapped between their bodies, and wet ichor soaked past the joints of his gauntlet to get in where his skin was exposed, making everything slippery. The sword must have gone straight through the daemon's body.

Trist tried to shove the daemon off of him, flares of orange fire running through the muscles of his arms as he pushed with all his improved strength. It wasn't enough, even now. Adrammelech caught his left wrist in a clawed grip that felt like Trist's bones were being ground in a mortar, and he gasped at the pain. His right hand was still trapped between their bodies, and he had no leverage. The daemon's free hand shot forward to clutch Trist around the throat, and suddenly he couldn't breathe, even with the leather stock to keep the claws off.

"Aggravating, mortal worm," the demon hissed in his face. Trist's eyelids fluttered, and the sounds of the battle dimmed. The only thing he could see were those horrid eyes, glowing like banked embers, and behind them the true heart of the creature, burning in orange-rimmed flames of bright yellow. Still more powerful than he was, than Acrasia was. How many Tithes would he have had to collect to truly fight this monster on equal footing? More than he'd had time for in only the span of a few weeks as an Exarch.

The familiar panic from boyhood days swimming in the River Rea, when Trist and Percy would compete to see who could hold their breath longer, overwhelmed him. He couldn't swim to the surface of the water, but he released the hilt of his sword to use his right hand to push against the daemon's bloody torso. It didn't matter; the weight on his chest, the grip on his neck did not move. Trist's vision darkened, and he wondered if Acrasia would Tithe his soul to the faerie king when he died.

Suddenly, the weight was off his chest, the claws no longer around his throat, and Trist gasped for air. His lungs burned, his vision swam, and he curled into himself in a fit of coughing.

"Get up, lad!" a gruff voice shouted, and he blinked away the darkness in his vision to see Bors backing Adrammelech away, holding the daemon at bay with great, heavy swings of his flail. With a snarl, the Prince of Plagues yanked Trist's sword from out of his chest and threw it aside. The spectral form of Tor De Lancey flanked the monster from the left, swinging his warhammer, forcing the wounded daemon to retreat again before the combined assault.

How much longer could he hold Tor here? Trist hacked up a great gob of phlegm and blood, and scrambled on his hands and knees for the hilt of his sword. He had to drag himself across the cold corpses of southernor and Narvonnian soldiers alike, stinking of emptied bowels and blood. The thread was already slipping, in truth, like his fingers from a rock too heavy to carry. The charge, then he'd come back around. How long had Adrammelech been choking him before the two of them regrouped and drove the daemon back? There might only be seconds left before Tor's form disappeared, and if Trist wasn't back on his feet by then, they were all lost.

His fingers closed around the leather-wrapped hilt, and Trist pushed himself back upright, lurched onto his feet, and swayed there, at the center of the slaughter. Longsword in hand, he turned back to see Tor bring his warhammer down in a great overhand sweep, directly on the head of the daemon... and dissolve. The brief moment of the ghost's incarnation passed, and only a trail of evanescent, shimmering motion swept over Adrammelech. The daemon flinched, but was unharmed, and now it was back to facing only Sir Bors: the fight it had been winning before Trist arrived. If Ismet hadn't been lost in the collapsing wall, if her general had been able to last a little longer, all of them together might have been able to end this by now.

Trist sucked a deep breath, blew it out again. He didn't feel the strength in his arms to hoist his sword into High Guard, above his head, so he kept it low, in Fool's Guard, extended in front of him and angled down toward the ground, inviting an attack.The older Exarch was retreating, now, with great sweeps of his flail meant to back the daemon off. Adrammelech, on the other hand, waited for the spiked ball to pass him, then leapt in, quick as a cat, to slash at Bors, forcing the knight to step back. Trist took a step forward, then another, and swung his blade up in an arc, only to bring it down again, shifting his hands on the hilt automatically to make his cut with the maximum possible speed. It wouldn't be enough: he knew from their last battle that the Prince of Plagues was faster than he was. Indeed, the daemon dodged to the side... but the tip of Trist's blade drew black blood from a new cut on its thigh.

Trist and the daemon both stopped, their eyes meeting, Trist's vision hazed in pulsing orange light. Trist's lips curved in a weary grin. Adrammelech could move faster than a charging horse could turn to compensate, that was true. But the monster was no longer as quick as Trist. Stronger, certainly; that had already been put to the test, and Trist had not the slightest chance of winning a grapple. But to his eye... yes. The monster seemed to be moving slower than before, which meant that, really, Trist was faster. Just like fighting normal men: he'd thought they looked like they were moving at only half speed. The degree wasn't as great, but it might be enough.

Hope lent strength and vigor to his tired, plague-wracked muscles, and Trist moved to attack, slashing in not single strokes, but combinations: feints, doubled cuts, thrusts flicked to the daemon's body faster than the shine of sun on water. Bors advanced at his side, and though they'd never fought together before, they did so now, the two exarchs turning the tide of battle and backing Adrammelech across the field of bodies, now. With nearly every stroke, Trist drew black ichor from the body of the daemon.

"Keep it up, boy!" Bors said, with a grin. They might never be friends, but in this moment, Trist was grateful to have the older man at his side.

"Enough of this," Adrammelech snarled. "My Ornes will finish you all, and both armies, soon enough. I am needed elsewhere!" With a great downstroke of his wings, the daemon leapt straight up into the air above their heads, out of reach of their weapons.

"No," a voice like thunder shook Trist's bones. "There will be no escape for you today, traitor." The sky exploded in light.

Adrammelech screamed. Trist had to shield his eyes with one gauntleted hand to get a glimpse of three burning entities above, lashing their whirls and threads of bright fire to wrap Adrammelech's limbs and bind him. Masheth, wings spread, in the center, his voice the same as Trist had heard it once before, when he'd first come to the camp at Falais. To the left, a second Angelus, which must have been Jibrīl, choosing to remain at the battlefield and face the daemon rather than depart to seek out a new Exarch. And on the right, her blonde tresses uplifted by a fresh breeze, Acrasia.

"I thought the faeries refused to take sides," Bors shouted, over the wails of the daemon. Its very form seemed to be blackening and burning under the assault of the three shining immortals, and it reminded Trist of when he'd plunged iron into Acrasia's flesh.

"I don't care about your war," Acrasia shouted back, her eyes burning, lashes burrowing into Adramelech now, sinking through his earthly form and past the flesh, spearing into the burning heart of the creature beyond. "But I'll kill anything that hurts my love!"

The daemon's wings were pierced by a dozen threads of fire, red and orange and yellow and white, and pinned against his sides. Adrammelech's body crashed down to the bloody ground.

"Now!" Jibrīl spoke, in a voice like ringing bells. "Strike, Exarchs!"

As one, Trist and Bors raised their weapons, and brought them down on the cowering Prince of Plagues.

Then, the battlefield was silent.

Chapter Fifty-Three

The Battle of Falais IX: The Tomb of Abatur

If you are familiar with Marius' theories, you will understand what I mean: the way in which an immortal binds itself to this world seems to influence the expression of physical power. Let me give an example: the Accord between Exarch and Angelus lends more than mortal physical capabilities - but the Exarch of an Angelus will never be as physically strong as a daemon, nor as quick as a faerie. For us, the anchor is most noticeable in increasing our raw physical stamina, our resistance to disease and ability to heal from injury.
-The Testament of Sir Baylin, Exarch of Kadosh

12th Day of the Flower Moon, 297 AC

"Good," Sir Divdan said, striding forward. "I was sick of talking to you anyway, you traitorous bitch." Henry watched in horror as Agrat leapt over the tomb, claws extended and wings spread, half-gliding to land on the knight's upraised shield, as if it were a bare rock face that she was about to climb. The fingers of her left hand had purchase over the top rim of the shield, and her feet and one knee supported her weight on it's broad surface. She swung down over the top with her right hand, then back up with her claws, ripping Divdan's helm from his head and sending it flying off into the dim crypt, clattering across the stones.

The weight of the daemon was more than Divdan could support, and given the option between collapsing to the ground under her or releasing the shield, he chose the latter. As the shield fell, Agrat beat her wings once and rose above him: Henry was certain that in a heartbeat more, she would fall upon his exposed face with her wicked claws, and that would be the end of the knight.

As he'd done a hundred times in the Ardenwood, when a quail took flight from the brush, Henry drew, nocked, and loosed in a single smooth motion, just as his father had taught him. The black wood of the longbow would have been beyond any untrained man to bend, but he'd been practicing every day since he was tall enough to follow his father's instructions, first with a bow sized for a child, then later with the same weapon he used now.

The arrow, black shaft of Iebara wood just like the bow, head of steel, and goose feather fletching from his brother-in-law's farm, entered the daemon woman's right eye, passed entirely through the socket, then into the back of her head, where it was stopped by the skull. The force of the powerful bow carried Agrat's body backwards, slamming it into the wall of the crypt; the daemon seemed to hang there for an interminable moment in time, then slid down the wall, leaving streaks of black ichor in her wake.

With an inarticulate, strangled cry, Lady Valeria rushed him. Henry, shocked that he'd actually put the daemon down, panicked when the noblewoman came at him, fumbled at his quiver, and scrambled backward. Killing a daemon was one thing; it was the sort of thing heroes and Exarchs did in stories, but it was done, and a noble thing to do indeed. But killing a noblewoman was death. His fingers, which had always been steady before, somehow failed to nock his arrow to the bowstring.

Sir Divdan appeared to have no such misgivings. The knight stepped into Valeria's path, drew the edge of his blade across her belly, and continued past her with the stroke.

Valeria bent double over the sword as it cut along her, then clutched herself as blood poured out over her fine, pale fingers.

"Every one of you is dead," she spat, her lifeblood splashing onto the floor. Sinking to the ground, Valeria du Champs d'Or sucked in a deep breath, held it a moment as her eyes fluttered, and then blew outward, like a child making a wish upon a dandelion. The noblewoman struggled to stay upright. "Plague," she gasped. "A plague upon all of you. I hope you all have great enjoyment of it!" Her once beautiful face was twisted into such an expression of hate and spite that Henry thought it was like watching someone pull off a mask.

Divdan coughed first, then Henry, and finally Yaél, from somewhere behind him. Henry swallowed, after the fit had passed, and found that his throat was sore at the motion. He raised a hand to his own forehead, and was amazed to find that it came away wet with sweat.

"We have to kill her now!" Sir Divdan shouted, spinning around to face Valeria again. He raised his sword, but swayed on his feet. If he felt anything like Henry did, the hunter thought, it was a miracle he could stand up straight at all, in that heavy plate armor.

Valeria, in the meanwhile, threw herself upright with a cry. Though she kept her left hand clenched over her bleeding stomach wound, with her right she caught Divdan's sword arm by the metal vambrace. The knight towered over the diminutive lady, and Henry could not imagine she had any muscle to speak of, but somehow, with hideous strength beyond that any mortal woman should have, she forced Divdan back. Not only did she prevent him from swinging the sword at her, she backed him to the wall of the crypt and then, to Henry's utter amazement, the shriek of bending, crumpling metal filled the air. Sir Divdan screamed as his steel vambrace bent in upon itself beneath the daemonic Exarch's fingers. It occurred to Henry that they were not winning this fight, after all, but he couldn't do anything about it but hack up gobs of phlegm and fall onto his side, against the cold stones.

"The ring!" Yaél gasped, and stumbled forward to the stairs which led down to the sarcophagus. The squire's body was wracked by a particularly bad fit of coughing, and, losing his balance, he tumbled down the steps to land at the bottom, where he gasped and wheezed for breath, pulling something off his finger. Auberon's ring, Henry remembered.

Valeria's head shot around so fast and far she seemed like an owl herself. "What do you have there, boy?" the woman hissed. "I can see it burning. Is that faerie magic? Give it to me, and I'll let you live."

Yaél shook his head, crawling to the sarcophagus, where he grasped at the stone, looking for some hand hold to support him in an attempt to stand up. With an exclamation of frustration, Valeria threw Sir Divdan aside, bouncing the knight's unprotected head off the stone wall. Divdan lay where he fell, unconscious at best, and she stalked back across the tomb to the steps. The cut to her belly seemed to hurt the daemonic woman less and less, while her plague ravaged the rest of them each passing breath. Fever shook Henry's body with alternating sweats and chills, and he struggled to fill his lungs with air.

"Stay away from the boy," Henry gasped, fumbled an arrow from his quiver, and fit it to his bowstring. He wasn't certain whether his body would fail him or remain true until the longbow bent, like his oldest friend, just as it always had.

"Impudent," Valeria snarled, and caught the arrow by the shaft in her right hand, where it quivered like a frightened bird. "Fine. I'll kill you first, then the boy." Henry felt for another arrow, but his eyes were growing dim, and he found it hard to see, hard to think. Then, he felt himself dragged upright, to his feet, then past, until he hung with only his tiptoes brushing the crypt floor. He tried to draw in a breath, but those delicate fingers squeezed the leather stock around his throat, and he couldn't make the air come in.

Henry gazed down into Valeria's eyes and saw no hint of compassion, or guilt, or mercy. She looked at him like he might have looked at a rat: nothing but vermin, to be exterminated before it got into the grain silos. This is it, then, Henry realized. He hoped that Sir Trist succeeded, because despite everything, they had failed him. He'll make a good lord, Henry comforted himself. He has a pure heart.

"I did what I said I would," Yaél's voice broke the dimness of Henry's mind, on the edge of consciousness, and then, clear and quiet, the softest clink of metal on stone.

Lady Valeria shrieked, and then the grip around Henry's throat was gone. He fell to the ground, and sucked in a breath, coughed it out, then sucked in another one. The darkness around his vision cleared, and Henry saw that the room was filled with light. It was not the warm glow of firelight, nor even the bright, pounding heat of a summer sun: it was the pale shine of moonlight, of stars in a night sky. The light came from whatever Yaél had placed on top of the sarcophagus, and it threw moving shadows onto the walls of the crypt, shadows that were long and sharp and inhuman.

"What have you done?" Valeria shrieked.

The snarling of hunting hounds filled the room, as great beasts emerged from those dancing shadows, coalescing from the very darkness itself. Cern, the Horned Hunter, took a knee in the center of the room, the butt of his spear planted on the stone.

"What would you have of me, my king?" he asked.

Valeria dashed for the stairs, scrambling up the stone steps in what Henry could only interpret as raw panic.

"Good lad," an unfamiliar voice intoned, echoing throughout the crypt. Henry turned his gaze from the stairwell Valeria had used to flee, back toward the sarcophagus. There stood a man impossibly tall, with fine sharp features, long black hair, and eyes that glittered like stars. He rested a hand on Yaél's head, patting the squire once and running his fingers through the boy's hair as if to soothe him. There was a kingly circlet about the man's brow, and he lifted whatever Yaél had put on the sarcophagus. A ring, Henry saw, now, as the man slipped it onto his finger.

The man turned to him, and for a moment, Henry met his eyes; they were vast, and seemed to draw him in, until he would be lost in them. "Look away, mortal," the man said, and Henry let his head fall back to the ground, screwing his eyes as tightly shut as he could. "Few there are of your race who can say they have gazed upon Auberon, King of Shadows. Take that blessing and be satisfied that I allow you to live. Cern," he continued. "Do as you were made to do. Hunt."

There was a great howling and rushing all about him, and Henry folded in on himself, begging the Angelus silently to preserve him. Soft fur and the scent of beasts passed him on every side, and then the sounds receded up the curved stairwell which led to the rest of the Church, and to Falais beyond. Finally the room dimmed, and the bright moonlight no longer stung his eyes through the lids.

"Come on," Yaél gasped, next to him, and clutching Henry's arm, helped him to his feet. "We need to go."

"Aye," Henry agreed. "The young lord may walk with faeries and return, but I would feel safer well away from them."

A groan from across the room caught their attention, and the two stumbled together over to where Sir Divdan stirred. "Can you walk?" Henry asked the knight, who could not answer for a fit of coughing. A part of his mind noted that the daemon of plagues was gone.

"Never mind," the hunter decided. "We'll help you." Between them, he and Yaél somehow pulled the wounded knight to his feet. Henry was never able to determine just how long it took them to climb the spiral stairwell back up to the main level of the church; once they'd set Divdan down on the floor, near the blood-stained altar, and once Henry had caught his breath, he looked up.

The stairwell continued to the Church steeple.

Without a word, Henry slumped back over to the stairs and began to climb. It was faster, now, without having to carry Sir Divdan, and at some point he heard Yaél coming up behind him. He had to stop three times: twice to hack up blood and Angelus knew what else, and once to lean against the curve of the outer wall, or else he was certain that a wave of dizziness would have pitched him all the way back down the stone steps, likely to land with a broken neck at the bottom.

Finally, Henry stepped out onto the steeple. It was located at the front of the church, and rose above the cliffs and the smoking town. He could see the streets spread out below, and the river, and the pass continuing south, and even the edges of the Ardenwood to the north.

He could see the Wild Hunt.

The Horned Lord and his hounds swept through the streets of Falais, and everywhere they went the daemon birds of Adrammelech died. The Hunter did not stop until he'd killed every monster in the city, and then he rode south through the gate, where even from this distance Henry could see men throw themselves aside in fear.

South into the Passe de Mûre rode the faerie host, and drove the flock of terrible birds before them.

Chapter Fifty-Four

The Battle of Falais X: Reunions

I've fed the crows often enough they should be my sigil, in truth. The lion is a lie, but it makes my men happy.
They speak of four great battles to turn aside the Cataclysm, but there were a dozen more skirmishes, ambushes, routs, and disasters besides. At the end of it all, I hope more people have lived than would have without me, but I am tired. All I want is an ending, and to sleep.
-The Campaign Journals of General Aurelius, volume IV

12th Day of the Flower Moon, 297 AC

Trist's longsword shivered and jerked, sending spurts of energy up his trembling arms as the daemon Adramelech died. Next to him, only an arm span away, Bors roared out loud as the Tithes poured into them both. How many souls had Adrammelech taken, in the short time he'd been free? Trist couldn't be certain, but he felt more power surging from the withering corpse of the Prince of Plagues than he'd felt at the death of Addanc.

Finally, in a flash of light, it was done. A wave of pressure blew out in a ring across the battlefield, scattering dust and other detritus like an autumn wind driving leaves before it. Trist fell to one knee, but kept a grip on his sword hilt with his right hand.

"How many Tithes?" he asked Acrasia, who floated down from the sky to land next to him. As she descended, she reeled in the loops and whirls of flame she'd extruded to fight the daemon.

"Five for each of us," Acrasia told him. "Adrammelech was quite powerful; perhaps on the level of my brother. Half the Tithes went to you, the other half to Bors."

"I would have thought it would be more," Trist gasped, after a moment.

"The monster had been bound away for a very long time," Bors responded gruffly. "We're fortunate we fought it now, before it had a chance to gain back more of its power. Use your Tithes now, lad," the older Exarch urged him. "You never know what danger is coming next, and we're still on a battlefield."

"Daemon Bane," Trist instructed Acrasia. "And Hunter of the Horned Lord."

"Good choices, my love," Acrasia murmured to him with a smile, then reached her hands into his chest. Two of the threads that pulsed inside of Trist stirred, grasped in her hands, and flicking out of his body to curl in the air around him. That same jolt of power followed, and Trist felt every muscle in his body tense. His eyes fluttered, and when the feeling had passed and he could see clearly again, the two threads retreating back into his chest burned a bright orange, instead of a dull red. He was able to see it happen more clearly, now, and also a thread of orange flaring to yellow down the length of his sword.

"That leaves you one put aside for later," Acrasia reminded him, and Trist nodded. He glanced over to Bors, who was getting to his feet, and wondered which Boons the older knight had improved. Since the man no longer seemed to want to kill him, perhaps Trist would even be able to ask for advice when this was all over.

With a start, Trist realized that he was no longer thinking as if they were going to lose the battle; he was even planning for after their victory. With Adrammelech's defeat, things no longer seemed hopeless. He could help end things more quickly if he was mounted.

"Caz!" Trist put two fingers to his mouth and whistled, and a moment later, the destrier trotted over. He staggered to his feet, clutched at Caz's saddle, and managed to keep himself upright, even while he coughed and hacked.

"Here." Bors was at his side. The older knight leaned down, caught Trist's boot, and boosted him up onto the destrier's back. "You look sick, boy."

"Lady Valeria," Trist explained. "I fear she is a daemonic Exarch. She breathed on me, and I have been ill ever since. She spoke of plague..."

"Ease your mind," Bors said. "I was an Exarch during the last plague, and I can tell you that not a single one of us died of it. Took a few days to recover, aye, but we are not only stronger than normal men, but harder to kill. Doesn't help you at this moment, but I would say a day or two of rest and you will be right again. Now," he said, turning to scan the field, "We have two tasks. Three, perhaps."

"I'm listening," Trist said.

"The fighting is dying down," Bors said, pointing a gauntleted fist. "Look there. See how the birds are dying?"

Trist looked. Ornes were dropping from the sky, plummeting as their wings ceased to function, and the ones who survived the fall were easily dispatched by combined groups of southern and northern soldiers, working together.

"With Adrammelech destroyed, his power no longer animates them," Acrasia explained.

"What I'm more worried about," Bors said, "Is the Great Cataclysm. Two of us won't be enough to kill it."

"There was another Exarch with me," Trist said. "Ismet. From the Caliphate. I lost track of her when the wall came down."

"That is where the Prince was, as well," Bors said. "Then that is where we go - to where the gate fell." It took only a moment for Sir Bors to find a horse without a rider and swing up into the saddle. Once mounted, the two knights set off, picking their way through the dead bodies strewn across the field.

As the fighting subsided, the ravens came, landing amidst the corpses and feasting. Piteous moans marked those soldiers wounded, perhaps dying, but not yet dead. As they approached the wall, Trist saw men who'd been killed not by Ornes, nor by the weapons of one army or the other, but with their heads or chests crushed by falling blocks of stone. The dust had settled enough to get a clear view of where the gate had once been.

To either side, the stone wall fell away, and the parapets and siege engines tumbled down in a great wreckage. Trist tried to count the bodies, but he'd never been as good at arithmetic as Percy, and he lost track quick enough.

"Prince Lionel!" Sir Bors shouted, his voice booming across the piles of stone and wood. "Is the Prince alive?"

"Here!" a man's voice sounded in return, and they directed their horses' steps around and between the fallen stones. There, atop a pile of crushed masonry, two figures sat, one drinking from a wineskin in his hand. Bors immediately slid down from the saddle, took three steps forward, and fell to one knee, head bowed.

"Your Royal Highness," he began. "It is good to see you alive." He turned to the woman sitting next to the Prince, and Trist could imagine the older man's confusion.

"Ismet," Trist called, "Exarch of Epinoia. Adrammelech is dead. Have I kept faith with you?" The Crown Prince offered his wineskin to her, and the southerner hesitated a moment before accepting.

"You have," she answered, after finishing a gulp of watered wine. Her red veil was covered in so much dust it looked to have been dipped in sand. "I count that as your ransom paid. More than paid," the southern woman admitted, with sparkling eyes. "We had a fight here, as well, though it did not end so well as yours."

Lionel Aurelianus laughed. "Our new friend is too modest. She stabbed the Great Cataclysm through the eye and drove it from the field."

"Sammā'ēl the Sun Eater still lives," Ismet complained.

"Lady Exarch," Sir Bors said, shaking his head. "Even for one of us, to stand against such a monster and live is a feat worthy of song. And it seems to me that we have you to thank for the survival of our Crown Prince."

"I only did what I came north to do," Ismet said, passing the wineskin back to Lionel.

"We will speak more of such things after the wounded have been seen to, and the dead given their honors," Lionel declared. "Has the General of the Caliphate Army been found? I would speak of peace with him."

"Lady Ismet," Trist answered, for he could guess how this news would strike her. "You have my deepest condolences in your sorrow. General Shadi fought bravely, but he was killed by the Prince of Plagues. If it is any comfort, Jibrīl remained with us during the battle, and joined with Masheth and Acrasia to bind Adramelech long enough for us to strike him down."

Ismet's shoulders slumped, and her eyes fell to the ground.

"There is more, and I fear you will not enjoy hearing it," Trist said, turning to his own Prince. "Your Royal Highness, my men and I, and Ismet as well, encountered Lady Valeria fleeing north through the pass."

"Good," Lionel said, with a sigh of relief. "I sent her away when it became clear the wall would not hold. It does my heart well to know she made it safely to Falais."

Ismet looked up, now, met Trist's eyes, and cocked her head to one side. She could not know the relationship between Lionel and the woman they'd fought, but now she could make a guess.

"My prince," Trist said, "Lady Valeria has betrayed us. When she saw us riding south, she revealed herself as Exarch of the daemon Agrat, who she called the Daemon Queen of Plagues. We drove them off, but not before I was infected."

Lionel's face paled, his eyes wide. "Valeria? But..." he turned to Ismet, searching for confirmation or denial in the southern woman's dark eyes.

"Your knight speaks truly," Ismet said. "We fought against her and the daemon together - though, at the time, I did not truly know who the woman was, save a lady of obvious high birth. She and her monster fled north to Falais, to work some wickedness."

"We sent Sir Divdan, my man Henry, and my squire Yaél to stop her," Trist explained.

"Two men and a child against an Exarch and a daemon?" Bors spun to face him, rising to his feet. "You sent them to their deaths, boy."

"I am not so certain of that," Trist said, after a moment, and a fit of coughing. "My squire bore a ring from the Faerie King of Shadows. But with your leave, Your Highness, I would ride north to Falais. If they have succeeded, they will be able to tell us what happened to Valeria. If they failed, we may have little time."

"Go," Lionel said with a wave of his hand. "And take Sir Bors with you."

"Your Highness," Bors protested. "My duty is to remain here with you. The field may be won, but it is not yet safe."

"I think I shall be safe enough here next to Lady Ismet," Lionel answered. "In any event, my lady, with General Shadi dead, I would treat with you. Unless there was a third Exarch with the Caliphate army?"

"No," Ismet admitted. "It was only the two of us."

"Then let us make a peace and a common cause here, this day," Lionel proposed. "There are at least two daemons still abroad in Narvonne, and I suspect that your sword-arm will be needed to bring them down, before all is said and done."

"Very well; we will speak." Ismet turned to Bors. "Your prince will be safe here with me; I swear it."

"As you say, then, m'lady." Bors swung back up into the saddle of his horse, and they all stopped at the sound of trumpets ringing across the field. Trist looked south, and saw a force of mounted knights, flying many banners, ride down out of the foothills and onto the battlefield, striking down the last of the Ornes as they came.

"Baron Urien," Lionel said, with a smile. "Arrived at last, though not to the purpose I had originally conceived."

"Meant to fall upon our rear and take us from behind, I assume?" Ismet asked, shaking her head. "Well, they can help secure the field now. I suppose I cannot be angry with you."

Trist and Bors turned the heads of their horses away, and after picking their way through the last stretch of debris, rode north toward Falais.

"I hope the boy is still alive," Acrasia said, settling into Trist's saddle and cuddling up against him.

"I thought mortals were like horses," Trist chided her. "Easily put down when they're of no more use, and not worth mourning."

"I think it is simple habit," Acrasia protested. "After traveling with the boy for days and days, I've grown accustomed to having him around."

When they reached the gate, they were approached by Baroness Arnive, who hailed them. "What news of the battle?" she asked, striding to where the two horses blew and trembled. "You would not believe what has transpired here in a hundred lifetimes."

"As much a victory as could be had," Bors responded. "Adrammelech is dead at our hands." He jerked his head to Trist, who was trying to catch his breath.

"Then my husband is finally avenged." The Baroness smiled. "The Crown Prince? The pass?"

"Alive and safe," Trist gasped out, "But the wall will need to be repaired. And there will be peace, at least for the moment, while we have daemons to hunt. Did my squire come through this way, with Sir Divdan?"

"They did, and your man with them, making haste to the Church in pursuit of Lady Valeria," the Baroness explained. "And whatever they did, it must have saved us all; for the Horned Hunter and his entire Host charged out of that church like an avalanche down from the cliffs."

Chapter Fifty-Five

The Battle of Falais XI: Auberon's Graal

It is said that Sir Maddoc laughed even at the loss of a hand, for when he returned to the bower of the Faerie King, all his wounds would be healed with a single sip from Auberon's Graal. Even after the Knight of the Wood's death, and his internment beneath the hills, many fortune-hunters and adventurers entered the Ardenwood in search of such a priceless treasure. Very few ever returned.

-François du Lutetia, A History of Narvonne

12th Day of the Flower Moon, 297 AC

When Trist came to the top of the stone steps that led up towards the cliffs looming over Falais, he stopped for a moment, to lean against the stone wall on the right side of the alley. With Baroness Arnive's assurance that no danger remained in the town - thanks in no small part to Cousin Lucan's efforts in halting saboteurs, apparently - Bors had remained at the southern gate to assist there, rounding up Lady Valeria's knights for questioning.

"Just a bit further, my love, and you can rest," Acrasia urged him from the street. She reached back a hand, but he didn't take it.

"It's not the coughing," Trist said, after catching his breath. "Look at the church."

"I know!" Acrasia smiled joyfully. It was the most pure expression of happiness he'd seen on her face since before the night of his brother's wedding to Clarisant, and Trist saw her again as he had for so many years: the sun in her hair, all aglow with some incomprehensible, incandescent beauty and life.

Hacking up a gob of phlegm, and not a little blood, and spitting it off to one side, Trist staggered toward the facade of the Church of Saint Abatur. It was still built out of the cliffs, of that same golden-brown and orange stone that ran through the hills and mountains all around the pass, but now the front was covered in ivy. It couldn't possibly have grown so quickly; the rock had been bare when Trist and Acrasia were here with Sir Divdan only eight days before. Now, the entire facade looked like the south wall of the monastery at Camaret-à-Arden, where the monks had stopped fighting to trim it back long before he was born.

A gentle breeze sighed down the high street, ruffling the green leaves of the ivy like the hairs on the back of a man's arm. As they came to the steps, Trist saw that the cobblestones and stairs were cracked, and that little mushrooms with white stocks, and bright red caps spotted with white, grew up there. They looked like they were still coming in, but Trist guessed that when they were done they would form a bright circle around the entrance to the church. He stepped over them carefully, rather than risk kicking them with his boot.

Inside, the sunlight streamed down golden through a shattered window that had once been stained glass. Vines and ivy covered the interior walls, as well as the exterior, and to Trist's amazement a great oak grew where the altar used to be, already high enough to brush the vaulted ceiling with its leaves. The knotted roots had ripped up chunks of the floor stones, and the entire thing had grown into a kind of cupped hand, where Auberon sat as on a throne, cradled by the divided boughs.

"Lady Acrasia and my Knight of Shadows," the Faerie King greeted them with a smile. "I told you they would survive, Cern. Have a bit more... faith." At the last word, he glanced around the overgrown church and laughed.

"Sister." Cern stepped forward from behind the trunk of the oak. "It is a comfort to see you in good health once again."

Trist took a knee. "Your Majesty," he addressed the King of Shadows. "Baroness Arnive tells me that your Wild Hunt saved the city. You have my personal gratitude, and I have no doubt that Crown Prince Lionel will wish to express his thanks, as well. But if I may..."

"Yes? You have a question?" Auberon prompted him, and reached into the tree's hollow to retrieve a silver goblet, from which he drank.

"Several," Trist admitted. "The first is what has become of our companions."

"Our companions, now, is it?" Auberon's eyes flicked to where Acrasia knelt at Trist's side. "You haven't made a habit of becoming too attached to mortals, my dear, have you?"

"Have they not served you well?" Acrasia answered, without lifting her eyes to meet her monarch's gaze. "The squire, at least, must have, for you to be here."

"True," Auberon admitted. "The child kept our bargain. Which, if you think on it, Trist du Camaret-à-Arden, provides the answer to your second question."

Trist frowned. "How - or perhaps why - is it that you are here? I understood that the faeries did not take a side, when daemon and Angelus fought."

"We do not," Auberon answered, and let the question hang for a moment, as he smirked.

"But we defend our territory," Acrasia hinted.

Trist looked around the room again, at the vines and the oak, the broken remnants of the altar, and the shattered stained glass window. "Your territory? It certainly looks like it. But is not this the tomb of an Angelus?"

"Yes, the withered old corpse of poor, tired and boring Abatur, watching over the prison of Adrammelech," Auberon elaborated, far more lightly than Trist was comfortable with, given the subject matter. "And so long as the Prince of Plagues remained imprisoned, it was necessary to leave those rattling bones in the basement of this place just so the monster couldn't break his chains. But you, my boy," the faerie king said, leaning forward and pinning Trist with his eyes, "Brought me word that Adrammelech had broken free."

"So there was nothing holding you back from - what?" Trist asked. "Taking this place?"

"Did you know that corpses can make excellent fertilizer?" Auberon asked, sitting back into his chair, and patting the boughs of the massive oak.

Trist decided that he wasn't going to think about that in any more detail. "And the ring?"

"My claim," Auberon explained. "My pennant, if you like. Delivered, of course, by an intermediary, as places sacred to the Angelus are not particularly comfortable to my people. Your squire got it here at the very last moment, by the by. Agrat and her Exarch had very nearly corrupted the entire place, and you would not have liked to see what that would have meant for all of the poor mortals living in the town."

"Are they alive?" Trist asked.

"For now," Cern growled. "If you would see them before Agrat's plague finishes its work, look for them in the steeple. Your hunter begged me to let them stay in the clean air, where they could look out over the city they've saved, as they die."

"Your Majesty," Trist begged, his voice hoarse. "Would you permit them to drink from the Graal?"

"How tiresome," Auberon sighed. "No, you will be running to me every time one of your people stubs a toe, at this rate. Where will it end? Your drink, my knight, was bought and paid for, and that bargain is done. I am disinclined to make another, though," he admitted, "I do appreciate the Tithes you have been sending."

"Then a Boon!" Acrasia suggested. Auberon turned to her, and she seemed to shrink into herself. "That is within the bounds of the Accords, is it not? To reward an Exarch whose services have pleased, with a Boon?"

"It is," Auberon said, drawing the words out slowly, considering.

"And he meets the conditions, does he not?" Acrasia pressed on. She hadn't yet been outright rejected, and Trist feared to make matters worse if he opened his mouth, since he knew so little of faerie courtesy.

"Oh, very well," the King of Shadows sighed. "I never could stand to see a creature as beautiful as you beg. Rise, boy, and approach me."

Trist stood, bowed, and closed the distance to the oak throne, keeping his eyes lowered the entire while. He was struck by another wave of dizziness and fever, but did his best not to let it show: he was so close to the end now, and if there was any chance that he could help Henry and Yaél and even Sir Divdan, he could stand all night.

"I see you have the one Tithe remaining, to pay for it," Auberon muttered to himself, and stretched a hand to Trist's chest. Their physical bodies did not touch, but a thread of blue-white flame reached out from Auberon's core of tightly wound fire, dipped into

Trist, and unspooled a new, deep, burning red cord from him. Trist shuddered, unable to breath for a moment, until the power receded and his body calmed.

"There," Auberon spoke, after a moment, withdrawing that piece of himself that shone so brightly. "Climb the stairs then, Graal Knight, and take a goblet with you. I believe the priest had one lying around, and a few bottles of wine. I expect you will know what to do."

"Thank you, Your Majesty," Trist said, and took three steps back. Acrasia rose from her knee to courtesy with him when he bowed, and then they departed the presence of the Faerie King.

"Don't get any closer, m'lord," Henry rasped when Trist and Acrasia emerged from the top of the stairwell onto the steeple.

"Henry," Trist said, as he strode over to where the two men and the boy slumped together on the floor, "I was infected before you were - do you not remember? In the pass, by the daemon?"

"It's the fever," Divdan mumbled. "Makes it hard to think straight. Come to die with us, then? Good. I want to hear about the battle." A fit of coughing took the knight, and his eyes fluttered closed.

"Come to you, but not to die." Trist set the goblet down, and the bottle of wine, and drew his longsword. He rubbed the edge of the blade up and down the neck of the glass bottle. "I could not find a corkscrew, so you are all lucky that Father Kramer kept a bottle of Cheverny White." Carefully, he pointed the bottle away from him, then with a single stroke, cut the top of the bottle off, causing the wine within to spill out in a bubbling froth. Setting the sword aside, he poured into the goblet, and allowed that new thread of deep red to extend along his hand and touch the wine as he did so. "Drink this," he urged Divdan, who lay closest to him.

Sir Divdan coughed, but accepted the wine and managed to swallow a gulp. Henry was next, and the hunter took a sip with a grin. "I suppose it's only fitting I get a taste of the good stuff before I pass," he joked.

"Help me with the boy," Trist said, and somehow between the three of the sick men they got Yaél upright.

"He's far gone, m'lord," Henry croaked. "Only a young lad, after all. I wish I could've have taken it for him," he mumbled.

"Yaél!" Trist called, and slapped the boy about the cheeks, from one side of the face to the other. "Wake up squire!"

"M'lord?" Yaél mumbled, eyes fluttering but not opening. His skin was burning hot to the touch, and Trist feared his brain would be cooked like an egg.

"Swallow," he said, putting the tip of the goblet to Yaél's lip, and pouring. The boy half-choked and coughed, but managed to gulp down some of it.

"Will it be enough?" he asked Acrasia, who was leaning against the rail, looking out over the city.

"Even the smallest sip should be enough," she said, "To begin, at least. Just keep giving them more as they improve."

"Enough for what?" Sir Divdan asked, narrowing his eyes in suspicion.

"What do you think?" Trist chided his companions. "To heal you all."

"The Graal?" Yaél asked, and Trist smiled to see the boy's eyes open.

"In a way," Trist said. "In a way. You see, an Exarch earns their boons not only by giving service and Tithing, but also by their accomplishments. What they have done, the victories they have won, the defeats they have survived."

"Riding with the Horned Hunter," Henry said, after a moment. "And then you could hunt like he can."

"Or drinking from Auberon's Graal," Trist confirmed, with a smile.

Chapter Fifty-Six

The Heart's Truth

We have little enough in the way of written testimony from Sir Maddoc himself - not a surprise, perhaps, given his status as an outlaw - but there is one letter that survives, from the knight to the Princess Helyan, in which he has this to say:

'I do not believe that any of the faeries truly comprehends what it is to be mortal, or to be human. They can play at eating and drinking, but they will not starve in a thousand years; they may take a human paramour for a time, but I do not think they are capable of feeling love, even if they wanted to. They are utterly and completely alien.'

-François du Lutetia, A History of Narvonne

1st Day of New Summer's Moon, 297 AC

"The carriage is here!" Yaël exclaimed, running into the central courtyard of Falais Castle, which lay between the Round Tower and the Central Tower. The

Round Tower, Trist had learned in conversation with Baroness Arnive, was the most recent, completed under the guidance of her father in law during her late husband's childhood.

Sir Bors dropped his shield and flail to one side, motioning for his squire to bring him a drink. The flail was not the one he used in battle; instead of a heavy, spiked metal ball, the end of the chain was affixed to a leather bag filled with sand. "You'd best get cleaned up, then, lad," he advised, then turned to peer at Yaél, flush and out of breath from running. "Did you run all the way from the north gate, squire?"

Yaél simply nodded his head up and down, hands on his knees, gasping for breath.

"Make that both of you should get cleaned up then," Bors said, shaking his head. "We'll continue another morning, Sir Trist."

"My thanks, Exarch," Trist said, setting his practice sword back on the rack. "Yaél, follow me," he said, and set off for the North Tower.

Baroness Arnive had been kind enough to lend rooms to Crown Prince Lionel, General Ismet, and the two Narvonnian Exarchs, as well as Baron Urien. Everyone else was camped either with the Narvonnian army, back where Trist, Henry and Yaél had first found them north of the city, or outside the southern gate, where the Caliphate forces had set up under their new commander's orders.

The idea, as Trist understood it, was to put a bit of distance between soldiers who had, not so long ago, been at each other's throats at the southern end of the pass. It would be easy enough to close off the southern or northern city gates as necessary, if tensions rose. In what everyone he'd spoken to considered a pleasant surprise, that hadn't been necessary. The shock of the daemonic attack, which had devastated both forces, had done more to break old ways of thinking than a hundred years of peace could have.

Reaching the stairwell, Trist took the stone steps two at a time, leaving Yaél to complain behind him. "Wait, m'lord!" the boy panted, but Trist kept on with a grin. Baron Urien's rooms were at the very top of the tower, and larger, but his were just the next floor down: a sitting room with space for Henry and Yaél to lay out their bedrolls next to the fire, a small private garderobe, and a bedchamber with tapestries on two walls, a feather mattress, and a four post bed currently hung with light, summer linen curtains. They had been keeping all of the windows open, and the door between the two chambers, so that the mountain breeze could blow through the rooms as much as possible.

Once in the bedchamber, Trist stripped out of his padded gambeson and chain, which he'd worn for practice with Sir Bors, and dipped a cloth in the basin of water and rose petals which had been left by the Baroness' servants. He wiped the sweat from his body, then donned a clean linen shirt with blackwork embroidered around the cuffs and collar, and only slightly moth-eaten. The Baroness had also been kind enough to open her late husband's wardrobe to him, as he'd brought hardly any spare clothes at all. By the time Yaél was at the top of the stairs, Trist had buckled on his sword belt and was passing him to head down again. "Get washed up and meet me in the courtyard," he called back, and took the steps down at a more sedate pace. It wouldn't do to get sweaty all over again.

Baroness Arnive was speaking to Baron Urien, in the courtyard, while his dogs lazed nearby, and her son Isdern grinned to see Trist when he approached. The boy was determined to be an Exarch one day, after feasting on tales of the battle for the past two weeks. Trist gave him a wave, then joined the group.

"I take it your squire brought you word?" Arnive asked him, eyebrows arched and lips quirked in amusement.

Urien laughed. "I think the entire castle saw him come rushing through. Saved me from having to post a lookout, at any rate."

"He did," Trist confirmed. "He is just cleaning up now; I expect him down in a moment." Indeed, Yaél managed to skid to a halt right next to Isdern, moments before the carriage rolled into the courtyard with a palfrey tied behind it. The two boys were of an age, and as long as the Baroness seemed willing to tolerate them spending time together, Trist thought it could only be a good thing.

The carriage, pulled by two horses and with two men-at-arms riding preceding it, was painted with the white shell of Baron Urien's family, on a blue field. That didn't surprise Trist; his family hadn't kept a carriage that he could recall for the entirety of his life. What did cause him to smile was that someone had attached a freshly sewn pennant, displaying a black Iebara tree, with white flowers, on a field of green, with the label along the top that marked the arms of the eldest son. Percy's arms, it should have been, and now Trist's: they fluttered, caught by the breeze, from where it was fastened to the carriage.

Once the small party had come to a halt, the coachman leapt down and opened the door. Both men at arms dismounted, and one made to approach the door, but Trist beat him to it.

"My lady wife," he murmured, peering into the carriage, and offered his hand.

"My lord husband," Clarisant du Camaret-à-Arden greeted him, with an answering smile. The sight of her face, and what Trist judged to be genuine relief, eased the knot in his stomach. She took his hand without hesitation, and stepped down out of the carriage into the courtyard. The mountain breeze, not satisfied with tossing the pennant, took her black hair as well, caught it up, and pulled it from her hairpins.

"Oh!" Clarisant exclaimed, reaching up to try to catch the black locks, and Trist wondered how he had ever overlooked her beauty. Before he could think it over, Trist wrapped his arms around her waist, drew her against him, and caught her lips with his own. On their wedding night, their kiss had been halting: now, there was no hesitation from her.

Behind him, Baron Urien coughed.

Trist released his wife, and was pleased to see that her cheeks were now red as if she'd been out riding in winter snow.

"Father," she said, squeezed Trist's hand once, and then stepped across the courtyard to embrace the Baron. The two dogs swarmed around her skirts, and would not desist until she scratched them under their ears, upon which they wagged their tails with such vigor the entire back of their bodies shook back and forth. Behind them, Clarisant's maid stepped down from inside the carriage and began seeing to her mistress's things.

"My little Claire," Urien said, with more warmth than Trist had ever heard from him before. "You are well?"

"I am," she assured the older man. "And you? Your letter said nothing of whether you'd taken a wound in the battle?"

Urien shook his head and huffed. "Not a scratch. His Royal Highness set me to command the cavalry reserve, to hit the southerners from behind and catch them against the wall. By the time we rode in, your husband had already killed just about everything worth killing."

Trist laughed. "We can talk about that later." He offered his arm to his wife, and she wrapped her hand around it, allowing him to steer her away from her father and to the other waiting noble. "Baroness Arnive, may I present my wife, Lady Clarisant du Camaret-à-Arden."

"Lady Clarisant," the Baroness said, kissing her on the cheek. "Welcome to Falais. My son, Isdern," she prodded the boy, and he gave a bow. "And the rascal attached to him at the hip is your husband's squire, whom I am told you have not yet met."

"M'lady," Yaél mumbled, and made the most atrocious bow Trist had ever seen. Another thing to practice with the boy.

"Yaél du Havre de Paix, I am told," Clarisant said, narrowing her brows as she glanced him over. "Do not worry," she said, after a moment, having clearly made a decision. "I will take you in hand."

The words seemed to utterly terrify Yaél, whom Trist had not seen so pale since he was dying of plague atop the steeple of the Church of Saint Abatur. The boy, eyes wide, swallowed as if he had been caught stealing wine from the cellars.

"You will want to have your things brought in, and recover from the journey," Arnive said. "I have given you and your husband rooms in the North Tower, just below your father's. I trust that will be satisfactory?"

"I am certain it will be lovely," Clarisant said. "And I look forward to becoming close friends with you, Baroness, if you are willing."

"Of course. Angelus know I could use help wrangling these two," the older woman said, glaring at Yaél and Isdern. "Boys. Help the maid take Lady Clarisant's things up."

"This way," Trist said, and, arm in arm, led his wife up into the tower.

Acrasia perched atop one of the stone crenellations that capped the outer walls of Falais Castle, weighing a fresh pear in her hand. The yellow skin, dusted brown, was crisp, and she could smell the juice within.

"You see," her brother said, stepping out of the shadow cast by the central tower to stand next to her. "He is not loyal to you, sister. He is not worthy of you." The hot breath of a wolf came with the Horned Hunter, the yellow gleam of a predator's eyes in the night, a discordant note.

"Oh, be silent," she shot at him with a scowl. Sweetbrier thorns pricked against thick fur, but did not draw blood; a fresh breeze rustled oak leaves, carrying away the reek of the wolf's breath.

"What?" Cern asked, spreading his hands as if to proclaim his innocence of any wrongdoing. The wolf's tongue lolled, and it rolled onto its back, showing a soft belly. "You are fully healed now, are you not? Then why is it that she is going to warm his bed tonight, and not you?"

"Because," Acrasia admitted, after a long silence, "He is never going to love me like he once did. Did you see the way he leapt to the carriage and kissed her? I've journeyed with him for a moon and more, waiting for him to forgive me, but he hasn't. We can finally touch again, kiss again, but we won't, because he will not choose to." The rose petals of the sweetbrier curled in on themselves, browned, died, and fell to the ground.

"As I told you." The wolf's tail wagged.

"And whose fault is that?" she spat at him, angrily. "Yours, for telling me to simply take what I wanted? The hunter who never thinks of anything but killing what our king sends you to kill? Or myself, for being fool enough to listen to you? They aren't like us. He isn't like us. He's still the same sweet boy I met in the Ardenwood years ago, and that boy will never forgive me, not if he lived as long as the hills. Leave me be, brother," Acrasia said, finally. "Leave me to stew in my own wretchedness." Flies settled on the rotting petals of the sweetbrier.

"You could leave," Cern said. "You need not be present every moment of every day for the Accord to function. And the King would be more than happy to kill the fool and have done with it." The wolf pawed at the ground, eager to race off on another hunt.

"Before, perhaps," she mused. "But now he's proven himself useful, and Auberon does not give up his toys easily once he has them in hand. I told you to leave me, Cern. Go." The sweetbrier grove thickened, the thorns grew long, barring passage.

A ripple of shadow was all that marked the passing of the Horned Hunter, leaving Acrasia alone atop the wall of the castle. She bit into the pear, tore a chunk off with her perfect white teeth, chewed and swallowed. It was the first food she'd had since regrowing her corporeal form, and she had been looking forward to it since the moment she'd realized the squire could hear her, up in the mountains, and that her recovery had begun.

"I saved his life," Acrasia said, looking down at the pear. She glanced over to the window of the tower, following the red strand of fire that bound her to Trist, and to his sword. Were they tumbling onto the bed even now, laughing and touching each other?

Acrasia looked down at the pear in disgust. It all tasted wrong, nothing like she'd imagined. It tasted like something already dead. She withdrew from her physical form, letting it scatter into motes of burning light, and the half-eaten pear fell off the wall, splattering on the stone of the courtyard below.

CHAPTER FIFTY-SEVEN

ONE NIGHT OF PEACE

Hereupon follows, as commanded to be set down by Aurelius, King of Narvonne, the list of daemons released from Vellatesia at the beginning of the Great Cataclysm, alone with all that we have learned about each. In number, they are two and seventy.
First, Aamon...
-The Marian Codex

1st Day of New Summer's Moon, 297 AC

"My friends," Crown Prince Lionel Aurelianus began, his voice echoing through the great hall of Falais Castle, "We have lost much, this past moon. But we have also gained much." He looked around the high table from where he stood at his seat, goblet of wine raised, and when the Prince's eyes met Trist's, in his turn, before sweeping on to the next person, he responded with a nod.

The Prince sat at the head of the table, in the place of honor, where Baroness Arnive's husband would have sat, had he been alive. To his left, the Baroness, and to his right, General Ismet ibnah Salah, who raised her goblet in turn. Baron Urien and his knights Sir Lucan and Sir Auron were there, as well as Dame Chantal and Sir Divdan, and Sir Florent of the Rive Ouest, who had ridden with Urien. The three knights who had come with Valeria from Champs d'Or were notably absent, awaiting their questioning with the Crown Prince.

"I thought that the Caliphate did not drink wine," Clarisant murmured, leaning in so close that her breath tickled Trist's ear. He caught the scent of the same perfume she'd worn the night of their wedding: cedarwood and fruit.

"Apple juice," Trist answered, softly. "From the orchards in the foothills outside the city. Though I did see her drink watered wine, once, right after the battle. From the Prince's own flask. But it was the only thing about, and she must have been parched from the fighting and the dust."

"His own flask, was it?"

Trist turned his head just far enough to see the grin on his wife's lips. "Yes?"

"That explains quite a bit, then," Clarisant said. "Look how close she sits to him."

Trist frowned. "You do not think-" he had to stop, because Prince Lionel wrapped up his speech right at that moment, and everyone in the great hall of Falais Castle rose from their seats to cheer and applaud. Once the Prince sat down again, the Baroness' servants flooded out from the kitchens, carrying platter after platter for the feast. The variety was astonishing: bowls of elvers, or baby eels, cooked with lemon, hot peppers, garlic, and olive oil; lamb stew with garlic, rosemary, onion, paprika, and roasted peppers; sheep's cheese; both cider and wine; salted rib steaks on the bone, again with peppers and garlic. It went on and on, dishes of the mountains and the river and of the sea that surrounded the Hauteurs Massif to east and west.

"I have never seen anything that would give me the idea that the Prince - that General Ismet," Trist stumbled over the words. "Lady Valeria was clinging to his arm every moment of the day!" With his belt knife, he cut a portion of his rib steak, and found it tender, juicy and flavorful.

"And yet, he never wed her," his wife observed, after swallowing a bite of stew. "Even before anyone knew that she had betrayed us. And let us remember, my lord husband," she said to him, with a smirk and glittering eyes, "That you are still under the impression that your squire is a boy. Perhaps your eyes are not to be trusted in such matters."

"What?" Trist said.

"Yaél," Carisant said, with all the certainty and finality of a landslide from the cliffs above the castle. "Is a girl. I knew it the moment I saw her."

"No, he isn't," Trist insisted.

"Has she ever taken her clothes off in front of you?" Clarisant lifted her fork, a bite of eel on the tines, and pointed it at him for emphasis. "I am certain you and your man Henry washed together more than once. At the lake, for instance, where you killed that monster?"

Trist squirmed in his chair.

"Do not worry," she continued. "I told you I would take her in hand, and I will. It is rare for a girl to be a squire, but not unheard of. I intend to speak with Dame Chantal about it tonight. I am certain she will be a wealth of advice and useful information."

"You are certain?" Trist asked again, unable to make the idea match up to his memory of a street urchin he'd met in the middle of a dark night. He looked down the length of the room to find a table near the entrance to the great hall, where all the squires, and Isdern besides, seemed to be having a grand time laughing and teasing each other. There was Yaél, with short chopped hair like a boy, pressed right up against the side of the Baroness' son, in the middle of a long bench. His jaw was delicate, it was true, in fact all his features fine, but that didn't mean that he would grow into any less a man.

Suddenly, Yaél turned his head, as if feeling Trist's eyes on him. Eyes wide, he blushed. Trist simply raised his goblet to the boy, across the hall. After a moment, Yaél followed suit; they drank, and shared a smile, and Trist turned back to his wife.

"By the Angelus, I see it now," he murmured. "Isdern is pressed right up against her. That is going to be trouble."

Clarisant laughed. "Perhaps. But trouble for another day."

"Trist, lad," a gruff voice came from behind them, and Sir Bors' hand thumped Trist in the middle of his back, causing a small bit of wine to slosh out of his goblet and onto the table. "This is your wife, then?"

"She is," Trist answered. "Sir Bors, please allow me to introduce Lady Clarisant du Camaret-à-Arden. My Lady, Sir Bors, Exarch of Masheth, and Champion of the Crown Prince."

"An honor to make the acquaintance of such an illustrious knight," Clarisant said, setting down her fork, and raising her hand to permit Sir Bors to bow over it.

"My lady." Borns nodded to her, then turns back to Trist. "I wanted to tell you, that I know I was not very welcoming when you arrived. Gave you a bit of a hard time, that I recall."

Trist credited years of etiquette training as a youth for his ability to keep his face calm and pleasant. A bit of a hard time - the man had wanted to kill him!

"But so far as I am concerned," Bors continued, "All of that is in the past now. I won't ever trust the faeries as far as I can throw them, but you stood beside me on the field, lad, and you didn't back down. That is a bond that cannot be broken. I will guard your back, Trist - you need not ever doubt that."

"Thank you," Trist said. "And I will guard yours."

"Good!" Bors slapped him on the shoulder again, then took a deep draught of wine. "We'll make a hardened soldier of you yet! Now, Lady Claire - may I call you Claire? - has your husband told you yet of how the daemon tackled him right off his horse? I was shouting at him to dismount, you see, but-"

"Sir Bors," Clarisant said, interrupting smoothly. "Please forgive me, but I fear the journey to Falais has exhausted me, and I feel a bit faint. Might you permit my husband to escort me back to our rooms?"

"Of course!" The big knight replied, backing away to give them room to stand. "Make way, you louts," he bullied the servants, who were scurrying past with more platters of food for the feast. "Sir Lucan!" he called over to Trist's cousin. "Tell me more about how you caught those saboteurs..."

Trist offered his arm to help Clarisant rise from her seat. As they walked past the long tables, toward the entrance of the grand hall, he leaned in to ask her, "Are you truly not feeling well?"

"The only thing that I am feeling," she murmured back, leaning her head into his shoulder, "Is a strong urge to be out of that particular conversation."

"Aye," Trist agreed, escorting her through the entranceway and out into the corridor, "Sir Bors can be a bit much, but he is a brave man on the field. You hardly ate anything. Will you be hungry?"

"You will just have to satisfy me in other ways," Clarisant said with a laugh, slipped out of his arms, and rushed up the stairs. Trist blinked for a moment, processing the words, then hurried after her.

Most of the platters were bare, now, and Urien's dogs gnawing on bones at the edges of the room. Lionel Aurelianus observed that many of the guests in the hall had slipped off singly or in pairs, and he suspected the moon was high in the sky. Even the table full of squires, flush with the strong wine they'd been allowed by special command of Baroness Arnive, had stumbled out into the night to find what trouble they could.

"And what is it called, again?" he asked Ismet ibnah Salah.

"Qahwa," she pronounced carefully, so that he could repeat it, mouthing the words to himself. Instead of the brigandine armor he'd first seen her wear, the Caliphate Exarch was dressed in a dizzying array of veils and shawls in complementing shades of scarlet and red, over some sort of long tunic or dress in heavy silk. Her eyes were outlined in dark paint, and red patterns adorned her hands. He would have thought her fingers delicate, save that he knew they were callused from long use of the sword. She offered the cup of steaming, deep brown liquid to him.

"Have a sip," she offered.

"I am not certain it is proper," Lionel said. He wished he could see her mouth, to tell whether or not she was smiling, but most of her face was hidden by the veil. "I do not wish to cause offense by disregarding the customs of the Caliphate."

"Did we not drink from the same wineskin on the field of battle?" Her veils rustled as she leaned toward him. Lionel was surprised to scent only the barest hint of perfume, and only because he was so close to her. Ambergris and clove. "I hardly think offering you your first sip of Qahwa will cause a diplomatic incident." Ismet pushed the cup across the table to him.

After a moment's hesitation, Lionel lifted the cup. It smelled heavenly, but when he tasted it, it was bitter. Nonetheless, there was something about it that he thought he could grow to like - much like the woman who had offered it to him.

"Lady Ismet," Lionel began, passing the cup back to her. Instead of sliding it across the table, he passed it, and her finger brushed his as she took hold of the cup. He froze there, in that moment, shocked by the touch of skin on skin.

"Your Royal Highness," Baron Urien said, at his shoulder, and the moment passed. Lionel released the cup of Qahwa, and withdrew his hand, to turn to the older man.

"Yes?" He tried not to be sharp with his tone at the interruption.

"A pigeon from Cheverny," Urien said, his voice low. "The castle has fallen."

"Who?" Lionel asked, his stomach roiling. "My father?"

"They say the heraldry was that of Champs d'Or," Urien said. "Lady Valeria's family. As to your father, the King... We do not know. The message left while two of the King's Exarchs were still fighting; they could have gotten His Majesty away safely."

"Only if we assume our enemy to be incompetent," Lionel said, calculating. "There are no coincidences. Our armies nearly destroyed, just as the capital is attacked? The plan becomes more and more clear. But for a few strokes of fortune which Valeria could not have predicted, Falais would have fallen, and I would have been captured or dead. Capture or kill my father, put Valeria in my bed, as she had clearly been seeking for so long, and they would soon have an infant in whose name they would rule."

"Do we muster and ride north for Lutetia, then?" Urien asked him. Ismet watched him, waiting for his answer behind those black-rimmed, enchanting eyes.

Lionel looked out over the hall, at what was left of the feast, and the few revelers who remained. "Not until morning," he decided. "Let them all have tonight, as a celebration of this victory that no one dared hope for. Let the heroes of the battle at the pass dream, for at least one night, that they have won us peace. There will be time enough tomorrow for me to tell them the war has only now begun."

GLOSSARY

A

Abatur, Saint (AH-ba-ter) - The Angelus of the North Star; Saint Abatur is said to weigh the souls of the deceased on his scales, to determine their fate after death. Abatur was slain during the Great Cataclysm, and the Angelus' corpse is interred beneath the Church of Saint Abatur in Falais, at the base of the Hauteurs Massif range that marks the southern border of the Kingdom of Narvonne. Saint Abatur's Feast Day is observed on the first day, or Kalends, of the Grey Moon.

Accolon, Brother (AE-ka-lon) - The first recorded Abbot of the Monastery of Saint Kadosh, located in the village of Camaret-à-Arden, on the edge of the Ardenwood.

Acrasia (ah-Kray-sya) - A faerie Lady in the service of Auberon, King of Shadows. She is the sister of Cern, the Horned Hunter.

Addanc (ah-DANK) - A daemon, bound to the bottom of a lake, by the faerie court of the Ardenwood, during the Great Cataclysm.

Adrammelech (ah-DROM-eh-lek) - A daemon known as the Prince of Plagues, bound long ago during the Cataclysm.

Alberic, Brother (AHL-ber-ik) - A middle-aged monk of the Monastery of Kadosh, who served as the personal tutor of Percival and Trist du Camaret-à-Arden.

Anais (ah-NY-as) - A young lady's maid to Clarisant du Rocher de la Garde.

Ardenwood (AHR-den-wood) - The great interior forest of the Kingdom of Narvonne, which has remained largely wild since even before the Etalan conquest. The Arden is said to shelter roving bands of brigands, and to be the haunted demesne of faeries and even stranger monsters. In addition to the usual stands of oak, beech, ash, sycamore and hazel, the Ardenwood is the only known source of Iebara, a black wood nearly as strong as stone. The village of Camaret-à-Arden lies within the edge of the Ardenwood.

Arnive, Lady (AHR-nyv) - Baroness du Hauteurs Massif, and a young widow; her family's heraldry is a black mountain on red. She is the mother of Isdern, the heir to the Barony, and acts as regent in his name.

Auberon (OH-ber-ahn) - The Fairie King of Shadows, said to hold court in the wild and haunted depths of the Ardenwood. Cern, the Horned Hunter, rides at Auberon's command with the Wild Hunt. Auberon is said to possess many treasures of great magical power.

Aurelius (OAR-el-ee-us) - Etalan General of the Ninth Legion, stationed in the Province of Narvonne at the time of the Great Cataclysm. Aurelius is said to have fought several major battle against the daemons released by the Cataclysm, commissioned the Marian Codex, the first and greatest work of daemonology extant in Telluria, and married a Narvonni tribal princess to secure his claim as the first King of Narvonne. As much a myth as a historical figure, Aurelius is said by the Narvonnians to sleep beneath the Hauteurs Massif to the current day, waiting only for the kingdom's greatest need to awaken.

Auron, Sir (OAR-on) - A knight sworn in fealty to Baron Urien de Rocher de la Garde. His knight's fee includes the small fishing village of Havre de Paix.

B

Baylin, Sir (BAE-lin) - One of the original seven Exarchs who fought for General Aurelius during the Great Cataclysm, Sir Baylin was the first Exarch of Saint Kadosh.

Bors du Chêne Fendu, Sir (BOARS-do-shaen-fen-do) - The current Exarch of Masheth the Destroyer, and one of the seven Exarchs charged with the defense of the royal family of Narvonne. Bors serves as the Champion of Lionel Aurelianus, the Crown Prince. He wears the arms of Masheth: golden wings on a white field, and below them a sword crossed with a lash.

C

Cador, Sir (KAY-door) - A trusted knight in the service of Baron Urien de Rocher de la Garde who often acts as his representative.

Caliphate of Maʿīn (MAH-in) - A former Etalan Province, located south of Narvonne, encompassing the Maghreb wastes and with the Hauteurs Massif marking its northernmost border. Instead of a monarchy, the government of the Caliphate is theocratic: the Exarch of the Angelus Isrāfīl always rules as Caliph, until their death, whereupon a new Exarch is chosen by the Angelus. Isrāfīl often chooses a son or daughter of the ruling Caliph, whom he will have groomed for the position over many years, but not always, occasionally deciding someone else is more suitable. The current Caliph, Rashid ibn Umar, rules from the city of Maʿīn, located in a valley beneath the western mountains.

Camaret-à-Arden (CAM-a-rey-a-AHR-den) - A small village on the edge of the Ardenwood, and the Knight's Fee of Sir Rience, who holds it in fealty to Baron Urien de Rocher de la Garde. Camaret-à-Arden is on the River Rea, which flows out of the Arden from its source in the mountains in the depths of the forest, and the river's current is used to operate a lumber mill. The village is important chiefly for the production of Iebara wood, a strategic resource for the Kingdom of Narvonne. Sir Rience's family rules from a manor named the Foyer Chaleureux, and the town is supported by the monks of the Monastery of Saint Kadosh.

Camiel, Saint (CAM-ee-el) - During the Great Cataclysm, Saint Camiel was Angelus of War. It is said that he was destroyed in battle with Sammāʾēl, and his corpse laid to rest beneath the Cathedral of Saint Camiel in Lutetia, the capital of Narvonne.

Cazador (CAZ-a-door) - A war trained destrier who serves as Trist du Camaret-à-Arden's mount. His name means 'Hunter' in the pre-Etalan language of the tribes of the Hauteurs Massif.

Cecilia du Camaret-à-Arden (Se-SEAL-ee-ah-do-CAM-a-rey-a-AHR-den) - The late wife of Sir Rience, and mother of Trist.

Cern, the Horned Hunter (KERN) - A faerie in service to Auberon, the leader of the Wild Hunt, and the brother of Acrasia. Also known as Hellequin or the Horned Lord.

Chantal, Dame (shan-TALL) - A knight in service to Baroness Arnive of Falais, and commander of the Tower of Tears.

Chapelle de Camiel (sha-PEL-de-CAM-y-el) - A ruined chapel outside the village of Camaret-à-Arden, once dedicated to the Angelus Saint Camiel.

Cheverny (sha-VER-nee) - The Castle of the King of Narvonne, located on an isand in the middle of the river that runs through Lutetia. The majority of the Exarchs of

Narvonne are stationed in Cheverny, to protect the monarch and their family, and court life revolves around events at the castle.

Circum Mare (sir-CUM-MAHR-eh) - The central sea that surrounds the island of Etalus and once hosted the shipping lanes which connected the six provinces of the old Etalan Empire. It is said by sailors that the Cirum Mare is much more calm than the western sea, and it is easily navigable even by ships which hug the coasts.

Clarisant du Rocher de la Garde (KLAIR-eh-sant-do-ROE-shehr-de-la-GUARD) - A young noblewoman betrothed to Percy du Camaret-à-Arden. She is the youngest daughter of Baron Urien du Rocher de la Garde, and the sister of both Gareth, the eldest son, and Kay, squire to the Crown Prince.

Clovis (KLOH-vis) - A blacksmith working as the Crown Prince's armorer, in the camp at Falais.

D

Decimus Avitus (DES-im-us AH-vih-tus) - One of the younger sons of the last Etalan Emperor, Sevrus the Fourth. Avitus was appointed provincial governor of Narvonne, and administered from the provincial capital of Vellatesia, until the Great Cataclysm.

Divdan, Sir (DIV-den) - A knight in service to Baroness Arnive of the Hauteurs Massif.

Durentia (DER-ent-ee-a)- A river that flows out of the heights of the Hauteurs Massif, and has eroded the Passe de Mûre, the only pass through the range that can accommodate an army of any size. Falais is the only significant settlement on the banks of the Durentia.

E

Enid De Lancey (EE-nid-deh-LAN-see) - The only daughter of Sir Tor and Lady Jeanette de Lancey, a knight in service to Baron Urien du Rocher de la Garde. Her family's arms are a red warhammer on white.

Epinoia (eh-pin-OY-ah) - The Angelus of Mothers, and one of the Angelus supporting the Caliphate of Maʿīn; her Exarch is the young Ismet ibnah Salah.

Etalan Empire / Etalus (eh-TALL-an) - The Etalan Empire grew from an island nation to control every significant landmass on the Circum Mare, including the six provinces of Etalia, Iberia, Kimerria, Narvonnia, Raetia, and Skandia. In each province, the Etalan Empire stationed a legion loyal to the Emperor, enforced the use of Etalan coinage, calendars and laws, and did its best to stamp out native languages. When the Great Cataclysm spread from the Provincia Narvonia to consume the Empire, local rulers turned the former provinces into petty kingdoms, where old, previously suppressed languages and traditions were reasserted.

Evarard du Rive Ouest (eh-ver-ARD-do-REEV-OH-west) - The Baron of the Kingdom of Narvonne's western shore, beyond the Ardenwood. His vassal, Sir Florent, leads his troops.

F

Falais (fah-LAY) - A town at the northern end of the Passe de Mûre, on the bank of the River Durentia. Falais is the seat of the Barony of the Hauteurs Massif, and as a result of its strategic importance has received funds from the Crown to see to the upkeep of its fortifications, including a southern wall and Falais Castle itself.

Fazil ibn Asad (fah-ZEEL-eb-en-ah-SAHD)- A young warrior of the Caliphate of Maʿīn, who is the brother of Shīrkūh ibn Asad.

Florent, Sir (FLOHR-ehnt) - A grizzled veteran knight, leading the troops from the Barony du Rive Ouest, sworn in fealty to Baron Everard.

G

Gareth du Rocher de la Garde (GAIR-eth) - Eldest son and heir of Baron Urien du Rocher de la Garde; brother of Kay and Clarisant.

Great Cataclysm, The - Common name for the event that ended the Etalan Empire, though often also used to refer to the daemon Sammā'ēl the Sun Eater. Historical records indicate the Great Cataclysm began in the Provincia Narvonia capital of Vellatesia, which was utterly destroyed by the arrival of the first daemons to Telluria. Some historians argue the Etalan Legions might have held the Empire together if Sammā'ēl had not crossed the Circum Mare to Etalus itself, destroying the capital of the Empire and devastating the population of the province. With no surviving emperor to rally the legions, the Empire itself fragmented and had ceased to exist in any practical sense by the end of the Cataclysm. Battles against daemonic forces were devastating, and accompanied by waves of plague that decimated the population. When Sammā'ēl the Sun Eater caused an entire week of darkness, so many crops died that a great famine followed. All told, the Great Cataclysm is said to have claimed the lives of fully half the people occupying the Empire at the time it began.

H

Hauteurs Massif, The (OH-ter-mah-SEEF) - Both a mountain range marking the border between the Kingdom of Narvonne and the Caliphate of Maʿīn, and a Narvonnian Barony encompassing the same region. While the mountains are navigable by small groups, the only route suitable for an army is the Passe de Mûre, a route carved by the River Durentia and paved with a road during the height of the Etalan Empire. Three towers, as well as the castle-town of Falais and various walls, protect the mountain chain from the threat of invasion, which has not stopped the Caliphate from making multiple attempts to claim the territory. The current Baron, Isdern, is not of age, and so the Barony is under the regency of his mother, Baroness Arnive. The arms of the Barony are a black mountain on red.

Havre de Paix (HAV-er-deh-PEH) - A small seaside town primarily supported by fishing. Havre de Paix is the Knight's Fee of Sir Auron, in fealty to the Baron of Rocher de la Garde.

Henry (hen-REE) - A young man-at-arms in the village of Camaret-à-Arden, in the service of Sir Rience. He is particularly skilled with a bow, and was taught to hunt by his father.

Hugh, Brother (HEW) - The current Abbot of the Monastery of Saint Kadosh in Camaret-à-Arden.

Hywel (HOW-uhl) - The local Blacksmith at Camaret-à-Arden.

I

Iebara Trees (I-eh-BAR-ah) - A rare and exotic species of trees valued for their black wood, which has a strength comparable to stone or metal. Iebara trees have black roots and bloom with white flowers, and are found only in the Ardenwood. Due to their unique hardness, woodsmen who cut Iebara trees use axes blessed by the monks of Saint Kadosh, and sing ancient tree-songs passed down from the Narvonni tribe before the days of the Etalan Empire. Iebara wood is the export of Camaret-à-Arden, and considered a strategic resource by the Narvonnian Crown.

Isdern (IS-durn) - The young Baron of the Hauteurs Massif, and the son of Lady Arnive and the late Baron Owain.

Ismet ibnah Salah (IS-met-IB-nah-SOL-ah) - The new Exarch of Epinoia, a young woman of the Caliphate recently graduated from the University of Maʿīn.

J

Jeanette De Lancey (JUH-net-deh-LAN-see) - The wife of Sir Tor De Lancey, and the mother of Enid.

John Granger (JON-GRANGE-er)- Master of Arms at Camaret-à-Arden, in the service of Sir Rience.

K

Kadosh, Saint (kah-DOSH) - Often named Saint Kadosh the Guardian, this Angelus' Feast Day is during the Wolf Moon.

Kay du Rocher de la Garde (KAY-do-ROE-shehr-de-la-GUARD)- Squire to Lionel Aurelianus, Crown Prince of Narvonne, and son of Baron Urien du Rocher de la Garde. Brother of Gareth and Clarisant.

Kramer, Father (KRAY-mur) - Priest of the Church of Saint Abatur in Falais.

L

Linette (LIN-eht) - A young woman who lives outside of Camaret-à-Arden with her elderly mother, in the ruins of the Chapelle de Camiel.

Lionel Aurelianus (LIE-oh-NEL-OAR-el-ee-AN-us) - Crown Prince of Narvonne, son of King Lothair, and cousin to Sir Lorengel. Widely considered the greatest tactical mind in the Kingdom of Narvonne, and the ideal of knighthood. Though many noblewomen have sought to catch his eye, he has not remarried since the loss of his first wife, Gwen, to plague. His arms are the same as his father's: a golden lion on a black field, with a label to mark him as eldest son and heir.

Lorengel, Sir (lor-EHNG-el)- The Exarch of Veischax, and the king's nephew. Cousin to Crown Prince Lionel Aurelianus.

Lothair Aurelianus (low-THAIR-OAR-el-ee-AN-us) - The King of Narvonne; father of Lionel Aurelianus, uncle of Sir Lorengel. The royal arms are a golden lion on a black field.

Luc (LUKE) - A man-at-arms in service to Sir Rience du Camaret-à-Arden, known for his exceptional size and strength.

Lucan, Sir (LUKE-en) - The older cousin of Percival and Trist, and the nephew of Sir Rience. Sir Lucan is a knight in the service of Baron Urien du Rocher de la Garde, and is recently wed to Miriam.

Lutetia (loo-TESH-ya) - The capital of the Kingdom of Narvonne, built by General Aurelius and Queen Elantia after his passing, to replace the former provincial capital of Vellatessia. Lutetia encompasses both banks of the Avainne River, as well as King's Island, in the middle of the river, where the castle Cheverny stands. Lutetia is also host to the Cathedral of Saint Camiel.

M

Marius (MAR-ee-us) - A staff officer of the Ninth Legion under General Aurelius. At the command of Aurelius, Marius compiled everything the Ninth Legion and the fledgling Kingdom of Narvonne could learn about the daemonic thread, and recorded the knowledge in what became known as the Marian Codex.

Masheth the Destroyer, Saint (ma-SHETH) - The Angelus who concerns himself with the punishment of crimes, particularly murder, incest, and other atrocities. His current Exarch is Sir Bors. The arms of Masheth are golden wings on a white field, and below them a sword crossed with a lash.

Monipodio (MON-eh-POE-dee-oh) - A businessman in Havre de Paix.

N

Narvonne (nahr-VONE) - The Kingdom that has emerged from the Etalan Provincia Narvonnia, which was effectively destroyed during the Great Cataclysm. The current Kingdom was founded by the Etalan General Aurelius and the Narvonni chief's daughter,

Elantia, who became his queen. Narvonne is the only state descended from Old Etalus which formally disqualifies any Exarch from sitting as a reigning Monarch.

Nasir al-Rashid (nah-SEER-al-rah-SHEED) - The eldest son of the current Caliph of Maʿīn, Rashid ibn Umar.

O

Owain du Hauteurs Massif (oh-WAIN-do-OH-ter-mah-SEEF) - The former Baron of the Hauteurs Massif; father of Isdern, and husband of Arnive. His arms were a black mountain on red, and are now carried by his wife and son.

P

Passe de Mûre (pah-SHAY-deh-MYUR) - A pass through the Hauteurs Massif which extends south from Falais, to the Tower of Tears, cut by the River Durentia.

Percival du Camaret-à-Arden (PURSE-eh-val-do-CAM-a-rey-a-AHR-den) - The eldest son of Sir Rience, elder half-brother of Trist, betrothed of Clarisant du Rocher de la Garde, cousin of Sir Lucan, and heir to Camaret-à-Arden. His arms are the same as his father's, marked with a label to signify his station as heir: a black Iebara tree, with white blossoms, on a green field.

R

Rience du Camaret-à-Arden, Sir (RYNS-do-CAM-a-rey-a-AHR-den) - The father of Percival and Trist, widower of Cecilia, uncle of Lucan, and a knight in service to Baron Urien du Rocher de la Garde. His Knight's Fee is the village of Camaret-à-Arden, and his arms are a black Iebara tree, with white blossoms, on a green field.

Rive Ouest (REEV-OH-west) - The Barony on the western shore of the Kingdom of Narvonne, currently held by Baron Everard. The barony is isolated from much of the rest of the kingdom by the Ardenwood to the east, and the harsh western ocean.

Rocher de la Garde (ROE-shehr-de-la-GUARD) - The largest and most prosperous Narvonnian port, the city of Rocher de la Garde is located on the Circum Mare, and known for the exotic goods and wealth that flow through its markets. Baron Urien holds the city and castle in fealty to the King of Narvonne.

S

Sammā'ēl the Sun Eater (sah-MY-ehl) - The first daemon to emerge into Telluria, often referred to as The Great Cataclysm due to the sheer destruction it wrought during the fall of the Etalan Empire. Sammā'ēl has been credited with the destruction of the provincial capital of Vellatessia, the ruin of Etalus, the death of both the last emperor and of the Angelus Saint Madiel, and even with blotting out the sun for a week.

Shadi ibn Yusuf (shaw-DEE-eb-en-YOU-sef) - The current Exarch of Jibrīl and the most favored General of the Caliph.

Shīrkūh ibn Asad (SHEER-kuh-eb-en-ah-SAHD) - A Caliphate scout and brother of Fazil ibn Asad.

T

Tor De Lancey, Sir (TOUR-deh-LAN-see) - A knight in service to Baron Urien du Rocher de la Garde. Husband of Jeanette, father of Enid. His heraldry is a red warhammer on white, and his knight's fee La Colline Isolé, a quarry town.

U

Urien, Baron du Rocher de la Garde (YUR-ee-ehn) - Knight and father of Gareth, Clarisant, and Kay. He rules Rocher de la Garde in the name of the King of Narvonne, and his arms are a white sea shell on a blue field.

V

Valeria du Champs d'Or (vah-LAIR-ee-uh-do-SHAMP-duh-OAR) - Daughter of Baron Maël du Champs d'Or, and heir to his Barony. Her arms, like her fathers, are a yellow sheaf of wheat on a green field, with a label to mark her as heir.

Vellatesia (VELL-ah-TESS-ee-ah) - The former capital of the Etalan Provincia Narvonia, destroyed in the Great Catacylsm. The daemon-haunted ruins are said to lie deep within the Ardenwood.

Vultures - A group of brigands who rebelled against the Baron du Champs d'Or, and were crushed by the Crown Prince.

Y

Yaél du Havre de Paix (YAEL-do-HAV-er-deh-PEH) - A young boy from a fishing village.

NOTES ON SOURCES

In writing this novel, I have drawn inspiration from a variety of sources, and included fragments of text adapted to this work to pay tribute to some of those inspirations. Most of the works listed below are long ago in the public domain, and often available online for free. For those who are curious, I hope that you might enjoy these things as much as I have.

Chapter 1: Acrasia's song is an adaptation of Rudyard Kipling's "A Tree Song," first published in *Puck of Pook's Hill* in 1906. I first heard it at the Connecticut Renaissance Faire, and it seems to have become something of a Ren Faire staple.

Chapter 2: The hymn that makes up the epigraph of this chapter is adapted from *The Medieval Latin Hymn*, by Ruth Ellis Messenger, available on Project Gutenberg.

Chapter 3: Johannes of Skandia is inspired by Johannes Lichtenauer, a historical 14th century German fencing master whose works I was introduced to when practicing the longsword at Sword in the Scroll Fencing Academy in Willimantic, Connecticut. The epigraph is a translation of his MS 3227a.

Chapter 5: The verses of this epigraph are adapted from the traditional ballad, "Scarborough Fair," made famous by Simon and Garfunkel. There have been a succession of lyrics over the centuries, going back to a Scottish Ballad named "The Elfin Knight."

Chapter 6: Acrasia's name is taken from the second volume of Spenser's *The Faerie Queene*; the Greek "Akrasia" means to act against one's better judgment.

Chapter 7: The Campaign Journals of General Aurelius were inspired by Julius Caesar's *Commentarii de Bello Gallico*, his firsthand account of the conquest of Gaul. Acrasia's home under the hill is inspired by John Keats' *La Belle Dame Sans Merci*.

Chapter 10: The Life and Times of Legionary Titus Nasica is inspired by the writings of Roger Lamb, a British soldier who wrote several books about his experiences during the American Revolution. Some doubt has been expressed among academics about whether Lamb could have possibly witnessed all of the battles he claims to have been present for, and to what extent his writings may have been exaggerated.

Chapter 13: The prayer in the epigraph is adapted from Psalm 147.

Chapter 16: The Narvonnian King Henry the Barnlock was inspired by Magnus Eriksson, King of Norway and Sweden, who was given the nickname after establishing country-wide laws which aimed to protect the property of farmers.

Chapter 20: The Addanc was inspired by Welsh mythology, and is based on a lake-monster first described in writing by Lewys Glyn Cothi, in the 15th century.

Chapter 21: The lyrics of the epigraph are from *Greensleeves*, a 16th century English ballad sometimes (falsely) attributed to Henry VIII.

Chapter 22: Trist's fencing manual, *The Flower of Battle*, is named after a real book by Italian fencing master Fiore dei Liberi.

Chapter 25: The Vultures were inspired by the historical 19th century Italian brigands Carmine Crocco and Ninco Nanco.

Chapter 31: The story of King Aurelius sleeping under the mountain is inspired by the Brothers Grimm tale of Frederick Barbarossa.

Chapter 36: The Leatherman's Cave is a reference to a northeast legend: Jules Bourglay, who walked a regular route between the Connecticut and the Hudson rivers for nearly thirty years, often living in caves.

Chapter 37: The ransom prices given are adapted from historical records, given in *Prisoners of War in the Hundred Years War*, by Rémy Ambühl.

Chapter 38: The Ornes are inspired by the mythical Stymphalian birds, who were said to be pets of Artemis, or perhaps Ares, depending on the myth.

Chapter 42: The idea of Auberon's magic ring comes from *Oberon*, an 18th century poem by Christoph Martin Wieland.

CALENDARS, CHRONOLOGY AND CLOCKS

The Etalan Empire numbered their years Year of the Empire (YOE), from the founding of their capital city, Rumen. The Cataclysm began in the 979th Year of the Empire, by their counting, and continued through the 981st.

Etalan roads in Narvonne are often said to be 'a thousand' years old; the Narvonni were conquered by the Etalans in the late 3rd century of the Empire, and remained under a provincial governor for the next six hundred years or so prior to the Cataclysm.

The Narvonnian Calendar was marked from the year of the founding of Aurelius' new kingdom, dubbed 'After Cataclysm,' and beginning with year 1 as 981 YoE; the fortuitous alignment of the number 'one' was said to have been suggested by his wife, Elantia of the Narvonni. It is likely also Elantia's influence that saw to the official use of the old Narvonni names for the moons, rather than the Etalan names.

The divisions of the day established by the Church of the Angelus are the same as those which were used in medieval Europe. In Narvonne and the rest of the Etalan successor kingdoms, most people get up at dawn, which is called prime, or the first hour. The third hour, terce, is about halfway between daybreak and noon. Sext, or noon, is the sixth hour. The ninth hour, nones, is about halfway between noon and sunset. Vespers is the twelfth hour, or sunset.

Church bells are rung at these times, though the precise timing often differs from village to village. If you are outside of hearing range from a bell, the only way to tell time is to estimate based on the sun, or to set up a sun-dial, such as the portable one Trust carries.

The year consists of thirteen Moons, each of twenty-eight days, for a total of 364 days in the year. The names are different from place to place. Under the Etalan system, the Kalends marked the first day of a moon, while the Ides marked the 14th. The list of Moons below gives approximate equivalent dates to the calendar most readers will be familiar with. The Feast Days of Narvonne are listed; the people of the Caliphate, for instance, would celebrate their own set of Angelus, rather than the ones given below.

Wolf Moon / Primus (January 19- February 15)

The first Moon of the year, when the winter wolves have free reign to hunt over the frozen, dark land. The Feast Day of Saint Kadosh the Guardian is celebrated during the Wolf Moon, and it is common for peasants to offer Wolfsbane at his altars.

Starving Moon / Secundus (February 16-March 15)

The Starving Moon is marked by the slow increase of light over dark and warmer temperatures, though it is still winter; it is named for the fate of those who have stored insufficient food to last the winter.

The Flood Moon /Tertius (March 15-April 11)

Storms and floods mark the beginning of Spring, and the Spring Equinox. As the days grow longer and warmer, and the snows turn to rain, even the high peaks melt, often leading to flooding rivers, washed out roads, and a morass of mud. It is considered foolish to undertake a military expedition before the Ides of the Flood Moon, which is the Feast Day of Saint Rahab, Angelus of the Sea. This is a fisherman's holiday, and marks the beginning of their season.

Planting Moon/Quartus (April 12-May 10)

Feast of Saint Lailahel on the Ides of Quartus

As the mud dries, the spring crop is planted; at the same time, the trees begin to blossom and flowers begin to bloom throughout Narvonne. The Feast of Saint Lailahel, Angelus of Fertility, is celebrated on the Ides of the Planting Moon. It is traditional to bathe in a river, and for women who hope to conceive to put sachets of mistletoe, mint, and cinnamon in their bedrooms.

Flower Moon /Quintilis (May 11-June 8)

The last moon of spring, as the world grows green and the seasons pass into summer. Any untended land is a riotous profusion of wildflowers and tree blossoms, and in many parts of Narvonne, lavender grows in profusion. The Feast of Saint Theliel, Angelus of Love, is celebrated on the Kalends, with flowers used to decorate cattle horns, and offerings made to propitiate the faeries of the Ardenwood.

New Summer's Moon / Sextilis (June 9-July 7)

New Summer's Moon brings the first days of summer. In the second week of this moon lies the Summer Solstice, a time of religious ceremony referred to as High Summer, and the Feast of Saint Madiel, Angelus of Fire. Bone-Fires are built to drive off witches and dragons, and in honor of Madiel's death fighting the Sun Eater. Dried lavender is often used in these rituals, to bless and protect houses, or thrown into the Bone-Fires.

High Summer Moon/September (July 8-August 5)

The hot summer sun warms Narvonne, especially in the south, and in coastal settlements such as Rocher de la Garde, swimming and bathing in the sea is common. The Kalends is celebrated with tourneys in honor of Camiel, Angelus of War, and his Feast Day.

Deep Summer Moon/October (August 6-September 3)

Toward the end of the summer, the crops grow tall and ripe, and a haze of heat lays upon the land. In the south, especially, little work is done during the day.

Harvest Moon /November (September 4-October 1)

The Autumn Equinox and its accompanying Bone-fires, especially, are a time of great Magical potential. The Feast Day of Saint Veischax, Angelus of the Seal, ends the harvest season, with the blessing of the Angelus invoked to seal the granaries. Cats, believed to be favored by Veischax as hunters of rats, are honored, and Priests of the Angelus perform rituals to maintain and strengthen the seals on the bindings which have held daemons since the Cataclysm.

Blood Moon/December (October 2-29)

Blood Moon ushers in Autumn, its leaves as red as the name would indicate. The Ardenwood, the greatest forest in Narvonne, is likened to a roaring fire of red, orange, and yellow leaves during this time. On the Ides, the Feast Day of Saint Masheth the Destroyer, the Angelus who punishes the guilty, is celebrated. It is a common time for executions to be held, or for prisoners to be released after serving their sentence.

Gray Moon/Undecimis (October 30-November 26)

Only the faeries of the Ardenwood speak the old name of this time – The Bone Moon, the moon when sacrifices were made in their honor. During their long withdrawal into the depths of the Ardenwood, the Etalans forbid the use of the old name, and Aurelius officially changed it to a less offensive description of this cold, gray season before the snows fall. On the Kalends, the Feast Day of Saint Abatur, Angelus of the North Star, is celebrated, who is said to weigh the souls of the deceased on his scales.

New Winter Moon /Tredecimis (November 24 -December 21)

In the more northern parts of Narvonne, as well as the Skandian March, the Principality of Raetia, and the Grand Duchy of Kimmeria, this is a picturesque time of new fallen snow, before the numbing chill of Deep Winter sets in.

Deep Winter Moon/Quattuordecimis (December 22-January 18)

The Kalends of Deep Winter marks the Winter Solstice, or Deep Winter Night, and the Feast Day of Penarys, Angelus of the Night. It is a time for feasting and celebration, as it marks not only the longest night of the year, but the days beginning to grow longer again and the eventual return of the sun.

AUTHOR'S NOTE

I began writing the Faerie Knight on April 27, 2023, about eight months after self-publishing my first novel, A Sea Cold and Deep, on Amazon. I spent much of that time fiddling with various projects that didn't seem to go anywhere, and realizing that I didn't know the first thing about how to actually get my writing out into spaces where people could find it.

I decided to try my hand at a time honored tradition - serial fiction - in a new form. Rather than releasing chapters in magazines, as Dickens did, I decided to try my hand at a website called Royal Road.

It has been an interesting challenge, and I think writing in this fashion has helped me to grow, especially in terms of structuring chapters, and writing consistently. As I write this note, I estimate that I'm about 73% finished with the sequel to this book, *The Graal Knight*. If I keep my current pace, I am on track to draft two novels in a year, which is frankly mind boggling to me.

A lot has happened during this time, including the loss of a very close friend who passed before her time. It is infuriating to see someone die at only 42 years old from a chronic medical condition that is manageable with consistent access to medicine. There is no excuse for a nation as wealthy as the United States to force people to scramble for insulin.

My wife pointed out that Clarisant was 'A Sarah Gabbey Character;' not deliberately or consciously modeled after her, but the sort of character she would create and portray in a roleplaying game. I like that; it means that I can remember her when I write, and that everyone who reads this will experience at least the smallest portion of her.

David Niemitz

March 7, 2024

If you're interested in news regarding my work, you can sign up for my newsletter by following the QR code below, and receive an exclusive short story:

ALSO BY

Books by the Author

The Faerie Knight - Available on Amazon

The Graal Knight - Forthcoming

A Sea Cold and Deep - Available on Amazon

THE GRAAL KNIGHT

THE FALL OF CHEVERNY

Who is to say there was not something rotten in the Province of Narvonne from the very beginning - perhaps rooted in that very Ardenwood where the Etalans built Vellatesia. Or perhaps Decimus Avitus was the one rotten from the start, which would explain why Emperor Severus passed him over for a younger brother.
-The Commentaries of Aram ibn Bashear

13th Day of the Flower Moon, 297 AC

Guiron, Exarch of Penarys, came back to himself with a sharp, panicked breath, and tasted smoke. The inhalation caused a stabbing pain in his right side, and he gasped, clutching at his steel cuirass to find it dented in and cracked.

"Your ribs are broken," Penarys told him. "At least. Take shallow breaths, and move carefully. You need to have them set and bound, if you do not want to risk a punctured lung."

"The King needs me," Guiron protested, and rolled onto his hands and knees. His twin arming swords he found close at hand; one beneath the corpse of a royal guard, the other under a broken wood beam. Until an hour before, it had barred the gate of the keep at the castle Cheverny. Penarys helped the knight to his feet, and together the pair followed a trail of corpses through the entranceway and toward the great hall, where King Lothair Aurelianus held court. To Guiron's left, the head of a squire had been crushed against the stone of the castle wall like a cracked egg; just three steps past, and lying on the right side of the hall, he winced to recognize Lady Blanche, the daughter of Sir Madoc, come from Dawn Spire not two months past to wait out the war with the Caliphate in safety. Guiron had danced with her more than once at the court masques, and found her light on her feet and as delicate as a bird.

Now, both her arms had been ripped entirely from her body and thrown aside; she lay, pale and lifeless, in a sticky puddle of her own blood. "Did you see who did this?" Guiron asked Penarys. He edged around the tacky blood, but couldn't entirely avoid it, and left bootprints the rest of the way down the hall.

"I did," Penarys admitted. "A man with short, dark curls, cut close to his skull. He wore a cuirass made in the old Etalan style, with the steel beaten into musculata, and then all of it enameled over with white, and gilt in gold. He strode through the broken gate after you fell, and then into the hall."

"By himself?" Guiron hissed.

"Yes," Penarys answered. "And Guiron, you must not fight him."

"I'm not going to fight him," Guiron spat. "I'm going to take his head for this. For all of this." He surged ahead to the entrance to the great hall, swinging his twin swords to get as loose and limber as he could. Sparks of orange power flickered at the edge of his vision. He would trust to his Boons to keep him moving, and deal with his cracked ribs once he had saved the King. If it was not too late.

Guiron heard the ring of steel with relief; someone, at least, was still fighting. He turned into the hall, and his stride faltered at the sight which confronted him.

King Lothair's head had rolled to a halt about halfway between the throne and the entrance to the hall, while the remainder of his corpse had been nailed to the stone wall behind the throne by a glaive through the chest. The glaive of Dame Margaret, as a matter of fact: Guiron recognized the fearsome weapon from countless mornings in the training yard. Margaret, herself, lay broken against one wall, but her Angelus, Rahab, hovered under the vaulted ceiling of the hall, and half a dozen of its burning whips were wrapped around the left arm of the man who stood before the throne. Like Penarys had said, he wore old-fashioned musculata painted white, and Guiron recognized him from many a court function.

"Baron Maël du Champs d'Or!" Guiron shouted across the room. "What low treachery is this?"

The Baron turned to regard him down the length of the hall, and Guiron saw now the man had the king's nephew, Sir Lorengel, Exarch of Veischax, caught by the throat. The knight's gauntleted fingers were wrapped around Baron Maël's unarmored hand, but all the strength of an Exarch seemed to cause the man no distress whatsoever. Veischax lay on the ground just beyond them, wings torn off the Angelus' back, leaving only stumps bleeding golden ichor.

"Of all the impertinence I have had to endure these long years," the villainous Baron intoned, "The use of pseudonyms has been, no doubt, one of the worst. The indignity of it; having to allow trash such as your pretender King to style themselves my superior. Any novelty has long since been lost. In hindsight, I killed him too quickly; he deserved time to appreciate his ending before it came."

Lorengal rasped out half a breath, the Exarch's eyes rolling back into his head, and rather than let a comrade die, Guiran knew he had to press the attack. "You admit your own treason, then; good. No need for a court. I will simply execute you myself."

Guiron slid forward smoothly, covering the distance of the long hall in only a few strides. He raised the right arming sword to his right ear, nearly parallel to the ground, while twisting his torso to advance the left arming sword, holding it out in front of him with the hilt about level with his waist. Both points were in line with the wicked Baron's center of mass, and left Guiron with the freedom to parry or cut using either hand.

"Too weak," Maël du Champs d'Or said, throwing Lorengal aside to skid across the stone floor. The man did not even have a weapon in hand! Guiron feinted a thrust with his left blade, then cut down at a diagonal with his right. The swing should have sliced through where the Baron's neck connected to his shoulder and collarbone, a killing blow. Instead, with a sneer, Maël caught Guiron by the wrist as easily as a grown man restrained a toddler. The cut never landed, and Guiron gasped in pain; he could feel the bones in his wrist grinding and cracking until the sword fell from his twitching fingers.

"Impossible," Guiron gasped. No normal man could possibly have such strength. He had slain daemons who did not have this kind of power.

"Look upon me, Exarch," Baron Maël whispered. "Truly look, and see, and comprehend."

A veil lifted from Guiron's eyes, and what had been hidden was now revealed to his sight. The seeing was not a thing of the mortal world, but of the Angelus, and he now perceived the numerous threads running through the Baron's body, meeting in a bundle at his core. The number was overwhelming, more than he could count in a glance, especially with the pain in his wrist, but it was the color that sent a shock of fear through his heart. Every single thread burned a bright, nearly white-hot blue.

No wonder this man was stronger than him: Guiron did not have a single Boon that burned brighter than yellow. With his left hand, he cut at the monster's arm, and Baron Maël reacted the way any man would: by letting go of Guiron's wrist, and pulling his hand out of the way of the blade. Guiron immediately scrambled back three paces, then raised the sword in his left hand, back into Plow Guard, hilt in front of his waist, tip pointed straight at the Baron's chest. He would have liked to get his other sword, but it was lying on the stone floor of the hall only a pace from the traitor.

"Where did this power come from?" Guiron asked, playing for time and for information. If he could stall until Lorengel was back on his feet, the two of them, plus the three Angelus who were hovering above, might still be able to pull out a victory here. Penarys had been with Guiron long enough to see what his partner was doing, and the relatively fresh Angelus was holding back the other two for the moment.

Baron Maël slipped the toe of his boot under the blade of Guiron's lost sword, kicked it up, and caught it by the hilt easily in his right hand. The knight had never heard that the Baron of Champs d'Or was much of a warrior, but the movements of the man in front of him proved that assumption a lie. This was clearly a warrior who had spent countless hours drilling with the blade.

"Where?" Maël shook his head. "Why, the same place as your power comes from, Exarch. An Accord. That is the only place that mortal men such as you and I can gain such power: from years upon years, and souls upon souls, of Tithes. You could not count the number of souls that have been sacrificed on the altar of my power, boy."

"No Angelus would make an Accord with a man such as you," Guiron declared, shaking his head. Admit it, man, he pleaded silently. Give me the name!

"Of course not; not at the beginning of it all, and certainly not now," the man said, with a thin smile and cold eyes. "If the name of my patron is what you wish to hear with your last breath of life, then it does me no harm to give it to you. Indeed, it is something of a relief, to finally reclaim my true identity, after all these years."

Guiron saw Lorengel rising, behind the traitor, but he kept his eyes fixed on the Baron so as to give no sign. "Out with it, then," he prodded. "Let there be no more lies between us, when we finish this."

"You will find me recorded in your history books as Decimus Avitus," the man answered. "Son of Emperor Sevrus the Fourth. Exarch," he continued, each word like the toll of a funeral bell in Guiron's heart, "Of Sammā'ēl, the Sun Eater, Cataclysm of Etalus."

"That is impossible," Guiron responded in disbelief, before he could help himself. "Avitus died centuries ago. He would be over three hundred years old by now. Not even an Exarch could live so long."

"With enough souls Tithed," the daemonic Exarch claimed, "One such as us can live a very long life, indeed. Not quite immortal, I think; but so close as makes little difference. Long enough to set this day in motion."

Guiron's eyes connected with Lorengel's. The other Exarch gave him the smallest nod, and then the two men moved together, as they had trained to do over so many hours in the practice yard. The King they had trained to defend lay dead on the stone, but somewhere in the Hauteurs Massif was a new monarch, and so long as Lionel Aurelianus lived, the Kingdom of Narvonne had not fallen.

Lorengel cut low, at Avitus' legs, while Guiron went high, and they not only came at him from front and back, but also swung from opposite sides. There should have been no way for the daemonic Exarch to avoid both of their strikes. With his right hand, the traitor used Guiron's own lost sword to set aside his strike with a ringing clang. An instant later, too quick to follow, he leapt over the blade that should have severed his legs at the calves. Then, reversing his grip on the stolen arming sword, Avitus stabbed backward, into Lorengel's chest.

"Go!" the dying Exarch choked, blood already spilling from his mouth. Lorengel wrapped his arms around Avitus, to hold him in place, and both the wounded Veischax and Dame Margaret's Rahab lashed out to aid him, wrapping tendrils of fire around the traitor's body as if they were spiders trussing an insect in silk. "Find the King! Warn him!"

Guiron hesitated only for a moment. He didn't want to admit that Cheverny had fallen, and with it the capital, but his duty was clear. With an inarticulate cry of frustration, he turned and dashed out of the throne room, Penarys flying above him, and then out through the shattered castle gate into the burning city of Lutetia. Panicked people ran in every direction, while Kimmerian mercenaries and men-at-arms wearing the heraldry of the Baron du Champs d'Or, a yellow sheaf of wheat on a green field, cut down the king's garrison in the streets.

South. He had to get south, and find Lionel Aurelianus.

For more of Trist, Acrasia, Clarisant and the rest, join us on Royal Road:

https://www.royalroad.com/fiction/81687/the-faerie-knight

If you would like to support my work, visit my Patreon:

https://www.patreon.com/DavidNiemitz

PATREON SUPPORTERS

Andrew Warfield
ARFConnor
Butters
Cryptiddies
Disgruntoad
Dora Jay
Emmy
Gabriela Fernandez
Kooooomakimi
Krosh
Manuel Bern
Merrybean
Nayruke
Neal Mayne
Nomad
Renimus Drago
Scholar of Endless Knowledge
SirToyJet
Steven Lemoine Jr
Susan Niemitz
Sven
Taylor Bouchard